Wild Thyme, Green Magic

Stories by Jack Vance

Edited by Terry Dowling and Jonathan Strahan

SUBTERRANEAN PRESS • 2009

First Edition

ISBN
978-1-59606-226-9

Subterranean Press
PO Box 190106
Burton, MI 48519

www.subterraneanpress.com

In loving memory of Norma Vance

Acknowledgements:

The editors would like to thank Jack Vance and John Vance for their generous and enthusiastic support of this project, as well as John Schwab and the VIE team. Quotes from Jack Vance originally appeared in "An Interview with Jack Vance," Jack Rawlins, *Demon Prince: The Dissonant Worlds of Jack Vance*, The Milford Series, Popular Writers of Today, Volume Forty, The Borgo Press, 1986.

Table of Contents

Introduction

Jack Vance: World-Thinker

"Never show anyone. They'll beg you, and they'll flatter you
for the secret. But as soon as you give it up you'll be nothing to
them, you understand? Nothing! The secret impresses no-one.
The trick you use it for is everything!"
—Alfred Borden in Christopher Nolan's film,
The Prestige, 2006

When Jack Vance set out to become a writer in the mid-1940s, a
"million-word-a-year man" as he put it so pragmatically at the time,
he also gave fantastic literature one of its most cherished and distinctive
voices. Though primarily a novelist throughout his long and distinguished
career, this Hugo, Nebula, Edgar and World Fantasy Award-winning Grand
Master also produced many short and mid-length works, sometimes as part
of continuing narratives, as with the adventures of one of his most famous
creations, Cugel the Clever.

Wild Thyme, Green Magic samples the range and exotic nature of this
shorter-length storytelling enterprise by presenting an alien's handful of often
wondrous, always interesting tales from the early to middle period of Vance's 59
years as a writer. To borrow from the title of another early Vance tale, what we
end up with is, by its nature, very much a 'practical guide' to the author's process
as storyteller, not as any kind of rigorous editorial agenda, but more as a fair
and appropriate appreciation of the pieces on offer.

The featured stories not only show the themes, preoccupations and signature
techniques in play, perhaps more noticeably in miniature than within the sheer
immersive scale of the longer works, but they also bring to the fore key aspects
of how characters are established, locales and mood created, how dialog is used
to further the action, and how conflict and crisis are introduced; in short, how
the coinage is spent when it comes to delivering story.

"Assault on a City" originally appeared in March 1974 in *Universe 4* and
concerns the fortunes of one of Vance's efficient and resourceful female leads in
what is a gently cautionary tale of how an overcivilized and over-subjective

approach to life can sometimes get in the way of living it fully. For an ethical pragmatist like Vance, any excess of parochialism, subjectivity and self-absorption is always the enemy, and we see it here in splendid contrast as "clever sophisticate" Waldo Walberg and Big Bo Histledine more than meet their match with the "culturally impoverished starlander" Alice Tynnott. Like other unforgettable Vance cities before it (Ambroy and Clarges readily spring to mind) the city of Hant is sketched for us with the sort of loving attention the author might well use to render his own beloved Bay area in Northern California.

"Green Magic" was first published in *The Magazine of Fantasy & Science Fiction* for June 1963, and is an inventive and assured take on the nature of magic. It has an interesting lead character in Howard Fair, a degree of social responsibility that is as commendable as it is welcome, and surprisingly hard edges.

"The World-Thinker" was Jack's first professional sale and appeared in the Summer 1945 issue of *Thrilling Wonder Stories*, with slight revisions made for its appearance in the 1982 Underwood-Miller collection *Lost Moons*. While it has the stellar empires and exotic creatures, the damsels in distress and the breakneck pace typical of so much 1940s space adventure, it also displays many of the signature touches that mark the author's later work. Lanarck, for instance, has the self-serving resourcefulness of Kirth Gersen, Ghyl Tarvoke and so many other Vance protagonists. As Jack put it in 1986: "I don't want to write about Conan or Tarzan; I want to write about human beings under the influence of some extraordinary motivation." Or to put it more succinctly: "Competence—they have competence."

We find this same kind of competent hero undergoing extraordinary motivation in "The Augmented Agent," an action novelette that, in large part, remains as fresh and modern as when it first appeared as "I-C-a-BeM" in *Amazing Stories* for October 1961. Jack recalls: "I wrote 'The Augmented Agent' to fit a cover. I went to a party, and a publisher…said she had gotten some artist's paintings cheap. I got two. One showed some giant moths attacking a person, so I wrote around that the story called 'Ecological Onslaught', which is a rotten title. The other one showed a row of missiles in silos in the water along a coast. I wrote 'Augmented Agent' for that one."

"Coup de Grace" was the tenth interstellar outing for Vance's most urbane effectuator, Magnus Ridolph, and originally appeared as "Worlds of Origin" in *Super Science Fiction* in February 1958. Published ten years after the first Ridolph adventure, it shows the author completely at ease with his in-series material, though having an older protagonist (and that character's preferred lifestyle) may have presented certain limitations. As a maturing writer, Vance would habitually turn to younger adventurers caught up, often against their wills, in all manner of dangerous predicaments in exotic realms and among the stars.

"Chateau d'If" was first published in *Thrilling Wonder Stories* in August 1950 as "New Bodies for Old," and again features a protagonist driven by crisis to excel, to become, indeed, the sort of practical, transcendent individual we find again and again at the center of so many Vance stories. Though some of the initial intrigue was compromised by an unfortunate editorial change of title, the plot-line remains compelling, and Vance's rendering of both the Empyrean Tower and the lead character's dilemma and subsequent transformation are impressive. Simply put, it is good storytelling.

"The Potters of Firsk" originally appeared in the May 1950 issue of *Astounding Science Fiction*. While very much an early 'gadget' story of the kind Jack soon took pains to avoid, it again shows the author's abiding interest in creating alien cultures and different mindsets, even if rendered minimally here for a simple narrative end. What makes the tale interesting, too, is that its scientific underpinning reflects Jack's own lifelong interest in ceramics, and comes from a period when the author and his wife actually spent time retailing pottery and glassware from the Ceramics Center, a rented storefront in Berkeley. Interestingly, the striking ceramic mask made by Jack that adorns the bar at his home in the hills above Oakland provides a fascinating template for so many of the alien races found in his stories.

"The Seventeen Virgins" was first published in *The Magazine of Fantasy & Science Fiction* for October 1974, and had its opening reworked for its 1983 appearance as part of *Cugel's Saga*. In many ways, the story is a typical, even quintessential, adventure featuring Jack's all-time favorite character getting up to his usual mischief in the far future of the Dying Earth.

"Ulward's Retreat" is one of the author's own favorites among his many stories and first appeared in *Galaxy* magazine in December 1958. With satire and irony in equal parts, it provides an interesting insight into the human condition and shows something of the same perils of subjectivity found in "Assault on a City".

At first glance, "Seven Exits from Bocz" might seem something of a departure for a writer long known to be a level-headed, pragmatic man after the manner of so many of his walk-the-walk protagonists. But Vance has always shown a keen interest in the workings of the mind and the possibility of extended mental powers in future human development, an interest in psionics explored in novels like *The Grey Prince*, *Marune: Alastor 933* and *Maske: Thaery* and in shorter works like "Parapsyche," "The Miracle Workers," even his first-ever sale, "The World-Thinker." We find it, too, at the center of this often underrated and elegant revenge tale first published in *The Rhodomagnetic Digest 21* in 1952 that has a wonderful gothic feel and a curiously satisfying finale.

As well as the completed and published works in the Vance canon, there are a number of unfinished titles that exist only as treatments and outlines, among them *The Genesee Slough Murders* (a third Sheriff Joe Bain novel), *The Stark*, concerning a generation starship, and *Wild Thyme and Violets*, a fanciful gothic romance set in medieval Italy. The latter appears here on its own merits as a moody and intriguing autumnal piece previously unseen by the great majority of Vance's readers, but also as another aspect of process: an example of how this working writer produced synopses either as a key part of generating publisher interest in a project or as work-in-progress frameworks for further development, complete with 'place-holders' and reminders of what needs to be done where.

As this present text shows, Jack's outlines were often surprisingly generous. Once the setting, mood and characters are in place and the "extraordinary motivation" that propels the story forward properly delineated, we have the bare-bones chapter by chapter business needed to take this bittersweet tale of Lucian and his love for Alicia to its intended length. It is telling that, even in outline, with the inevitable coolness and detachment such overviews bring, there is still a classic narrative force at work. Perhaps it was the absence of a happier ending that doomed the project; then again, Jack has long been known for departing from such outlines and for being gifted at providing grace notes of hope. Who knows what *Wild Thyme and Violets* might have become?

"Rumfuddle" first appeared in *Three Trips in Time and Space: Original Novellas of Science Fiction* in 1973. While it never does to seize too eagerly on autobiographical tidbits in a given story, there are personal touches here that are more overt than usual. Gilbert Duray's home-town of Montclair above Oakland is Vance's home-town, and Jack's son and grandchildren attended the same Thornhill School Duray visits to fetch his own children. So, too, our protagonist has named parts of his private domain the Silver River, the Robber Woods and the Sounding Sea after a Robert Louis Stevenson verse much-loved by Jack, while the musical favorites played by Bix Beiderbecke and the Wolverines are among Jack's own and remind us of his great love of traditional jazz.

For many years, Jack Vance remained famously reclusive when it came to discussing background, influences and process, and most of the biographical insights that do exist come from later in his career. The two included here are by Jack's late wife, Norma. "A Jack Vance Biography" appeared in the *Norwescon 25 Program Book* in March 2002, "A Different View of Jack Vance" in August

2003 in Volume 41 of the fanzine *Cosmopolis*. In another way entirely, they provide tantalizing glimpses at how the task of storyteller came to be played out for this particular writer.

But the stories are the thing, and for now they stand to remind us that whatever the circumstances, whatever the motivations and influences or the techniques used in their creation, it is the trick such things are used for that matters, since, where the fiction of Jack Vance is concerned, the trick, most assuredly, is everything.

Terry Dowling and Jonathan Strahan
Sydney and Perth, July 2008

Assault on a City

A certain Angus Barr, officer's steward aboard the spaceship *Danaan Warrior*, had taken his pay and gone forth into that district of the city Hant known as Jillyville in search of entertainment. There, according to information received by the police, he fell into the company of one Bodred Histledine, a well-known bravo of the North River district. The two had entertained themselves briefly at the Epidrome, where Angus Barr won two hundred dollars at a gambling machine. They then sauntered along the Parade to the Black Opal Café, where they drank lime beer and tried to pick up a pair of women tourists without success. Continuing north along the Parade, they crossed the River Louthe by the Boncastle Bridge and rode the clanking old escalator up Semaphore Hill to Hongo's Blue Lamp Tavern and Angus Barr was seen no more.

The disappearance of Angus Barr was reported to the police by the chief steward of the *Danaan Warrior*. Acting on a tip, Detectives Clachey and Delmar located Bo Histledine, whom they knew well, and took him to Central Authority for examination.

Mind-search produced no clear evidence. According to Bo's memory, he had spent an innocent evening in front of his term. Unluckily for Bo, his memory also included fragmentary recollections of the Epidrome, the Parade and the Black Opal Café. The female tourists not only described the missing Angus Barr, but also positively identified Bo.

Delmar nodded with grim satisfaction and turned to Bo. "What do you say to that?"

Bo hunched down in the chair, his face a mask of belligerent obstinacy. "I told you already. I know nothing about this case. Those backwads got me mixed with somebody else. Do you think I'd work on a pair like that? Look at her!" Bo jerked his head toward the closer of the angry women. "Face like a plateful of boiled pig's feet. She's not wearing a sweater; that's the hair on her arms. And her cross-eyed mother—"

"I'm not her mother! We're not related!"

"—she's no better; she walks with her legs bent, as if she's sneaking up on somebody."

Delmar chuckled; Clachey nodded gravely. "I see. And how do you know the way she walks? They were sitting down when we brought you in. Your bad mouth has brought you trouble."

Delmar said, "That's all, ladies. Thank you for your help."

"It's been a pleasure. I hope he gets sent out to Windy River." She referred to a penal colony on the far planet Resurge.

"It might well be," said Delmar. The tourists departed. Clachey said to Bo: "Well then, what about it? What did you do to Barr?"

"Never heard of him."

"You had your memory blanked," said Delmar. "It won't do you any good. Windy River, get ready."

"You haven't got a thing on me," said Bo. "Maybe I was drunk and don't remember too well, but that doesn't mean I scragged Barr."

Clachey and Delmar, who recognized the limitations of their case as well as Bo, vainly sought more direct evidence. In the end Bo was arraigned on the charge of memory-blanking without a permit: not a trivial offense when committed by a person with an active criminal record. The magistrate fined Bo a thousand dollars and placed him upon stringent probation. Bo resented both provisions to the depths of his passionate soul, and he detested the probation officer, Inspector Guy Dalby, at sight.

For his part, Inspector Dalby, an ex-spacefarer, liked nothing about Bo: neither his dense blond-bronze curls, his sullenly handsome features—marred perhaps by a chin a trifle too heavy and a mouth a trifle too rich and full— nor his exquisitely modish garments, nor the devious style of Bo's life. Dalby suspected that for every offense upon Bo's record, a dozen existed which had never come to official attention. As a spaceman he took an objective attitude toward wrong-doing, and held Bo to the letter of his probationary requirements. He subjected Bo's weekly budget to the most skeptical scrutiny. "What is this figure—one hundred dollars—repayment of old debt?"

"Exactly that," said Bo, sitting rigid on the edge of the chair.

"Who paid you this money?"

"A man named Henry Smith: a gambling debt."

"Bring him in here. I'll want to check this."

Bo ran a hand through his cap of golden curls. "I don't know where he is. I happened to meet him on the street. He paid me my money and went his way."

"That's your total income of the week?"

"That's it."

Guy Dalby smiled grimly and flicked a sheet of paper with his fingertips. "This is a statement from a certain Polinasia Glianthe, occupation: prostitute. 'Last week I paid Big Bo Histledine one hundred and seventy-five dollars, otherwise he said he would cut my ears.'"

Bo made a contemptuous sound. "Who are you going to believe? Me or some swayback old she-dog who never made a hundred and seventy-five the best week of her life?"

Dalby forbore a direct response. "Get yourself a job. You are required to support yourself in an acceptable manner. If you can't find work, I'll find it for you. There's plenty out on Jugurtha." He referred to that world abhorred by social delinquents for its rehabilitation farms.

Bo was impressed by Dalby's chilly succinctness. His last probation officer had been an urbanite, whose instinctive tactic was empathy. Bo found it a simple matter to explain his lapses. The probation officer in turn was cheered by Bo's ability to distinguish between right and wrong, at least verbally. Inspector Dalby, however, obviously cared not a twitch for the pain or travail which afflicted Bo's psyche. Cursing and seething, Bo took himself to the City Employment Office and was dispatched to the Orion Spaceyards as an apprentice metal-worker, at a wage he considered a bad joke. One way or another he'd outwit Dalby! In the meantime he found himself under the authority of a foreman equally unsympathetic: another ex-spaceman named Edmund Sarkane. Sarkane explained to Bo that to gain an hour's pay he must expend an hour's exertion, which Bo found a novel concept. Sarkane could not be serious! He attempted to circumvent Sarkane's precepts by a variety of methods, but Sarkane had dealt with a thousand apprentices and Bo had known only a single Sarkane. Whenever Bo thought to relax in the shadows, or ignore a troublesome detail, Sarkane's voice rasped upon his ears, and Bo began to wonder if after all he must accept the unacceptable. The work, after all, was not in itself irksome; and Sarkane's contempt was almost a challenge to Bo to prove himself superior in every aspect, even the craft of metal-working, to Sarkane himself. At times to his own surprise and displeasure he found himself working diligently.

The spaceyards themselves he found remarkable. His eye, like that of most urbanites, was sensitive; he noted the somber concord of color: black structures, ocher soil, grey concrete, reds, blues and olive greens of signs and symbols, all animated by electric glitters, fires and steams, the constant motion of stern-faced workmen. The hulls loomed upon the sky; for these Bo felt a curious emotion: half-awe, half-antipathy; they symbolized the far worlds which Bo, as an urbanite, had no slightest intention of visiting, not even as a tourist.

Why probe these far regions? He knew the look, odor and feel of these worlds through the agency of his term; he had seen nothing which wasn't done better here in Hant.

If one had money. Money! A word resonant with magic. From where he worked with his buffing machine he could see south to Cloudhaven, floating serene and golden in the light of afternoon. Here was where he would live, so he promised himself, and muttered slow oaths of longing as he looked. Money was what he needed.

The rasp of Sarkane's voice intruded upon his daydreams. "Put a No. Five head on your machine and bring it over to the aerie bays. Look sharp; there's a hurry-up job we've got to get out today." He made what Bo considered an unnecessarily brusque gesture.

Bo slung the machine over his shoulder and followed Sarkane, walking perforce with the bent loose-kneed stride of a workman carrying a load. He knew the look of his gait; introversion and constant self-evaluation are integral adjuncts to the urbanite's mental machinery; he felt humiliation and fury: he, Bo Histledine, Big Bo the Boodlesnatch, hunching along like a common workman! He longed to shout at Sarkane, something like: "Hey! Slow down, you old gutreek; do you think I'm a camel? Here, carry the damn machine yourself, or put it in your ear!" Bo only muttered the remarks, and loped to catch up with Sarkane: through the clangor of the cold-belling shop, across the pulsion-pod storage yard with the great hulls massive overhead; over the gantry ways to a cluster of three platforms at the southern edge of the yard. On one of the platforms rested a glass-domed construction which Bo recognized for an aerie: the honorary residence of a commander in the Order of the Terrestrial Empire, and reserved for the use of such folk alone.

Sarkane motioned to Bo, and indicated the underside of the peripheral flange. "Polish that metal clean, get all that scurf and oxide off, so the crystallizer can lay on a clean coat. They'll be arriving at any time and we want it right for them."

"Who is 'them'?"

"A party from Rampold: an O.T.E. and his family. Get cracking now, we don't have much time."

Sarkane moved away. Bo considered the aerie. Rampold? Bo thought he had heard the place mentioned: a far half-savage world where men strove against an elemental environment and hostile indigenes to create new zones of habitability. Why didn't they stay out there if they liked it so much? But they always came swanking back to Earth with their titles and prerogatives, and here he was, Bo Histledine, polishing metal for them.

Bo jumped up to the deck and went to peer into the interior. He saw a pleasant but hardly lavish living room with white walls, a scarlet and blue rug, an open fireplace. In the center of the room a number of cases had been stacked. Bo read the name stenciled on the sides: Commander M.R. Tynnott, S.E.S.— the S.E.S. for *Space Exploration Service.*

Sarkane's voice vibrated against his back. "Hey! Histledine! Get down from there! What do you think you're up to?"

"Just looking," said Bo. "Keep your shirt on." He jumped to the ground. "Nothing much to see anyway. They don't even have a TV let alone a term. Still, I'd take one if they gave it to me."

"There's no obstacle in your way." Sarkane's tone was edged with caustic humor. "Just go work out back of beyond for twenty or thirty years; they'll give you an aerie."

"Bo Histledine isn't about to start out there."

"I expect not. Buff down that flange now, and make a clean job of it."

While Bo applied his machine, Sarkane wandered here and there, inspecting the repairs which had been made on the aerie's underbody, waiting for the crystallizer crew and keeping an eye on Bo.

The work was tiresome; Bo was forced to stand in a cramped position, holding the machine above him. His zeal, never too keen, began to flag. Whenever Sarkane was out of sight, Bo straightened up and relaxed. Commander Tynnott and his family could wait another hour or two, or two or three days, so far as Bo was concerned. Starlanders were much too haughty and self-satisfied for Bo's taste. They acted as if the simple process of flying space made them somehow superior to the folk who chose to stay home in the cities.

During one of his rest periods he watched a cab glide down to a halt nearby. A girl alighted and walked toward the aerie. Bo stared in fascination. This was a girl of a sort he had never seen before: a girl considerably younger than himself, perfectly formed, slender but lithe and supple, a creature precious beyond value. She approached with an easy jaunty stride, as if already in her short life she had walked far and wide, across hill and dale, forest trails and mountain ridges: wherever she chose to go. Her polished copper hair hung loose, just past her jaw-line; she was either ignorant or heedless of the intricate coiffures currently fashionable in Hant. Her clothes were equally simple: a blue-gray frock, white sandals, no ornaments whatever. She halted beside the aerie and Bo was able to study her face. Her eyes were dark blue and deep as lakes; her cheeks were flat; her mouth was wide and through some charming mannerism seemed a trifle wry and crooked. Her skin was a clear pale tan; her features could not have been more exquisitely formed. She spoke to Bo without actually looking at him. "I wonder where I get aboard."

Instantly gallant, Bo stepped forward. "Here; let me give you a leg up." To touch her, to caress (even for an instant) one of those supple young legs would be a fine pleasure indeed. The girl seemed not to hear him; she jumped easily up to the rail and swung herself over.

Sarkane came forward. He made a brusque gesture toward Bo, then turned to the girl. "I expect you're one of the owners. Tynnott I think is the name?"

"My father is Commander Tynnott. I thought he'd already be here with my mother. I suppose they'll be along soon." The girl's voice was as easy and light-hearted as her appearance, and she addressed gray old Ed Sarkane as if they had been friends for years. "You're no urbanite; where did you get your cast?" She referred to the indefinable aspect by which starlanders and spacemen were able to identify their own kind.

"Here, there and everywhere," said Sarkane. "Most of my time I worked for Slade out in the Zumberwalts."

The girl looked at him with admiration. "Then you must have known Vode Skerry and Ribolt Troil, and all the others."

"Yes, Miss, well indeed."

"And now you're living in Hant!" The girl spoke in a marveling voice. Bo's lips twitched. What, he wondered, was so wrong about living in Hant?

"Not for long," said Sarkane. "Next year I'm going out to Tinctala. My son farms a station out there."

The girl nodded in comprehension. She turned to inspect the aerie. "This is all so exciting; I've never lived in such splendor before."

Sarkane smiled indulgently. "It's not all that splendid, Miss, or I should say not compared to the way the rich folk live up there." He gestured toward Cloudhaven. "Still, they'd trade for aeries anytime, or so I'm told."

"There's not all that many aeries then?"

"Two thousand is all there'll ever be; that's the law. Otherwise they'd be hanging in the sky thick as jellyfish. Every cheap-jack and politician and pluto-crat around the world would want his aerie. No Miss, they're reserved to the O.T.E. and that's how it should be. Are you to be here long?"

"Not too long; my father has business with the Agency, and I'll undertake a bit of research while I'm here."

"Ah, you'll be a student at the Academy? It's an interesting place, the last word on everything, or so they say."

"I'm sure it is. I plan to visit the Hall of History tomorrow, as a matter of fact." She pointed toward a descending cab. "Here they are at last."

Bo, who had worked to within casual earshot, wielded his machine until Sarkane went off to confer with the Tynnotts. He buffed along the flange to where the girl stood leaning on the rail; raising his eyes he glimpsed a pair of smooth slender brown legs, a glint of thigh. She was only peripherally aware of his existence. Bo straightened up and put on that expression of mesmeric masculinity which had served him so well in the past. But the girl, rather than heeding him, went down the deck a few steps. "I'm already here," she called, "but I don't know how to get in."

Bo quivered with wrath. So the girl wouldn't look at him! So she thought him a stupid laborer! Couldn't she tell he was Bo Histledine, the notorious Big Boo, known up and down the North Shore, from Dipshaw Heights to Swarling Park?

He moved along the rail. Halting beside the girl he contrived to drop his adjustment wrench on her foot. She yelped in pain and surprise. "Sorry," said Bo. He could not restrain a grin. "Did it hurt?"

"Not very much." She looked down at the black smear of grease on her white sandal, then she turned and joined her parents who were entering the aerie.

She said in a puzzled voice: "Do you know, I believe that workman purposely dropped his tool on my foot."

Tynnott said after a moment: "He probably wanted to attract your attention."

"I wish he'd thought of some other way…It still hurts."

Two hours later, with the sun low in the west, Tynnott took the aerie aloft. The spaceyards dwindled below; the black buildings, the skeletal spaceships, the ramps, docks and gantries, became miniatures. The Louthe lay across the panorama in lank mustard-silver sweeps, with a hundred bridges straddling. Dipshaw Heights rose to the west with white structures stepping up and down the slope; beyond and away to the north spread residential suburbs among a scatter of parks and greenways. In the east stood the decaying towers of the Old City; in the south, golden among a tumble of cumulus clouds, Cloudhaven floated like a wonderful fairy castle.

The aerie drifted full in the light of sunset. The Tynnotts, Merwyn, Jade and Alice, leaned on the railing looking down upon the city.

"Now you've seen old Hant," said Merwyn Tynnott, "or at least the scope of it. What do you think?"

"It's a wild confusion," said Alice. "At least it seems that way. So many incongruous elements: Cloudhaven, the Old City, the working class slums…"

"Not to mention Jillyville, which is just below us," said Jade, "and College Station, and the Alien Quarter."

"And Dipshaw Heights, and Goshen, and River Meadow, and Elmhurst, and Juba Valley."

"Exactly," said Alice. "I wouldn't even try to generalize."

"Wise girl!" said Merwyn Tynnott. "In any event, generalization is a job for the subconscious, which has a very capable integrating apparatus."

Alice found the idea interesting. "How do you distinguish between generalization and emotion?"

"I never bother."

Alice laughed at her father's whimsy. "I use my subconscious whenever I can, but I don't trust it. For instance, my subconscious insists that a workman carefully dropped his wrench on my foot. My common sense doesn't believe it."

"Your common sense isn't common enough," said Merwyn Tynnott. "It's perfectly simple. He fell in love and wanted to let you know."

Alice, half-amused, half-embarrassed, shook her head. "Ridiculous! I'd only just jumped aboard the boat!"

"Some people make up their minds in a hurry. As a matter of fact, you were unusually cordial with Waldo Walberg last night."

"Not really," said Alice airily. "Waldo of course is a pleasant person, but certainly neither of us has the slightest romantic inclination. In the first place, I couldn't spare the time, and secondly I doubt if we have anything in common."

"You're right, of course," said Jade. "We're only teasing you because you're so pretty and turn so many heads and then pretend not to notice."

"I suppose I could make myself horrid," mused Alice. "There's always the trick Shikabay taught me."

"Which trick? He's taught you so many."

"His new trick is rather disgusting, but he insists that it works every time."

"I wonder how he knows," said Jade with a sniff. "Wretched old charlatan! And lewd to boot."

"In this connection," said Merwyn Tynnott, "I want to warn you: be careful around this old city. The people here are urbanites. The city festers with subjectivity."

"I'll be careful, although I'm sure I can take care of myself. If I couldn't, Shikabay would feel very humiliated...I'll get it." She went in to answer the telephone. Waldo's face looked forth from the screen: a handsome face, with an aquiline profile, the eyes stern, the nose straight, the droop of the mouth indicating sensitivity, or charm, or self-indulgence, or impatience, or all, or none, depending upon who made the appraisal and under what circumstances. In accordance with the current mode, Waldo's hair had been shorn to a stubble, then enameled glossy black, and carefully carved into a set of rakish curves, cusps, and angles. His teeth were enameled black; he wore silver lip-enamel and his ears were small flat tabs, with a golden bauble dangling from his right ear. To a person schooled in urban subtleties, Waldo's costume indicated upper-class lineage and his mannerisms were those of Cloudhaven alone.

"Hello Waldo," said Alice. "I'll call Father."

"No, no, wait! It's you I want."

"Oh? For what?"

Waldo licked his lips and peered into the screen. "I was right."

"How so?"

"You're the most exciting, entrancing, exhilarating person in, on, above or below the city Hant."

"How ridiculous," said Alice. "I'm just me."

"You're fresh as a flower, an orange marigold dancing in the wind."

"Please be serious, Waldo. I assume you called about that book *Cities of the Past*."

"No. I'm calling about cities of the present, namely Hant. Since you'll be here so short a time, why don't we look the old place over?"

"That's just what we're doing," said Alice. "We can see all the way south to Elmhurst, north to Birdville, east to the Old Town, west to the sunset."

Waldo peered into the screen. Flippancy? Ponderous humor? Sheer stupidity? Utter naïveté? Waldo could not decide. He said politely: "I meant that we should look in on one of the current presentations, something that you might not see out on Rampold. For instance, a concert? an exhibition? a percept?...What's that you're doing?"

"I'm noting down an idea before I forget it."

Waldo raised his expressive eyebrows. "Then afterwards we could take a bite of supper somewhere and get acquainted. I know an especially picturesque place, the Old Lair, which I think you might enjoy."

"Waldo, I really don't want to leave the aerie; it's so peaceful up here, and we're having such a nice talk."

"You and your parents?" Waldo was amazed.

"There's no one else here."

"But you'll be in Hant such a very short time!"

"I know...Well, perhaps I should make the most of my time. I can enjoy myself later."

Waldo's voice became thick. "But I want you to enjoy yourself tonight!"

"Oh, very well. But let's not stay out late. I'm visiting the Academy tomorrow morning."

"We'll let circumstances decide. I'll be across in about an hour. Will that give you time to do your primping?"

"Come sooner, if you like. I'll be ready in ten minutes."

II

Waldo arrived half an hour later to find Alice waiting for him. She wore a simple gown of dull dark green stuff; a fillet of flat jade pebbles bound with gold wire confined her hair. She inspected Waldo with curiosity, and for a fact Waldo's habiliments were remarkable both for elegance and intricacy. His trousers, of a light material patterned in black, brown and maroon, bagged artfully at the hips, gripped the calves, and hung carelessly awry over the slippers of black- and red-enameled metal. Waldo's blouse was a confection of orange, gray and black; above this he wore a tight-waisted black jacket, pinched at the elbow, flaring at the sleeve, and a splendid cravat of silk, which shimmered with the colors of an oil-film on water. "What an interesting costume!" Alice exclaimed. "I suppose each detail has its own symbological value."

"If so, I'm not aware of it," said Waldo. "Good evening, Commander."

"Good evening, Waldo. And where are you bound tonight?"

"It depends upon Alice. There's a concert at the Contemporanea: the music of Vaakstras, highly interesting."

"Vaakstras?" Alice reflected. "I've never heard of him. Of course that means nothing."

Waldo laughed indulgently. "A cult of dissident musicians emigrated to the coast of Greenland. They raised their children without music of any sort, without so much as knowledge of the word 'music'. At adolescence they gave the children a set of instruments and required that they express themselves, and in effect create a musical fabric based upon their innate emotive patterns. The music which resulted is indeed challenging. Listen." From his pocket he brought a small black case. A window glowed to reveal an index; Waldo set dials. "Here's a sample of Vaakstras; it's not obvious music."

Alice listened to the sounds from the music-player. "I've heard better cat fights."

Waldo laughed. "It's demanding music, and certainly requires empathy from the participant. He must search his own file of patterns, rummaging and discarding until he finds the set at the very bottom of the pile, and these should synthesize within his mind the wild emotions of the Vaakstras children."

"Let's not bother tonight," said Alice. "I'd never be sure that I'd uncovered the proper patterns and I might feel all the wrong emotions, and anyway I'm not all that interested in feeling someone else's emotions; I've got enough of my own."

"We'll find something you'll like, no fear of that." Waldo bowed politely to Merwyn and Jade, and conducted Alice into the cab. They slanted down toward the city.

Waldo looked sidewise at Alice. He declared, "Tonight you're an enchanted princess from a fairy tale. How do you do it?"

"I don't know," said Alice. "I didn't try anything special. Where are we going?"

"Well, there's an exhibition of Latushenko's spirit crystals, which he grows in new graves; or we could go to the Arnaud Intrinsicalia, where there's a very clever performance, which I've already seen three times; I know you'd enjoy it. Operators are prosthetically coupled to puppets, who perform the most adventurous and outrageous acts. There's a performance of *Salammbô* on tonight, with *The Secret Powder-puff*, which is rather naughty, if you like such things."

Alice smiled and shook her head. "I happened upon the mammoth atrachids of Didion Swamp in a state of oestrus, and since then I've lost all interest in voyeurism."

Waldo was taken aback. He blinked and adjusted his cravat. "Well—there's always the Perceptory—but you're not wired and you'd miss a great deal. There's an exhibit at the Hypersense: John Shibe's *Posturings* . Or we might luck into a couple seats at the Conservatory; tonight they're doing Oxtot's *Generation of Fundamental Pain*, with five music machines."

"I'm not really all that interested in music," said Alice. "I just don't care to sit still that long, wondering why someone saw fit to perform this or that particular set of notes."

"My word," said Waldo in astonishment. "Isn't there any music on Rampold?"

"There's music enough, I suppose. People sing or whistle when the mood strikes them. Out on the stations there's always someone with a banjo."

"That's not quite what I mean," said Waldo. "Music, and in fact, art in general, is the process of consciously communicating an emotional judgment or point of view in terms of abstract symbology. I don't believe whistling a jig fits this definition."

"I'm sure you're right," said Alice. "I know it's never occurred to me when I'm whistling. When I was very little we had a school teacher from Earth— an elderly lady who was dreadfully afraid of everything. She tried to teach us subjectivity; she played us plaque after plaque of music without effect; all of us enjoyed our own emotions more than someone else's."

"What a little barbarian you are, for a fact!"

Alice only laughed. "Poor old Miss Burch! She was so upset with us! The only name I remember is Bargle, or Bangle, or something like that, who always ended his pieces with a great deal of pounding and fanfares."

"'Bargle'? 'Bangle'? Was it possibly Baraungelo?"

"Why yes, I'm sure that's the name! How clever of you!"

Waldo laughed ruefully. "One of the greatest composers of the last century. Well—you don't want to go to concerts or exhibitions, or to the Perceptory," said Waldo plaintively. "What are you doing? Making more notes?"

"I have a bad memory," said Alice. "When an idea arrives, I've got to record it."

"Oh," said Waldo flatly. "Well—what do you suggest we do?"

Alice tried to soothe Waldo's feelings. "I'm a very impatient person. I just don't care for subjectivizing, or vicarious experience…Oh my, I've done it again, and made it even worse. I'm sorry."

Waldo was dazed by the whirl of ideas. "Sorry for what?"

"Perhaps you didn't notice, which is just as well."

"Oh come now. It couldn't have been all that bad. Tell me!"

"It's not important," said Alice. "Where do spacemen go for amusement?"

Waldo responded in a measured voice. "They drink in saloons, or escort fancy ladies to the High Style Restaurant, or prowl Jillyville, or gamble in the Epidrome."

"What is Jillyville?"

"It's the old market plaza, and I suppose it's sometimes amusing. The Alien Quarter is just down Light-year Road; the jeeks and wampoons and tinkos all have shops along the Parade. There are little bistros and drunken spacemen, mystics, charlatans and inverts, gunkers and gunk peddlers and all sorts of furtive desperate people. It's more than a trifle vulgar."

"Jillyville might be interesting," said Alice. "At least it's alive. Let's go there."

What an odd girl! thought Waldo. Beautiful to melt a man's mind, a daughter of Commander Merwyn Tynnott, O.T.E., a member of the galactic nobility with a status far superior to his own; yet how provincial, how incredibly self-assured for her age, which could hardly be more than seventeen or eighteen! She seemed at times almost patronizing, as if he were the culturally impoverished starlander and she the clever sophisticate! Well then, thought Waldo, let's divert matters into a more amusing channel. He leaned close, put his hand to her cheek and sought to kiss her, which would re-establish his initiative. Alice ducked back and Waldo was thwarted. She asked in astonishment, "Why did you do that?"

"The usual reasons," said Waldo in a muffled voice. "They're quite well known. Haven't you ever been kissed before?"

"I'm sorry if I hurt your feelings, Waldo. But let's just be casual friends."

Waldo said largely: "Why should we limit ourselves in any way? There's scope for whatever relationship we want! Let's start over. Pretend now that we've just met, but already we've become interested in one another!"

"The last person I want to deceive is myself," said Alice. She hesitated. "I hardly know how to advise you."

Waldo looked at Alice with a slack jaw. "As to what?"

"Subjectivity."

"I'm afraid I don't understand you."

Alice nodded. "It's like talking to a fish about being wet…Let's speak of something else. The lights of the city are really magnificent. Old Earth is certainly picturesque! Is that the Epidrome down there?"

Looking askance at the charming features, Waldo responded in a somewhat metallic voice. "That's Meridian Circle, at the end of the Parade, where the cults and debating societies meet. See that bar of white luciflux? That marks the Parade. The luminous green circle is the Epidrome. See those colored lights across the Parade? That's the Alien Quarter. The jeeks like blue lights, the tinkos insist on yellow, the wampoons won't have any lights at all, which accounts for that rather strange effect."

The cab landed; Waldo gallantly assisted Alice from the craft. "We're at the head of the Parade; that's all Jillyville ahead of us…What's that you're carrying?"

"My camera. I want to record some of those beautiful costumes, and yours too."

"Costume?" Waldo looked down at his garments. "Barbarians wear costumes. These are just clothes."

"Well, they're very interesting in any event…What a remarkable assortment of people!"

"Yes," said Waldo glumly. "You'll see everybody and everything along the Parade. Don't walk too closely behind the jeeks. They have a rather noxious defensive mechanism right above their tail horn. If you see a man with a red hat, he's a bonze of the External Magma. Don't look at him or he'll want an 'enlightenment fee' for divining his thoughts. Those three men yonder are spacemen—drunk, of course. Down at the end of the Parade is Spaceman's Rest: a jail reserved for over-exuberant spacemen. Out yonder is the Baund, the most garish section of Jillyville: saloons, bordellos, shampoo parlors, cult studios, curio shops, mind-readers, evangelists and prophets, gunk-peddlers— all in the Baund."

"What a picturesque place!"

"Yes indeed. Here's the Black Opal Café, and there's a table; let's sit and watch for a bit."

For a period they sat and sipped drinks: Waldo a clear cold Hyperion Elixir, Alice a goblet of the popular Tanglefoot Punch. They watched the passersby: tourists from the backlands, spacemen, the young folk of Hant. Ladies of the night sauntered past with an eye for the spacemen, their wrist-chains jingling with socket adapters. They dressed in the most modish extremes, hair piled high and sprinkled with sparkling lights. Some varnished their skins, others wore cheek-plates plumed with jaunty feathers. Their ears were uniformly clipped into elf-horns; their shoulder finials rose in grotesque spikes. Waldo suggested that Alice take their picture, and she did so. "But I'm really more interested in representative pictures of representative folk, such as yourself and that fine young couple yonder. Aren't they picturesque? My word, what are those creatures?"

"Those are jeeks," said Waldo. "From Caph III. There's quite a colony here. Notice the organ above the dorsal horn? It ejects body-tar, which smells like nothing on Earth…Look yonder, those tall whitish creatures. They're wampoons from Argo Navis. About five hundred live in an old brick warehouse. They don't walk out too often. I don't see any tinkos, and the spangs won't appear until just before dawn."

A tall man stumbled against the railing and thrust a hairy face over their table. "Can you spare a dollar or two, your lordships? We're poor backlanders looking for work, and hungry so that we can hardly walk."

"Why not try gunk," suggested Waldo, "and take your mind off your troubles."

"Gunk is not free either, but if you'll oblige with some coins, I'll make myself merry and gay."

"Try that white building across the Parade. They'll fix you up."

The gunker roared an obscenity. He looked at Alice. "Somewhere, my lovely darling, we've met. Out there somewhere, in some lovely land of glory; I'll never forget your face. For old times' sake, a dollar or two!"

Alice found a five dollar bill. The gunker, chuckling in mad glee, seized it and shambled away.

"Money wasted," said Waldo. "He'll buy gunk, some cheap new episode."

"I suppose so…Why isn't wiring illegal?"

Waldo shook his head. "The perceptories would go out of business. And never discount the power of love."

"Love?"

"Lovers wire themselves with special sockets, so that they can plug into one another. You don't do this on Rampold?"

"Oh no indeed."

"Aha. You're shocked."

"Not really. I'm not even surprised. Just think, you could even make love by telephone or television, or even by a recording; all you need is the right kind of wiring."

"It's been done. In fact, the gunk producers have gone far beyond: brain-wiring plus a percept equals gunk."

"Oh. That's what gunk is. I thought it was a hallucinatory drug."

"It's controlled hallucination. The more you turn up the voltage, the more vivid it becomes. To the gunker life is gray; the colors come back when he dials up the gunk. Real life is a dismal interlude between the sumptuous experiences of gunk…Oh, it's seductive!"

"Have you tried it?"

Waldo shrugged. "It's illegal—but most everybody tries it. Are you interested?"

Alice shook her head. "In the first place I'm not wired. In the second place—but no matter." She became busy with her notes.

Waldo asked, "What are you writing about now? Gunk?"

"Just an idea or two."

"Such as?"

"You probably wouldn't be interested."

"Oh but I would! I'd be interested in all your notes."

"You might not understand them."

"Try me."

Alice shrugged and read: "'Urbanites as explorers of inner space: i.e.—subjectivity. The captains: psychologists. The pioneers: abstractionists. The creed: perceptiveness, control of ideas. The fuglemen: critics. The paragons: the 'well-read man', the 'educated listener', the 'perceptive spectator'.

"'Precursive to gunk: theater-attendance, percepts, music, books: all urbanite cult-objects.

"'Abstraction: the work of urbanity. Vicarious experience: the life-flow of urbanity. Subjectivity: the urban mind-flow.'"

She looked at Waldo. "These are only a few rough notes. Do you want to hear any more?"

Waldo sat with a grim expression. "Do you really believe all that?"

"'Belief' is not quite the right word." Alice reflected a moment. "I've simply arranged a set of facts into a pattern. For an urbanite the implications go very far—in fact very far indeed. But let's talk of something else. Have you ever visited Nicobar?"

"No," said Waldo, looking off across the Baund.

"I've heard that the Sunken Temple is very interesting. I'd like to try to decipher the glyphs."

"Indeed?" Waldo lifted his eyebrows. "Are you acquainted with Ancient Gondwanese?"

"Of course not! But glyphs usually have a symbolic derivation. Don't stare at those lights, Waldo; they'll put you to sleep."

"What?" Waldo sat up in his chair. "Nothing of the sort. They're just the lights of a carousel."

"I know, but passing behind those pillars they fluctuate at about ten cycles a second, or so I'd estimate."

"And what of that?"

"The lights send impulses to your brain which create electrical waves. At that particular frequency, if the waves are strong enough or continue long enough, you'll very likely become dazed. Most people do."

Waldo gave a skeptical grunt. "Where did you learn that?"

"It's common knowledge—at least among neurologists."

"I'm no neurologist. Are you?"

"No. But our odd-jobs man on Rampold is, or at least claims to be. He's also a magician, bear wrestler, cryptologist, boat-builder, herbalist, and half a dozen other wonderful things. Mother considers him bizarre, but I admire him tremendously, because he is competent. He's taught me all kinds of useful skills." Alice picked a pink flower from a potted plant beside the table. She placed it on the table, and put her hands down flat, covering the flower. "Which hand is it under?"

Waldo somewhat condescendingly pointed to her left hand. Alice lifted her right hand to reveal a red flower.

"Aha," said Waldo. "You picked two flowers! Lift your other hand."

Alice lifted her left hand. On the table glittered the gold ornament which had hung at Waldo's ear. Waldo blinked, felt his ear, then stared at Alice. "How did you get hold of that?"

"I took it while you were watching the lights. But where is the pink flower?" She looked up, grinning like an imp. "Do you see it?"

"No."

"Touch your nose."

Waldo blinked once more and touched his nose. "There's no flower there."

Alice laughed in great merriment. "Of course not. What did you expect?" She sipped from her goblet of punch, and Waldo, somewhat annoyed, leaned back with his own glass of punch, to find within the pink flower. "Very clever." He rose stiffly to his feet. "Shall we continue?"

"As soon as I photograph the picturesque couple at the table yonder. They seem to know you. At least they've been watching us."

"I've never seen them before in my life," said Waldo. "Are you ready? Let's go on."

They continued along the Parade.

"There's a really big jeek," said Alice. "What's that it's carrying?"

"Probably garbage for its soup. Don't stand too close behind it…Well, we're behind it anyway. Just don't jostle it, or—"

An arm reached in from the side and dealt the jeek's tail horn a vigorous blow. Alice ducked aside; the spurt of body tar missed her and struck Waldo on the neck and chest.

III

After his day's work Bo Histledine rode a slideway to the transit tube, and was whisked northwest to Fulchock, where he inhabited a small apartment in an ancient concrete warren. Waiting for him was Hernanda Degasto Confurias whom he had only recently wooed and won. Bo stood in the doorway looking at her. She was perfectly turned out, he thought; no one was more sensitive to the latest subtleties of fashion; no one surpassed her at adapting them to herself, so that she and the style were indistinguishable; with every change of clothes she assumed a corresponding temperament. A toque or cylinder of transparent film clasped the top of her head and contained a froth of black curls, artfully mingled with bubbles of pale green glass. Her ears were concave shells three inches high, rounded on top, with emerald plugs. Her skin was marmoreal; her lips were enameled black; her eyes and eyebrows, both black, could not be improved upon and remained in their natural condition. Hernanda was a tall girl. Her breasts had been artificially reduced to little rounded hummocks; her torso was a rather gaunt cylinder over which she had drawn a tube of coarse white cloth, which compressed her haunches. On her shoulders stood small bronze ornaments, like urns or finials, into each of which she had placed a dram of her personal scent. On her hands she wore greaves of black metal clustered with green jewels. Under her right armpit was a socket and the bottom terminal was decorated with a pink heart on which were inscribed the initials *B H.*

Hernanda stood proud and silent before Bo's inspection, knowing herself perfect. Bo gave her no word of greeting; she said nothing to him. He strode into his inner room, bathed, and changed into a black and white diapered blouse, loose lime-green pantaloons, the legs long over his heels and tucked into sandals to expose his long white toes. He tied a purple and blue kerchief at a rakish angle to his head, and hung a string of black pearls from his right ear. When he returned to the living room Hernanda apparently had not moved. Silent as an obelisk she waited beside the far wall. Bo stood brooding. Hernanda was just right in every aspect. He was a lucky man to own the private plug to her socket. And yet…And yet what? Bo angrily thrust aside the thought.

"I want to go to the Old Lair," said Hernanda.

"Do you have money?"

"Not enough."

"I'm short as well. We'll go down to Fotzy's."

They left the apartment and carefully adjusted the alarms; only last week gunkers had broken in and stolen Bo's expensive term.

At Fotzy's they pressed buttons to order the dishes of their choice: hot gobbets of paste in spice-sauce, a salad of nutrient crisps on a bed of natural lettuce from the hydroponic gardens of Old Town. After a moment or two Bo said: "The spaceyards are no good. I'm going to get out."

"Oh? Why?"

"A man stands watching me. Unless I work like a kaffir he harangues me. It's simply not comfortable."

"Poor old Bo."

"But for that flashing probation I'd tie him in a knot and kite off. I was built for beauty, not toil."

"You know Suanna? Her brother has gone off into space."

"It's like jumping into nothing. He can have all he wants."

"If I got money I'd like to take an excursion. Give me a thousand dollars, Bo."

"You give me a thousand dollars. I'll go on the excursion."

"But you said you wouldn't go!"

"I don't know what I want to do."

Hernanda accepted the rejoinder in silence. They left the restaurant and walked out upon Shermond Boulevard. South beyond Old Town, Cloudhaven rode among the sunset clouds; in the halcyon light it seemed as if it might have been, or should have been, the culminating glory of human endeavor; but everyone knew differently.

"I'd rather have an aerie," muttered Bo.

One of Hernanda's few faults was a tendency to enunciate the obvious with the air of one transmitting a startling new truth. "You're not licensed for an aerie. They only give them to O.T.E.'s."

"That's all tripe. They should go to whoever can pay for them."

"You still wouldn't have one."

"I'd get the money, never fear."

"Remember your probation."

"They'll never fix on me again."

Hernanda thought her private thoughts. She wanted Bo to take a cottage in Galberg, and work in the artificial flavor factory. Tonight the prospect seemed as flimsy as smoke. "Where are we going?"

"I thought we'd look into Hongo's for the news."

"I don't like Hongo's all that much."

Bo said nothing. If Hernanda did not like Hongo's she could go somewhere else. And only as recently as yesterday she had seemed such a prize!

They rode the slideway to the Prospect Escalator and up to Dipshaw Knob. Hongo's Blue Lamp Tavern commanded a fine view of the River Louthe, the spaceyards and most of West Hant, and was old beyond record or calculation. The woodwork was stained black, the brick floors were worn with the uneven passage of footsteps; the ceiling was lost in the dark blur of time. Tall windows looked across the far vistas of Hant, and on a rainy day Hongo's was a tranquil haven from which to contemplate the city.

Hongo's reputation was not altogether savory; curious events had occurred on the premises or shortly after patrons had departed. The Blue Lamp was known as a place where one must keep his wits about him, but the reputation incurred no loss of patronage; indeed the suffusion of vice and danger attracted folk from all Hant, as well as backland tourists and spacemen.

Bo led Hernanda to his usual booth, and found there a pair of his cronies: Raulf Dido and Paul Amhurst. Bo and Hernanda seated themselves without words of greeting, according to the tenets of current custom.

Bo presently said: "The spaceyard keeps me off punition, but this aside, it's just too bad."

"You're earning an honest wage," said Raulf Dido.

"Hah! Bah! Bo Histledine, a sixteen-dollar-a-day apprentice? You give me fits!"

"Talk to Paul. He's on to something good."

"It's a beautiful new line of gunk," said Paul Amhurst. "It's produced in Aquitaine and it's as good as the best." He displayed a selection of stills; the views were vivid and provocative. "Ow-wow," said Bo. "That's good stuff. I'll take some of that myself."

Hernanda made a restless movement and pouted; it was bad manners to talk of gunk in front of one's lady friend, inasmuch as gunk inevitably included erotic and hyper-erotic episodes.

"Somebody will get the Hant distributorship," said Paul, "and I'm hoping it's me. If so I'll need help: you and Raulf, maybe a few more if we have to bust into Julio's territory."

"Hmm," said Bo. "What about the Old Man?"

"I put through an application a week ago. He hasn't bounced it back. I saw Jantry yesterday and he gave me an up-sign. So it looks good."

"Genine won't fix it with Julio."

"No. We'd have to gut it through by ourselves. It might get warm."

"And wet," said Paul referring to the bodies sometimes found floating in the Louthe.

"That flashing probation," spat Bo. "I've got to worry about that. In fact, look over there! My personal vermin, Clachey and Delmar. Hide that gunk! They're coming by."

The two detectives halted beside the table; they looked down with mercury-colored eyes, back and forth between Bo, Raulf and Paul. "A fine lot of thugs," said Clachey. "What deviltry are you working up now?"

"We're planning a birthday party for our mothers," said Raulf. "Would you care to come?"

Delmar scrutinized Bo. "Your probation, as I recall, depends on avoiding bad company. Yet here you sit with a pair of gunk merchants."

Bo returned a stony gaze. "They've never mentioned such things to me. In fact we're all planning to enter the Police Academy."

Clachey reached to the seat between Bo and Paul and came up with the stills. "Now what have we here? Could it be gunk?"

"It looks like some photographs," said Raulf. "They were on the seat when we arrived."

"Indeed," said Clachey. "So you think you're going to import Aquitanian gunk? Do you have any tablets on you?"

"Of course not," said Raulf. "What do you take us for? Criminals?"

"Empty your pockets," said Delmar. "If there's gunk in the group, somebody's probation is in bad trouble."

Paul, Raulf and Bo wordlessly arranged the contents of their pockets on the table. One at a time they stood up while Delmar deftly patted them up and down. "Oh, what's this?" From Paul's waistband he extracted one of those devices known as stingers, capable of hurling needles of lethal or anaesthetic drugs across a room or a street and into a man's neck. Bo and Raulf were clean.

"Pay your respects to all," Clachey told Paul. "I believe that this is up and out, Amhurst."

"It might well be," Paul agreed dolefully.

A drunk lurched away from the bar and careened into the two detectives. "Can't a man drink in peace without you noses breathing down his neck?"

A waiter tugged at his arm and muttered a few words.

"So they're after gunkers!" stormed the drunk. "What of that? Up in Cloudhaven there's fancy gunk-parlors; why don't the noses go raid up there? It's always the poor scroffs what get the knocks."

The waiter managed to lead him away.

Bo said, "For a fact, how come you don't raid Cloudhaven?"

"We got our hands full with the scroffs, like the man said," replied Delmar, without heat.

Clachey amplified the remark. "They pay; they have the money. The scroffs don't have the money. They loot to get it. They're the problem, them and you merchants."

Delmar said to Bo: "This is a final notification, which will be inserted into your record. I warn you that you have been observed in the company of known criminals. If this occurs again, it's up and out."

"Thank you for your concern," said Bo in a heavy voice. He rose to his feet and jerked his hand at Hernanda. "Come along. We can't even take a drink in a respectable tavern without persecution."

Delmar and Clachey led away the despondent Paul Amhurst.

"Just as well," said Raulf. "He's too erratic."

Bo grunted. "I'm going to have to lay low. Until I think of something."

Raulf made a sign of comprehension; Bo and Hernanda departed Hongo's. "Where now?" asked Hernanda.

"I don't know...I don't feel like much. There's nowhere to go." As if involuntarily he glanced up to the stars which burnt through the night-glare. Rampold? Where was Rampold?

Hernanda took Bo's arm and led him down the escalator to the Shermond slideway. "I haven't been over to Jillyville for a while. It's just across the bridge."

Bo grumbled automatically, but could think of nothing better.

They crossed River Louthe by the Vertes Avenue Bridge, and sauntered through the flower market which for centuries had created a zone of clotted color in the shadow of the Epidrome.

Hernanda wanted to wander through the Epidrome and perhaps risk a dollar or two at one of the games of chance. "So long as you use your own money," said Bo gracelessly. "I don't intend to throw gold down a rat-hole. Not at sixteen dollars a day on that buffing machine."

Hernanda became sulky and refused to enter the Epidrome, which suited Bo well enough. The two moodily walked up to the Parade. As they passed the Black Opal Café, Bo noticed Alice's copper-glinting hair. He stopped short, then led Hernanda to a table. "Let's have a drink."

"Here? It's the most expensive place along the Parade!"

"Money means nothing to Big Bo the Histle."

Hernanda shrugged, but made no objection.

Bo selected a table twenty feet from where Waldo sat with Alice. He punched buttons, deposited coins; a moment later a waitress brought out their refreshment: lime beer for Bo and frozen rum for Hernanda.

Alice saw them and raised her camera; in irritation Bo put his head down on his hand. Hernanda stared at Alice and the camera. Tourists everywhere, taking photographs.

"We should be flattered." Bo gave Waldo a baleful examination. "Toffs out slumming—him, anyway. She's off-world. A starlander."

Hernanda scrutinized each detail of Alice's gown, hair, face and her fillet of jade pebbles. "She's just a child and a bit tatty. She looks as if she'd never seen a stylist in her life."

"Probably hasn't."

Hernanda looked at him suspiciously sidelong. "Are you interested?"

"Not all so much. She looks happy. I wonder why. It's probably her first time to Hant; soon she'll be heading back into nowhere. What has she got to live for?"

"She's probably rolling in money. I could have it too if I were willing to put up with her kind of life."

Bo chuckled. "It's remarkable, for a fact. Well, she's harmless, or so I suppose."

"Certainly nothing much to look at. All young eagerness and dancing around the maypole. Hair like a straw pile...Bo!"

"What?"

"You're not listening to me."

"My mind is roving the star lanes."

Waldo and Alice rose from their table and left the café. Bo's lewd conjectures caused him to suck in his breath. "Come along."

Hernanda sulkily swung her head away, and remained in her seat. Bo paid her no heed. Speechless with indignation she watched him go.

Waldo and Alice halted to avoid a jeek. Bo reached from the side and gave the jeek's tail horn a hard slap. The jeek voided upon Waldo. Alice glanced at Bo in consternation, then turned to Waldo. "It's that man there who did it!"

"Where? Which man?" croaked Waldo.

Suddenly alive to the danger of apprehension and police charges, Bo slid away through the crowd. Reeking and smarting, Waldo pursued him. Bo ran across the Parade, off into one of the rancid little alleys of the Alien Quarter. Wild with rage, Waldo followed.

Bo ran across the plaza where a dozen or more jeeks stood at a chest-high bench ingesting salt-froth. Waldo halted, looking here and there; Bo darted forth and thrust him into the group of jeeks; Waldo's impetus overturned the bench. Bo ran fleetly away, while the jeeks trampled Waldo, struck him with their secondary stubs, squirted him with tar.

Alice appeared with a pair of patrolmen, who flashed red lights at the jeeks and froze them into rigidity.

Waldo crept across the plaza on his hands and knees, and vomited the contents of his stomach.

"Poor Waldo," said Alice.

"Leave him to us, Miss," said the corporal. "Just a question or two, then I'll call down a cab. Who is this gentleman?"

Alice recited Waldo's name and address.

"And how did he get in this mess?"

Alice explained as best she could.

"Was this man in the green pants known to either of you?"

"I'm sure not. The whole affair seems so strange."

"Thank you, Miss. Come along, I'll call the cab."

"What of poor Waldo?"

"He'll be all right. We'll take him to the dispensary to be cleaned up. Tomorrow he'll be as good as new."

Alice hesitated. "I don't like to leave him, but I'd better be getting home; I've a great deal to do tomorrow."

IV

Bo gave no thought to Hernanda; he strode along the Parade in a strange savage mood, comprehensible to himself least of all. Why had he acted so? Not that he was sorry; to the contrary, he had hoped to soil the girl as well.

He returned to his Fulchock apartment, where he thought of Hernanda for the first time. She was nowhere in evidence, nor had he expected her, nor did he want her. What he craved was something unattainable, something indescribable.

He wanted the red-haired girl, and for the first time in his life he thought not in terms of sheer submission, but admiration and affection and a manner of living he could only sluggishly imagine.

He flung himself upon his couch and fell into a torpor.

>•‹

Gray-blue light awoke Bo. He groaned, rolled over on his couch and sat up.

He went to look at himself in the mirror. The sullen heavy-jawed face under the tangle of blond ringlets provided him neither distress nor joy; Bo Histledine merely looked at Bo Histledine.

He showered, dressed, drank a mug of bitter mayhaw tea, and ruminated.

Why not? Bo rasped at himself. He was as good as anyone, and better than most. If not one way, then another—but own her, possess her he would. The aspirations of the night before were flimsy shadows; Bo was a practical man.

The spaceyards? The buffing machine? As remote as the winds of last summer.

Bo dressed with care in gray and white pantaloons, a loose dark blue shirt with a dark red cravat, a soft gray cap pulled low over his forehead. Examining himself in the mirror Bo found himself oddly pleased with his appearance. He looked, so he thought, less bulky and even somewhat younger: perhaps because he felt excited.

He removed the cravat and opened the collar of his shirt. The effect pleased him: he looked—so he thought—casual and easy, less heavy in the chin and jaw. What of the tight blond curls which clustered over his ears and gave his face—so he thought—a sullen, domineering look? Bo yanked the cap down over his forehead and left his apartment.

At a nearby studio, a hairdresser trimmed away clustering curls and rubbed brown toner into the hair remaining. Different, thought Bo. Better? Hard to say. But different.

He rode the tube south to Lake Werle in Elmhurst, then went by slideway to the Academy.

Bo now moved tentatively; never before had he visited the Academy. He passed under the Gate of the Universe and stood looking across the campus. Giant elms stood dreaming in the wan morning sunlight; beyond rose the halls of the various academic disciplines. Students streamed past him: young men and women from the backlands and the far worlds, a few from Cloudhaven and the patrician suburbs, others from the working-class areas to the north.

The business of the day was only just beginning. Bo asked a few questions and was directed to the central cab landing; here he leaned against a wall and composed himself for a possibly long wait.

An hour passed. Bo frowned through a discarded student journal, wondering why anyone considered such trivia worth the printing.

A cab dropped from the sky; Alice stepped to the ground. Bo dropped the journal and watched her, keen as a hawk. She wore a black jacket, a gray skirt, black stockings reaching up almost to her knees; at her waist hung her note-taking apparatus. For a moment she stood looking about her, alert and attentive, mouth curved in a half-smile.

Bo leaned forward, encompassing her with the hot force of his will. He scrutinized her inch by inch, memorizing each of her attributes. Body: supple, slender; delightful slim legs. Hair flowing and glowing like brushed copper. Face: calm, suffused with—what? gayety? merriment? optimism? The air around her quivered with the immediacy of her presence.

Bo resented her assurance. This was the whole point! She was smug! Arrogant! She thought herself better than ordinary folk because her father was a commander of the O.T.E....Bo had to admit that this was not true. He would have preferred that it were. Her self-sufficiency was inherent. Bo envied her: a bubble of self-knowledge opened into his brain. He wanted to be like her: easy, calm, magnificent. The inner strength of the starlander was such that he never thought to measure himself against someone else. True! Alice was neither smug nor arrogant; to the contrary, she knew no vanity, nor even pride. She was herself; she knew herself to be intelligent, beautiful and good; nothing more was necessary.

Bo compressed his lips. She must concede him equality. She must know his strength, recognize his fierce virility.

Tragedy might be latent in the situation. If so, let it come! He was Bo Histledine, Big Boo the Blond Brute, who did as he pleased, who drove through life, reckless, feckless, giving way to no one.

Alice walked toward the halls of learning. Bo followed, twenty feet behind, admiring the jaunty motion of her body.

V

That morning, immediately after breakfast, Alice had telephoned Waldo at Cloudhaven. The Waldo who appeared on the screen was far different from that handsome, serene and gallant Waldo who had arrived by cab the previous evening to show her the city. This Waldo was pale, gaunt and grim, and met Alice's sympathetic inspection with a shifting darting gaze.

"No bones broken," he said in a muffled voice. "I'm lucky there. Once the jeeks start on a man they'll kill him, and they can't be punished because they're aliens."

"And this stuff they squirted on you: is it poisonous?"

Waldo made a guttural sound and directed one of his burning suspicious glances into the screen. "They scoured me and scrubbed me, and shaved all my hair. Still I smell it. The stuff apparently reacts with skin protein, and stays until a layer of skin wears off."

"Certainly a remarkable affair," mused Alice. "I wonder who would do a thing like that? And why?"

"I know who, at least. It was the fellow in green pantaloons at the table opposite. I've been meaning to ask you: didn't you photograph that couple?"

"Yes indeed I did! They seemed such a typical pair! I don't think you can identify the man; his head is turned away. But the woman is clear enough."

Waldo thrust his head forward with something of his old animation. "Good! Will you bring over the photograph? I'll show it to the police; they'll work up an identification fast enough. Somebody's going to suffer."

"I'll certainly send over the photograph," said Alice. "But I'm afraid that I don't have time to drop by. The Academy is on my schedule for today."

Waldo drew back, eyes glittering. "You won't learn much in one day. It usually takes a week just for orientation."

"I think I can find the information I want in just an hour or two; anyway, that's all the time I can spare."

"And may I ask the nature of this information?" Waldo's voice now had a definite edge. "Or is it a secret?"

"Of course not!" Alice laughed at the thought. "I'm mildly curious as to the formal methods of transmitting the urbanite ideology. Academicians are naturally a diverse lot, but in general they are confirmed urbanites: in fact, I suppose this is the basis upon which they attain their positions. After all, rabbits don't hire lions to teach their children."

"I don't follow you," said Waldo haughtily.

"It's perfectly simple. The Academy indoctrinates young rabbits in rabbitry, to pursue the metaphor, and I'm mildly curious as to the techniques."

"You'll be wasting your time," said Waldo. "I attend the Academy and I'm not aware of any 'rabbitry', as you put it."

"You would be more apt to notice its absence," said Alice. "Goodbye, Waldo. It was kind of you to show me Jillyville; I'm sorry the evening ended unpleasantly."

Waldo stared at the fresh young face, so careless and gay. "'Goodbye'?"

"I may not be seeing you again. We won't be in Hant all that long. But perhaps some day you'll come out to the starlands."

"Not bloody likely," Waldo muttered.

➤◄

A curious affair, Alice reflected, as she rode the cab down to the Academy. The man in the green pantaloons probably mistook Waldo for someone else. Or he might have acted out of sheer perversity; such folk were probably not uncommon in the psychological stew of the great city Hant.

The cab discharged her on a plat at the center of the campus. She stood a moment admiring the prospect: the walks and slideways leading here and there across landscaped vistas, the white halls under great elms, the great Enoie Memorial Clock Tower, formed from a single quartz crystal four hundred and sixty feet high. Students passed in their picturesque garments, each a small lonely cosmos exquisitely sensitive to the psychic compulsions of his environment. Alice gave her head a wistful shake and went to an information placard where the component structures of the Academy were identified: the Halls of Physical Science, Biologics, Mathematics, Human History, Anthropology and Comparative Culture, Xenology, Cosmology, Human Ideas and Arts, a dozen others. She read an informational notice addressed to visitors:

> Each hall consists of a number of conduits, or thematic passages, equipped with efficient pedagogical devices. The conduits are interconnected, to provide a flexible passage through any particular discipline, in accordance with the needs of the individual. The student determines his special field of interest, and is issued a chart designating his route through the hall. He moves at a rate dictated by his assimilative ability; his comprehension is continuously verified; when the end is reached he has mastered his subject.

Alice proceeded to the Hall of History. Entering, she gazed in awe around the splendid lobby, which enforced upon the visitor an almost stupefying awareness of the human adventure. Under a six-inch floor of clear crystal spread a luminous map of the terrestrial surface, projected by some curious shifting means which minimized distortion. The dark-blue dome of the ceiling scintillated with constellations. Around the walls, somewhat above eye-level, ran a percept-continuum where marched a slow procession of men, women and children: straggling peasants; barbarians in costumes of feathers and leather; clansmen marching to a music of clarions and drums; heroes striding alone; prelates and sacerdotes; hetairae, flower-maidens and dancing girls; blank-faced folk in drab garments, from any of a dozen ages; Etruscans, Celts, Scythians, Zumbelites, Dagonites, Mennonites; posturing priests of Babylon, warriors of the Caucasus. At one side of the hall they appeared from a blur of fog; as they marched they turned an occasional glance out toward those who had come to visit the Hall of History; to the far side of the great room they faded into the blur and were gone.

Alice went to the information desk where she bought a catalogue. Listed first were the basic routes through the conduits, then more complicated routes to encompass the aspects of special studies. Alice settled upon the basic survey course: 'Human History: from the origin of man to the present'. She paid the three dollar fee for non-credit transit, received a chart indicating her route through the conduits. A young man in a dark shirt immediately behind her, so she chanced to notice, elected the same course: evidently a subject popular with the students.

Her route proved to be simple enough: a direct transit of Conduit 1, with whatever detours, turn-offs, loops into other conduits, which happened to arouse her interest.

The young man in the dark shirt went on ahead. When she entered the conduit she discovered him studying the display of human precursors. He glanced at Alice and politely moved aside so that she might inspect the diorama as well. "Rough-looking thugs!" he commented in a jocular voice. "All hairy and dirty."

"Yes, quite so." Alice moved along the diorama.

The young man kept pace with her. "Excuse me, but aren't you a star-lander? From Engsten, or more likely Rampold?"

"Why yes! I'm from Rampold. How did you know?"

"Just a lucky guess. How do you like Hant?"

"It's interesting, certainly." Alice, rather primly erect, moved on along the display.

"Ugh," said Bo. "What's that they're eating?"

"Presumably some sort of natural food," said Alice.

"I guess you're right," said Bo. "They weren't too fussy in those days. Are you a student here?"

"No."

"Oh I see. Just sightseeing."

"Not exactly that either. I'm curious as to the local version of history."

"I thought history was history," said Bo.

Alice turned him a quick side-glance. "It's hard for the historian to maintain objectivity, especially for the urban historian."

"I didn't know there was all that much to it," said Bo. "I thought they just showed a lot of percepts and charts. Don't they do it the same way on Rampold?"

"We have nothing quite so elaborate."

"It all amounts to the same thing," said Bo generously. "What's done is dead and gone, but here they call it history and study it."

Alice gave a polite shrug and moved on. Bo understood that he had struck the wrong tone, which annoyed him. Oh why must he pussyfoot? Why must he appease? He said: "Of course I don't know all that much about the subject. That's why I'm here; I want to learn!"

The statement was uttered in a mincing over-delicate voice which Alice found amusing, and hence worth some small exploration. "All very well, if you learn anything useful. In your case, I doubt if..." Alice let her voice trail off; why discourage the poor fellow? She asked: "I take it you're not a student either?"

"Well no. Not exactly."

"What do you do?"

"I—well, I work in the spaceyards."

"That's useful work," Alice said brightly. "And it's work you can be proud of. I hope you profit from your studies." She gave him a gracious nod and passed on down the conduit, to a percept detailing the daily activities of a mesolithic family. Bo looked after her with a frown. He had pictured the encounter going somewhat differently, with Alice standing wide-eyed and coy, enthralled by the magnetism of his personality. He had worried only that she might recognize him, for she had seen him on two previous occasions. His fears were groundless. Evidently she had paid no attention to him. Well, she'd make up for that. And her attitude now was far too casual; she treated him as if he were a small boy. He'd fix that, as well.

Bo followed her slowly along the conduit. He considered the percept, then sidled a step closer. In a bluff voice he said: "Sometimes we don't realize how lucky we are, and that's a fact."

"'Lucky'?" Alice spoke in an abstracted voice. "Who? The people of Hant? Or the Cro-magnons?"

"Us, of course."

"Oh."

"You don't think so?" Bo spoke indulgently.

"Not altogether."

"Look at them! Living in caves. Dancing around a campfire. Eating a piece of dead bear. That doesn't look so good."

"Yes, their lives lacked delicacy." Alice continued along the conduit, moving briskly, and frowning just a trifle. She glanced into percepts depicting aspects of the proto-civilizations; she halted at a percept presenting in a time-compression sequence the development of Hialkh, the first city known to archaeologists. The annunciator commented: "At this particular instant in the human epic, civilization has begun. Behind: the long gray dawn ages. Ahead: the glories which culminate in Hant! Achievement then as now derives from the energies concentrated by the urban environment. But beware! Look yonder across the Pontus! The cruel barbarians of the steppes, those expert wielders of sword and axe who time and time again have ravaged the cities!"

Bo's now familiar voice spoke: "The only ravagers nowadays are the tourists."

Alice made no comment, and continued along the conduit. She looked into the faces of Xerxes, Subotai, Napoleon, Shgulvarsko, Jensen, El Jarm. She saw battles, sieges, slaughters and routs. Cities developed from villages, grew great, collapsed into ruins, disappeared into flames. Bo enunciated his impressions and opinions, to which Alice made perfunctory acknowledgments. He was something of a nuisance, but she was too kind to snub him directly and hurt his feelings. Altogether she found him somewhat repulsive, a curious mixture of innocence and cynicism; of ponderous affability and sudden sinister silences. She wondered if he might not be a trifle deranged; odd for a person of his attributes to be studying the history of man! The percepts and displays, for all their splendor, began to bore her; there was simply too much to be encompassed at a casual inspection, and long ago she had learned what she wanted to know. She said to Bo: "I think I'll be leaving. I hope you profit by your studies; in fact I know you will if you apply yourself diligently. Goodbye."

"Wait," said Bo. "I've seen enough for today." He fell into step beside her. "What are you going to do now?"

Alice looked at him sidewise. "I'm going to find some lunch. I'm hungry. Why do you ask?"

"I'm hungry too. We're not all that different, you and I."

"Just because we're both hungry? That's not logical. Crows, vultures, rats, sharks, dogs: they all get hungry. I don't identify myself with any of these."

Bo frowned, examining the implications of the remark. They left the Hall of History and came out into the daylight. Bo asked gruffly: "You mean that you think I'm like a bird or a rat or a dog?"

"No, of course not!" Alice laughed at the quaint conceit. "I mean that we're people of different societies. I'm a starlander; you're an urbanite. Yours is a very old way of life, which is perhaps a bit—well, let's say, passive, or introverted."

Bo grunted. "If you say so. I never thought about it that way. Anyway just yonder is a branch of the Synthetique. Do you care to eat there? It's on me."

"No, I think not," said Alice. "I've seen those colored pastes and nutritious shreds of bark and they don't look very good. I think I'll go up home for lunch. So once again: goodbye. Have a good lunch."

"Wait!" cried Bo. "I've got a better idea! I know another place, an old tavern where spacemen and all kinds of people go. It's very old and famous: Hongo's Blue Lamp. It would be a shame if you didn't see it." He modulated his voice into that husky cajoling tone which had always dissolved female will-power like warm water on sugar. "Come along, I'll buy you a nice lunch and we'll get to know each other better."

Alice smiled politely and shook her head. "I think I'll be getting on. Thank you anyway."

Bo stood back, mouth compressed. He turned glumly away, raising a hand to his face. The gesture closed a circuit in Alice's memory-bank. Why, this was the man who had victimized Waldo! How very odd! What a strange coincidence that she should meet him at the Academy! Coincidence? The chances seemed remote. She asked, "What is your name?"

Bo spoke in a grumbling resentful voice. "Bo, short for Bodred. The last name is Histledine."

"Bodred Histledine. And you work at the spaceyards?"

Bo nodded. "What's your name?"

Alice seemed not to hear. "Perhaps I'll have lunch at this tavern after all— if you care to show me the way."

"It's not exactly a big expedition, with me running ahead like a guide," growled Bo. "I'll take you there as my guest."

"No, I wouldn't care for that," said Alice. "But I'll visit this tavern: yes. I think I'd like to talk with you."

VI

Waldo pushed the photograph across the desk to Inspector Vole, who examined it with care. "The man isn't identifiable, as you can see for yourself," said Vole. "The woman—I don't recognize her, but I'll put her through identification procedure and maybe something will show up." He departed the room. Waldo sat drumming his fingers. From time to time a faint waft of jeek body-tar odor reached his nostrils, causing him to wince and twist his head.

Inspector Vole returned with the photograph and a print-out bearing the likenesses of a dozen women. He pushed the sheet across the desk. "This is what the machine gave me. Do you recognize any of them?"

Waldo nodded. "This is the one." He touched a face on the sheet.

"I thought so too," said Vole. "Do you intend to place criminal charges?"

"Maybe. But not just yet. Who is she?"

"Her name is Hernanda Degasto Confurias. Her address is 214-19-64, Bagram. If you plan to confront this woman and her friend I advise you to go in company with a police officer."

"Thank you; I'll keep your advice in mind," said Waldo. He left the office.

Vole reflected a moment, then punched a set of buttons. He watched the display screen, which flashed a gratifying run of green lights: the name Hernanda Confurias was not unknown to the criminal files. Instead of a data read-out, the screen flickered to show the face of Vole's colleague Inspector Delmar.

"What have you got on Hernanda Confurias?" asked Delmar.

"Nothing of import," said Vole. "Last night on the Parade—" Vole described the occurrence. "A senseless matter, or so it seems offhand."

"Put through the photograph," said Delmar. Vole facsimilated across a copy of the photograph.

"I wouldn't swear to it," said Delmar, "but that looks to me like Big Bo Histledine."

Waldo found the apartment numbered 214-19-64, then went to a nearby park where he approached a pair of adolescent girls. "I need your help," said Waldo. "A certain lady friend is angry with me, and I don't think she'll answer the door if she sees my face in the robber's portrait, so I want one, or both, of you to press the door button for me." Waldo produced a five-dollar note. "I'll pay you, of course, for your trouble."

The girls looked at each other and giggled. "Why not? Where does she live?"

"Just yonder," said Waldo. "Come along." He gave the girls instructions and led them to the door, while he waited beyond the range of the sensor eye, which produced the 'robber portrait' on the screen within.

The girls pressed the button, and waited while the person within scrutinized their images.

"Who do you want?"

"Hernanda Degasto Confurias. We're from the charm school."

"Charm school?" The door opened; Hernanda looked forth. "Which charm school?"

Waldo stepped forward. "You girls come some other time. Hernanda, I want to speak with you."

She tried to close the door, but Waldo pushed through the opening. Hernanda ran across the room to the alarm button. "Get out of here! Or I'll press for the police!"

"I am the police," said Waldo.

"No, you're not! I know who you are."

"Who am I?"

"Never mind. Leave here at once!"

Waldo tossed the photograph to the table. "Look at that."

Hernanda gingerly examined the picture. "Well—what of it?"

"Who's the man?"

"What's it to you?"

"You say you know who I am."

Hernanda gave her head a half-fearful half-defiant jerk of assent. "He shouldn't have done it—but I'm not saying anything."

"You'll either tell me or the police."

"No! He'd cut my ears; he'd sell me to the gunkers."

"He won't get the chance. You can either tell me now in secret, or the police will take you in as his accomplice."

"In secret?"

"Yes. He won't know where I got his name."

"You swear this?"

"I do."

Hernanda came a timid step forward. She picked up the photograph, glanced at it, threw it contemptuously back down on the table. "Bodred Histledine. He lives in Fulchock: 663-20-99. He works in the spaceyards."

"Bodred Histledine." Waldo noted the name and address. "Why did he do what he did?"

Hernanda gave her head a meditative stroke. "He's a strange man. Sometimes he's like a little boy, sad and sweet; then sometimes he's a beast of the jungle. Have you noticed his eyes? They're like the eyes of a tiger."

"That may be. But why did he victimize me?"

Hernanda's own eyes flashed. "Because of the girl you were with! He's a crazy man!"

Waldo gave a grunt of bitter amusement. He inspected Hernanda thoughtfully; in her turn she looked at him. A patrician for certain: one of those Cloudhaven types.

"He's always up at the Blue Lamp Tavern," said Hernanda. "That's his headquarters. He's on probation, you know. Just yesterday the detectives warned him." Hernanda, relaxing, had become limpid and charming; she came forward to the table.

Waldo looked her over without expression. "What did they warn him for?"

"Consorting with gunkers."

"I see. Anything else you care to tell me?"

"No." Hernanda now was almost arch. She came around the table. "You won't tell him that you saw me?"

"No, definitely not." Waldo once again caught a breath of that hateful odor. Rolling his eyes up and around, he turned and left the apartment.

VII

Entering the Blue Lamp Tavern Alice halted and peered through the gloom. For possibly the first time in her brash young life she felt the living presence of time. Upon that long black mahogany bar men of ten centuries had rested their elbows. The old wood exhaled vapors of the beer and spirits they had quaffed; their ghosts were almost palpable and their conversations hung in the gloom under the age-blackened ceiling. Alice surveyed the room, then crossed to a table under one of the tall windows which overlooked the many-textured expanse of Hant. Bo came at a rather foolish trot behind her, to pluck at her arm and urge her toward his usual booth. Alice paid him no heed, and seated herself placidly at the table she had chosen. Bo, drooping an eyelid and mouth, settled into the seat across from her. For a long moment he stared at her. Her features were fine and clean, but hardly extraordinary; how did she produce so much disturbance? Because she was insufferably confident, he told himself; because she enforced her own evaluation of herself upon those who admired her…He'd do more than admire her; she'd remember him to the last day of her life. Because he was Bo Histledine! Bo the Histle! Big Boo the Whangeroo! who accepted nothing but the best. So now: to work, to attract her interest, to dominate her with his own pride. He said: "You haven't told me your name."

Alice turned from the window and looked at Bo as if she had forgotten his presence. "My name? Miss Tynnott. My father is Commander Tynnott."

"What is your first name?" Bo asked patiently.

Alice ignored the question. Signaling the waiter, she ordered a sandwich and a mug of Tanglefoot. She looked around at the other patrons. "Who are these people? Workmen like yourself?"

"Some are workmen," said Bo in a measured voice. "Those two—" he nodded his head "—are off a sea-ship from the river docks. That tall thin man is from the backlands. But I'm more interested in you. What's your life like out on Rampold?"

"It's always different. My father's work takes him everywhere. We go out into the wilderness to plan canals and aquifers; sometimes we camp out for weeks. It's a very exciting life. We're about finished on Rampold; it's becoming quite settled, and we may move on to a new wild planet; in fact that's why we're here on Earth."

"Hmmf," said Bo. "Seems as if you'd want to stay in Hant and enjoy yourself a while; take in the percepts, meet people, buy new clothes, get your hair fixed in the latest style, things like that."

Alice grinned. "I don't need clothes. I like my hair as it is. As for percepts, I don't have either time or inclination for vicarious living. Most urbanites, of course, don't have much choice; it's either vicarious experience or none."

Bo looked at her blankly. "I don't altogether understand you. Are you sure you know what you're talking about?"

"Of course. Passive, fearful, comfort-loving people tend to live in cities. They have no taste for real existence; they make do with second-hand second-best experience. When they realize this, as most do consciously or subconsciously, sometimes they become hectic and frantic."

"Bah," growled Bo. "I live in Hant; I'd live nowhere else. Second-best isn't good enough for me. I go after the best; I always get the best."

"The best what?"

Bo looked sharply at the girl. Was she mocking him? But no, above the sandwich her eyes were guileless.

"The best of whatever I want," said Bo.

"What you think you want is a shadow of what you really do want. Urbanites are dissatisfied people; they're all lonesome for the lost paradise, but they don't know where to find it. They search all the phases of subjectivity: they try drugs, music, percepts—"

"And gunk. Don't forget gunk!"

"Urban life is the ultimate human tragedy," said Alice. "People can't escape except through catastrophe. Wealth can't buy objectivity; the folk in Cloudhaven are the most subjective of any in Hant. You're lucky to work in the space-yards; you have contact with something real."

Bo shook his head in wonder. "How old are you?"

"It's really not relevant."

"You certainly didn't figure all that stuff out by yourself. You're too young."

"I've learned from my father and mother. Still, the truth is obvious, if you dare to look at it."

Bo felt baffled and savage. "I'd say that maybe you're not all that experienced yourself. Have you ever had a lover?"

"Last night," said Alice, "someone put the question rather more delicately. He asked me if I'd ever been in love, and of course I didn't care to discuss the matter."

Bo drank deep from a tankard of lime beer. "And what do you think of me?"

Alice gave him a casual appraisal. "I'd say that you are an individual of considerable energy. If you directed and disciplined yourself you might someday become an important person: a foreman or even a superintendent."

Bo looked away. He picked up his tankard, drank and set it down with a carefully measured effort. He looked back at Alice. "What are you writing about?"

"Oh—I'm just jotting down ideas as they occur to me."

"In regard to what?"

"Oh—the folk of the city and their customs."

Bo sat glowering at her. "I suppose you've been studying me all morning. Am I one of the picturesque natives?"

Alice laughed. "I must be starting home."

"One moment," said Bo. "I see a man I want to talk to." He crossed to a booth from which Raulf Dido quietly observed comings and goings.

Bo spoke in a harsh clipped voice. "You notice who I'm sitting with?"

Raulf nodded impassively. "Very tasty, in an odd sort of way. What is she?"

"She's a starlander, and to talk to her you'd think she owns all Hant. I've never seen such conceit."

"She looks like she's dressed for a masquerade."

"That's the style out back of beyond. She's absolutely innocent, pure as the morning dew. I'll deliver. How much?"

"Nothing whatever. The heat's on. It's just too much of a hassle."

"Not if it's handled right."

"I'd have to ship her off to Nicobar or Mauritan. It wouldn't be worth the risk."

"Come now. Why not work up a quick sequence over in the studio like we did with that set of twins?"

Raulf gave his head a dubious shake. "There's no scenery; we don't have a script; we'd need a buck—"

"I'll be the buck. All we need is the studio. No story, no sets: just the situation. She's so arrogant, so haughty! She'll throw a first-class display! Outrage. Apprehension. Fury. The works! I'm itching to lay hands on her beautiful body."

"She'll turn you in. If she's around to do so."

"She'll be around. I want her to remember a long time. I'll have to wear a clown-mask; I can't risk having Clachey or Delmar look at the gunk and say 'Hey! there's Bo!' Here's how we can arrange it so we're both clear—"

Raulf inclined his head toward Alice. "You're too late. She's leaving."

"The wicked little wench, I told her to wait!"

"I guess she just remembered," said Raulf mildly. "Because suddenly now she's waiting."

Alice had seen enough of the Blue Lamp Tavern, more than enough of Hant; she wanted to be back up on the aerie, high in the clear blue air. But a man had entered the room, to take an unobtrusive seat to the side, and Alice peered in wonder. Surely it wasn't Waldo? But it was! though he wore a loose golden brown slouch-hat, bronze cheek-plates, a voluminous parasol cape of beetle-back green, all of which had the effect of disguising his appearance. Now why had Waldo come to the Blue Lamp Tavern? Alice curbed a mischievous impulse to cross the room and put the question directly. Bo and his friend had their heads together; they were obviously plotting an escapade of some sort, probably to the discredit of both. Alice glanced back to Waldo to find him staring at her with furtive astonishment. Alice found his emotion highly amusing, and she decided to wait another few minutes to learn what eventuated.

Two other men approached Waldo and joined him at his table. One of the two directed Waldo's attention to Bo with an almost imperceptible inclination of the head. Waldo darted a puzzled look across the room, then returned to his informant. He seemed to be saying: "But he's not blond! The photograph showed blond hair!" And his friend perhaps remarked: "Hair dye is cheap." To which Waldo gave a dubious nod.

Alice began to quiver with merriment. Waldo had been surprised to find her at the Blue Lamp Tavern, but in a moment Bo would come swaggering back across the room, and indeed Bo now rose to his feet. For a moment he stood looking off into nothing, with what Alice thought a rather unpleasant smirk on his face. His bulk, his meaty jaw, the round stare of his eyes, the flaring nostrils, suggested the portrayal of a Minoan man-bull she had noticed earlier in the day; the resemblance was fascinating.

Bo crossed the room to the table where Alice sat. Waldo leaned forward, jaw sagging in shock.

Bo seated himself. Alice was more than ever conscious of his new mood. The rather obsequious manner he had cultivated at the Academy was gone; now he seemed to exude a reek of bravado and power. Alice said, "I'm just about ready to go. Thank you for showing me the tavern here; it's really a quaint old place, and I'm glad to have seen it."

Bo sat looking at her, with rather more intimacy than she liked. He said in a husky voice: "My friend yonder is a police agent. He wants to show me a gunk studio they've just raided; perhaps you'd like to come along."

"What's a gunk studio?"

"A place where fanciful percepts are made. Sometimes they're erotic; sometimes they're wonderful experiences, and the person who wires into them becomes the person who takes part in the adventures. It's illegal, naturally; a gunk addict can't do much else but stay wired into gunk once he's had a taste of it."

Alice considered. "It sounds interesting, if one is in the mood for depravity. But I think I've had enough for today."

"Enough what?" asked Bo jocularly. "Depravity? You haven't seen anything yet."

"Still, I'll be leaving for home." Alice rose to her feet. "It was pleasant meeting you, and I hope you do well at the spaceyards."

Bo joined her. "I'll show you the cab pad. This way, out the back. It's just around the corner."

Alice somewhat dubiously went with Bo along a dim corridor, down concrete steps to an iron door, which opened into an alley. Alice paused, glanced sidewise at Bo who was standing rather closer than she liked. He lifted his hand and stroked her hair. Alice moved back with raised eyebrows. "And where is the cab pad?"

Bo grinned. "Just around the corner."

Keeping a wary eye on Bo, Alice marched off down the alley, with Bo a pace or two behind. She noticed a small van parked to the side. As she passed, footsteps pounded behind her; she swung around to see two men bearing Bo to the ground. Another man threw a blanket over her head, looped a strap around her knees; she was picked up and tossed into the van. The door closed and a moment later the van moved off.

Alice rolled over and made herself as comfortable as possible. She found no difficulty breathing and her first emotion was outrage. How dared anyone treat her with such disrespect! She began to speculate as to the purpose of the deed, and her probable prospects; she was not at all cheered.

Kicking and elbowing, she worked the blanket loose, and freed herself, but her situation was hardly improved. The interior of the van was dark and the doors were locked.

The van halted; the back door opened to reveal the interior of a concrete-walled room. Two men looked in at her; Alice was somewhat reassured by the hoods which concealed their faces, which would seem to indicate that they planned to spare her life, if nothing else.

She jumped out of the van and looked about her. "What's the reason for all this?"

"Come along; this way. You're going to be famous."

"Oh? In what way?"

"You're to be the star of an exciting new percept."

"I see. Is this what is called 'gunk'?"

"I've heard it called 'gunk'. I like to think of it as 'art'."

"I'm afraid you'll find me an uncooperative performer. The production will be a failure."

"Nothing in life is a sure thing. Still it's worth trying. Come along this way."

Alice went as she was directed, along a hall and into a large windowless room illuminated by panels in the ceiling and around the walls. From four angles and from above recording apparatus surveyed the room. A man in a white beret, a domino and cheek-plates stood waiting. He came to inspect Alice. "You don't seem concerned."

"I'm not, particularly."

Raulf Dido, the man in the white beret, was momentarily disconcerted. "Maybe you like the idea?"

"I wouldn't quite go that far."

"Are you wired?"

Alice smiled, as if at the naïve question of a child. "No."

"We'll want you to wear this induction device. It's not as accurate as the direct connection but better than nothing."

"Just what do you propose to do?" asked Alice.

"We plan to produce an erotic percept with emotional accompaniment. As you see, we have no exotic props, but we feel that your special personality will make the production interesting. Before you indulge in any tantrums or hysterics, we'll want to attach this induction device to your neck."

Alice looked at the adjuncts of the room: a couch, a chair, a case containing several objects which caused Alice to compress her lips in wry disgust. "You don't understand my 'special personality' as you put it. The percept will be very uninteresting. I wonder if you have a magazine or a newspaper I might read while you're trying to make your percept?"

"You won't be bored, never fear." This was the comment of another man who had entered the room: a man tall and strong, bulky about the shoulders, with a head shaved bald. A mask of gold foil clung to his face; he wore loose black pantaloons, a blouse checked red, white and black; he looked almost monumental in his strength. Alice instantly recognized Bo, and burst out laughing.

"What's so funny?" he growled.

"The whole affair is ridiculous. I really don't care to be a party to such a farce. After all I have my pride."

The man in the gold mask stood looking at her sullenly. "You'll find whether it's ridiculous or not." He spoke to the man in the domino. "Check my signals." He pushed a clip into the socket under his right arm.

"Signals fine. You're in good shape."

"Put on her induction; we'll get on with the business."

The man in the domino advanced; Alice gestured, took the induction-cell, waved her hands and the cell was gone. Bo and Raulf Dido stared in annoyance. "What did you do with it?" asked Bo in a hard voice.

"It's gone," said Alice. "Forever. Or maybe it's somewhere up here." She jumped up to the recorder platform and pushed over equipment. Cameras, recorders crashed to the floor, evoking cries of rage from Raulf and Bo. They ran to catch her, then stopped short at the sound of contention: calls and curses, the thud of blows. Into the room burst four men. Waldo stood to the side while his companions advanced upon Raulf and Bo and commenced to beat them with leather truncheons. Raulf and Bo bellowed in rage and sought to defend themselves, with only small success, as the blows fell upon them from all sides.

Alice said, "Hello Waldo. What are you doing here?"

"I might ask you the same thing."

"Bodred brought me here in a van," said Alice. "He seemed to want my help in making percepts; I was about to go when you arrived."

"You were about to go?" Waldo laughed scornfully. He put his arm around Alice's waist and drew her toward him. She put her hands on his chest and held him away. "Now Waldo, control yourself. I don't need reassurance."

"Do you know what they were going to do?" asked Waldo in a thick voice.

"I wasn't particularly interested. Please, Waldo, don't be amorous. I'm sure women of your own race are adequate to your needs."

Waldo made a guttural sound. He called to his hirelings. "Hold off. Don't kill them. Bring that man over here."

The men pushed Bo across the room. Waldo held a small gun which he waved carelessly. "You were about to produce some gunk, evidently."

"What if we were?" Bo panted. "Is it any of your affair? Why did you come busting in on us?"

"Think back to last night."

"Oh. You were the geezer behind the jeek."

"Correct. Go on with your gunk." Waldo jerked his head toward Alice. "Take her. Use her. I don't want her."

Bo glanced uncertainly toward Raulf, still on the floor. He looked back to Waldo, glaring sidelong at Waldo's gun. "What then?"

"I'm not done with you, if that's what you're worried about. You've got a lot coming, and you're going to get it."

Alice spoke in a puzzled voice: "Waldo, are you suggesting that these nasty creatures continue with what they were doing?"

Waldo grinned. "Why not? A little humility might do you good."

"I see. Well, Waldo, I don't care to participate in anything so sordid. I'm surprised at you."

Waldo leaned forward. "I'll tell you exactly why I'm doing this. It's because your arrogance and your vanity absolutely rub me raw."

"Hear, hear!" croaked Bo. "You talk the way I feel."

Alice spoke in a soft voice, "Both you boys are mistaken. I'm not vain and arrogant. I'm merely superior." She could not control her mirth at the expressions on the faces of Waldo and Bo. "Perhaps I'm unkind. It's really not your fault; you're both rather pitiful victims of the city."

"A 'victim'? Hah!" cried Waldo. "I live in Cloudhaven!"

And almost in the same instant: "Me, Big Bo, a victim? Nobody fools with me!"

"Both of you, of course, understand this—subconsciously. The result is guilt and malice."

Waldo listened with a sardonic smile, Bo with a lowering sneer.

"Are you finished?" Waldo asked. "If so—"

"Wait! One moment," said Alice. "What of the cameras and the induction-cell?"

Raulf, limping and groaning, went to one of the cameras which Alice had not thrown to the floor. "This one will work. The cell is gone; I guess we'll have to dub in her track."

Bo looked around the room. "I don't know as I like all this company. Everybody's got to go. I can't concentrate."

"I'm not going," said Waldo. "You three wait in the hall. There'll be more work for you after a bit."

"Well, don't beat me any more," whined Raulf. "I didn't do anything."

"Quit sniveling!" Bo snarled. "Fire up that camera. This isn't quite like I planned, but if it's not good, we'll do a retake."

"Wait!" said Alice. "One thing more. Watch my hands. Are you watching?" She stood erect, and performed a set of apparently purposeless motions. She halted, held her palms toward Bo and Waldo, and each held a small mechanism. From the object in her right hand burst a gush of dazzling light, pulsating ten times per second; the mechanism in the left hand vented an almost solid tooth-chattering mass of sound: a throbbing scream in phase with the light: *erreek erreek erreek!* Waldo and Bo flinched and sagged back, their brain circuits overloaded and rendered numb. The gun dropped from Waldo's hand. Prepared for the event, Alice was less affected. She placed the beacon on the table, picked up the gun. Waldo, Bo and Raulf staggered and lurched, their brain-waves now surging at disorientation frequency.

Alice, her face taut with concentration, left the room. In the hall she sidled past Waldo's three hireling thugs, who stood indecisively, and so gained the street. From a nearby public telephone, she called the police, who dropped down from the sky two minutes later. Alice explained the circumstances; the police in short order brought forth a set of sullen captives.

Alice watched as they were loaded into the conveyance. "Goodbye Waldo. Goodbye Bo. At least you evaded your beating. I don't know what's going to happen to you, but I can't extend too much sympathy, because you've both been rascals."

Waldo asked sourly: "Do you make as much trouble as this wherever you go?"

Alice decided that the question had been asked for rhetorical effect and required no exact or accurate reply; she merely waved and watched as Waldo, Bo, Raulf Dido and the three thugs were wafted aloft and away.

Alice arrived back at the aerie halfway through the afternoon, to find that her father had completed his business. "I was hoping you'd get back early," said Merwyn Tynnott, "so that we could leave tonight. Did you have a good day?"

"It's been interesting," said Alice. "The teaching processes are spectacular and effective, but I wonder if by presenting events so categorically they might not stifle the students' imaginations?"

"Possible. Hard to say."

"Their point of view is urbanite, naturally. Still, the events speak for themselves and I suspect that the student of history falls into urbanite doctrine through social pressure."

"Very likely so. Social pressure is stronger than logic."

"I had lunch at the Blue Lamp Tavern, a spooky old place."

"Yes. I know it well. It's a back-eddy of ancient times, and also something of an underworld hangout. Dozens of spacemen have disappeared from the Blue Lamp."

"I had an adventure there myself; in fact, Waldo Walberg misbehaved rather badly and I believe he's now been taken away for penal processing."

"I'm sorry to hear that," said Merwyn Tynnott. "He'll miss Cloudhaven, especially if he's sent out to the starlands."

"It's a pity about poor Waldo, and Bodred as well. Bodred is the workman who flung his wrench upon my foot. You were quite right about his motives. I'm a trifle disillusioned, although I know I shouldn't be."

Merwyn Tynnott hugged his daughter and kissed the top of her head. "Don't worry another instant. We're off and away from Hant, and you never need come back."

"It's a strange wicked place," said Alice, "though I rather enjoyed Jillyville."

"Jillyville is always amusing."

They went into the dome; Commander Tynnott touched the controls, and the aerie drifted away to the southeast.

Afterword to "Assault on a City"

"I wanted freedom, and the only way I could think of to be free was to be a writer. I started in university as a mining engineer, changed to a physics major, but I just couldn't see myself in it—both those occupations seemed too claustrophobic—so I changed to English, History, journalism. And about that time I figured I'd better take this career thing seriously. In my sophomore English class, I had to do a paper every week, so I decided to write a story, turn it in, and try to sell it. When the batch of stories was returned, the instructor said to the class, 'This week, we run the gamut. On the one hand, we have, written by Mr. Smith, this beautiful, pungent story of a prize fight, in which you can smell the rosin and feel every blow. On the other hand, written by a person who shall be nameless, we have this piece of so-called science fiction.'"

—Jack Vance 1986

Green Magic

Howard Fair, looking over the relicts of his great-uncle Gerald McIntyre, found a large ledger entitled:

WORKBOOK & JOURNAL
Open at Peril!

Fair read the journal with interest, although his own work went far beyond ideas treated only gingerly by Gerald McIntyre.

"The existence of disciplines concentric to the elementary magics must now be admitted without further controversy," wrote McIntyre. "Guided by a set of analogies from the white and black magics (to be detailed in due course), I have delineated the basic extension of purple magic, as well as its corollary, Dynamic Nomism."

Fair read on, remarking the careful charts, the projections and expansions, the transpolations and transformations by which Gerald McIntyre had conceived his systemology. So swiftly had the technical arts advanced that McIntyre's expositions, highly controversial sixty years before, now seemed pedantic and overly rigorous.

"Whereas benign creatures: angels, white sprites, merrihews, sandestins— are typical of the white cycle; whereas demons, magners, trolls and warlocks are evinced by black magic; so do the purple and green cycles sponsor their own particulars, but these are neither good nor evil, bearing, rather, the same relation to the black and white provinces that these latter do to our own basic realm."

Fair re-read the passage. The 'green cycle'? Had great-uncle McIntyre wandered into regions overlooked by modern workers?

He reviewed the journal in the light of this suspicion, and discovered additional hints and references. Especially provocative was a bit of scribbled marginalia: "More concerning my latest researches I may not state, having been promised an infinite reward for this forbearance."

The passage was dated a day before Gerald McIntyre's death, which had occurred on March 21, 1898, the first day of spring. McIntyre had enjoyed very little of his 'infinite reward', whatever had been its nature...Fair returned to a consideration of the journal, which, in a sentence or two, had opened a chink on an entire new panorama. McIntyre provided no further illumination, and Fair set out to make a fuller investigation.

His first steps were routine. He performed two divinations, searched the standard indexes, concordances, handbooks and formularies, evoked a demon whom he had previously found knowledgeable: all without success. He found no direct reference to cycles beyond the purple; the demon refused even to speculate.

Fair was by no means discouraged; if anything, the intensity of his interest increased. He re-read the journal, with particular care to the justification for purple magic, reasoning that McIntyre, groping for a lore beyond the purple, might well have used the methods which had yielded results before. Applying stains and ultraviolet light to the pages, Fair made legible a number of notes McIntyre had jotted down, then erased.

Fair was immensely stimulated. The notes assured him that he was on the right track and further indicated a number of blind alleys from which Fair profited by avoiding. He applied himself so successfully that before the week was out he had evoked a sprite of the green cycle. It appeared in the semblance of a man with green glass eyes and a thatch of young eucalyptus leaves in the place of hair. It greeted Fair with cool courtesy, would not seat itself, and ignored Fair's proffer of coffee. After wandering around the apartment inspecting Fair's books and curios with an air of negligent amusement, it agreed to respond to Fair's questions.

Fair asked permission to use his tape-recorder, which the sprite allowed, and Fair set the apparatus in motion. (When subsequently he replayed the interview, no sound could be heard.)

"What realms of magic lie beyond the green?" asked Fair.

"I can't give you an exact answer," replied the sprite, "because I don't know. There are at least two more, corresponding to the colors we call rawn and pallow, and very likely others."

Fair arranged the microphone where it would more directly intercept the voice of the sprite. "What," he asked, "is the green cycle like? What is its physical semblance?"

The sprite paused to consider. Glistening mother-of-pearl films wandered across its face, reflecting the tinge of its thoughts. "I'm rather severely restricted by your use of the word 'physical'. And 'semblance' involves a subjective interpretation, which changes with the rise and fall of the seconds."

"By all means," Fair said hastily, "describe it in your own words."

"Well—we have four different regions, two of which floresce from the basic skeleton of the universe, and so subsede the others. The first of these is compressed and isthiated, but is notable for its wide pools of mottle which we use sometimes for deranging stations. We've transplanted club-mosses from Earth's Devonian and a few ice-fires from Perdition. They climb among the rods which we call devil-hair—" he went on for several minutes but the meaning almost entirely escaped Fair. And it seemed as if the question by which he had hoped to break the ice might run away with the entire interview. He introduced another idea.

"Can we freely manipulate the physical extensions of Earth?"

The sprite seemed amused. "You refer, so I assume, to the various aspects of space, time, mass, energy, life, thought and recollection."

"Exactly."

The sprite raised its green cornsilk eyebrows. "I might as sensibly ask, can you break an egg by striking it with a club? The response is on a similar level of seriousness."

Fair had expected a certain amount of condescension and impatience, and was not abashed. "How may I learn these techniques?"

"In the usual manner: through diligent study."

"Ah, indeed—but where could I study, and who would teach me?"

The sprite made an easy gesture, and whorls of green smoke trailed from his fingers to spin through the air. "I could arrange the matter, but since I bear you no particular animosity, I'll do nothing of the sort. And now, I must be gone."

"Where do you go?" Fair asked in wonder and longing. "May I go with you?"

The sprite, swirling a drape of bright green dust over its shoulders, shook his head. "You would be less than comfortable."

"Other men have explored the worlds of magic!"

"True: your uncle Gerald McIntyre, for instance."

"My uncle Gerald learned green magic?"

"To the limit of his capabilities. He found no pleasure in his learning. You would do well to profit by his experience and modify your ambitions." The sprite turned and walked away.

Fair watched it depart. The sprite receded in space and dimension, but never reached the wall of Fair's room. At a distance which might have been fifty yards, the sprite glanced back, as if to make sure that Fair was not following, then stepped off at another angle and disappeared.

Fair's first impulse was to take heed and limit his explorations. He was an adept in white magic, and had mastered the black art—occasionally he evoked a demon to liven a social gathering which otherwise threatened to become dull—but he had by no means illuminated every mystery of purple magic, which is the realm of Incarnate Symbols.

Howard Fair might have turned away from the green cycle except for three factors.

First was his physical appearance. He stood rather under medium height, with a swarthy face, sparse black hair, a gnarled nose, a small heavy mouth. He felt no great sensitivity about his appearance, but realized that it might be improved. In his mind's eye he pictured the personified ideal of himself: he was taller by six inches, his nose thin and keen, his skin cleared of its muddy undertone. A striking figure, but still recognizable as Howard Fair. He wanted the love of women, but he wanted it without the interposition of his craft. Many times he had brought beautiful girls to his bed, lips wet and eyes shining; but purple magic had seduced them rather than Howard Fair, and he took limited satisfaction in such conquests.

Here was the first factor which drew Howard Fair back to the green lore; the second was his yearning for extended, perhaps eternal, life; the third was simple thirst for knowledge.

The fact of Gerald McIntyre's death, or dissolution, or disappearance—whatever had happened to him—was naturally a matter of concern. If he had won to a goal so precious, why had he died so quickly? Was the 'infinite reward' so miraculous, so exquisite, that the mind failed under its possession? (If such were the case, the reward was hardly a reward.)

Fair could not restrain himself, and by degrees returned to a study of green magic. Rather than again invoke the sprite whose air of indulgent contempt he had found exasperating, he decided to seek knowledge by an indirect method, employing the most advanced concepts of technical and cabalistic science.

He obtained a portable television transmitter which he loaded into his panel truck along with a receiver. On a Monday night in early May, he drove to an abandoned graveyard far out in the wooded hills, and there, by the light of a waning moon, he buried the television camera in graveyard clay until only the lens protruded from the soil. With a sharp alder twig he scratched on the ground a monstrous outline. The television lens served for one eye, a beer bottle pushed neck-first into the soil the other.

During the middle hours, while the moon died behind wisps of pale cloud, he carved a word on the dark forehead; then, standing back, recited the activating incantation.

The ground rumbled and moaned, the golem heaved up to blot out the stars.

The glass eyes stared down at Fair, secure in his pentagon.

"Speak!" called out Fair. "*Enteresthes, Akmai Adonai Bidemgir! Elohim, pa rahulli! Enteresthes, HVOI!* Speak!"

"Return me to earth, return my clay to the quiet clay from whence you roused me."

"First you must serve."

The golem stumbled forward to crush Fair, but was halted by the pang of protective magic.

"Serve you I will, if serve you I must."

Fair stepped boldly forth from the pentagon, strung forty yards of green ribbon down the road in the shape of a narrow V. "Go forth into the realm of green magic," he told the monster. "The ribbons reach forty miles; walk to the end, turn about, return, and then fall back, return to the earth from which you rose."

The golem turned, shuffled into the V of green ribbon, shaking off clods of mold, jarring the ground with its ponderous tread. Fair watched the squat shape dwindle, recede, yet never reach the angle of the magic V. He returned to his panel truck, tuned the television receiver to the golem's eye, and surveyed the fantastic vistas of the green realm.

Two elementals of the green realm met on a spun-silver landscape. They were Jaadian and Misthemar, and they fell to discussing the earthen monster which had stalked forty miles through the region known as Cil; which then, turning in its tracks, had retraced its steps, gradually increasing its pace until at the end it moved in a shambling rush, leaving a trail of clods on the fragile moth-wing mosaics.

"Events, events, events," Misthemar fretted, "they crowd the chute of time till the bounds bulge. Or then again, the course is as lean and spare as a stretched tendon…But in regard to this incursion…" He paused for a period of reflection, and silver clouds moved over his head and under his feet.

Jaadian remarked, "You are aware that I conversed with Howard Fair; he is so obsessed to escape the squalor of his world that he acts with recklessness."

"The man Gerald McIntyre was his uncle," mused Misthemar. "McIntyre besought, we yielded; as perhaps now we must yield to Howard Fair."

Jaadian uneasily opened his hand, shook off a spray of emerald fire. "Events press, both in and out. I find myself unable to act in this regard."

"I likewise do not care to be the agent of tragedy."

A Meaning came fluttering up from below: "A disturbance among the spiral towers! A caterpillar of glass and metal has come clanking; it has thrust electric eyes into the Portinone and broke open the Egg of Innocence. Howard Fair is the fault."

Jaadian and Misthemar consulted each other with wry disinclination. "Very well, both of us will go; such a duty needs two souls in support."

They impinged upon Earth and found Howard Fair in a wall booth at a cocktail bar. He looked up at the two strangers. One of them asked, "May we join you?"

Fair examined the two men. Both wore conservative suits and carried cashmere topcoats over their arms. Fair noticed that the left thumb-nail of each man glistened green, in accordance with precept.

Fair rose politely to his feet. "Will you sit down?"

The green sprites hung up their overcoats and slid into the booth. Fair looked from one to the other. He addressed Jaadian. "Aren't you he whom I interviewed several weeks ago?"

Jaadian assented. "You have not accepted my advice."

Fair shrugged. "You asked me to remain ignorant, to accept my stupidity and ineptitude."

"And why should you not?" asked Jaadian gently. "You are a primitive in a primitive realm; nevertheless not one man in a thousand can match your achievements."

Fair agreed, smiling faintly. "But knowledge creates a craving for further knowledge. Where is the harm in knowledge?"

Misthemar, the more mercurial of the sprites, spoke angrily. "Where is the harm? Consider your earthen monster! It befouled forty miles of delicacy, the record of ten million years. Consider your caterpillar! It trampled our pillars of carved milk, our dreaming towers, damaged the nerve-skeins which extrude and waft us our Meanings."

"I'm dreadfully sorry," said Fair. "I meant no destruction."

The sprites nodded. "But your apology conveys no guarantee of restraint."

Fair toyed with his glass. A waiter approached the table, addressed the two sprites. "Something for you two gentlemen?"

Jaadian ordered a glass of charged water, as did Misthemar. Fair called for another highball.

"What do you hope to gain from this activity?" inquired Misthemar. "Destructive forays teach you nothing!"

Fair agreed. "I have learned little. But I have seen miraculous sights. I am more than ever anxious to learn."

The green sprites glumly watched the bubbles rising in their glasses. Jaadian at last drew a deep sigh. "Perhaps we can obviate toil on your part and disturbance on ours. Explicitly, what gains or advantages do you hope to derive from green magic?"

Fair, smiling, leaned back into the red imitation-leather cushions. "I want many things. Extended life—mobility in time—comprehensive memory—augmented perception, with vision across the whole spectrum. I want physical charm and magnetism, the semblance of youth, muscular endurance…Then there are qualities more or less speculative, such as—"

Jaadian interrupted. "These qualities and characteristics we will confer upon you. In return you will undertake never again to disturb the green realm. You will evade centuries of toil; we will be spared the nuisance of your presence, and the inevitable tragedy."

"Tragedy?" inquired Fair in wonder. "Why tragedy?"

Jaadian spoke in a deep reverberating voice. "You are a man of Earth. Your goals are not our goals. Green magic makes you aware of our goals."

Fair thoughtfully sipped his highball. "I can't see that this is a disadvantage. I am willing to submit to the discipline of instruction. Surely a knowledge of green magic will not change me into a different entity?"

"No. And this is the basic tragedy!"

Misthemar spoke in exasperation. "We are forbidden to harm lesser creatures, and so you are fortunate; for to dissolve you into air would end all the annoyance."

Fair laughed. "I apologize again for making such a nuisance of myself. But surely you understand how important this is to me?"

Jaadian asked hopefully, "Then you agree to our offer?"

Fair shook his head. "How could I live, forever young, capable of extended learning, but limited to knowledge which I already see bounds to? I would be bored, restless, miserable."

"That well may be," said Jaadian. "But not so bored, restless and miserable as if you were learned in green magic."

Fair drew himself erect. "I must learn green magic. It is an opportunity which only a person both torpid and stupid could refuse."

Jaadian sighed. "In your place I would make the same response." The sprites rose to their feet. "Come then, we will teach you."

"Don't say we didn't warn you," said Misthemar.

Time passed. Sunset waned and twilight darkened. A man walked up the stairs, entered Howard Fair's apartment. He was tall, unobtrusively muscular. His face was sensitive, keen, humorous; his left thumb-nail glistened green.

Time is a function of vital processes. The people of Earth had perceived the motion of their clocks. On this understanding, two hours had elapsed since Howard Fair had followed the green sprites from the bar.

Howard Fair had perceived other criteria. For him the interval had been seven hundred years, during which he had lived in the green realm, learning to the utmost capacity of his brain.

He had occupied two years training his senses to the new conditions. Gradually he learned to walk in the six basic three-dimensional directions, and accustomed himself to the fourth-dimensional short-cuts. By easy stages the blinds over his eyes were removed, so that the dazzling over-human intricacy of the landscape never completely confounded him.

Another year was spent training him to the use of a code-language—an intermediate step between the vocalizations of Earth and the meaning-patterns of the green realm, where a hundred symbol-flakes (each a flitting spot of delicate iridescence) might be displayed in a single swirl of import. During this time Howard Fair's eyes and brain were altered, to allow him the use of the many new colors, without which the meaning-flakes could not be recognized.

These were preliminary steps. For forty years he studied the flakes, of which there were almost a million. Another forty years was given to elementary permutations and shifts, and another forty to parallels, attenuations, diminishments and extensions; and during this time he was introduced to flake patterns, and certain of the more obvious displays.

Now he was able to study without recourse to the code-language, and his progress became more marked. Another twenty years found him able to recognize more complicated Meanings, and he was introduced to a more varied program. He floated over the field of moth-wing mosaics, which still showed the footprints of the golem. He sweated in embarrassment, the extent of his wicked willfulness now clear to him.

So passed the years. Howard Fair learned as much green magic as his brain could encompass.

He explored much of the green realm, finding so much beauty that he feared his brain might burst. He tasted, he heard, he felt, he sensed, and each one of his senses was a hundred times more discriminating than before. Nourishment came in a thousand different forms: from pink eggs which burst into a hot sweet gas, suffusing his entire body; from passing through a rain of stinging metal crystals; from simple contemplation of the proper symbol.

Homesickness for Earth waxed and waned. Sometimes it was insupportable and he was ready to forsake all he had learned and abandon his hopes for the future. At other times the magnificence of the green realm permeated him, and the thought of departure seemed like the threat of death itself.

By stages so gradual he never realized them he learned green magic.

But the new faculty gave him no pride: between his crude ineptitudes and the poetic elegance of the sprites remained a tremendous gap—and he felt his innate inferiority much more keenly than he ever had in his old state. Worse, his most earnest efforts failed to improve his technique, and sometimes, observing the singing joy of an improvised manifestation by one of the sprites, and contrasting it to his own labored constructions, he felt futility and shame.

The longer he remained in the green realm, the stronger grew the sense of his own maladroitness, and he began to long for the easy environment of Earth, where each of his acts would not shout aloud of vulgarity and crassness. At times he would watch the sprites (in the gossamer forms natural to them) at play among the pearl-petals, or twining like quick flashes of music through the forest of pink spirals. The contrast between their verve and his brutish fumbling could not be borne and he would turn away. His self-respect dwindled with each passing hour, and instead of pride in his learning, he felt a sullen ache for what he was not and could never become. The first few hundred years he worked with the enthusiasm of ignorance, for the next few he was buoyed by hope. During the last part of his time, only dogged obstinacy kept him plodding through what now he knew for infantile exercises.

In one terrible bitter-sweet spasm, he gave up. He found Jaadian weaving tinkling fragments of various magics into a warp of shining long splines. With grave courtesy, Jaadian gave Fair his attention, and Fair laboriously set forth his meaning.

Jaadian returned a message. "I recognize your discomfort, and extend my sympathy. It is best that you now return to your native home."

He put aside his weaving and conveyed Fair down through the requisite vortices. Along the way they passed Misthemar. No flicker of meaning was expressed or exchanged, but Howard Fair thought to feel a tinge of faintly malicious amusement.

Howard Fair sat in his apartment. His perceptions, augmented and sharpened by his sojourn in the green realm, took note of the surroundings. Only two hours before, by the clocks of Earth, he had found them both restful and stimulating; now they were neither. His books: superstition, spuriousness, earnest nonsense. His private journals and workbooks: a pathetic scrawl of infantilisms. Gravity tugged at his feet, held him rigid. The shoddy construction of the house, which heretofore he never had noticed, oppressed him. Everywhere he looked he saw slipshod disorder, primitive filth. The thought of the food he must now eat revolted him.

He went out on his little balcony which overlooked the street. The air was impregnated with organic smells. Across the street he could look into windows where his fellow humans lived in stupid squalor.

Fair smiled sadly. He had tried to prepare himself for these reactions, but now was surprised by their intensity. He returned into his apartment. He must accustom himself to the old environment. And after all there were compensations. The most desirable commodities of the world were now his to enjoy.

Howard Fair plunged into the enjoyment of these pleasures. He forced himself to drink quantities of expensive wines, brandies, liqueurs, even though they offended his palate. Hunger overcame his nausea, he forced himself to the consumption of what he thought of as fried animal tissue, the hypertrophied sexual organs of plants. He experimented with erotic sensation, but found that beautiful women no longer seemed different from the plain ones, and that he could barely steel himself to the untidy contacts. He bought libraries of erudite books, glanced through them with contempt. He tried to amuse himself with his old magics; they seemed ridiculous.

He forced himself to enjoy these pleasures for a month; then he fled the city and established a crystal bubble on a crag in the Andes. To nourish himself, he contrived a thick liquid, which, while by no means as exhilarating as the substances of the green realm, was innocent of organic contamination.

After a certain degree of improvisation and make-shift, he arranged his life to its minimum discomfort. The view was one of austere grandeur; not even the condors came to disturb him. He sat back to ponder the chain of events which had started with his discovery of Gerald McIntyre's workbook. He frowned. Gerald McIntyre? He jumped to his feet, looked far over the crags.

He found Gerald McIntyre at a wayside service station in the heart of the South Dakota prairie. McIntyre was sitting in an old wooden chair, tilted back against the peeling yellow paint of the service station, a straw hat shading his eyes from the sun. He was a magnetically handsome man, blond of hair, brown of skin, with blue eyes whose gaze stung like the touch of an icicle. His left thumbnail glistened green.

Fair greeted him casually; the two men surveyed each other with wry curiosity.

"I see you have adapted yourself," said Howard Fair.

McIntyre shrugged. "As well as possible. I balance between solitude and the pressure of humanity." He looked into the bright blue sky where crows flapped and called. "For many years I lived in isolation. I began to detest the sound of my own breathing."

Along the highway came a glittering automobile, rococo as a hybrid goldfish. With the perceptions now available to them, Fair and McIntyre could see the driver to be red-faced and truculent, his companion a peevish woman in expensive clothes.

"There are other advantages to residence here," said McIntyre. "For instance, I am able to enrich the lives of passers-by with an occasional trifle of novel adventure." He made a small gesture; two dozen crows swooped down and flew beside the automobile. They settled on the fenders, strutted back and forth along the hood, fouled the windshield.

The automobile squealed to a halt, the driver jumped out, put the birds to flight. He threw an ineffectual rock, waved his arms in outrage, returned to his car, proceeded.

"A paltry affair," said McIntyre with a sigh. "The truth of the matter is that I am bored." He pursed his mouth and blew forth three bright puffs of smoke: first red, then yellow, then blazing blue. "I have arrived at the estate of foolishness, as you can see."

Fair surveyed his great-uncle with a trace of uneasiness. McIntyre laughed. "Enough; no more pranks. I predict, however, that you will presently share my malaise."

"I share it already," said Fair. "Sometimes I wish I could abandon all my magic and return to my former innocence."

"I have toyed with the idea," McIntyre replied thoughtfully. "In fact I have made all the necessary arrangements. It is really a simple matter." He led Fair to a small room behind the station. Although the door was open, the interior showed only a thick darkness.

McIntyre, standing well back, surveyed the darkness with a quizzical curl to his lip. "You need only enter. All your magic, all your recollections of the green realm will depart. You will be no wiser than the next man you meet. And with your knowledge will go your boredom, your melancholy, your dissatisfaction."

Fair contemplated the dark doorway. A single step would resolve his discomfort.

He glanced at McIntyre; the two surveyed each other with sardonic amusement. They returned to the front of the building.

"Sometimes I stand by the door and look into the darkness," said McIntyre. "Then I am reminded how dearly I cherish my boredom, and what a precious commodity is so much misery."

Fair made himself ready for departure. "I thank you for this new wisdom, which a hundred more years in the green realm would not have taught me. And now—for a time, at least—I go back to my crag in the Andes."

McIntyre tilted his chair against the wall of the service station. "And I—for a time, at least—will wait for the next passer-by."

"Good-by, then, Uncle Gerald."

"Good-by, Howard."

The World-Thinker

i

Through the open window came sounds of the city—the swish of passing air-traffic, the clank of the pedestrian-belt on the ramp below, hoarse undertones from the lower levels. Cardale sat by the window studying a sheet of paper which displayed a photograph and a few lines of type:

FUGITIVE!
Isabel May—Age 21; height 5 feet 5 inches; medium physique.
Hair: black (could be dyed).
Eyes: blue.
Distinguishing characteristics: none.

Cardale shifted his eyes to the photograph and studied the pretty face with incongruously angry eyes. A placard across her chest read: 94e-627. Cardale returned to the printed words.

> Sentenced to serve three years at the Nevada Women's Camp, in the first six months of incarceration Isabel May accumulated 22 months additional punitive confinement. Caution is urged in her apprehension.

The face, Cardale reflected, was defiant, reckless, outraged, but neither coarse nor stupid—a face, in fact, illuminated by intelligence and sensitivity. Not the face of a criminal, thought Cardale.

He pressed a button. The telescreen plumbed into sharp life. "Lunar Observatory," said Cardale.

The screen twitched to a view across an austere office, with moonscape outside the window. A man in a rose-pink smock looked into the screen. "Hello, Cardale."

"What's the word on May?"

"We've got a line on her. Quite a nuisance, which you won't want to hear about. One matter: please, in the future, keep freighters in another sector when you want a fugitive tracked. We had six red herrings to cope with."

"But you picked up May?"

"Definitely."

"Keep her in your sights. I'll send someone out to take over." Cardale clicked off the screen.

He ruminated a moment, then summoned the image of his secretary. "Get me Detering at Central Intelligence."

The polychrome whirl of color rose and fell to reveal Detering's ruddy face.

"Cardale, if it's service you want—"

"I want a mixed squad, men and women, in a fast ship to pick up a fugitive. Her name is Isabel May. She's fractious, unruly, incorrigible—but I don't want her hurt."

"Allow me to continue what I started to say. Cardale, if you want service, you are out of luck. There's literally no one in the office but me."

"Then come yourself."

"To pick up a reckless woman, and get my hair pulled and my face slapped? No thanks…One moment. There's a man waiting outside my office on a disciplinary charge. I can either have him court-martialed or I can send him over to you."

"What's his offense?"

"Insubordination. Arrogance. Disregard of orders. He's a loner. He does as he pleases and to hell with the rule-book."

"What about results?"

"He gets results—of a sort. His own kind of results."

"He may be the man to bring back Isabel May. What's his name?"

"Lanarck. He won't use his rank, which is captain."

"He seems something of a free spirit…Well, send him over."

Lanarck arrived almost immediately. The secretary ushered him into Cardale's office.

"Sit down, please. My name is Cardale. You're Lanarck, right?"

"Quite right."

Cardale inspected his visitor with open curiosity. Lanarck's reputation, thought Cardale, was belied by his appearance. He was neither tall nor heavy, and carried himself unobtrusively. His features, deeply darkened by the hard waves of space, were regular and dominated by a cold directness of the gray eyes and a bold jutting nose. Lanarck's voice was pleasant and soft.

"Major Detering assigned me to you for orders, sir."

"He recommended you highly," said Cardale. "I have a ticklish job on hand. Look at this." He passed over the sheet with the photograph of Isabel May. Lanarck scrutinized it without comment and handed it back.

"This girl was imprisoned six months ago for assault with a deadly weapon. She escaped the day before yesterday into space—which is more or less trivial in itself. But she carries with her a quantity of important information, which must be retrieved for the economic well-being of Earth. This may seem to you an extravagant statement, but accept it from me as a fact."

Lanarck said in a patient voice: "Mr. Cardale, I find that I work most efficiently when I am equipped with facts. Give me details of the case. If you feel that the matter is too sensitive for my handling, I will retire and you may bring in operatives better qualified."

Cardale said crossly: "The girl's father is a high-level mathematician, at work for the Exchequer. By his instruction an elaborate method of security to regulate transfer of funds was evolved. As an emergency precaution he devised an over-ride system, consisting of several words in a specific sequence. A criminal could go to the telephone, call the Exchequer, use these words and direct by voice alone the transfer of a billion dollars to his personal account. Or a hundred billion."

"Why not cancel the over-ride and install another?"

"Because of Arthur May's devilish subtlety. The over-ride is hidden in the computer; it is buried, totally inaccessible, that it might be protected from someone ordering the computer to reveal the over-ride. The only way the over-ride can be voided is to use the over-ride first and issue appropriate orders."

"Go on."

"Arthur May knew the over-ride. He agreed to transfer the knowledge to the Chancellor and then submit to a hypnotic process which would remove the knowledge from his brain. Now occurred a rather sordid matter in regard to May's remuneration, and in my mind he was absolutely in the right."

"I know the feeling," said Lanarck. "I've had my own troubles with the scoundrels. The only good bursar is a dead bursar."

"In any event there follows an incredible tale of wrangling, proposals, estimates, schemes, counter-proposals, counter-schemes and conniving, all of which caused Arthur May a mental breakdown and he forgot the over-ride. But he had anticipated something of the sort and he left a memorandum with his daughter: Isabel May. When the authorities came for her father, she refused to let them in; she performed violent acts; she was confined in a penal institution, from which she escaped. Regardless of rights and wrongs she must be captured, more or less gently, and brought back—with the over-ride. You will surely understand the implications of the situation."

"It is a complicated business," said Lanarck. "But I will go after the girl, and with luck I will bring her back."

Six hours later Lanarck arrived at Lunar Observatory. The in-iris expanded; the boat lurched through.

Inside the dome Lanarck unclamped the port, stepped out. The master astronomer approached. Behind came the mechanics, one of whom bore an instrument which they welded to the hull of Lanarck's spaceboat.

"It's a detector cell," the astronomer explained. "Right now it's holding a line on the ship you're to follow. When the indicator holds to the neutral zone, you're on her track."

"And where does this ship seem to be headed?"

The astronomer shrugged. "Nowhere in Tellurian space. She's way past Fomalhaut and lining straight out."

Lanarck stood silent. This was hostile space Isabel May was entering. In another day or so she would be slicing the fringe of the Clantlalan System, where the space patrol of that dark and inimical empire without warning destroyed all approaching vessels. Further on opened a region of black stars, inhabited by nondescript peoples little better than pirates. Still farther beyond lay unexplored and consequently dangerous regions.

The mechanics were finished. Lanarck climbed back into the boat. The out-iris opened; he drove his craft through, down the runway, and off into space.

A slow week followed, in which distance was annihilated. Earth empire fell far astern: a small cluster of stars. To one side the Clantlalan System grew ever brighter, and as Lanarck passed by the Clantlalan space-spheres tried to close with him. He threw in the emergency bank of generators and whisked the war-boat far ahead. Someday, Lanarck knew, he would slip down past the guard ships to the home planet by the twin red suns, to discover what secret was held so dear. But now he kept the detector centered in the dial, and day by day the incoming signals from his quarry grew stronger.

They passed through the outlaw-ridden belt of dark stars, and into a region of space unknown but for tales let slip by drunken Clantlalan renegades— reports of planets covered with mighty ruins, legends of an asteroid littered with a thousand wrecked spaceships. Other tales were even more incredible. A dragon who tore spaceships open in its jaws purportedly wandered through this region, and it was said that alone on a desolate planet a godlike being created worlds at his pleasure.

The signals in the detector cell presently grew so strong that Lanarck slackened speed for fear that, overshooting his quarry, the cell would lose its thread of radiation. Now Isabel May began to swing out toward the star-systems which drifted past like fireflies, as if she sought a landmark. Always the signals in the detector cell grew stronger.

A yellow star waxed bright ahead. Lanarck knew that the ship of Isabel May was close at hand. Into that yellow star's system he followed her, and lined out the trail toward the single planet. Presently, as the planet globed out before him, the signals ceased entirely.

The high clear atmosphere braked the motion of Lanarck's spaceboat. He found below a dun, sun-baked landscape. Through the telescope the surface appeared to be uniformly stony and flat. Clouds of dust indicated the presence of high winds.

He had no trouble finding Isabel May's ship. In the field of his telescope lay a cubical white building: the only landmark visible from horizon to horizon. Beside the building sat Isabel May's silver spaceboat. Lanarck swooped to a landing, half-expecting a bolt from her needle-beam. The port of the spaceboat hung open, but she did not show herself as he came down on his crash-keel close by.

The air, he found, was breathable. Buckling on his needle-beam, he stepped out on the stony ground. The hot gale tore at him, buffeting his face, whipping tears from his eyes. Wind-flung pebbles bounding along the ground stung his legs. Light from the sun burned his shoulders.

Lanarck inspected the terrain, to discover no sign of life, either from the white building or from Isabel May's spaceboat. The ground stretched away, bare and sundrenched, far into the dusty distances. Lanarck looked to the lonely white structure. She must be within. Here was the end of the chase which had brought him across the galaxy.

ii

Lanarck circled the building. On the leeward side, he found a low dark archway. From within came the heavy smell of life: an odor half-animal, half-reptile. He approached the entrance with his needle-beam ready.

He called out: "Isabel May!" He listened. The wind whistled by the corner of the building; little stones clicked past, blowing down the endless sun-dazzled waste. There was no other sound.

A sonorous voice entered his brain.

"The one you seek is gone."

Lanarck stood stock-still.

"You may come within, Earthman. We are not enemies."

The archway loomed dark before him. Step by step he entered. After the glare of the white sun the dimness of the room was like a moonless night. Lanarck blinked.

Slowly objects about him assumed form. Two enormous eyes peered through the gloom; behind appeared a tremendous domelike bulk. Thought surged into Lanarck's brain. "You are unnecessarily truculent. Here will be no occasion for violence."

Lanarck relaxed, feeling slightly at a loss. Telepathy was not often practised upon Earth. The creature's messages came like a paradoxically silent voice, but he had no knowledge how to transmit his own messages. He hazarded the experiment.

"Where is Isabel May?"

"In a place inaccessible to you."

"How did she go? Her spaceboat is outside, and she landed but a half-hour ago."

"I sent her away."

Keeping his needle-beam ready, Lanarck searched the building. The girl was nowhere to be found. Seized by a sudden fearful thought, he ran to the entrance and looked out. The two spaceboats were as he had left them. He shoved the needle-beam back into the holster and turned to the leviathan, in whom he sensed benign amusement.

"Well, then—who are you and where is Isabel May?"

"I am Laoome," came the reply. "Laoome, the one-time Third of Narfilhet—Laoome the World-Thinker, the Final Sage of the Fifth Universe...As for the girl, I have placed her, at her own request, upon a pleasant but inaccessible world of my own creation."

Lanarck stood perplexed.

"Look!" Laoome said.

Space quivered in front of Lanarck's eyes. A dark aperture appeared in midair. Looking through, Lanarck saw hanging apparently but a yard before his eyes a lambent sphere—a miniature world. As he watched, it expanded like a toy balloon.

Its horizons vanished past the confines of the opening. Continents and oceans assumed shape, flecked with cloud-wisps. Polar ice-caps glinted blue-white in the light of an unseen sun. Yet all the time the world seemed to be but a yard distant. A plain appeared, rimmed by black, flinty mountains. The color of the plain, a ruddy ocher he saw presently, was due to a forest-carpet of rust-colored foliage. The expansion ceased.

The World-Thinker spoke: "That which you see before you is matter as real and tangible as yourself. I have indeed created it through my mind. Until I dissolve it in the same manner, it exists. Reach out and touch it."

Lanarck did so. It was actually only a yard from his face, and the red forest crushed like dry moss under his fingertips.

"You destroyed a village," commented Laoome, and caused the world to expand once more at a breathtaking rate, until the perspectives were as if Lanarck hung a hundred feet above the surface. He was looking into the devastation which his touch had wrought a moment before. The trees, far larger than he had supposed, with boles thirty or forty feet through, lay tossed and shattered. Visible were the ruins of rude huts, from which issued calls and screams of pain, thinly audible to Lanarck. Bodies of men and women lay crushed. Others tore frantically at the wreckage.

Lanarck stared in disbelief. "There's life! Men!"

"Without life, a world is uninteresting, a lump of rock. Men, like yourself, I often use. They have a large capacity for emotion and initiative, a flexibility to the varied environments which I introduce."

Lanarck gazed at the tips of his fingers, then back to the shattered village. "Are they really alive?"

"Certainly. And you would find, should you converse with one of them, that they possess a sense of history, a racial heritage of folklore, and a culture well-adapted to their environment."

"But how can one brain conceive the detail of a world? The leaves of each tree, the features of each man—"

"That would be tedious," Laoome agreed. "My mind only broadly conceives, introduces the determinate roots into the hypostatic equations. Detail then evolves automatically."

"You allowed me to destroy hundreds of these—men."

Curious feelers searched his brain. Lanarck sensed Laoome's amusement.

"The idea is repugnant? In a moment I shall dissolve the entire world…Still, if it pleases you, I can restore it as it was. See!"

Immediately the forest was unmarred, the village whole again, secure and peaceful in a small clearing.

Awareness came to Lanarck of a curious rigidity in the rapport he had established with the World-Thinker. Looking about, he saw that the great eyes had glazed, that the tremendous black body was twitching and jerking. Now Laoome's dream-planet was changing. Lanarck leaned forward in fascination. The noble red trees had become gray rotten stalks and were swaying drunkenly. Others slumped and folded like columns of putty.

On the ground balls of black slime rolled about with vicious energy pursuing the villagers, who in terror fled anywhere, everywhere.

From the heavens came a rain of blazing pellets. The villagers were killed, but the black slime-things seemed only agonized. Blindly they lashed about, burrowed furiously into the heaving ground to escape the impacts. More suddenly than it had been created, the world vanished. Lanarck tore his gaze from the spot where the world had been. He looked about and found Laoome as before.

"Don't be alarmed." The thoughts came quietly. "The seizure is over. It occurs only seldom, and why it should be I do not know. I imagine that my brain, under the pressure of exact thought, lapses into these reflexive spasms for the sake of relaxation. This was a mild attack. The world on which I am concentrating is usually totally destroyed."

The flow of soundless words stopped abruptly. Moments passed. Then thoughts gushed once more into Lanarck's brain.

"Let me show you another planet—one of the most interesting I have ever conceived. For almost a million Earth years it has been developing in my mind."

The space before Lanarck's eyes quivered. Out in the imaginary void hung another planet. As before, it expanded until the features of the terrain assumed an earthly perspective. Hardly a mile in diameter, the world was divided around the equator by a belt of sandy desert. At one pole glimmered a lake, at the other grew a jungle of lush vegetation.

From this jungle now, as Lanarck watched, crept a semi-human shape. A travesty upon man, its face was long, chinless and furtive, with eyes beady and quick. The legs were unnaturally long; the shoulders and arms were undeveloped. It slunk to the edge of the desert, paused a moment, looking carefully in both directions, then began a mad dash through the sand to the lake beyond.

Halfway across, a terrible roar was heard. Over the close horizon bounded a dragon-like monster. With fearsome speed it pursued the fleeing man-thing, who outdistanced it and gained the edge of the desert by two hundred feet. When the dragon came to the limits of the sandy area, it halted and bellowed an eery mournful note which sent shivers along Lanarck's spine. Casually now, the man-thing loped to the lake, threw himself flat and drank deeply.

"An experiment in evolution," came Laoome's thought. "A million years ago those creatures were men like yourself. This world is oddly designed. At one end is food, at the other drink. In order to survive, the 'men' must cross the desert every day or so. The dragon is prevented from leaving the desert by actinic boundaries. Hence, if the men can cross the desert, they are safe.

"You have witnessed how admirably they have adapted to their environment. The women are particularly fleet, for they have adjusted to the handicap of caring for their young. Sooner or later, of course, age overtakes them and their speed gradually decreases until finally they are caught and devoured.

"A curious religion and set of taboos have evolved here. I am worshipped as the primary god of Life, and Shillal, as they call the dragon, is the deity of

Death. He, of course, is the basic concern of their lives and colors all their thoughts. They are close to elementals, these folk. Food, drink, and death are intertwined for them into almost one concept.

"They can build no weapons of metal against Shillal, for their world is not endowed with the raw materials. Once, a hundred thousand years ago, one of their chiefs contrived a gigantic catapult, to hurl a sharp-pointed tree-trunk at Shillal. Unluckily, the fibers of the draw-cord snapped and the chief was killed by the recoil. The priests interpreted this as a sign and—

"Look there! Shillal catches a weary old woman, sodden with water, attempting to return to the jungle!"

Lanarck witnessed the beast's great gulping.

"To continue," Laoome went on, "a taboo was created, and no further weapons were ever built."

"But why have you forced upon these folk a million years of wretched existence?" asked Lanarck.

Laoome gave an untranslatable mental shrug. "I am just, and indeed benevolent," he said. "These men worship me as a god. Upon a certain hillock, which they hold sacred, they bring their sick and wounded. There, if the whim takes me, I restore them to health. So far as their existence is concerned, they relish the span of their lives as much as you do yours."

"Yet, in creating these worlds, you are responsible for the happiness of the inhabitants. If you were truly benevolent, why should you permit disease and terror to exist?"

Laoome again gave his mental shrug. "I might say that I use this universe of our own as a model. Perhaps there is another Laoome dreaming out the worlds we ourselves live on. When man dies of sickness, bacteria live. Dragon lives by eating man. When man eats, plants and animals die."

Lanarck was silent, studiously preventing his thoughts from rising to the surface of his mind.

"I take it that Isabel May is upon neither of these planets?"

"That is correct."

"I ask that you make it possible for me to communicate with her."

"But I put her upon a world expressly to assure her safety from such molestation."

"I believe that she would profit by hearing me."

"Very well," said Laoome. "In justice I should accord to you the same opportunity that I did her. You may proceed to this world. Remember, however, the risk is your own, exactly as it is for Isabel May. If you perish upon Markavvel, you are as thoroughly dead as you might be upon Earth. I can not play Destiny to influence either one of your lives."

There was a hiatus in Laoome's thoughts, a whirl of ideas too rapid for Lanarck to grasp. At last Laoome's eyes focused upon him again. An instant of faintness as Lanarck felt knowledge forced into his brain.

As Laoome silently regarded him, it occurred to Lanarck that Laoome's body, a great dome of black flesh, was singularly ill-adapted to life on the planet where he dwelt.

"You are right," came the thoughts of Laoome. "From a Beyond unknown to you I came, banished from the dark planet Narfilhet, in whose fathomless black waters I swam. This was long ago, but even now I may not return." Laoome lapsed once more into introspection.

Lanarck moved restlessly. Outside the wind tore past the building. Laoome continued silent, dreaming perhaps of the dark oceans of ancient Narfilhet. Lanarck impatiently launched a thought.

"How do I reach Markavvel? And how do I return?"

Laoome fetched himself back to the present. His eyes settled upon a point beside Lanarck. The aperture which led into his various imaginary spaces was now wrenched open for the third time. A little distance off in the void, a space-boat drifted. Lanarck's eyes narrowed with sudden interest.

"That's a 45-G—my own ship!" he exclaimed.

"No, not yours. One like it. Yours is still outside." The craft drew nearer, gradually floated within reach.

"Climb in," said Laoome. "At present, you will find Isabel May in the city which lies at the apex of the triangular continent."

"But how do I get back?"

"Aim your ship, when you leave Markavvel, at the brightest star visible. You will then break through the mental dimensions into this universe."

Lanarck reached his arm into the imaginary universe and pulled the imagined spaceboat close to the aperture. He opened the port and gingerly stepped in as Laoome's parting thoughts reached him.

"Should you fall into danger, I cannot modify the natural course of events. On the other hand, I will not intentionally place dangers in your way. If such befall you, it will be due solely to circumstance."

iii

Lanarck slammed shut the port, half-expecting the ship to dissolve under his feet. But the ship was solid enough. He looked back. The gap into his own universe had disappeared, leaving in its place a brilliant blue star. He found himself in space. Below glimmered the disk of Markavvel, much like other planets he had approached from the void. He tugged at the throttle, threw the nose hard over and down. Let the abstracts take care of themselves. The boat dropped down at Markavvel.

It seemed a pleasant world. A hot white sun hung off in space; blue oceans covered a large part of the surface. Among the scattered land masses he found the triangular continent. It was not large. There were mountains with green-forested slopes and a central plateau: a not un-Earthlike scene, and Lanarck did not feel the alien aura which surrounded most extra-terrestrial planets.

Sighting through his telescope Lanarck found the city, sprawling and white, at the mouth of a wide river. He sent his ship streaking down through the upper atmosphere, then slowed and leveled off thirty miles to sea. Barely skimming the sparkling blue waves, he flew toward the city.

A few miles to the left an island raised basalt cliffs against the ocean. In his line of sight there heaved up on the crest of a swell a floating black object. After an instant it disappeared into the trough: a ramshackle raft. Upon it a girl with tawny golden hair desperately battled sea-things which sought to climb aboard.

Lanarck dropped the ship into the water beside the raft. The wash threw the raft up and over and down on the girl.

Lanarck slipped through the port and dived into clear green water. He glimpsed only sub-human figures paddling downward, barely discernible. Bobbing to the surface, he swam to the raft, ducked under, grasped the girl's limp form, pulled her up into the air.

For a moment he clung to the raft to catch his breath, while holding the girl's head clear of the water. He sensed the return of the creatures from below. Dark forms rose in the shadow cast by the raft, and a clammy, long-fingered hand wound around his ankle. He kicked and felt his foot thud into something like a face. More dark forms came up from the depths. Lanarck measured the distance to his spaceboat. Forty feet. Too far. He crawled onto the raft, and pulled the girl after him. Leaning far out, he recovered the paddle and prepared to smash the first sea-thing to push above water. But instead, they swam in tireless circles twenty feet below.

The blade of the paddle had broken. Lanarck could not move the unwieldy bulk of the raft. The breeze, meanwhile, was easing the spaceboat ever farther away. Lanarck exerted himself another fifteen minutes, pushing against the water with the splintered paddle, but the gap increased. He cast down the paddle in disgust and turned to the girl who, sitting cross-legged, regarded him thought-fully. For no apparent reason, Lanarck was reminded of Laoome in the dimness of his white building, on the windy world. All this, he thought, looking from clear-eyed girl to heaving sun-lit sea to highlands of the continent ahead, was an idea in Laoome's brain.

He looked back at the girl. Her bright wheat-colored hair frothed around her head in ringlets, producing, thought Lanarck, a most pleasant effect. She returned his gaze for a moment, then, with jaunty grace, stood up.

She spoke to Lanarck who found to his amazement that he understood her. Then, remembering Laoome's manipulation of his brain, extracting ideas, altering, instilling new concepts, he was not so amazed.

"Thank you for your help," she said. "But now we are both in the same plight."

Lanarck said nothing. He knelt and began to remove his boots.

"What will you do?"

"Swim," he answered. The new language seemed altogether natural.

"The Bottom-people would pull you under before you went twenty feet." She pointed into the water, which teemed with circling dark shapes. Lanarck knew she spoke the truth.

"You are of Earth also?" she asked, inspecting him carefully.

"Yes. Who are you and what do you know of Earth?"

"I am Jiro from the city yonder, which is Gahadion. Earth is the home of Isabel May, who came in a ship such as yours."

"Isabel May arrived but an hour ago! How could you know about her?"

"'An hour'?" replied the girl. "She has been here three months!" This last a little bitterly.

Lanarck reflected that Laoome controlled time in his universes as arbitrarily as he did space. "How did you come to be here on this raft?"

She grimaced toward the island. "The priests came for me. They live on the island and take people from the mainland. They took me but last night I escaped."

Lanarck looked from the island to the city on the mainland. "Why do not Gahadion authorities control the priests?"

Her lips rounded to an O. "They are sacred to the Great God Laoome, and so inviolate."

Lanarck wondered what unique evolutionary process Laoome had in progress here.

"Few persons thus taken return to the mainland," she went on. "Those who win free, and also escape the Bottom-people, usually live in the wilderness. If they return to Gahadion they are molested by fanatics and sometimes recaptured by the priests."

Lanarck was silent. After all, it concerned him little how these people fared. They were beings of fantasy, inhabiting an imaginary planet. And yet, when he looked at Jiro, detachment became easier to contemplate than to achieve.

"And Isabel May is in Gahadion?"

Jiro's lips tightened. "No. She lives on the island. She is the Thrice-Adept, the High Priestess."

Lanarck was surprised. "Why did they make her High Priestess?"

"A month after she arrived, the Hierarch, learning of the woman whose hair was the color of night, even as yours, tried to take her to Drefteli, the Sacred Isle, as a slave. She killed him with her weapon. Then when the lightnings of Laoome did not consume her, it was known that Laoome approved, and so she was made High Priestess in place of the riven Hierarch."

The philosophy, so Lanarck reflected, would have sounded naive on Earth, where the gods were more covert in their supervision of human affairs.

"Is Isabel May a friend of yours—or your lover?" asked Jiro softly.

"Hardly."

"Then what do you want with her?"

"I've come to take her back to Earth." He looked dubiously across the ever-widening gap between the raft and his spaceboat. "That at least was my intention."

"You shall see her soon," said Jiro. She pointed to a long black galley approaching from the island. "The Ordained Ones. I am once more a slave."

"Not yet," said Lanarck, feeling for the bulk of his needle-beam.

The galley, thrust by the force of twenty long oars, lunged toward them. On the afterdeck stood a young woman, her black hair blowing in the wind. As her features became distinct, Lanarck recognized the face of Cardale's photograph, now serene and confident.

Isabel May, looking from the silent two on the raft to the wallowing spaceboat a quarter-mile distant, seemed to laugh. The galley, manned by tall, golden-haired men, drew alongside.

"So Earth Intelligence pays me a visit?" She spoke in English. "How you found me, I cannot guess." She looked curiously at Lanarck's somber visage. "How?"

"I followed your trail, and then explained the situation to Laoome."

"Just what is the situation?"

"I'd like to work out some kind of compromise to please everyone."

"I don't care whether I please anyone or not."

"Understandable."

The two studied each other. Isabel May suddenly asked, "What is your name?"

"Lanarck."

"Just Lanarck? No rank? No first name?"

"Lanarck is enough."

"Just as you like. I hardly know what to do with you. I'm not vindictive, and I don't want to handicap your career. But ferrying you to your spaceboat would be rather quixotic. I'm comfortable here, and I haven't the slightest intention of turning my property over to you."

Lanarck reached for his needle-beam.

She watched him without emotion. "Wet needle-beams don't work well."

"This one is the exception." Lanarck blasted the figurehead from the galley.

Isabel May's expression changed suddenly. "I see that I'm wrong. How did you do it?"

"A personal device," replied Lanarck. "Now I'll have to request that you take me to my spaceboat."

Isabel May stared at him a moment, and in those blue eyes Lanarck detected something familiar. Where had he seen eyes with that expression? On Fan, the Pleasure Planet? In the Magic Groves of Hycithil? During the raids on the slave-pens of Starlen? In Earth's own macropolis Tran?

She turned and muttered to her boatswain, a bronzed giant, his golden hair bound back by a copper band. He bowed and moved away.

"Very well," said Isabel May. "Come aboard."

Jiro and Lanarck clambered over the carven gunwale. The galley swept ahead, foaming up white in its wake.

Isabel May turned her attention to Jiro, who sat looking disconsolately toward the island Drefteli. "You make friends quickly," Isabel told Lanarck. "She's very beautiful. What are you planning for her?"

"She's one of your escaped slaves. I don't have any plans. This place belongs to Laoome; he makes all plans. I'm interested only in getting you out. If you don't want to come back to Earth, give me the document which you brought with you, and stay here as long as you like."

"Sorry. The document stays with me. I don't carry it on my person, so please don't try to search me."

"That sounds quite definite," said Lanarck. "Do you know what's in the document?"

"More or less. It's like a blank check on the wealth of the world."

"That's a good description. As I understand this sorry affair, you became angry at the treatment accorded your father."

"That's a very quiet understatement."

"Would money help soothe your anger?"

"I don't want money. I want revenge. I want to grind faces into the mud; I want to kick people and make their lives miserable."

"Still…don't dismiss money. It's nice to be rich. You have your life ahead of you. I don't imagine you want to spend it here, inside Laoome's head."

"Very true."

"So name a figure."

"I can't measure anger and grief in dollars."

"Why not? A million? Ten million? A hundred million?"

"Stop there. I can't count any higher."

"That's your figure."

"What good will money do me? They'll take me back to Nevada."

"No. I'll give you my personal guarantee of this."

"Meaningless. I know nothing about you."

"You'll learn during the trip back to Earth."

Isabel May said: "Lanarck, you are persuasive. If the truth be known, I'm homesick." She turned away and stood looking over the ocean. Lanarck stood watching her. She was undeniably attractive and he found it difficult to take his eyes from her. But as he settled on the bench beside Jiro, he felt a surge of a different, stronger, feeling. It irritated him, and he tried to put it aside.

iv

Wallowing in the swells, the spaceboat lay dead ahead. The galley scudded through the water at a great rate, and the oarsmen did not slacken speed as they approached. Lanarck's eyes narrowed; he jumped upright shouting orders. The galley, unswerving, plowed into the spaceboat, grinding it under the metal-shod keel. Water gushed in through the open port; the spaceboat shuddered and sank, a dark shadow plummeting into green depths.

"Too bad," remarked Isabel. "On the other hand, this puts us more on an equal footing. You have a needle-beam, I have a spaceboat."

Lanarck silently seated himself. After a moment he spoke. "Where is your own needle-beam?"

"I blew it up trying to recharge it from the spaceboat generators."

"And where is your spaceboat?"

Isabel laughed at this. "Do you expect me to tell you?"

"Why not? I wouldn't maroon you here."

"Nevertheless, I don't think I'll tell you."

Lanarck turned to Jiro. "Where is Isabel May's spaceboat?"

Isabel spoke in a haughty voice: "As High Priestess to Almighty Laoome, I command you to be silent!"

Jiro looked from one to the other. She made up her mind. "It is on the plaza of the Malachite Temple in Gahadion."

Isabel was silent. "Laoome plays tricks," she said at last. "Jiro has taken a fancy to you. You're obviously interested in her."

"Laoome will not interfere," said Lanarck.

She laughed bitterly. "That's what he told me—and look! I'm High Priestess. He also told me he wouldn't let anyone come to Markavvel from the outside to molest me. But you are here!"

"My intention is not to molest you," said Lanarck curtly. "We can as easily be friends as enemies."

"I don't care to be a friend of yours. And as an enemy, you are no serious problem. Now!" Isabel called, as the tall boatswain came near.

The boatswain whirled on Lanarck. Lanarck twisted, squirmed, heaved, and the golden-haired boatswain sprawled back into the bilge, where he lay dazed.

A soft hand brushed Lanarck's thigh. He looked around, smoothing his lank black hair, and found Isabel May smiling into his face. His needle-beam dangled from her fingers.

Jiro arose from the bench. Before Isabel could react, Jiro had pushed a hand into her face, and with the other seized the needle-beam. She pointed the weapon at Isabel.

"Sit down," said Jiro.

Weeping with rage, Isabel fell back upon the bench.

Jiro, her young face flushed and happy, backed over to the thwart, needle-beam leveled.

Lanarck stood still.

"I will take charge now," said Jiro. "You—Isabel! Tell your men to row toward Gahadion!"

Sullenly Isabel gave the order. The long black galley turned its bow toward the city.

"This may be sacrilege," Jiro observed to Lanarck. "But then I was already in trouble for escaping from Drefteli."

"What do you plan in this new capacity of yours?" Lanarck inquired, moving closer.

"First, to try this weapon on whomever thinks he can take it away from me." Lanarck eased back. "Secondly—but you'll see soon enough."

White-tiered Gahadion rapidly drew closer across the water.

Isabel sulked on the bench. Lanarck had little choice but to let matters move on their own momentum. He relaxed against a thwart, watching Jiro from the corner of his eye. She stood erect behind the bench where Isabel sat, her clear eyes looking over the leaping sparkles of the ocean. Breeze whipped her hair behind and pressed the tunic against her slim body. Lanarck heaved a deep sad sigh. This girl with the wheat-colored hair was unreal. She would vanish into oblivion as soon as Laoome lost interest in the world Markavvel. She was less than a shadow, less than a mirage, less than a dream. Lanarck looked over at Isabel, the Earth girl, who glared at him with sullen eyes. She was real enough.

They moved up the river and toward the white docks of Gahadion. Lanarck rose to his feet. He looked over the city, surveyed the folk on the dock who were clad in white, red and blue tunics, then turned to Jiro. "I'll have to take the weapon now."

"Stand back or I'll—" Lanarck took the weapon from her limp grasp. Isabel watched in sour amusement.

A dull throbbing sound, like the pulse of a tremendous heart, came down from the heavens. Lanarck cocked his head, listening. He scanned the sky. At the horizon appeared a strange cloud, like a band of white-gleaming metal, swelling in rhythm to the celestial throbbing. It lengthened with miraculous speed, until in all directions the horizon was encircled. The throb became a vast booming. The air itself seemed heavy, ominous. A terrible idea struck Lanarck. He turned and yelled to the awestruck oarsmen who were trailing their oars in the river.

"Quickly—get to the docks!"

They jerked at their oars, frantic, yet the galley moved no faster. The water of the river had become oily smooth, almost syrupy. The boat inched close to the dock. Lanarck was grimly aware of the terrified Isabel on one side of him, Jiro on the other.

"What is happening?" whispered Isabel. Lanarck watched the sky. The cloud-band of bright metal quivered and split into another which wabbled, bouncing just above.

"I hope I'm wrong," said Lanarck, "but I suspect that Laoome is going mad. Look at our shadows!" He turned to look at the sun, which jerked like a dying insect, vibrating through aimless arcs. His worst fears were realized.

"It can't be!" cried Isabel. "What will happen?"

"Nothing good."

The galley lurched against a pier. Lanarck helped Isabel and Jiro up to the dock, then followed.

Masses of tall golden-haired people milled in panic along the avenue.

"Lead me to the spaceboat!" Lanarck had to shout to make himself heard over the tumult of the city. His mind froze at a shocking thought: what would happen to Jiro?

He pushed the thought down. Isabel pulled at him urgently. "Come, hurry!"

Taking Jiro's hand, he ran off after Isabel toward the black-porticoed temple at the far end of the avenue.

A constriction twisted the air; down came a rain of warm red globules: small crimson jellyfish which stung naked flesh like nettles. The din from the city reached hysterical pitch. The red plasms increased to become a cloud of pink slime, now oozing ankle-deep on the ground.

Isabel tripped and fell headlong in the perilous mess. She struggled until Lanarck helped her to her feet.

They continued toward the temple, Lanarck supporting both girls and keeping an uneasy eye on the structures to either side.

The rain of red things ceased, but the streets flowed with ooze.

The sky shifted color—but what color? It had no place in any spectrum. The color only a mad god could conceive.

The red slime curdled and fell apart like quicksilver, to jell in an instant to millions upon millions of bright blue manikins three inches high. They ran, hopped, scuttled; the streets were a quaking blue carpet of blank-faced little homunculi. They clung to Lanarck's garments, they ran up his legs like mice. He trod them under, heedless to their squeals.

The sun, jerking in small spasmodic motions, slowed, lost its glare, became oblate. It developed striations and, as the stricken population of Gahadion quieted in awe, the sun changed to a segmented white slug, as long as five suns, as wide as one. It writhed its head about and stared down through the strange-colored sky at Markavvel.

In a delirium, the Gahadionites careened along the wide avenues. Lanarck and the two girls almost were trod under as they fought past a cross-street.

In a small square, beside a marble fountain, the three found refuge. Lanarck had reached a state of detachment: a conviction that this experience was a nightmare.

A blue man-thing pulled itself into his hair. It was singing in a small clear baritone. Lanarck set it upon the ground. His mind grew calmer. This was no nightmare; this was reality, however the word could be interpreted! Haste! The surge of people had passed; the way was relatively open. "Let's go!" He pulled at the two girls, who had been watching the slug which hung across the sky.

As they started off, there came the metamorphosis Lanarck had been expecting, and dreading. The matter of Gahadion, and all Markavvel, altered into unnatural substances. The buildings of white marble became putty, slumped beneath their own weight. The Malachite Temple, an airy dome on green malachite pillars, sagged and slid to a sodden lump. Lanarck urged the gasping girls to greater speed.

The Gahadionites no longer ran; there was no destination. They stood staring up, frozen in horror by the glittering slug in the sky. A voice screamed: "Laoome, Laoome!" Other voices took up the cry: "Laoome, Laoome!"

If Laoome heard, he gave no sign.

Lanarck kept an anxious eye on these folk, dreading lest they also, as dream-creatures, alter to shocking half-things. For should they change, so would Jiro. Why take her to the spaceboat? She could not exist outside the mind of Laoome…But how could he let her go?

The face of Markavvel was changing. Black pyramids sprouted through the ground and, lengthening tremendously, darted upward, to become black spikes, miles high.

Lanarck saw the spaceboat, still sound and whole, a product of more durable mind-stuff, perhaps, than Markavvel itself. Tremendous processes were transpiring beneath his feet, as if the core of the planet itself were degenerating. Another hundred yards to the spaceboat! "Faster!" he panted to the girls.

All the while they ran, he watched the folk of Gahadion. Like a cold wind blowing on his brain, he knew that the change had come. He almost slowed his steps for despair. The Gahadionites themselves knew. They staggered in unbelieving surprise, regarding their hands, feeling their faces.

Too late! Unreasonably Lanarck had hoped that once in space, away from Markavvel, Jiro might retain her identity. But too late! A blight had befallen the Gahadionites. They clawed their shriveling faces, tottered and fell, their shrunken legs unable to support them.

In anguish Lanarck felt one of the hands he was holding become hard and wrinkled. As her legs withered, he felt her sag. He paused and turned, to look sadly upon what had been Jiro.

The ground beneath his feet lurched. Around him twisted dying Gahadionites. Above, dropping through the weird sky, came the slug. Black spikes towered tremendously over his head. Lanarck heeded none of these. Before him stood Jiro—a Jiro gasping and reeling in exhaustion, but a Jiro sound and golden still! Dying on the marble pavement was the shriveled dream-thing he had known as Isabel May. Taking Jiro's hand, he turned and made for the spaceboat.

Hauling back the port, he pushed Jiro inside. Even as he touched the hull, he realized that the spaceboat was changing also. The cold metal had acquired a palpitant life of its own. Lanarck slammed shut the port, and, heedless of fracturing cold thrust-tubes, gushed power astern.

Off careened the spaceboat, dodging through the forest of glittering black spines, now hundreds of miles tall, swerving a thousand miles to escape the great slug falling inexorably to the surface of Markavvel. As the ship darted free into space, Lanarck looked back to see the slug sprawled across half a hemisphere. It writhed, impaled on the tall black spikes.

Lanarck drove the spaceboat at full speed toward the landmark star. Blue and luminous it shone, the only steadfast object in the heavens. All else poured in turbulent streams through black space: motes eddying in a pool of ink.

Lanarck looked briefly toward Jiro, and spoke. "Just when I decided that nothing else could surprise me, Isabel May died, while you, Jiro the Gahadionite, are alive."

"I am Isabel May. You knew already."

"I knew, yes, because it was the only possibility." He put his hand against the hull. The impersonal metallic feel had altered to a warm vitality. "Now, if we escape from this mess, it'll be a miracle."

Changes came quickly. The controls atrophied; the ports grew dull and opaque, like cartilage. Engines and fittings became voluted organs; the walls were pink moist flesh, pulsing regularly. From outside came a sound like the flapping of pinions; about their feet swirled dark liquid. Lanarck, pale, shook his head. Isabel pressed close to him.

"We're in the stomach of—something."

Isabel made no answer.

A sound like a cork popped from a bottle, a gush of gray light. Lanarck had guided the spaceboat aright; it had continued into the sane universe and its own destruction.

The two Earth-creatures found themselves stumbling on the floor of Laoome's dwelling. At first they could not comprehend their deliverance; safety seemed but another shifting of scenes.

Lanarck regained his equilibrium. He helped Isabel to her feet; together they surveyed Laoome, who was still in the midst of his spasm. Rippling tremors ran along his black hide, the saucer eyes were blank and glazed.

"Let's go!" whispered Isabel.

Lanarck silently took her arm; they stepped out on the glaring wind-whipped plain. There, the two spaceboats, just as before. Lanarck guided Isabel to his craft, opened the port and motioned her inside. "I'm going back for one moment."

Lanarck locked the power-arm. "Just to guard against any new surprises."

Isabel said nothing.

Walking around to the spaceboat in which Isabel May had arrived, Lanarck similarly locked the mechanism. Then he crossed to the white concrete structure.

Isabel listened, but the moaning of the wind drowned out all other sounds. The chatter of a needle-beam? She could not be sure.

Lanarck emerged from the building. He climbed into the boat and slammed the port. They sat in silence as the thrust-tubes warmed, nor did they speak as he threw over the power-arm and the boat slanted off into the sky.

Not until they were far off in space did either of them speak.

Lanarck looked toward Isabel. "How did you know of Laoome?"

"Through my father. Twenty years ago he did Laoome some trifling favor— killed a lizard which had been annoying Laoome, or something of the sort."

"And that's why Laoome shielded you from me by creating the dream Isabel?"

"Yes. He told me you were coming down looking for me. He arranged that you should meet a purported Isabel May, that I might assess you without your knowledge."

"Why don't you look more like the photograph?"

"I was furious; I'd been crying; I was practically gnashing my teeth. I certainly hope I don't look like that."

"How about your hair?"

"It's bleached."

"Did the other Isabel know your identity?"

"I don't think so. No, I know she didn't. Laoome equipped her with my brain and all its memories. She actually was I."

Lanarck nodded. Here was the source of the inklings of recognition. He said thoughtfully: "She was very perceptive. She said that you and I were, well, attracted to each other. I wonder if she was right."

"I wonder."

"There will be time to consider the subject…One last point: the documents, with the over-ride."

Isabel laughed cheerfully. "There aren't any documents."

"No documents?"

"None. Do you care to search me?"

"Where are the documents?"

"Document, in the singular. A slip of paper. I tore it up."

"What was on the paper?"

"The over-ride. I'm the only person alive who knows it. Don't you think I should keep the secret to myself?"

Lanarck reflected a moment. "I'd like to know. That kind of knowledge is always useful."

"Where is the hundred million dollars you promised me?"

"It's back on Earth. When you get there you can use the over-ride."

Isabel laughed. "You're a most practical man. What happened to Laoome?"

"Laoome is dead."

"How?"

"I destroyed him. I thought of what we just went through. His dream-creatures—were they real? They seemed real to me, and to themselves. Is a person responsible for what happens during a nightmare? I don't know. I obeyed my instincts, or conscience, whatever it's called, and killed him."

Isabel May took his hand. "My instincts tell me that I can trust you. The over-ride is a couplet:

Tom, Tom, the piper's son
Stole a pig and away he run.

V

Lanarck reported to Cardale. "I am happy to inform you that the affair is satisfactorily concluded."

Cardale regarded him skeptically. "What do you mean by that?"

"The over-ride is safe."

"Indeed? Safe where?"

"I thought it best to consult with you before carrying the over-ride on my person."

"That is perhaps over-discreet. What of Isabel May? Is she in custody?"

"In order to get the over-ride I had to make broad but reasonable concessions, including a full pardon, retraction of all charges against her, and official apologies as well as retributive payments for false arrest and general damage. She wants an official document, certifying these concessions. If you will prepare the document, I will transmit it, and the affair will be terminated."

Cardale said in a cool voice: "Who authorized you to make such far-reaching concessions?"

Lanarck spoke indifferently. "Do you want the over-ride?"

"Of course."

"Then do as I suggest."

"You're even more arrogant than Detering led me to expect."

"The results speak for themselves, sir."

"How do I know that she won't use the over-ride?"

"You can now call it up and change it, so I'm given to understand."

"How do I know that she hasn't used it already, to the hilt?"

"I mentioned compensatory payments. The adjustment has been made."

Cardale ran his fingers through his hair. "How much damages?"

"The amount is of no great consequence. If Isabel May had chosen to make in-temperate demands, they would only partially balance the damage she has suffered."

"So you say." Cardale could not decide whether to bluster, to threaten, or to throw his hands in the air. At last he leaned back in his chair. "I'll have the document ready tomorrow, and you can bring in the over-ride."

"Very well, Mr. Cardale."

"I'd still like to know, unofficially, if you like, just how much she took in settlement."

"We requisitioned a hundred and one million, seven hundred and sixty-two dollars into a set of personal accounts."

Cardale stared. "I thought you said that she'd made a temperate settlement!"

"It seemed as easy to ask for a large sum as a small."

"No doubt even easier. It's a strange figure. Why seven hundred and sixty-two dollars?"

"That, sir, is money owing to me for which the bursar refuses to issue a voucher. It represents expenses in a previous case: bribes, liquor and the services of a prostitute, if you want the details."

"Any why the million extra?"

"That represents a contingency fund for my own convenience, so that I won't be harassed in the future. In a quiet and modest sense it also reflects my annoyance with the bursar."

Lanarck rose to his feet. "I'll see you tomorrow at the same time, sir."

"Until tomorrow, Lanarck."

Afterword to "The World-Thinker"

"I've got my writing down, and I'm pretty disciplined, so I don't have to do a lot of re-writing. I like to write about two or three thousand words a day, and I like to write straight through the whole first draft of the book without rewriting, then go back and do the whole second at once. But I find that in the morning [if] I glance at the stuff of the day before, see something needing to be changed, and get caught up—pretty soon I'm completely rewriting the day's work. The word processor has really increased my volume. I used to write longhand, my wife would type it out, I'd go through it again and she'd type it out again. Damn, she did a lot of work. But that was the only way to do it, because I couldn't type—it's too rigid."

—Jack Vance 1986

The Augmented Agent

Across a period of seven months, James Keith had undergone a series of subtle and intricate surgeries, and his normally efficient body had been altered in many ways: 'augmented', to use the jargon of the Special Branch, CIA.

Looking into the mirror, he saw a face familiar only from the photographs he had studied—dark, feral and harsh: the face, literally, of a savage. His hair, which he had allowed to grow long, had been oiled, stranded with gold tinsel, braided and coiled; his teeth had been replaced with stainless-steel dentures; from his ears dangled a pair of ivory amulets. In each case, adornment was the secondary function. The tinsel strands in his head-dress were multi-laminated accumulators, their charge maintained by thermo-electric action. The dentures scrambled, condensed, transmitted, received, expanded and unscrambled radio waves of energies almost too low to be detected. The seeming ivory amulets were stereophonic radar units, which not only could guide Keith through the dark, but also provided a fractional second's warning of a bullet, an arrow, a bludgeon. His fingernails were copper-silver alloy, internally connected to the accumulators in his hair. Another circuit served as a ground, to protect him against electrocution—one of his own potent weapons. These were the more obvious augmentations; others more subtle had been fabricated into his flesh.

As he stood before the mirror two silent technicians wound a narrow darshba turban around his head, draped him with a white robe. Keith no longer recognized the image in the mirror as himself. He turned to Carl Sebastiani, who had been watching from across the room—a small man, parchment-pale, with austere cheek-bones and a fragile look to his skull. Sebastiani's title, Assistant to the Under Director, understated his authority just as his air of delicacy misrepresented his inner toughness.

"Presently you'll become almost as much Tamba Ngasi as you are James Keith," said Sebastiani. "Quite possibly more. In which case your usefulness ends, and you'll be brought home."

Keith made no comment. He raised his arms, feeling the tension of new connections and conduits. He clenched his right fist, watched three metal stingers appear above his knuckles. He held up his left palm, felt the infra-red radiation emitted by Sebastiani's face. "I'm James Keith. I'll act Tamba Ngasi—but I'll never become him."

Sebastiani chuckled coolly. "A face is an almost irresistible symbol. In any event you'll have little time for introspection…Come along up to my office."

The aides removed Keith's white robe; he followed Sebastiani to his official suite, three rooms as calm, cool and elegant as Sebastiani himself. Keith settled into a deep-cushioned chair, Sebastiani slipped behind his desk, where he flicked at a row of buttons. On a screen appeared a large-scale map of Africa. "A new phase seems to be opening up and we want to exploit it." He touched another button, and a small rectangle on the underpart of the great Mauretanian bulge glowed green. "There's Lakhadi. Fejo is that bright point of light by Tabacoundi Bay." He glanced sidelong at Keith. "You remember the floating ICBM silos?"

"Vaguely. They were news twenty years or so ago. I remember the launchings."

Sebastiani nodded. "In 1963. Quite a boondoggle. The ICBM's—Titans—were already obsolete, the silos expensive, maintenance a headache. A month ago they went for surplus to a Japanese salvage firm, warheads naturally not included. Last week Premier Adoui Shgawe of Lakhadi bought them, apparently without the advice, consent or approval of either Russians or Chinese."

Sebastiani keyed four new numbers; the screen flickered and blurred. "Still a new process," said Sebastiani critically. "Images recorded by the deposition of atoms on a light-sensitive crystal. The camera is disguised, effectively if whimsically, as a common house-fly." A red and gold coruscation exploded upon the screen. "Impurities—rogue molecules, the engineers call them." The image steadied to reveal a high-domed council chamber, brightly lit by diffused sunlight. "The new architecture," said Sebastiani sardonically. "Equal parts of Zimbabwe, Dr. Caligari and the Bolshoi Ballet."

"It has a certain wild charm," said Keith.

"Fejo's the showplace of all Africa; no question but what it's a spectacular demonstration." Sebastiani touched a Hold button, freezing the scene in the council chamber. "Shgawe is at the head of the table, in gold and green. I'm sure you recognize him."

Keith nodded. Shgawe's big body and round muscular face had become almost as familiar as his own.

"To his right is Leonide Pashenko, the Russian ambassador. Opposite is the Chinese ambassador Hsia Lu-Minh. The others are aides." He set the image in motion. "We weren't able to record sound; the lip-reading lab gave us a rough translation…Shgawe is now announcing his purchase. He's bland and affable, but watching Pashenko and Hsia like a hawk. They're startled and annoyed, agreeing possibly for the first time in years…Pashenko inquires the need for such grandiose weapons…Shgawe replies that they were cheap and will contribute both to the defense and prestige of Lakhadi. Pashenko says that the U.S.S.R. has guaranteed Lakhadi's independence, that such concerns are superfluous. Hsia sits thinking. Pashenko is more volatile. He points out that the Titans are not only obsolete and unarmed, but that they require an extensive technical complex to support them.

"Shgawe laughs. 'I realize this and I hereby request this help from the U.S.S.R. If it is not forthcoming, I will make the same request of the Chinese People's Democracy. If still unsuccessful, I shall look elsewhere.'

"Pashenko and Hsia close up like clams. There's bad blood between them; neither trusts the other. Pashenko manages to announce that he'll consult his government, and that's all for today."

The image faded. Sebastiani leaned back in his chair. "In two days Tamba Ngasi leaves his constituency, Kotoba on the Dasa River, for the convening of the Grand Parliament at Fejo." He projected a detailed map on the screen, indicated Kotoba and Fejo with a dot of light. "He'll come down the Dasa River by launch to Dasai, continue to Fejo by train. I suggest that you intercept him at Dasai. Tamba Ngasi is a Leopard Man, and took part in the Rhodesian Extermination. To win his seat in the Grand Parliament he killed his uncle, a brother, and four cousins. Extreme measures should cause you no compunction." With a fastidious gesture Sebastiani blanked out the screen. "The subsequent program we've discussed at length." He reached into a cabinet, brought forth a battered fiber case. "Here's your kit. You're familiar with all the contents except—these." He displayed three phials, containing respectively white, yellow and brown tablets. "Vitamins, according to the label." He regarded Keith owlishly. "We call them Unpopularity Pills. Don't dose yourself, unless you want to be unpopular."

"Interesting," said Keith. "How do they work?"

"They induce body odor of a most unpleasant nature. Not all peoples react identically to the same odor; there's a large degree of social training involved, hence the three colors." He chuckled at Keith's skeptical expression. "Don't underestimate these pills. Odors create a subconscious back-drop to our impressions; an offensive odor induces irritation, dislike, distrust. Notice the color of the pills: they indicate the racial groups most strongly affected. White for Caucasians, yellow for Chinese, brown for Negroes."

"I should think that a stench is a stench," said Keith.

Sebastiani pursed his lips didactically. "These naturally are not infallible for-mulations. North Chinese and South Chinese react differently, as do Laplanders, Frenchmen, Russians and Moroccans. American Negroes are culturally Caucasians. But I need say no more; I'm sure the function of the pills is clear to you. A dose persists two or three days, and the person affected is unaware of his condition." He replaced the phials in the case, and as if by afterthought brought forth a battered flashlight. "And this of course—absolutely top-secret. I marvel that you are allowed the use of it. When you press this button—a flash-light. Slip over the safety, press the button again—" he tossed the flashlight back into the case "—a death-ray. Or if you prefer, a laser, projecting red and infra-red at high intensity. If you try to open it you'll blow your arm off. Recharge by plugging into any AC socket. The era of the bullet is at an end." He snapped shut the case, rose to his feet, gave a brusque wave of his hand. "Wait in the outside office for Parrish; he'll take you to your plane. You know your objectives. This is a desperate business, a fool-hardy business. You must like it or you'd have a job in the post office."

At Latitude 6° 34' N, Longitude 13° 30' W, the plane made sunrise ren-dezvous with a wallowing black submarine. Keith drifted down on a jigger consisting of a seat, a small engine, four whirling blades. The submarine submerged with Keith aboard, surfaced twenty-three hours later to set him afloat in a sailing canoe, and once more submerged.

Keith was alone on the South Atlantic. Dawn ringed the horizon, and there to the east lay the dark mass of Africa. Keith trimmed his sail to the breeze and wake foamed up astern.

Daybreak illuminated a barren sandy coast, on which a few fishermen's huts could be seen. To the north, under wads of black-green foliage, the white build-ings of Dasai gleamed. Keith drove his canoe up on the beach, plodded across sand dunes to the coast highway.

There was already considerable traffic abroad: women trudging beside don-keys, young men riding bicycles, an occasional small automobile of antique vin-tage; once an expensive new Amphitrite Air-Boat slid past on its air-cushion, with a soft whispered whoosh.

At nine o'clock, crossing the sluggish brown Dasa River, he entered Dasai, a small sun-dazzled coastal port, as yet untouched by the changes which had transformed Fejo. Two- and three-storied buildings of white stucco, with arcades below, lined the main street, and a strip planted with palms, rhododendrons and oleanders ran down the middle. There were two hotels, a bank, a garage, miscellaneous shops and office buildings. A dispirited police officer in a white helmet directed traffic: at the moment two camels led by a ragged Bedouin. A squat pedestal supported four large photographs of Adoui Shgawe, the "Beloved Premier of our Nation, the Great Beacon of Africa". Below, conspicuously smaller, were photographs of Marx, Lenin, and Mao Tse-Tung.

Keith turned into a side street, walked to the river-bank. He saw ramshackle docks, a half-dozen restaurants, beer-gardens and cabarets built over the water on platforms and shaded by palm-thatched roofs. He beckoned to a nearby boy, who approached cautiously. "When the launch comes down the river from Kotoba, where does it land?"

The boy pointed a thin crooked finger. "That is the dock, sir, just beyond the Hollywood Café."

"And when is the launch due to arrive?"

"That I do not know, sir."

Keith flipped the boy a coin and made his way to the dock, where he learned that indeed the river-boat from Kotoba would arrive definitely at two P.M., certainly no later than three, beyond any question of doubt by four.

Keith considered. If Tamba Ngasi should arrive at two or even three he would probably press on to Fejo, sixty miles down the coast. If the boat were late he might well decide to stay in Dasai for the night—there at the Grand Plaisir Hotel, only a few steps away.

The question: where to intercept Tamba Ngasi? Here in Dasai? At the Grand Plaisir Hotel? En route to Fejo?

None of these possibilities appealed to Keith. He returned to the main street. A tobacconist assured him that no automobiles could be hired except one of the town's three ancient taxicabs. He pointed up the street to an old black Citroën standing in the shade of an enormous sapodilla. The driver, a thin old man in white shorts, a faded blue shirt and canvas shoes, lounged beside a booth which sold crushed ice and syrup. The proprietress, a large woman in brilliant black, gold and orange gown prodded him with her fly-whisk, directing his attention to Keith. He moved reluctantly across the sidewalk. "The gentleman wishes to be conveyed to a destination?"

Keith, in the role of the back-country barbarian, pulled at his long chin dubiously. "I will try your vehicle, provided you do not try to cheat me."

"The rates are definite," said the driver, unenthusiastically. "Three rupiahs for the first kilometer, one rupiah per kilometer thereafter. Where do you wish to go?"

Keith entered the cab. "Drive up the river road."

They rattled out of town, along a dirt road which kept generally to the banks of the river. The countryside was dusty and barren, grown over with thorn, with here and there a massive baobab. The miles passed and the driver became nervous. "Where does the gentleman intend to go?"

"Stop here," said Keith. The driver uncertainly slowed the cab. Keith brought money from the leather pouch at his belt. "I wish to drive the cab. Alone. You may wait for me under that tree." The driver protested vehemently. Keith pressed a hundred rupiahs upon him. "Do not argue; you have no choice. I may be gone several hours, but you shall have your cab back safely and another hundred rupiahs—if you wait here."

The driver alighted and limped through the dust to the shade of the tall yellow gum tree and Keith drove off up the road.

The country became more pleasant. Palm trees lined the river-bank; there were occasional garden-patches, and he passed three villages of round mud-wall huts with conical thatched roofs. Occasionally canoes moved across the dull brown water, and he saw a barge stacked with cord-wood, towed by what seemed a ridiculously inadequate rowboat with an outboard motor. He drove another ten miles and the country once more became inhospitable. The river, glazed by heat, wound between mud-banks where small crocodiles basked; the shores were choked with papyrus and larch thickets. Keith stopped the car, consulted a map. The first town of any consequence where the boat might be expected to discharge passengers was Mbakouesse, another twenty-five miles—too far.

Replacing the map in his suitcase, Keith brought out a jar containing brilliantine, or so the label implied. He considered it a moment, and arrived at a plan of action.

He now drove slowly and presently found a spot where the channel swung close in under the bank. Keith parked beside a towering clump of red-jointed bamboo and made his preparations. He wadded a few ounces of the waxy so-called brilliantine around a strangely heavy lozenge from a box of cough drops, taped the mass to a dry stick of wood. He found a spool of fine cord, tied a rock to the end, unwound twenty feet, tied on the stick. Then, wary of adders, crocodiles, and the enormous clicking-wing wasps which lived in burrows along the river-bank, he made his way through the larches to the shore of the river. Unreeling a hundred feet of cord, he flung stick and stone as far across the river as possible. The stone sank to the bottom, mooring the stick which now floated at the far edge of the channel, exactly where Keith had intended.

An hour passed, two hours. Keith sat in the shade of the larches, surrounded by the resinous odor of the leaves, the swampy reek of the river. At last: the throb of a heavy diesel engine. Down the river came a typical boat of the African rivers. About seventy feet long, with first-class cabins on the upper deck, second-class cubicles on the main deck, the remainder of the passengers sitting, standing, crouching or huddling wherever room offered itself.

The boat approached, chugging down the center of the channel. Keith gathered in the slack of the cord, drew the stick closer. On the top deck stood a tall gaunt man, his face dark, feral and clever under a darshba turban: Tamba Ngasi? Keith was uncertain. This man walked with head bent forward, elbows jutting at a sharp angle. Keith had studied photographs of Tamba Ngasi, but confronted by the living individual…There was no time for speculation. The boat was almost abreast, the bow battering up a transparent yellow bow-wave. Keith drew in the cord, pulled the stick under the bow. He held up the palm of his right hand, in which lay coiled a directional antenna. He spread his fingers, an impulse struck out to the detonator in the little black lozenge. A dull booming explosion, a gout of foam, sheets of brown water, shrill cries of surprise and fear. The boat nosed down into the water, swerved erratically.

Keith pulled back and rewound what remained of his cord.

The boat, already overloaded, was about to sink. It swung toward the shore, ran aground fifty yards down-stream.

Keith backed the taxi out of the larches, drove a half-mile up the road, waited, watching through binoculars.

A straggle of white-robed men and women came through the larches and presently a tall man in a darshba turban strode angrily out on the road. Keith focused the binoculars: there were the features he himself now wore. The posture, the stride seemed more angular, more nervous; he must remember to duplicate these mannerisms…Now, to work. He pulled the hood of his cloak forward to conceal his face, shifted into gear. The taxi approached the knot of people standing by the roadside. A portly olive-skinned man in European whites sprang out, flagged him to a stop. Keith looked out in simulated surprise.

Keith shrugged. "I have a fare; I am going now to pick him up."

Tamba Ngasi came striding up. He flung open the door. "The fare can wait. I am a government official. Take me to Dasai."

The portly little Hindu made a motion as if he would likewise seek to enter the cab. Keith stopped him. "I have room only for one." Tamba Ngasi threw his suitcase into the cab, leapt in. Keith moved off, leaving the group staring disconsolately after him.

"An insane accident," Tamba Ngasi complained peevishly. "We ride along quietly; the boat strikes a rock; it seems like an explosion, and we sink! Can you imagine that? And I, an important member of the government, riding aboard! Why are you stopping?"

"I must see to my other fare." Keith turned off the road, along a faint track leading into the scrub.

"No matter about your other fare, I wish no delay. Drive on."

"I must also pick up a can of petrol, otherwise we will run short."

"Petrol, here, out in the thorn bushes?"

"A cache known only to the taxi drivers." Keith halted, alighted, opened the rear door. "Tamba Ngasi, come forth."

Tamba Ngasi stared under Keith's hood into his own face. He spit out a passionate expletive, clawed for the dagger at his waist. Keith lunged, tapped him on the forehead with his copper-silver fingernails. Electricity burst in a killing gush through Ngasi's brain; he staggered sidelong and fell into the road.

Keith dragged the corpse off the track, out into the scrub. Tamba Ngasi's legs were heavy and thick, out of proportion to his sinewy torso. This was a peculiarity of which Keith had been ignorant. But no matter; who would ever know that Keith's shanks were long and lean?

Jackals and vultures would speedily dispose of the corpse.

Keith transferred the contents of the pouch to his own, sought but found no money-belt. He returned to the taxi, drove back to the tall gum tree. The driver lay asleep; Keith woke him with a blast of the horn. "Hurry now, take me back to Dasai, I must be in Fejo before nightfall."

In all of Africa, ancient, medieval and modern, there never had been a city like Fejo. It rose on a barren headland north of Tabacoundi Bay, where twenty years before not even fishermen had deigned to live. Fejo was a bold city, startling in its shapes, textures and colors. Africans determined to express their unique African heritage had planned the city, rejecting absolutely the architectural traditions of Europe and America, both classical and contemporary. Construction had been financed by a gigantic loan from the U.S.S.R., Soviet engineers had translated the sketches of fervent Lakhadi students into space and solidity.

Fejo, therefore, was a remarkable city. Certain European critics dismissed it as a stage-setting; some were fascinated, others repelled. No one denied that Fejo was compellingly dramatic. "In contrast to the impact of Fejo, Brasilia seems sterile, eclectic, prettified," wrote an English critic. "Insane fantasies, at which Gaudi himself might be appalled," snapped a Spaniard. "Fejo is the defiant challenge of African genius, and its excesses are those of passion, rather than of style," declared an Italian. "Fejo," wrote a Frenchman, "is hideous, startling, convoluted, pretentious, ignorant, oppressive, and noteworthy only for the tortured forms to which good building material has been put."

Fejo centered on the fifty-story spire of the Institute of Africa. Nearby stood the Grand Parliament, held aloft on copper arches, with oval windows and a blue-enameled roof like a broad-brimmed derby hat. Six tall warriors of polished basalt representing the six principal tribes of Lakhadi fronted a plaza; and beyond, the Hôtel des Tropiques, the most magnificent in Africa, and ranking with any in the world. The Hôtel des Tropiques was perhaps the most conventional building of the central complex, but even here the architects had insisted on pure African style. Vegetation from the roof-garden trailed down the white and blue walls; the lobby was furnished in padauk, teak and ebony; columns of structural glass rose from silver-blue carpets and purple-red rugs to support a ceiling of stainless steel and black enamel.

At the far end of the plaza stood the official palace, and beyond, the first three of a projected dozen apartment buildings, intended for the use of high officials. Of all the buildings in Fejo, these had been most favorably received by foreign critics, possibly because of their simplicity. Each floor consisted of a separate disk twelve feet in height, and was supported completely apart from the floors above and below by four stanchions piercing the disks. Each disk also served as a wide airy deck, and the top deck functioned as a heliport.

On the other side of the Hôtel des Tropiques spread another plaza, to satisfy the African need for a bazaar. Here were booths, hawkers, and entertainers of every sort, selling autochron wrist-watches powered and synchronized by 60-cycle pulse originating in Greenwich, as well as jujus, elixirs, potions and talismans.

Through the plaza moved a cheerful and volatile mixture of people: negro women in magnificently printed cottons, silks and gauzes, Mohammedans in white djellabas, Tuaregs and Mauretanian Blue Men, Chinese in fusty black suits, ubiquitous Hindu shopkeepers, an occasional Russian grim and aloof from the crowd. Beyond this plaza lay a district of stark white three-story apartment cubicles. The people looking from the windows seemed irresolute and uncertain, as if the shift from mud and thatch to glass, tile, and air-conditioning were too great to be encompassed in a lifetime.

Into Fejo, at five in the afternoon, came James Keith, riding first class on the train from Dasai. From the terminal he marched across the bazaar to the Hôtel des Tropiques, strode to the desk, brushed aside a number of persons who stood waiting, pounded his fist to attract the clerk, a pale Eurasian who looked around in annoyance. "Quick!" snapped Keith. "Is it fitting that a Parliamentarian waits at the pleasure of such as you? Conduct me to my suite."

The clerk's manner altered. "Your name, sir?"

"I am Tamba Ngasi."

"There is no reservation, Comrade Ngasi. Did you—"

Keith fixed the man with a glare of outrage. "I am a Parliamentarian of the State. I need no reservation."

"But all the suites are occupied!"

"Turn someone out, and quickly."

"Yes, Comrade Ngasi. At once."

Keith found himself in a sumptuous set of rooms furnished in carved woods, green glass, heavy rugs. He had not eaten since early morning; a touch on a button flashed the restaurant menu on a screen. No reason why a tribal chieftain should not enjoy European cuisine, thought Keith, and he ordered accordingly. Awaiting his lunch he inspected walls, floor, drapes, ceiling, furniture. Spy cells might or might not be standard equipment here in intrigue-ridden Fejo. They were not apparent, nor did he expect them to be. The best of modern equipment was dependably undetectable.

He stepped out on the deck, pushed with his tongue against one of his teeth, spoke in a whisper for several minutes. He returned the switch to its former position, and his message was broadcast in a hundredth-second coded burst indistinguishable from static. A thousand miles overhead hung a satellite, rotating with the Earth; it caught the signal, amplified and rebroadcast it to Washington.

Keith waited, and minutes passed, as many as were required to play back his message, and frame a reply. Then came the almost imperceptible click marking the arrival of the return message. It communicated itself in the voice of Sebastiani by way of Keith's jaw-bone to his auditory nerve, soundlessly, but with all of Sebastiani's characteristic inflections.

"So far so good," said Sebastiani. "But I've got some bad news. Don't try to make contact with Corty. Apparently he's been apprehended and brainwashed by the Chinese. So you're on your own."

Keith grunted glumly, returned to the sitting room. His lunch was served; he ate, then he opened the case he had taken from Tamba Ngasi. It was similar to his own, even to the contents: clean linen, toilet articles, personal effects, a file of documents. The documents, printed in florid New African type, were of no particular interest: a poll list, various official notifications. Keith found a directive which read, "…When you arrive in Fejo, you will take up lodgings at Rue Arsabatte 453, where a suitable suite has been prepared for you. Please announce your presence to the Chief Clerk of Parliament as soon as possible."

Keith smiled faintly. He would simply declare that he preferred the Hôtel des Tropiques. And who would question the whim of a notoriously ill-tempered back-country chieftain?

Replacing the contents of Tamba Ngasi's suitcase, Keith became aware of something peculiar. The objects felt—strange. This fetish-box for instance—just a half-ounce too heavy. Keith's mind raced along a whole network of speculations. This rather battered ball-point pencil…He inspected it closely, pointed it away from himself, pressed the extensor-button. A click, a hiss, a spit of cloudy gas. Keith jerked back, moved across the room. It was a miniature gas-gun, designed to puff a drug into and through the pores of the skin. Confirmation for his suspicions—and in what a strange direction they led!

Keith replaced the pencil, closed the suitcase. He paced thoughtfully back and forth a moment or two, then locked his own suitcase and left the room.

He rode down to the lobby on a twinkling escalator of pink and green crystal, stood for a moment surveying the scene. He had expected nothing so splendid; how, he wondered, would Tamba Ngasi have regarded this glittering room and its hyper-sophisticated guests? Not with approval, Keith decided. He walked to the entrance, twisting his face into a leer of disgust. Even by his own tastes, the Hôtel des Tropiques seemed over-rich, a trifle too fanciful.

He crossed the plaza, marched along the Avenue of the Six Black Warriors to the grotesque but oddly impressive Grand Parliament of Lakhadi. A pair of glossy black guards, wearing metal sandals and greaves, pleated kirtles of white leather, sprang out, crossed spears in front of him.

Keith inspected them haughtily. "I am Tamba Ngasi, Grand Parliamentarian from Kotoba Province."

The guards twitched not a muscle; they might have been carved of ebony. From a side cubicle came a short fat white man in limp brown slacks and shirt. He barked, "Tamba Ngasi. Guards, admit!"

The guards with a single movement sprang back across the floor. The little fat man bowed politely, but it seemed as if his gaze never veered from Keith. "You have come to register, Sir Parliamentarian?"

"Precisely. With the Chief Clerk."

The fat man bowed his head again. "I am Vasif Doutoufsky, Chief Clerk. Will you step into my office?"

Doutoufsky's office was hot and stuffy and smelled sweet of rose incense. Doutoufsky offered Keith a cup of tea. Keith gave Tamba Ngasi's characteristic brusque shake, Doutoufsky appeared faintly surprised. He spoke in Russian. "Why did you not go to Rue Arsabatte? I awaited you there until ten minutes ago."

Keith's mind spun as if on ball-bearings. He said gruffly, in his own not-too-facile Russian, "I had my reasons…There was an accident to the river-boat, possibly an explosion. I hailed a taxi, and so arrived at Dasai."

"Aha," said Doutoufsky in a soft voice. "Do you suspect interference?"

"If so," said Keith, "it could only come from one source."

"Aha," said Doutoufsky again, even more softly. "You mean—"

"The Chinese."

Doutoufsky regarded Keith thoughtfully. "The transformation has been done well," he said. "Your skin is precisely correct, with convincing tones and shadings. You speak rather oddly."

"As might you, if your head were crammed with as much as mine."

Doutoufsky pursed his lips, as if at a secret joke. "You will change to Rue Arsabatte?"

Keith hesitated, trying to sense Doutoufsky's relationship to himself: inferior or superior? Inferior, probably, with the powers and prerogatives of the contact, from whom came instructions and from whom, back to the Kremlin, went evaluations. A chilling thought: Doutoufsky and he who had walked in the guise of Tamba Ngasi might both be renegade Russians, both Chinese agents in this most fantastic of all wars. In which case Keith's life was even more precarious than it had been a half-hour previous…But this was the hypothesis of smaller probability. Keith said in a voice of authority, "An automobile has been placed at my disposal?"

Doutoufsky blinked. "To my knowledge, no."

"I will require an automobile," said Keith. "Where is your car?"

"Surely, sir, this is not in character?"

"I am to be the judge of that."

Doutoufsky heaved a sigh. "I will call out one of the Parliamentary limousines."

"Which, no doubt, is efficiently monitored."

"Naturally."

"I prefer a vehicle in which I can transact such business as necessary without fear of witnesses."

Doutoufsky nodded abruptly. "Very well." He tossed a key to the table of his desk. "This is my own Aerofloat. Please use it discreetly."

"This car is not monitored?"

"Definitely not."

"I will check it intensively nonetheless." Keith spoke in a tone of quiet menace. "I hope to find it as you describe."

Doutoufsky blinked, and in a subdued voice explained where the car might be found. "Tomorrow at noon Parliament convenes. You are naturally aware of this."

"Naturally. Are there supplementary instructions?"

Doutoufsky gave Keith a dry side-glance. "I was wondering when you would ask for them, since this was specified as the sole occasion for our contact. Not to hector, not to demand pleasure-cars."

"Contain your arrogance, Vasif Doutoufsky. I must work without interference. Certain slight doubts regarding your ability already exist; spare me the necessity of corroborating them."

"Aha," said Doutoufsky softly. He reached in his drawer, tossed a small iron nail down upon the desk. "Here are your instructions. You have the key to my car, you have refused to use your designated lodgings. Do you require anything further?"

"Yes," said Keith, grinning wolfishly. "Funds."

Doutoufsky tossed a packet of rupiah notes on the desk. "This should suffice until our next contact."

Keith rose slowly to his feet. There would be difficulties if he failed to make prearranged contacts with Doutoufsky. "Certain circumstances may make it necessary to change the routine."

"Indeed? Such as?"

"I have learned—from a source which I am not authorized to reveal—that the Chinese have apprehended and brain-washed an agent of the West. He was detected by the periodicity of his actions. It is better to make no precise plans."

Doutoufsky nodded soberly. "There is something in what you say."

By moonlight the coast road from Fejo to Dasai was beautiful beyond imagination. To the left spread an endless expanse of sea, surf and wan desolate sand; to the right grew thorn-bush, baobabs, wire cactus—angular patterns in every tone of silver, gray and black.

Keith felt reasonably sure that he had not been followed. He had carefully washed the car with the radiation from his flashlight, to destroy a spy-cell's delicate circuits by the induced currents. Halfway to Dasai he braked to a halt, extinguished his lights, searched the sky with the radar in his ear-amulets. He could detect nothing; the air was clear and desolate, nor did he sense any car behind him. He took occasion to despatch a message to the hovering satellite. There was a five minute wait; then the relay clicked home. Sebastiani's voice came clear and distinct into his brain: "The coincidence, upon consideration, is not astonishing. The Russians selected Tamba Ngasi for the same reasons we did: his reputation for aggressiveness and independence, his presumable popularity with the military, as opposed to their suspicion of Shgawe.

"As to the Arsabatte address, I feel you have made the correct decision. You'll be less exposed at the hotel. We have nothing definite on Doutoufsky. He is ostensibly a Polish emigrant, now a Lakhadi citizen. You may have overplayed your hand taking so strong an attitude. If he seeks you out, show a degree of contrition and remark that you have been instructed to cooperate more closely with him."

Keith searched the sky once more, but received only a signal from a low-flying owl. Confidently he continued along the unreal road, and presently arrived at Dasai.

The town was quiet, with only a sprinkling of street-lights, a tinkle of music and laughter from the cabarets. Keith turned along the river-road and proceeded inland.

The country became wild and forlorn. Twenty miles passed; Keith drove slowly. Here, the yellow gum tree where he had discharged the taxi-driver. Here, where he had grounded the river-boat. He swung around, returned down the road. Here— where he had driven off the road with the man he had thought to be Tamba Ngasi. He turned, drove a space, then stopped, got out of the car. Off in the brush a dozen yellow eyes reflected back his headlights, then swiftly retreated.

The jackals had been busy with the body. Three of them lay dead, mounds of rancid fur, and Keith was at a loss to account for their condition. He played his flashlight up and down the corpse, inspected the flesh at which the jackals had been tearing. He bent closer, frowning in puzzlement. A peculiar pad of specialized tissue lay along the outside of the thighs, almost an inch thick. It was organized in orderly strips and fed plentifully from large arteries, and here and there Keith detected the glint of metal. Suddenly he guessed the nature of the tissue and knew why the jackals lay dead. He straightened up, looked around through the moon-drenched forest of cactus and thorn-scrub and shivered. The presence of death alone was awesome, the more so for the kind of man who lay here so far from his home, so strangely altered and augmented. Those pads of gray flesh must be electro-organic tissue, similar to that of the electric eel, somehow adapted to human flesh by Russian biologists. Keith felt a sense of oppression. How far they exceed us! he thought. My power source is chemical, inorganic; that of this man was controlled by the functioning of his body, and remained at so high a potential that three jackals had been electrocuted tearing into it.

Gritting his teeth he bent over the corpse, and set about his examination.

Half an hour later he had finished, and stood erect with two films of semi-metalloid peeled from the inside of the corpse's cheeks: communication circuits certainly as sophisticated as his own.

He scrubbed his hands in the sand, returned to the car and drove back into the setting moon. He came to the dark town of Dasai, turned south along the coast road, and an hour later returned to Fejo.

The lobby of the Hôtel des Tropiques was now illuminated only by great pale green and blue globes. A few groups sat talking and sipping drinks; to the hushed mutter of their conversation Keith crossed to the escalator, was conveyed to his room.

He entered with caution. Everything seemed in order. The two cases had not been tampered with; the bed had been turned back, pajamas of purple silk had been provided for him.

Before he slept, Keith touched another switch in his dentures, and the radar mounted guard. Any movement within the room would awaken him. He was temporarily secure; he slept.

An hour before the first session of the Grand Parliament Keith sought out Vasif Doutoufsky, who compressed his mouth into a pink rosette. "Please. It is not suitable that we seem intimate acquaintances."

Keith grinned his vulpine unpleasant grin. "No fear of that." He displayed the devices he had taken from the body of the so-called Tamba Ngasi. Doutoufsky peered curiously.

"These are communication circuits." Keith tossed them to the desk. "They have failed, and I cannot submit my reports. You must do this for me, and relay my instructions."

Doutoufsky shook his head. "This was not to be my function. I cannot compromise myself; the Chinese already suspect my reports."

Ha, thought Keith, Doutoufsky functioned as a double-agent. The Russians seemed to trust him, which Keith considered somewhat naïve. He ruminated a moment, then reaching in his pouch brought forth a flat tin. He opened it, extracted a small woody object resembling a clove. He dropped it in front of Doutoufsky. "Eat this."

Doutoufsky looked up slowly, brow wrinkled in plaintive protest. "You are acting very strangely. Of course I shall not eat this object. What is it?"

"It is a tie which binds our lives together," said Keith. "If I am killed, one of my organs broadcasts a pulse which will detonate this object."

"You are mad," muttered Doutoufsky. "I shall make a report to this effect."

Keith moved forward, laid his hand on Doutoufsky's shoulder, touched his neck. "Are you aware that I can cause your heart to stop?" He sent a trickle of electricity into his copper-silver fingernails.

Doutoufsky seemed more puzzled than alarmed. Keith emitted a stronger current, enough to make any man wince. Doutoufsky merely reached up to disengage Keith's arm. His fingers clamped on Keith's wrist. They were cold, and clamped like steel tongs. And into Keith's arm came a hurting surge of current.

"You are an idiot," said Doutoufsky in disgust. "I carry weapons you know nothing about. Leave me at once, or you will regret it."

Keith departed, sick with dismay. Doutoufsky was augmented. His rotundity no doubt concealed great slabs of electro-generative tissue. He had blundered; he had made a fool of himself.

A gong rang; other Parliamentarians filed past him. Keith took a deep breath, swaggered into the echoing red, gold, and black paneled hall. A doorkeeper saluted. "Name, sir?"

"Tamba Ngasi, Kotoba Province."

"Your seat, Excellency, is Number 27."

Keith seated himself, listened without interest to the invocation. What to do about Doutoufsky?

His ruminations were interrupted by the appearance on the rostrum of a heavy moon-faced man in a simple white robe. His skin was almost blue-black, the eyelids hung lazily across his protuberant eyeballs, his mouth was wide and heavy. Keith recognized Adoui Shgawe, Premier of Lakhadi, Benefactor of Africa.

He spoke resonantly, in generalities and platitudes, with many references to Socialist Solidarity. "The future of Lakhadi is the future of Black Africa! As we look through this magnificent chamber and note the colors of the tasteful decoration, can we not fail to be impressed by the correctness of the symbolism? Red is the color of blood, which is the same for all men, and also the color of International Socialism. Black is the color of our skins, and it is our prideful duty to ensure that the energy and genius of our race is respected around the globe. Gold is the color of success, of glory, and of progress; and golden is the future of Lakhadi!"

The chamber reverberated with applause.

Shgawe turned to more immediate problems. "While spiritually rich, we are in certain ways impoverished. Comrade Nambey Faranah—" he nodded toward a squat square-faced man in a black suit "—has presented an interesting program. He suggests that a carefully scheduled program of immigration might provide us a valuable new national asset. On the other hand—"

Comrade Nambey Faranah bounded to his feet and turned to face the assembly. Shgawe held up a restraining hand, but Faranah ignored him. "I have conferred with Ambassador Hsia Lu-Minh of our comrade nation, the Chinese People's Democracy. He has made the most valuable assurances, and will use all his influence to help us. He agrees that a certain number of skilled agricultural technicians can immeasurably benefit our people, and can accelerate the political orientation of the non-political back-regions. Forward to progress!" bellowed Faranah. "Hail the mighty advance of the colored races, arm in arm, united under the red banner of International Socialism!" He looked expectantly around the hall for applause, which came only in a perfunctory spatter. He sat down abruptly. Keith studied him with a new somber speculation. Comrade Faranah—an augmented Chinese?

Adoui Shgawe had placidly continued his address. "—some have questioned the practicality of this move," he was saying. "Friends and comrades, I assure you that no matter how loyal and comradely our brother nations, they cannot provide us prestige! The more we rely on them for leadership, the more we diminish our own stature among the nations of Africa."

Nambey Faranah held up a quivering finger. "Not completely correct, Comrade Shgawe!"

Shgawe ignored him. "For this reason I have purchased eighteen American weapons. Admittedly they are cumbersome and outmoded. But they are still terrible instruments—and they command respect. With eighteen intercontinental missiles poised against any attack, we consolidate our position as the leaders of black Africa."

There was another spatter of applause. Adoui Shgawe leaned forward, gazed blandly over the assembly. "That concludes my address. I will answer questions from the floor...Ah, Comrade Bouassede."

Comrade Bouassede, a fragile old man with a fine fluffy white beard, rose to his feet. "All very fine, these great weapons, but against whom do we wish to use them? What good are they to us, who know nothing of such things?"

Shgawe nodded with vast benevolence. "A wise question, Comrade. I can only answer that one never knows from which direction some insane militarism may strike."

Faranah leapt to his feet. "May I answer the question, Comrade Shgawe?"

"The assembly will listen to your opinions with respect," Shgawe declared courteously.

Faranah turned toward old Bouassede. "The imperialists are at bay, they cower in their rotting strongholds, but still they can muster strength for one final feverish lunge, should they see a chance to profit."

Shgawe said, "Comrade Faranah has expressed himself with his customary untiring zeal."

"Are not these devices completely beyond our capacity to maintain?" demanded Bouassede.

Shgawe nodded. "We live in a swiftly changing environment. At the moment this is the case. But until we are able to act for ourselves, our Russian allies have offered many valuable services. They will bring great suction dredges, and will station the launching tubes in the tidal sands off our coast. They have also undertaken to provide us a specially designed ship to supply liquid oxygen and fuel."

"This is all nonsense," growled Bouassede. "We must pay for this ship; it is not a gift. The money could be better spent building roads and buying cattle."

"Comrade Bouassede has not considered the intangible factors involved," declared Shgawe equably. "Ah, Comrade Maguemi. Your question, please."

Comrade Maguemi was a serious bespectacled young man in a black suit. "Exactly how many Chinese immigrants are envisioned?"

Shgawe looked from the corner of his eye toward Faranah. "The proposal so far is purely theoretical, and probably—"

Faranah jumped to his feet. "It is a program of great urgency. However many Chinese are needed, we shall welcome them."

"This does not answer my question," Maguemi persisted coldly. "A hundred actual technicians might in fact be useful. A hundred thousand peasants, a colony of aliens in our midst, could only bring us harm."

Shgawe nodded gravely. "Comrade Maguemi has illuminated a very serious difficulty."

"By no means," cried Faranah. "Comrade Maguemi's premises are incorrect. A hundred, a hundred thousand, a million, ten million—what is the difference? We are Communists together, striving toward a common goal!"

"I do not agree," shouted Maguemi. "We must avoid doctrinaire solutions to our problems. If we are submerged in the Asiatic tide, our voices will be drowned."

Another young man, thin as a starved bird, with a thin face and blade-like nose, sprang up. "Comrade Maguemi has no sense of historical projection. He ignores the teachings of Marx, Lenin, and Mao. A true Communist takes no heed of race or geography."

"I am no true Communist," declared Maguemi coldly. "I have never made such a humiliating admission. I consider the teachings of Marx, Lenin and Mao even more obsolete than the American weapons with which Comrade Shgawe has unwisely burdened us."

Adoui Shgawe smiled broadly. "We may safely pass on from the subject of Chinese immigration, as in all likelihood it will never occur. A few hundred technicians, as Comrade Maguemi suggests, of course will be welcome. A more extended program would certainly lead to difficulties."

Nambey Faranah glowered at the floor.

Shgawe spoke on, in a soothing voice, and presently adjourned the Parliament for two days.

Keith returned to his room at the des Tropiques, settled himself on the couch, considered his position. He could feel no satisfaction in his performance to date. He had blundered seriously with Doutoufsky, might well have aroused his suspicions. There was certainly small reason for optimism.

Two days later Adoui Shgawe reappeared in the Grand Chamber, to speak on a routine matter connected with the state-operated cannery. Nambey Faranah could not resist a sardonic jibe: "At last we perceive a use for the cast-off American missile-docks: they can easily be converted into fish-processing plants, and we can shoot the wastes into space."

Shgawe held up his hands against the mutter of appreciative laughter. "This is no more than stupidity; I have explained the importance of these weapons. Persons inexperienced in such matters should not criticize them."

Faranah was not to be subdued so easily. "How can we be anything other than inexperienced? We know nothing of these American cast-offs, they float unseen in the ocean. Do they even exist?"

Shgawe shook his head in pitying disgust. "Are there no extremes to which you will not go? The docks are at hand for any and all to inspect. Tomorrow I will order the Lumumba out, and I now request the entire membership to make a trip of inspection. There will be no further excuse for skepticism—if, indeed, there is now."

Faranah was silenced. He gave a petulant shrug, settled back into his seat.

Almost two-thirds of the chamber responded to Shgawe's invitation, and on the following morning, trooped aboard the single warship of the Lakhadi navy, an ancient French destroyer. Bells clanged, whistles sounded, water churned up aft and the Lumumba eased out of Tabacoundi Bay, to swing south over long blue swells.

Twenty miles the destroyer cruised, paralleling the wind-beaten shore; then at the horizon appeared seventeen pale humps—the floating missile silos. But the Lumumba veered in toward shore, where the eighteenth of the docks had been raised on buoyancy tanks, floated in toward the beach, lowered to the sub-tidal sand. Alongside was moored a Russian dredge which pumped jets of water below the silo, dislodging sand and allowing the dock to settle.

The Parliamentarians stood on the Lumumba's foredeck, staring at the admittedly impressive cylinder. All were forced to agree that the docks existed. Premier Shgawe came out on the wing of the bridge, with beside him the Grand Marshal of the Army, Achille Hashembe, a hard-bitten man of sixty, with close-cropped gray hair. While Shgawe addressed the Parliamentarians Hashembe scrutinized them carefully, first one face, then another.

"The helicopter assigned to this particular dock is under repair," said Shgawe. "It will be inconvenient to inspect the missile itself. But no matter; our imaginations will serve us. Picture eighteen of these great weapons ranged at intervals along the shores of our fatherland; can a more impressive defense be conceived?"

Keith standing near Faranah heard him mutter to those near at hand. Keith watched with great attention. Two hours previously, stewards had served small cups of black coffee, and Keith, stationing himself four places above Faranah, had dropped an Unpopularity Pill into the fourth cup. The steward passed along the line; each intervening Parliamentarian took a cup and Faranah received the cup with the pill. Now Faranah's audience regarded him with fastidious distaste and moved away. A whiff of odor reached Keith himself: American biochemists, he thought, had wrought effectively. Faranah smelled very poorly indeed. And Faranah glared about in bafflement.

The Lumumba slowly circled the dock, which now had reached a permanent bed in the sand. Aboard the dredge the Russian engineers were disengaging the pumps, preparatory to performing the same operation upon a second dock.

A steward approached Keith. "Adoui Shgawe wishes a word with you."

Keith followed the steward to the officers' mess, and as he entered met one of his colleagues on the way out.

Adoui Shgawe rose to his feet, bowed gravely. "Tamba Ngasi, please be seated. Will you take a glass of brandy?"

Keith shook his head brusquely: one of Ngasi's idiosyncrasies.

"You have met Grand Marshal Hashembe?" Shgawe asked politely.

Keith had been briefed as thoroughly as possible but on this point had no information. He evaded the question. "I have a high regard for the Grand Marshal's abilities."

Hashembe returned a curt nod, but said nothing.

"I take this occasion," said Shgawe, "to learn if you are sympathetic to my program, now that you have had an opportunity to observe it more closely."

Keith took a moment to reflect. In Shgawe's words lay the implication of previous disagreement. He submerged himself in the role of Tamba Ngasi, spoke with the sentiments Tamba Ngasi might be expected to entertain. "There is too much waste, too much foreign influence. We need water for the dry lands, we need medicine for the cattle. These are lacking while treasures are squandered on the idiotic buildings of Fejo." From the corner of his eye he saw Hashembe's eyes narrow a trifle. Approval?

Shgawe answered, ponderously suave. "I respect your argument, but there is also this to be considered: the Russians lent us the money for the purpose of building Fejo into a symbol of progress. They would not allow the money to be used for less dramatic purposes. We accepted, and I feel that we have benefited. Prestige nowadays is highly important."

"Important, to whom? To what end?" grumbled Keith. "Why must we pretend to a glory which is not ours?"

"You concede defeat before the battle begins," said Shgawe more vigorously. "Unfortunately this is our African heritage, and it must be overcome."

Keith, in the role of Ngasi, said, "My home is Kotoba, at the backwaters of the Dasa, and my people live in mud huts. Is not the idea of glory for the people of Kotoba ridiculous? Give us water and cattle and medicine."

Shgawe's voice dropped in pitch. "For the people of Kotoba, I too want water and cattle and medicine. But I want more than this, and glory perhaps is a poor word to use."

Hashembe rose to his feet, bowed stiffly to Shgawe and to Keith, and left the room. Shgawe shook his round head. "Hashembe cannot understand my vision. He wants me to expel the foreigners: the Russians, the French, the Hindus, especially the Chinese."

Keith rose to his feet. "I am not absolutely opposed to your views. Perhaps you have some sort of document I might read?" He took a casual step across the room. Shgawe shrugged, looked among his papers. Keith seemed to stumble and his knuckles touched the nape of Shgawe's plump neck. "Your pardon, Excellency," said Keith. "I am clumsy."

"No matter," said Shgawe. "Here: this and this—papers which explain my views for the development of Lakhadi and of the New Africa." He blinked. Keith picked up the papers, studied them. Shgawe's eyes drooped shut, as the drug which Keith had blasted through his skin began to permeate his body. A minute later he was asleep.

Keith moved quickly. Shgawe wore his hair in short oiled clusters; at the base of one of these Keith tied a black pellet no larger than a grain of rice, then stepped back to read the papers.

Hashembe returned to the room. He halted, looked from Shgawe to Keith. "He seems to have dozed off," said Keith and continued to read the papers.

"Adoui Shgawe!" called Hashembe. "Are you asleep?"

Shgawe's eyelids fluttered; he heaved a deep sigh, looked up. "Hashembe... I seem to have napped. Ah, Tamba Ngasi. Those papers, you may keep them, and I pray that you deal sympathetically with my proposals in Parliament. You are an influential man, and I depend upon your support."

"I take your words to heart, Excellency." Leaving the mess-hall Keith climbed quickly to the flying bridge. The Lumumba was now heading back up the coast toward Fejo. Keith touched one of his internal switches, and into his auditory channel came the voice of Shgawe: "—has changed, and on the whole become a more reasonable man. I have no evidence for this, other than what I sense in him."

Hashembe's voice sounded more faintly. "He does not seem to remember me, but many years ago when he belonged to the Leopard Society, I captured him and a dozen of his fellows at Engassa. He killed two of my men and escaped, but I bear him no grudge."

"Ngasi is a man worth careful attention," said Shgawe. "He is more subtle than he appears, and I believe, not so much of the back-country tribesman as he would have us believe."

"Possibly not," said Hashembe.

Keith switched off the connections, spoke for the encoder: "I'm aboard the Lumumba, we've just been out for a look at the missile docks. I've attached my No. 1 transmitter to the person of Adoui Shgawe; you'll now be picking up Shgawe's conversations. I don't dare listen in; they could detect me by the resonance. If anything interesting occurs, notify me."

He snapped back the switch; the pulse of information whisked up to the satellite and bounced down to Washington.

The Lumumba entered Tabacoundi Bay, docked. Keith returned to the Hôtel des Tropiques, rode the sparkling escalator to the second floor, strode along the silk and marble corridor to the door of his room. Two situations saved his life: an ingrained habit never to pass unwarily through a door, and the radar in his ear-amulets. The first keyed him to vigilance; the second hurled him aside and back, as through the spot his face had occupied flitted a shower of little glass needles. They tinkled against the far wall, fell to the floor in fragments.

Keith picked himself up, peered into the room. It was empty. He entered, closed the door. A catapult had launched the needles, a relatively simple mechanism. Someone in the hotel would be on hand to observe what had happened and remove the catapult—necessarily soon.

Keith ran to the door, eased it open, looked into the corridor. Empty—but here came footsteps. Leaving the door open, Keith pressed against the wall.

The footsteps halted. Keith heard the sound of breathing. The tip of a nose appeared through the doorway; it moved inquiringly this way and that. The face came through; it turned and looked into Keith's face, almost eye to eye. The mouth opened in a gasp, then a crooked wince as Keith reached forth, grasped the neck. The mouth opened but made no sound.

Keith pulled the man into the room, shut the door. He was a mulatto, about forty years old. His cheeks were fleshy and expansive, his nose a lumpy beak. Keith recognized him: Corty, his original contact in Fejo. He looked deep into the man's eyes; they were stained pink and the pupils were small; the gaze seemed leaden.

Keith sent a tingle of electricity through the rubbery body. Corty opened his mouth in agony, but failed to cry out. Keith started to speak, but Corty made a despairing sign for silence. He seized the pencil from Keith's pocket, scribbled in English: "Chinese, they have a circuit in my head, they drive me mad."

Keith stared. Corty suddenly opened his eyes wide. Yelling soundlessly he lunged for Keith's throat, clawing, tearing. Keith killed him with a gush of electricity, stood looking down at the limp body.

Heaven help the American agent who fell into Chinese hands, thought Keith. They ran wires through his brain, into the very core of the pain processes; then instructing and listening through transceivers, they could tweak, punish, or drive into frantic frenzy at will. The man was happier dead.

The Chinese had identified him. Had someone witnessed the placing of the tap on Shgawe? Or the dosing of Faranah? Or had Doutoufsky passed a broad hint? Or—the least likely possibility—did the Chinese merely wish to expunge him, as an African Isolationist?

Keith looked out into the corridor, which was untenanted. He rolled out the corpse, and then in a spirit of macabre whimsy, dragged it by the heels to the escalator, and sent it down into the lobby.

He returned to his room in a mood of depression. North vs. East vs. South vs. West: a four-way war. Think of all the battles, campaigns, tragedies: grief beyond calculation. And to what end? The final pacification of Earth? Improbable, thought Keith, considering the millions of years ahead. So why did he, James Keith, American citizen, masquerade as Tamba Ngasi, risking his life and wires into the pain centers of his brain? Keith pondered. The answer evidently was this: all of human history is condensed into each individual lifetime. Each man can enjoy the triumphs or suffer the defeats of all the human race. Charlemagne died a great hero, though his empire immediately split into fragments. Each man must win his personal victory, achieve his unique and selfish goal.

Otherwise, hope could not exist.

The sky over the fantastic silhouette of Fejo grew smoky purple. Colored lights twinkled in the plaza. Keith went to the window, looked off into the dreaming twilight skies. He wished no more of this business; if he fled now for home, he might escape with his life. Otherwise—he thought of Corty. In his own mind a relay clicked. The voice of Carl Sebastiani spoke soundlessly, but harsh and urgent. "Adoui Shgawe is dead—assassinated two minutes ago. The news came by your transmitter No. 1. Go to the palace, act decisively. This is a critical event."

Keith armed himself, tested his accumulators. Sliding back the door, he looked into the corridor. Two men in the white tunic of the Lakhadi Militia stood by the escalator. Keith stepped out, walked toward them. They became silent, watched his approach. Keith nodded with austere politeness, started to descend, but they halted him. "Sir, have you had a visitor this evening? A mulatto of early middle-age?"

"No. What is all this about?"

"We are trying to identify this man. He died under strange circumstances."

"I know nothing about him. Let me pass; I am Parliamentarian Tamba Ngasi."

The militia-men bowed politely; Keith rode the escalator down into the lobby.

He ran across the plaza, passed before the six basalt warriors, approached the front of the palace. He marched up the low steps, entered the vestibule. A doorman in a red and silver uniform, wearing a plumed head-dress with a silver nose-guard, stepped forward. "Good evening sir."

"I am Tamba Ngasi, Parliamentarian. I must see His Excellency immediately."

"I am sorry, sir, Premier Shgawe has given orders not to be disturbed this evening."

Keith pointed into the foyer. "Who then is that person?"

The doorman looked, Keith tapped him in the throat with his knuckles, held him at the nerve junctions under the ears until he stopped struggling, then dragged him back into his cubicle. He peered into the foyer. At the reception desk sat a handsome young woman in a Polynesian lava-lava. Her skin was golden-brown, she wore her hair piled in a soft black pyramid.

Keith entered, the young woman smiled politely up at him.

"Premier Shgawe is expecting me," said Keith. "Where may I find him?"

"I'm sorry sir, he has just given orders that he is not to be disturbed."

"Just given orders?"

"Yes, sir."

Keith nodded judiciously. He indicated her telephone. "Be so good as to call Grand Marshal Achille Hashembe, on an urgent matter."

"Your name, sir?"

"I am Parliamentarian Tamba Ngasi. Hurry."

The girl bent to the telephone.

"Ask him to join me and the Premier Shgawe at once," Keith ordered curtly.

"But, sir—"

"Premier Shgawe is expecting me. Call Marshal Hashembe at once."

"Yes sir." She punched a button. "Grand Marshal Hashembe from the State Palace."

"Where do I find the Premier?" inquired Keith, moving past.

"He is in the second-floor drawing room, with his friends. A page will conduct you." Keith waited; better a few seconds delay than a hysterical receptionist.

The page appeared: a lad of sixteen in a long smock of black velvet. Keith followed him up a flight of stairs to a pair of carved wooden doors. The page made as if to open the doors but Keith stopped him. "Return and wait for Grand Marshal Hashembe; bring him here at once."

The page retreated uncertainly, looking over his shoulder. Keith paid him no further heed. Gently he pressed the latch. The door was locked. Keith wadded a trifle of plastic explosive against the door jamb, attached a detonator, pressed against the wall.

Crack! Keith reached through the slivers, slammed the door open, stepped inside. Three startled men looked at him. One of them was Adoui Shgawe. The other two were Hsia Lu-Minh, the Chinese Ambassador, and Vasif Doutoufsky, Chief Clerk of the Grand Lakhadi Parliament.

Doutoufsky stood with his right fist clenched and slightly advanced. On his middle finger glittered the jewel of a large ring.

Steps pounded down the corridor: the doorman and a warrior in the black leather uniform of the Raven Elite Guard.

Shgawe asked mildly, "What is the meaning of all this?"

The doorkeeper cried fiercely, "This man attacked me; he has come with an evil heart!"

"No," cried Keith in confusion. "I feared that Your Excellency was in danger; now I see that I was misinformed."

"Seriously misinformed," said Shgawe. He motioned with his fingers. "Please go."

Doutoufsky leaned over, whispered into Shgawe's ear. Keith's gaze focused on Shgawe's hand, where he also wore a heavy ring. "Tamba Ngasi, stay if you will; I wish to confer with you." He dismissed the doorkeeper and the warrior. "This man is trustworthy. You may go."

They bowed, departed. And the confusion in Keith's mind had disappeared. Shgawe started to rise to his feet, Doutoufsky sidled thoughtfully forward. Keith flung himself to the carpet; the laser beam from his flashlight slashed across Doutoufsky's face, over against Shgawe's temple. Doutoufsky croaked, clutched his burnt-out eyes; the beam from his own ring burnt a furrow up his face. Shgawe had fallen on his back. The fat body quaked, jerked and quivered. Keith struck them again with his beam and they both died. Hsia Lu-Minh, pressing against the wall stood motionless, eyes bulging in horror. Keith jumped to his feet, ran forward. Hsia Lu-Minh made no resistance as Keith pumped anaesthetic into his neck.

Keith stood back panting, and once again the built-in radar saved his life. An impulse, not even registered by his brain, convulsed his muscles and jerked him aside. The bullet tore through his robe, grazing his skin. Another bullet sang past him. Keith saw Hashembe standing in the doorway, the bug-eyed page behind.

Hashembe took leisurely aim. "Wait," cried Keith. "I did not do this!"

Hashembe smiled faintly, and his trigger-finger tightened. Keith dropped to the floor, slashed the laser beam down over Hashembe's wrist. The gun dropped, Hashembe stood stern, erect, numb. Keith ran forward, hurled him to the floor, seized the page, blasted anaesthetic gas into the nape of his neck, pulled him inside, slammed shut the door.

He turned to find Hashembe groping for the gun with his left hand. "Stop!" cried Keith hoarsely. "I tell you I did not do this."

"You killed Shgawe."

"This is not Shgawe." He picked up the gun. "It is a Chinese agent, his face molded to look like Shgawe."

Hashembe was skeptical. "That is hard to believe." He looked down at the corpse. "Adoui Shgawe was not as fat as this man." He bent, lifted the thick fingers, then straightened up. "This is not Adoui Shgawe!" He inspected Doutoufsky. "The Chief Clerk, a renegade Pole."

"I thought that he worked for the Russians. The mistake almost cost me my life."

"Where is Shgawe?"

Keith looked around the room. "He must be nearby."

In the bathroom they found Shgawe's corpse. A sheet of fluoro-silicon plastic lined the tub, into which had been poured hydrofluoric acid from two large carboys. Shgawe's body lay on its back in the tub, already blurred, unrecognizable.

Choking from the fumes, Hashembe and Keith staggered back, slammed the door.

Hashembe's composure had departed. He tottered to a chair, nursing his wounded arm, muttered, "I understand nothing of these crimes."

Keith looked across to the limp form of the Chinese Ambassador. "Shgawe was too strong for them. Or perhaps he learned of the grand plan."

Hashembe shook his head numbly.

"The Chinese want Africa," said Keith. "It's as simple as that. Africa will support a billion Chinese. In fifty years there may well be another billion."

"If true," said Hashembe, "it is monstrous. And Shgawe, who would tolerate none of this, is dead."

"Therefore," said Keith, "we must replace Shgawe with a leader who will pursue the same goals."

"Where shall we find such a leader?"

"Here. I am such a leader. You control the army; there can be no opposition."

Hashembe sat for two minutes looking into space. Then he rose to his feet. "Very well. You are the new premier. If necessary, we shall dissolve the Parliament. In any event it is no more than a pen for cackling chickens."

The assassination of Adoui Shgawe shocked the nation, all of Africa. When Grand Marshal Achille Hashembe appeared before the Parliament, and announced that the body had the choice either of electing Tamba Ngasi Premier of Lakhadi, or submitting to dissolution and martial law, Tamba Ngasi was elected premier without a demur.

Keith, wearing the black and gold uniform of the Lion Elite, addressed the chamber.

"In general, my policies are identical to those of Adoui Shgawe. He hoped for a strong United Africa; this is also my hope. He tried to avoid a dependence upon foreign powers, while accepting as much genuine help as was offered. This is also my policy. Adoui Shgawe loved his native land, and sought to make Lakhadi a light of inspiration to all Africa. I hope to do as well. The missile docks will be emplaced exactly as Adoui Shgawe planned, and our Lakhadi technicians will continue to learn how to operate these great devices."

Weeks passed. Keith restaffed the palace, and burned every square inch of floor, wall, ceiling, furniture and fixtures clear of spy-cells. Sebastiani had sent him three new operatives to function as liaison and provide technical advice. Keith no longer communicated directly with Sebastiani; without this direct connection with his erstwhile superior, the distinction between James Keith and Tamba Ngasi sometimes seemed to blur.

Keith was aware of this tendency, and exercised himself against the confusion. "I have taken this man's name, his face, his personality. I must think like him, I must act like him. But I cannot be that man!" But sometimes, if he were especially tired, uncertainty plagued him. Tamba Ngasi? James Keith? Which was the real personality?

Two months passed quietly, and a third month. The calm was like the eye of a hurricane, thought Keith. Occasionally protocol required that he meet and confer with Hsia Lu-Minh, the Chinese Ambassador. During these occasions, decorum and formality prevailed; the murder of Adoui Shgawe seemed nothing more than the wisp of an unpleasant dream. "Dream," thought Keith, the word persisting. "I live a dream." In a sudden spasm of dread, he called Sebastiani. "I'm going stale, I'm losing myself."

Sebastiani's voice was cool and reasonable. "You seem to be doing the job very well."

"One of these days," said Keith gloomily, "you'll talk to me in English and I'll answer in Swahili. And then—"

"And then?" Sebastiani prompted.

"Nothing important," said Keith. And then you'll know that when James Keith and Tamba Ngasi met in the thorn bushes beside the Dasa River, Tamba Ngasi walked away alive and jackals ate the body of James Keith.

Sebastiani made Keith a slightly improper suggestion: "Find yourself one of those beautiful Fejo girls and work off some of your nervous energy."

Keith somberly rejected the idea. "She'd hear relays clanking and buzzing and wonder what was wooing her."

A day arrived when the missile docks were finally emplaced. Eighteen great concrete cylinders, washed by the Atlantic swells, stretched in a line along the Lakhadi coast. Keith ordained a national holiday to celebrate the installation, and presided at an open air banquet in the plaza before the Parliament House. Speeches continued for hours, celebrating the new grandeur of Lakhadi:

"—a nation once subject to the cruel imperial yoke, and now possessed of a culture superior to any west of China!" These were the words of Hsia Lu-Minh, with a bland side-glance for Leon Pashenko, the Russian Ambassador.

Pashenko, in his turn, spoke with words equally mordant. "With the aid of the Soviet Union, Lakhadi finds itself absolutely secure against the offensive maneuvers of the West. We now recommend that all technicians, except those currently employed in the training programs, be withdrawn. African manpower must shape the future of Africa!"

James Keith sat only half-listening to the voices, and without conscious formulation, into his mind came a scheme so magnificent in scope that he could only marvel. It was a policy matter; should he move without prior conference with Sebastiani? But he was Tamba Ngasi as well as James Keith. When he arose to address the gathering, Tamba Ngasi spoke.

"Comrades Pashenko and Hsia have spoken and I have listened with interest. Especially I welcome the sentiments expressed by Comrade Pashenko. The citizens of Lakhadi must perform excellently in every field, without further guidance from abroad. Except in one critical area. We still are unable to manufacture warheads for our new defense system. I therefore take this happy occasion to formally request from the Soviet Union the requisite explosive materials."

Loud applause, and now, while Hsia Lu-Minh clapped with zest, Leon Pashenko showed little enthusiasm. After the banquet, he called upon Keith, and made a blunt statement.

"I regret that the fixed policy of the Soviet Union is to retain control over all its nucleonic devices. We cannot accede to your request."

"A pity," said Keith.

Leon Pashenko appeared puzzled, having expected protests and argument.

"A pity, because now I must make the request of the Chinese."

Leon Pashenko pointed out the contingent dangers. "The Chinese make hard masters!"

Keith bowed the baffled Russian out of his apartment. Immediately he sent a message to the Chinese Embassy, and half an hour later Hsia Lu-Minh appeared.

"The ideas expressed by Comrade Pashenko this evening seemed valuable," said Keith. "I assume you agree?"

"Wholeheartedly," declared Hsia Lu-Minh. "Naturally the program for agricultural reform we have long discussed would not come under these restraints."

"Most emphatically they would," said Keith. "However a very limited pilot program might be launched, provided that the Chinese People's

Democracy supplies warheads, immediately and at once, for our eighteen missiles."

"I must communicate with my government," said Hsia Lu-Minh.

"Please use all possible haste," said Keith, "I am impatient."

Hsia Lu-Minh returned the following day. "My government agrees to arm the missiles provided that the pilot program you envision consists of at least two hundred thousand agricultural technicians."

"Impossible! How can we support so large an incursion?"

The figure was finally set at one hundred thousand, with six missiles only being supplied with nucleonic warheads.

"This is an epoch-making agreement," declared Hsia Lu-Minh.

"It is the beginning of a revolutionary process," Keith agreed.

There was further wrangling about the phasing of delivery of the warheads vis-à-vis the arrival of the technicians, and negotiations almost broke down. Hsia Lu-Minh seemed aggrieved to find that Keith wanted actual and immediate delivery of the warheads, rather than merely a symbolic statement of intent. Keith, in his turn, experienced surprise when Hsia Lu-Minh objected to a proviso that the incoming 'technicians' be granted only six-month visas marked TEMPORARY, with option of renewal at the discretion of the Lakhadi government. "How can these technicians identify themselves with the problems? How can they learn to love the soil which they must till?"

The difficulties were eventually ironed out; Hsia Lu-Minh took his leave. Almost at once Keith received a call from Sebastiani, who had only just learned of the projected China-Lakhadi treaty. Sebastiani's voice was cautious, tentative, probing. "I don't quite understand the rationale of this project."

When Keith was tired, the Tamba Ngasi element of his personality exerted greater influence. The voice which answered Sebastiani sounded impatient, harsh and rough to Keith himself.

"I did not plan this scheme by rationality, but by intuition."

Sebastiani's voice became even more cautious. "I fail to see any advantageous end to the business."

Keith, or Tamba Ngasi—whoever was dominant—laughed. "The Russians are leaving Lakhadi."

"The Chinese remain in control. Compared with the Chinese, the Russians are genteel conservatives."

"You make a mistake. I am in control!"

"Very well, Keith," said Sebastiani thoughtfully. "I see that we must trust your judgment."

Keith—or Tamba Ngasi—made a brusque reply, and took himself to bed. Here the tension departed and James Keith lay staring into the dark.

A month passed; two warheads were delivered by the Chinese, flown in from the processing plants at Ulan Bator. Cargo helicopters set them in place, and Keith made a triumphant address to Lakhadi, to Africa, and to the world. "From this day forward, Lakhadi, the Helm of Africa, must be granted its place in the world's councils. We have sought power, not for the sake of power alone, but to secure for Africa the representation our people only nominally have enjoyed. The South no longer must defer to West, to North or to East!"

The first contingent of Chinese 'technicians' arrived three days later: a thousand young men and women, uniformly clad in blue coveralls and white canvas shoes. They marched in disciplined platoons to buses, and were conveyed to a tent city near the lands on which they were to be settled.

On this day Leon Pashenko called to deliver a confidential memorandum from the President of the U.S.S.R. He waited while Keith glanced through the note.

"It is necessary to point out," read the note, "that the government of the U.S.S.R. adversely regards the expansion of Chinese influence in Lakhadi, and holds itself free to take such steps as are necessary to protect the interests of the U.S.S.R."

Keith nodded slowly. He raised his eyes to Pashenko, who sat watching with a glassy thin-lipped smile. Keith punched a button, spoke into a mesh. "Send in the television cameras, I am broadcasting an important bulletin."

A crew hurriedly wheeled in equipment. Pashenko's smile became more fixed, his skin pasty.

The director made a signal to Keith. "You're on the air."

Keith looked into the lens. "Citizens of Lakhadi, and Africans. Sitting beside me is Leon Pashenko, Ambassador of the U.S.S.R. He has just now presented me with an official communication which attempts to interfere with the internal policy of Lakhadi. I take this occasion to issue a public rebuke to the Soviet Union. I declare that the government of Lakhadi will be influenced only by measures designed to benefit its citizens, and that any further interference by the Soviet Union may lead to a rupture of diplomatic relations."

Keith bowed politely to Leon Pashenko, who had sat full in view of the camera with a frozen grimace on his face. "Please accept this statement as a formal reply to your memorandum of this morning."

Without a word Pashenko rose to his feet and left the room.

Minutes later Keith received a communication from Sebastiani. The soundless voice was sharper than ever Keith had heard it. "What the devil are you up to? Publicity? You've humiliated the Russians, perhaps finished them in Africa—but have you considered the risks? Not for yourself, not for Lakhadi, not even for Africa—but for the whole world?"

"I have not considered such risks. They do not affect Lakhadi."

Sebastiani's voice crackled with rage. "Lakhadi isn't the center of the universe merely because you've been assigned there! From now on—these are orders, mind you—make no moves without consulting me!"

"I have heard all I care to hear," said Tamba Ngasi. "Do not call me again, do not try to interfere in my plans." He clicked off the receiver, sighed, slumped back in his chair. Then he blinked, straightened up as the memory of the conversation echoed in his brain.

For a moment he thought of calling back and trying to explain, then rejected the idea. Sebastiani would think him mad for a fact—when he had merely been over-tired, over-tense. So Keith assured himself.

The following day he received a report from a Swiss technical group, and snorted in anger, though the findings were no more than he had expected.

The Chinese Ambassador unluckily chose this moment to pay a call, and was ushered into the premier's office. Round-faced, prim, brimming with affability, Hsia Lu-Minh came forward.

He takes me for a back-country chieftain, thought the man who was now entirely Tamba Ngasi—a man relentless as a crocodile, sly as a jackal, dark as the jungle.

Hsia Lu-Minh was full of gracious compliments. "How clearly you have discerned the course of the future! It is no mere truism to state that the colored races of the world share a common destiny."

"Indeed?"

"Indeed! And I carry the authorization of my government to permit the transfer of another group of skillful, highly trained workers to Lakhadi!"

"What of the remaining warheads for the missiles?"

"They will assuredly be delivered and installed on schedule."

"I have changed my mind," said Tamba Ngasi. "I want no more Chinese immigrants. I speak for all of Africa. Those already in this country must leave, and likewise the Chinese missions in Mali, Ghana, Sudan, Angola, the

Congolese Federation—in fact in all of Africa. The Chinese must leave Africa, completely and inalterably. This is an ultimatum. You have a week to agree. Otherwise Lakhadi will declare war upon the Chinese People's Republic."

Hsia Lu-Minh listened in astonishment, his mouth a doughnut of shock. "You are joking?" he quavered.

"You think I am joking? Listen!" Once again Tamba Ngasi called for the television crew, and again issued a public statement.

"Yesterday I cleansed my country of the Russians; today I expel the Chinese. They helped us from our post-colonial chaos—but why? To pursue their own advantage. We are not the fools they take us to be." Tamba Ngasi jerked a finger at Hsia Lu-Minh. "Speaking on behalf of his government, Comrade Hsia has agreed to my terms. The Chinese are withdrawing from Africa. They will leave at once. Hsia Lu-Minh has graciously consented to this. Lakhadi now has a stalwart defense, and no longer needs protection from anyone. Should anyone seek to thwart this purge of foreign influence, these weapons will be instantly used, without remorse. I cannot speak any plainer." He turned to the limp Chinese ambassador. "Comrade Hsia, in the name of Africa, I thank you for your promise of cooperation, and I shall hold you to it!"

Hsia Lu-Minh tottered from the room. He returned to the Chinese Embassy and put a bullet through his head.

Eight hours later a Chinese plane arrived in Fejo, loaded with ministers, generals and aides. Tamba Ngasi received them immediately. Ting Sieuh-Ma, the leading Chinese theoretician, spoke vehemently. "You put us into an intolerable position. You must reverse yourself!"

Tamba Ngasi laughed. "There is only one road for you to travel. You must obey me. Do you think the Chinese will profit by going to war with Lakhadi? All Africa will rise against you; you will face disaster. And never forget our new weapons. At this moment they are aimed at the most sensitive areas in China."

Ting Sieuh-Ma's laugh was mocking. "It is the least of our worries. Do you think we would trust you with active warheads? Your ridiculous weapons are as harmless as mice."

Tamba Ngasi displayed the Swiss report. "I know this. The detonators: ninety-six percent lead, four percent radioactive waste. The lithium hydride—ordinary hydrogen. You cheated me; therefore I am expelling you from Africa. As for the warheads, I have dealt with a certain European power; even now they are installing active materials in these missiles you profess to despise. You have no choice. Get out of Africa within the week or prepare for disaster."

"It is disaster either way," said Ting Sieuh-Ma. "But ponder: you are a single man, we are the East. Can you really hope to best us?"

Tamba Ngasi bared his stainless-steel teeth in a wolfish grin. "That is my hope."

Keith leaned back in his chair. The deputation had departed; he sat alone in the conference chamber. He felt drained of energy, lax and listless. Tamba Ngasi, temporarily at least, had been purged.

Keith thought of the last few days, and felt a pang of terror at his own recklessness. The recklessness rather, of Tamba Ngasi, who had humiliated and confused two of the great world powers. They would not forgive him. Adoui Shgawe, a relatively mild adversary, had been dissolved in acid. Tamba Ngasi, author of absolutely intolerable policies, could hardly expect to survive.

Keith rubbed his long harsh chin and tried to formulate a plan for survival. For perhaps a week he might be safe, while his enemies decided upon a plan of attack...

Keith jumped to his feet. Why should there be any delay whatever? Minutes now were precious to both Russians and Chinese; they must have arranged for any and all contingencies.

His communication screen tinkled; the frowning face of Grand Marshal Achille Hashembe appeared. He spoke curtly. "I cannot understand your orders. Why should we hesitate now? Clear the vermin out, send them back to their own land—"

"What orders are you talking about?" Keith demanded.

"Those you issued five minutes ago in front of the palace, relative to the Chinese immigrants."

"I see," said Keith. "You are correct. There was a misunderstanding. Ignore those orders, proceed as before."

Hashembe nodded with brusque satisfaction; the screen faded. There would be no delay whatever, thought Keith. The Chinese already were striking. He twisted a knob on the screen, and his reception clerk looked forth. She seemed startled.

"Has anyone entered the palace during the last five minutes?"

"Only yourself, sir...How did you get upstairs so quickly?"

Keith cut her off. He went to the door, listened, and heard the hum of the rising elevator. He ran to his private apartments, snatched open a drawer. His weapons—gone. Betrayed by one of his servants.

Keith went to the door which led out into the terrace garden. From the garden he could make his way to the plaza and escape if he so chose. To his ears came a soft flutter of sound. Keith stepped out into the dark, searched the sky. The night was overcast; he could see only murk. But his radar apprised him of a descending object, and the infra-red detector in his hand felt heat.

From behind him, in his bedroom, came another soft sound. He turned, watched himself step warily through the door, glance around the room. They had done a good job, thought Keith, considering the shortness of the time. This version of Tamba Ngasi was perhaps a half-inch shorter than himself, the face was fuller, the skin a shade darker and not too subtly toned. He moved without the loose African swing, on legs thicker and shorter than Keith's own. Keith decided inconsequentially that in order to simulate a Negro, it was best to begin with a Negro. In this respect at least the United States had an advantage.

The new Tamba left the bedroom. Keith slipped over to the door, intending to stalk him, attack with his bare hands, but now down from the sky came the object he had sensed on his radar: a jigger-plane, little more than a seat suspended from four whirling air-foils. It landed softly on the dark terrace; Keith pressed against the wall, ducked behind an earthenware urn.

The man from the sky approached, went to the sliding door, slipped into the bedroom. Keith stared. Tamba Ngasi once more, leaner and more angular than the first interloper. This Tamba from the sky looked quickly around the room, peered through the door into the corridor, stepped confidently through.

Keith followed cautiously. The Tamba from the sky jogged swiftly down the corridor, stopped at the archway giving on the tri-level study. Keith could not restrain a laugh at the farce of deadly misconceptions which now must ensue.

Sky-Tamba leapt into the study like a cat. Instantly there was an ejaculation of excitement, a sputter of deadly sound. Silence.

Keith ran to the doorway, and standing back in the shadow, peered into the study. Sky-Tamba stood holding some sort of gun or projector in one hand and a polished disc in the other. He sidled along the wall. Tamba Short-legs had ducked behind a bookcase, where Keith could hear him muttering under his breath. Sky-Tamba made a quick leap forward; from behind the bookcase came a sparkling line of light and ions. Sky-Tamba caught the beam on his shield, tossed a grenade which Tamba Short-legs thrust at the bookcase; it toppled forward; Sky-Tamba jerked back to avoid it. He tripped and sprawled awkwardly. Tamba Short-legs was on him, hacking with a hatchet, which gave off sparks and smoke where it struck.

Sky-Tamba lay dead, his mission a failure, his life ended. Tamba Short-legs rose in triumph. He saw Keith, uttered a guttural expletive of surprise. He bounded like a rubber ball down to the second landing, intending to outflank Keith.

Keith ran to the body of Sky-Tamba, tugged at his weapon, but it was caught under the heavy body. A line of ionizing light sizzled across his face; he fell flat. Tamba Short-legs came running up the steps; Keith yanked furiously at the weapon, but there would be no time: his end had come.

Tamba Short-legs stopped short. In the doorway opposite stood a lean harsh-visaged man in white robes—still another Tamba. This one was like Keith, in skin, feature, and heft, identical except for an indefinable difference of expression. The three gazed stupefied at each other; then Tamba Short-legs aimed his electric beam. New Tamba slipped to the side like a shadow, slashing the air with his laser. Tamba Short-legs dropped, rolled over, drove forward in a low crouch. New Tamba waited for him; they grappled. Sparks flew from their feet as each sought to electrocute the other; each had been equipped with ground circuits, and the electricity dissipated harmlessly. Tamba Short-legs disengaged himself, swung his hatchet. New Tamba dodged back, pointed his laser. Tamba Short-legs threw the hatchet, knocked the laser spinning. The two men sprang together. Keith picked up hatchet and laser and prepared to deal with the survivor. "Peculiar sort of assassination," he reflected. "Everyone gets killed but the victim."

Tamba Short-legs and New Tamba were locked in a writhing tangle. There was a clicking sound, a gasp. One of the men stood up, faced Keith: New Tamba.

Keith aimed the laser. New Tamba held up his hands, moved back. He cried, "Don't shoot me, James Keith. I'm your replacement."

Coup De Grâce

The Hub, a cluster of bubbles in a web of metal, hung in empty space, in that region known to Earthmen as Hither Sagittarius. The owner was Pan Pascoglu, a man short, dark and energetic, almost bald, with restless brown eyes and a thick mustache. A man of ambition, Pascoglu hoped to develop the Hub into a fashionable resort, a glamor-island among the stars—something more than a mere stopover depot and junction point. Working to this end, he added two dozen bright new bubbles—"cottages", as he called them—around the outer meshes of the Hub, which already resembled the model of an extremely complex molecule.

The cottages were quiet and comfortable; the dining saloon offered an adequate cuisine; a remarkable diversity of company met in the public rooms. Magnus Ridolph found the Hub at once soothing and stimulating. Sitting in the dim dining saloon, the naked stars serving as chandeliers, he contemplated his fellow-guests. At a table to his left, partially obscured by a planting of dendrons, sat four figures. Magnus Ridolph frowned. They ate in utter silence and three of them, at least, hulked over their plates in an uncouth fashion.

"Barbarians," said Magnus Ridolph, and turned his shoulder. In spite of the mannerless display he was not particularly offended; at the Hub one must expect to mingle with a variety of peoples. Tonight they seemed to range the whole spectrum of evolution, from the boors to his left, across a score of more or less noble civilizations, culminating with—Magnus Ridolph patted his neat white beard with a napkin—himself.

From the corner of his eye he noticed one of the four shapes arise, approach his own table.

"Forgive my intrusion, but I understand that you are Magnus Ridolph."

Magnus Ridolph acknowledged his identity and the other, without invitation, sat heavily down. Magnus Ridolph wavered between curtness and civility. In the starlight he saw his visitor to be an anthropologist, one Lester Bonfils, who had been pointed out to him earlier. Magnus Ridolph, pleased with his own perspicacity, became civil. The three figures at Bonfils' table were savages in all reality: palaeolithic inhabitants of S-Cha-6, temporary wards of Bonfils.

Their faces were dour, sullen, wary; they seemed disenchanted with such of civilization as they had experienced. They wore metal wristlets and rather heavy metal belts: magnetic pinions. At necessity, Bonfils could instantly immobilize the arms of his charges.

Bonfils himself was a large fair man with thick blond hair, heavy and vaguely flabby. His complexion should have been florid; it was pale. He should have exhaled easy good-fellowship, but he was withdrawn and diffident. His mouth sagged, his nose was pinched; there was no energy to his movements, only a nervous febrility. He leaned forward. "I'm sure you are bored with other people's troubles, but I need help."

"At the moment I do not care to accept employment," said Magnus Ridolph in a definite voice.

Bonfils sat back, looked away, finding not even the strength to protest. The stars glinted on the whites of his eyes; his skin shone the color of cheese. He muttered, "I should have expected no more."

His expression held such dullness and despair that Magnus Ridolph felt a pang of sympathy. "Out of curiosity—and without committing myself—what is the nature of your difficulty?"

Bonfils laughed briefly—a mournful empty sound. "Basically—my destiny."

"In that case, I can be of little assistance," said Magnus Ridolph.

Bonfils laughed again, as hollowly as before. "I use the word 'destiny' in the largest sense, to include—" he made a vague gesture "—I don't know what. I seem predisposed to failure and defeat. I consider myself a man of good-will— yet there is no one with more enemies. I attract them as if I were the most vicious creature alive."

Magnus Ridolph surveyed Bonfils with a trace of interest. "These enemies, then, have banded together against you?"

"No…at least I think not. I am harassed by a woman. She is busily engaged in killing me."

"I can give you some rather general advice," said Magnus Ridolph. "It is this: have nothing more to do with this woman."

Bonfils spoke in a desperate rush, with a glance over his shoulder toward the palaeolithics. "I had nothing to do with her in the first place! That's the difficulty! Agreed that I'm a fool; an anthropologist should be careful of such things, but I was absorbed in my work. This took place at the southern tip of Kharesm, on Journey's End; do you know the place?"

"I have never visited Journey's End."

"Some people stopped me on the street—'We hear you have engaged in intimate relations with our kinswoman!'

"I protested: 'No, no, that's not true!'—because naturally, as an anthropologist, I must avoid such things like the plague."

Magnus Ridolph raised his brows in surprise. "Your profession seems to demand more than monastic detachment."

Bonfils made his vague gesture; his mind was elsewhere. He turned to inspect his charges; only one remained at the table. Bonfils groaned from the depths of his soul, leapt to his feet—nearly overturning Magnus Ridolph's table—and plunged away in pursuit.

Magnus Ridolph sighed, and after a moment or two departed the dining saloon. He sauntered the length of the main lobby, but Bonfils was nowhere to be seen. Magnus Ridolph seated himself, ordered a brandy.

The lobby was full. Magnus Ridolph contemplated the other occupants of the room. Where did these various men and women, near-men and near-women, originate? What were their purposes, what had brought them to the Hub? That rotund moon-faced bonze in the stiff red robe, for instance. He was a native of the planet Padme, far across the galaxy: why had he ventured so far from home? And the tall angular man whose narrow shaved skull carried a fantastic set of tantalum ornaments: a Lord of the Dacca. Exiled? In pursuit of an enemy? On some mad crusade? And the anthrope from the planet Hecate sitting by himself: a walking argument to support the theory of parallel evolution. His outward semblance caricatured humanity; internally he was as far removed as a gastropod. His head was bleached bone and black shadow, his mouth a lipless slit. He was a Meth of Maetho, and Magnus Ridolph knew his race to be gentle and diffident, with so little mental contact with human beings as to seem ambiguous and secretive…Magnus Ridolph focused his gaze on a woman, and was taken aback by her miraculous beauty. She was dark and slight, with a complexion the color of clean desert sand; she carried herself with a self-awareness that was immensely provoking…

Into the chair beside Magnus Ridolph dropped a short nearly-bald man with a thick black mustache: Pan Pascoglu, proprietor of the Hub. "Good evening, Mr. Ridolph; how goes it with you tonight?"

"Very well, thank you…That woman: who is she?"

Pascoglu followed Magnus Ridolph's gaze. "Ah. A fairy-princess. From Journey's End. Her name—" Pascoglu clicked his tongue. "I can't remember. Some outlandish thing."

"Surely she doesn't travel alone?"

Pascoglu shrugged. "She says she's married to Bonfils, the chap with the three cave-men. But they've got different cottages, and I never see them together."

"Astonishing," murmured Magnus Ridolph.

"An understatement," said Pascoglu. "The cave-men must have hidden charms."

The next morning the Hub vibrated with talk, because Lester Bonfils lay dead in his cottage, with the three palaeolithics stamping restlessly in their cages. The guests surveyed each other nervously. One among them was a murderer!

II

Pan Pascoglu came to Magnus Ridolph in an extremity of emotion. "Mr. Ridolph, I know you're here on vacation, but you've got to help me out. Someone killed poor Bonfils dead as a mackerel, but who it was—" He held out his hands. "I can't stand for such things here, naturally."

Magnus Ridolph pulled at his little white beard. "Surely there is to be some sort of official inquiry?"

"That's what I'm seeing you about!" Pascoglu threw himself into a chair. "The Hub's outside all jurisdiction. I'm my own law—within certain limits, of course. That is to say, if I was harboring criminals, or running vice, someone would interfere. But there's nothing like that here. A drunk, a fight, a swindle—we take care of such things quietly. We've never had a killing. It's got to be cleaned up!"

Magnus Ridolph reflected a moment or two. "I take it you have no criminological equipment?"

"You mean those truth machines, and breath-detectors and cell-matchers? Nothing like that. Not even a fingerprint pad."

"I thought as much," sighed Magnus Ridolph. "Well, I can hardly refuse your request. May I ask what you intend to do with the criminal after I apprehend her—or him?"

Pascoglu jumped to his feet. Clearly the idea had not occurred to him. He held out his clenched hands. "What should I do? I'm not equipped to set up a law court. I don't want to just shoot somebody."

Magnus Ridolph spoke judiciously. "The question may resolve itself. Justice, after all, has no absolute values."

Pascoglu nodded passionately. "Right! Let's find out who did it. Then we'll decide the next step."

"Where is the body?" asked Magnus Ridolph.

"Still in the cottage, just where the maid found it."

"It has not been touched?"

"The doctor looked him over. I came directly to you."

"Good. Let us go to Bonfils' cottage."

Bonfils' 'cottage' was a globe far out on the uttermost web, perhaps five hundred yards by tube from the main lobby.

The body lay on the floor beside a white chaise-longue, lumpy, pathetic, grotesque. In the center of the forehead was a burn; no other marks were visible. The three palaeolithics were confined in an ingenious cage of flexible splines, evidently collapsible. The cage of itself could not have restrained the muscular savages; the splines apparently were charged with electricity.

Beside the cage stood a thin young man, either inspecting or teasing the palaeolithics. He turned hastily when Pascoglu and Magnus Ridolph stepped into the cottage.

Pascoglu performed the introductions. "Dr. Scanton, Magnus Ridolph."

Magnus Ridolph nodded courteously. "I take it, doctor, that you have made at least a superficial examination?"

"Sufficient to certify death."

"Could you ascertain the time of death?"

"Approximately midnight."

Magnus Ridolph gingerly crossed the room, looked down at the body. He turned abruptly, rejoined Pascoglu and the doctor who waited by the door.

"Well?" asked Pascoglu anxiously.

"I have not yet identified the criminal," said Magnus Ridolph. "However, I am almost grateful to poor Bonfils. He has provided what appears to be a case of classic purity."

Pascoglu chewed at his mustache. "Perhaps I am dense—"

"A series of apparent truisms may order our thinking," said Magnus Ridolph. "First, the author of this act is currently at the Hub."

"Naturally," said Pascoglu. "No ships have arrived or departed."

"The motives to the act lie in the more or less immediate past."

Pascoglu made an impatient movement. Magnus Ridolph held up his hand, and Pascoglu irritably resumed the attack on his mustache.

"The criminal in all likelihood had had some sort of association with Bonfils."

Pascoglu said, "Don't you think we should be back in the lobby? Maybe someone will confess, or—"

"All in good time," said Magnus Ridolph. "To sum up, it appears that our primary roster of suspects will be Bonfils' shipmates en route to the Hub."

"He came on the *Maulerer Princeps;* I can get the debarkation list at once." And Pascoglu hurriedly departed the cottage.

Magnus Ridolph stood in the doorway studying the room. He turned to Dr. Scanton. "Official procedure would call for a set of detailed photographs; I wonder if you could make these arrangements?"

"Certainly. I'll do them myself."

"Good. And then—there would seem no reason not to move the body."

III

Magnus Ridolph returned along the tube to the main lobby, where he found Pascoglu at the desk.

Pascoglu thrust forth a paper. "This is what you asked for."

Magnus Ridolph inspected the paper with interest. Thirteen identities were listed:

1. Lester Bonfils, with
a. Abu
b. Toko
c. Homup
2. Viamestris Diasporus
3. Thorn 199
4. Fodor Impliega
5. Fodor Banzoso
6. Scriagl
7. Hercules Starguard
8. Fiamella of Thousand Candles
9. Clan Kestrel, 14th Ward, 6th Family, 3rd Son
10. (No name)

"Ah," said Magnus Ridolph. "Excellent. But there is a lack. I am particularly interested in the planet of origin of these persons."

"Planet of origin?" Pascoglu complained. "What is the benefit of this?"

Magnus Ridolph inspected Pascoglu with mild blue eyes. "I take it that you wish me to investigate this crime?"

"Yes, of course, but—"

"You will then cooperate with me, to the fullest extent, with no further protests or impatient ejaculations." And Magnus Ridolph accompanied the words with so cold and clear a glance that Pascoglu wilted and threw up his hands. "Have it your own way. But I still don't understand—"

"As I remarked, Bonfils has been good enough to provide us a case of definitive clarity."

"It's not clear to me," Pascoglu grumbled. He looked at the list. "You think the murderer is one of these?"

"Possibly, but not necessarily. It might be me, or it might be you. Both of us have had recent contact with Bonfils."

Pascoglu grinned sourly. "If it were you, please confess now and save me the expense of your fee."

"I fear it is not quite so simple. But the problem is susceptible to attack. The suspects—the persons on this list and any other Bonfils had dealt with recently—are from different worlds. Each is steeped in the traditions of his unique culture. Police routine might solve the case through the use of analyzers and detection machines. I hope to achieve the same end through cultural analysis."

Pascoglu's expression was that of a castaway on a desert island watching a yacht recede over the horizon. "As long as the case gets solved," he said in a hollow voice, "and there's no notoriety."

"Come then," said Magnus Ridolph briskly. "The worlds of origin."

The additions were made; Magnus Ridolph scrutinized the list again. He pursed his lips, pulled at his white beard. "I must have two hours for research. Then—we interview our suspects."

IV

Two hours passed, and Pan Pascoglu could wait no longer. He marched furiously into the library to find Magnus Ridolph gazing into space, tapping the table with a pencil. Pascoglu opened his mouth to speak, but Magnus Ridolph turned his head, and the mild blue gaze seemed to operate some sort of relay within Pascoglu's head. He composed himself, and made a relatively calm inquiry as to the state of Magnus Ridolph's investigations.

"Well enough," said Magnus Ridolph. "And what have you learned?"

"Well—you can cross Scriagl and the Clan Kestrel chap off the list. They were gambling in the game-room and have fool-proof alibis."

Magnus Ridolph said thoughtfully, "It is of course possible that Bonfils met an old enemy here at the Hub."

Pascoglu cleared his throat. "While you were here studying, I made a few inquiries. My staff is fairly observant; nothing much escapes them. They say that Bonfils spoke at length only to three people. They are myself, you and that moon-faced bonze in the red robes."

Magnus Ridolph nodded. "I spoke to Bonfils, certainly. He appeared in great trouble. He insisted that a woman—evidently Fiamella of Thousand Candles—was killing him."

"What!" cried Pascoglu. "You knew all this time?"

"Calm yourself, my dear fellow. He claimed that she was engaged in the process of killing him—vastly different from the decisive act whose effect we witnessed. I beg of you, restrain your exclamations; they startle me. To continue, I spoke to Bonfils, but I feel secure in eliminating myself. You have requested my assistance and you know my reputation: hence with equal assurance I eliminate you."

Pascoglu made a guttural sound, and walked across the room.

Magnus Ridolph spoke on. "The bonze—I know something of his cult. They subscribe to a belief in reincarnation, and make an absolute fetish of virtue, kindness and charity. A bonze of Padme would hardly dare such an act as murder; he would expect to spend several of his next manifestations as a jackal or a sea-urchin."

The door opened, and into the library, as if brought by some telepathetic urge, came the bonze himself. Noticing the attitudes of Magnus Ridolph and Pascoglu, their sober appraisal of himself, he hesitated. "Do I intrude upon a private conversation?"

"The conversation is private," said Magnus Ridolph, "but inasmuch as the topic is yourself, we would profit by having you join us."

"I am at your service." The bonze advanced into the room. "How far has the discussion advanced?"

"You perhaps are aware that Lester Bonfils, the anthropologist, was murdered last night."

"I have heard the talk."

"We understand that last evening he conversed with you."

"That is correct." The bonze drew a deep breath. "Bonfils was in serious trouble. Never had I seen a man so despondent. The bonzes of Padme—especially we of the Isavest Ordainment—are sworn to altruism. We render constructive service to any living thing, and under certain circumstances to inorganic objects as well. We feel that the principle of life transcends protoplasm; and in fact has its inception with simple—or perhaps not so simple—motion. A molecule brushing past another—is this not one aspect of vitality? Why can we not conjecture consciousness in each individual molecule? Think what a ferment of thought surrounds us; imagine the resentment which conceivably arises when we tread on a clod! For this reason we bonzes move as gently as possible, and take care where we set our feet."

"Aha, hum," said Pascoglu. "What did Bonfils want?"

The bonze considered. "I find it difficult to explain. He was a victim of many anguishes. I believe that he tried to live an honorable life, but his precepts were contradictory. As a result he was beset by the passions of suspicion, eroticism, shame, bewilderment, dread, anger, resentment, disappointment and confusion. Secondly, I believe that he was beginning to fear for his professional reputation—"

Pascoglu interrupted. "What, specifically, did he require of you?"

"Nothing specific. Reassurance and encouragement, perhaps."

"And you gave it to him?"

The bonze smiled faintly. "My friend, I am dedicated to serious programs of thought. We have been trained to divide our brains left lobe from right, so that we may think with two separate minds."

Pascoglu was about to bark an impatient question, but Magnus Ridolph interceded. "The bonze is telling you that only a fool could resolve Lester Bonfils' troubles with a word."

"That expresses something of my meaning," said the bonze.

Pascoglu stared from one to the other in puzzlement, then threw up his hands in disgust. "I merely want to find who burnt the hole in Bonfils' head. Can you help me, yes or no?"

The bonze smiled. "I will be glad to help you, but I wonder if you have considered the source of your impulses? Are you not motivated by an archaic quirk?"

Magnus Ridolph interpreted smoothly. "The bonze refers to the Mosaic Law. He warns against the doctrine of extracting an eye for an eye, a tooth for a tooth."

"Again," declared the bonze, "you have captured the essence of my meaning."

Pascoglu threw up his hands, stamped to the end of the room and back. "Enough of this foolery!" he roared. "Bonze, get out of here!"

Magnus Ridolph once more took it upon himself to interpret. "Pan Pascoglu conveys his compliments, and begs that you excuse him until he can find leisure to study your views more carefully."

The bonze bowed and withdrew. Pascoglu said bitterly, "When this is over, you and the bonze can chop logic to your heart's content. I'm sick of talk; I want to see some action." He pushed a button. "Ask that Journey's End woman— Miss Thousand Candles, whatever her name is—to come into the library."

Magnus Ridolph raised his eyebrows. "What do you intend?"

Pascoglu refused to meet Magnus Ridolph's gaze. "I'm going to talk to these people and find out what they know."

"I fear that you waste time."

"Nevertheless," said Pascoglu doggedly. "I've got to make a start somewhere. Nobody ever learned anything lying low in the library."

"I take it then that you no longer require my services?"

Pascoglu chewed irritably at his mustache. "Frankly, Mr. Ridolph, you move a little too slow to suit me. This is a serious affair. I've got to get action fast."

Magnus Ridolph bowed in acquiescence. "I hope you have no objection to my witnessing the interviews?"

"Not at all."

A moment passed, then the door opened and Fiamella of Thousand Candles stood looking in.

Pan Pascoglu and Magnus Ridolph stared in silence. Fiamella wore a simple beige frock, soft leather sandals. Her arms and legs were bare, her skin only slightly paler than the frock. In her hair she wore a small orange flower.

Pascoglu somberly gestured her forward; Magnus Ridolph retired to a seat across the room.

"Yes, what is it?" asked Fiamella in a soft, sweet voice.

"You no doubt have learned of Mr. Bonfils' death?" asked Pascoglu.

"Oh yes!"

"And you are not disturbed?"

"I am very happy, of course."

"Indeed." Pascoglu cleared his throat. "I understand that you have referred to yourself as Mrs. Bonfils."

Fiamella nodded. "That is how you say it. On Journey's End we say he is Mr. Fiamella. I pick him out. But he ran away, which is a great harm. So I came after him, I tell him I kill him if he will not come back to Journey's End."

Pascoglu jumped forward like a terrier, stabbed the air with a stubby forefinger. "Ah! Then you admit you killed him!"

"No, no," she cried indignantly. "With a fire gun? You insult me! You are so bad as Bonfils. Better be careful, I kill you."

Pascoglu stood back startled. He turned to Magnus Ridolph. "You heard her, Ridolph?"

"Indeed, indeed."

Fiamella nodded vigorously. "You laugh at a woman's beauty; what else does she have? So she kills you, and no more insult."

"Just how do you kill, Miss Fiamella?" asked Magnus Ridolph politely.

"I kill by love, naturally. I come like this—" she stepped forward, stopped, stood rigid before Pascoglu, looking into his eyes. "I raise my hands—" she slowly lifted her arms, held her palms toward Pascoglu's face. "I turn around, I walk away." She did so, glancing over her shoulder. "I come back." She came running back. "And soon you say, 'Fiamella, let me touch you, let me feel your skin.' And I say, 'No!' And I walk around behind you, and blow on your neck—"

"Stop it!" said Pascoglu uneasily.

"—and pretty soon you go pale and your hands shake and you cry, 'Fiamella, Fiamella of Thousand Candles, I love you, I die for love!' Then I come in when it is almost dark and I wear only flowers, and you cry out, 'Fiamella!' Next I—"

"I think the picture is clear," said Magnus Ridolph suavely. "When Mr. Pascoglu recovers his breath, he surely will apologize for insulting you. As for myself, I can conceive of no more pleasant form of extinction, and I am half-tempted to—"

She gave his beard a playful tweak. "You are too old."

Magnus Ridolph agreed mournfully. "I fear that you are right. For a moment I had deceived myself…You may go, Miss Fiamella of Thousand Candles. Please return to Journey's End. Your estranged husband is dead; no one will ever dare insult you again."

Fiamella smiled in a kind of sad gratification and with soft lithe steps went to the door, where she halted, turned. "You want to find out who burned poor Lester?"

"Yes, of course," said Pascoglu eagerly.

"You know the priests of Cambyses?"

"Fodor Impliega, Fodor Banzoso?"

Fiamella nodded. "They hated Lester. They said, 'Give us one of your savage slaves. Too long a time has gone past, we must send a soul to our god.' Lester said, 'No!' They were very angry, and talked together about Lester."

Pascoglu nodded thoughtfully. "I see. I'll certainly make inquiries of these priests. Thank you for your information."

Fiamella departed. Pascoglu went to the wall mesh. "Send Fodor Impliega and Fodor Banzoso here, please."

There was a pause, then the voice of the clerk responded: "They are busy, Mr. Pascoglu, some sort of rite or other. They said they'll only be a few minutes."

"Mmph…Well, send in Viamestris Diasporus."

"Yes, sir."

"For your information," said Magnus Ridolph, "Viamestris Diasporus comes from a world where gladiatorial sports are highly popular, where successful gladiators are the princes of society, especially the amateur gladiator, who may be a high-ranking nobleman, fighting merely for public acclamation and prestige."

Pascoglu turned around. "If Diasporus is an amateur gladiator, I would think he'd be pretty callous. He wouldn't care who he killed!"

"I merely present such facts as I have gleaned through the morning's research. You must draw your own conclusions."

Pascoglu grunted.

In the doorway appeared Viamestris Diasporus, the tall man with the ferocious aquiline head whom Magnus Ridolph had noticed in the lobby. He inspected the interior of the library carefully.

"Enter, if you please," said Pascoglu. "I am conducting an inquiry into the death of Lester Bonfils. It is possible that you may help us."

Diasporus' narrow face elongated in surprise. "The killer has not announced himself?"

"Unfortunately, no."

Diasporus made a swift gesture, a nod of the head, as if suddenly all were clear. "Bonfils was evidently of the lowest power, and the killer is ashamed of his feat, rather than proud."

Pascoglu rubbed the back of his head. "To ask a hypothetical question, Mr. Diasporus, suppose you had killed Bonfils, what reason—"

Diasporus cut the air with his hand. "Ridiculous! I would only mar my record with a victory so small."

"But, assuming that you had reason to kill him—"

"What reason could there be? He belonged to no recognized gens, he had issued no challenges, he was of stature insufficient to drag the sand of the arena."

Pascoglu spoke querulously: "But if he had done you an injury—"

Magnus Ridolph interjected a question: "For the sake of argument, let us assume that Mr. Bonfils had flung white paint on the front of your house."

In two great strides Diasporus was beside Magnus Ridolph, the feral bony face peering down. "What is this, what has he done?"

"He has done nothing. He is dead. I ask the question merely for the enlightenment of Mr. Pascoglu."

"Ah! I understand. I would have such a cur poisoned. Evidently Bonfils had committed no such solecism, for I understand that he died decently, through a weapon of prestige."

Pascoglu turned his eyes to the ceiling, held out his hands. "Thank you, Mr. Diasporus, thank you for your help."

Diasporus departed; Pascoglu went to the wall-mesh. "Please send Mr. Thorn 199 to the library."

They waited in silence. Presently Thorn 199 appeared, a wiry little man with a rather large round head, evidently of a much mutated race. His skin was a waxy yellow; he wore gay garments of blue and orange, with a red collar and rococo red slippers.

Pascoglu had recovered his poise. "Thank you for coming, Mr. Thorn. I am trying to establish—"

Magnus Ridolph said in a thoughtful voice, "Excuse me. May I make a suggestion?"

"Well?" snapped Pascoglu.

"I fear Mr. Thorn is not wearing the clothes he would prefer for so important an inquiry as this. For his own sake he will be the first to wish to change into black and white, with, of course, a black hat."

Thorn 199 darted Magnus Ridolph a glance of enormous hatred.

Pascoglu was puzzled. He glanced from Magnus Ridolph to Thorn 199 and back.

"These garments are adequate," rasped Thorn 199. "After all, we discuss nothing of consequence."

"Ah, but we do! We inquire into the death of Lester Bonfils."

"Of which I know nothing!"

"Then surely you will have no objection to black and white."

Thorn 199 swung on his heel and left the library.

"What's all this talk about black and white?" demanded Pascoglu.

Magnus Ridolph indicated a strip of film still in the viewer. "This morning I had occasion to review the folkways of the Kolar Peninsula on Duax. The symbology of clothes is especially fascinating. For instance, the blue and orange in which Thorn 199 just now appeared induces a frivolous attitude, a light-hearted disregard for what we Earthmen would speak of as 'fact'. Black and white, however, are the vestments of responsibility and sobriety. When these colors are supplemented by a black hat, the Kolarians are constrained to truth."

Pascoglu nodded in a subdued fashion. "Well, in the meantime, I'll talk to the two priests of Cambyses." He glanced rather apologetically at Magnus Ridolph. "I hear that they practice human sacrifice on Cambyses; is that right?"

"Perfectly correct," said Magnus Ridolph.

The two priests, Fodor Impliega and Fodor Banzoso, presently appeared, both corpulent and unpleasant-looking, with red flushed faces, full lips, eyes half-submerged in the swelling folds of their cheeks.

Pascoglu assumed his official manner. "I am inquiring into the death of Lester Bonfils. You two were fellow passengers with him aboard the *Maulerer Princeps;* perhaps you noticed something which might shed some light on his death."

The priests pouted, blinked, shook their heads. "We are not interested in such men as Bonfils."

"You yourselves had no dealings with him?"

The priests stared at Pascoglu, eyes like four knobs of stone.

Pascoglu prompted them. "I understand you wanted to sacrifice one of Bonfils' palaeolithics. Is this true?"

"You do not understand our religion," said Fodor Impliega in a flat plangent voice. "The great god Camb exists in each one of us, we are all parts of the whole, the whole of the parts."

Fodor Banzoso amplified the statement. "You used the word 'sacrifice'. This is incorrect. You should say, 'go to join Camb'. It is like going to the fire for warmth, and the fire becomes warmer the more souls that come to join it."

"I see, I see," said Pascoglu. "Bonfils refused to give you one of his palaeolithics for a sacrifice—"

"Not 'sacrifice'!"

"—so you became angry, and last night you sacrificed Bonfils himself!"

"May I interrupt?" asked Magnus Ridolph. "I think I may save time for everyone. As you know, Mr. Pascoglu, I spent a certain period this morning in research. I chanced on a description of the Cambygian sacrificial rites. In order for the rite to be valid, the victim must kneel, bow his head forward. Two skewers are driven into his ears, and the victim is left in this position, kneeling, face down, in a state of ritual composure. Bonfils was sprawled without regard for any sort of decency. I suggest that Fodor Impliega and Fodor Banzoso are guiltless, at least of this particular crime."

"True, true," said Fodor Impliega. "Never would we leave a corpse in such disorder."

Pascoglu blew out his cheeks. "Temporarily, that's all."

At this moment Thorn 199 returned, wearing skin-tight black pantaloons, white blouse, a black jacket, a black tricorn hat. He sidled into the library, past the departing priests.

"You need ask but a single question," said Magnus Ridolph. "What clothes was he wearing at midnight last night?"

"Well?" asked Pascoglu. "What clothes were you wearing?"

"I wore blue and purple."

"Did you kill Lester Bonfils?"

"No."

"Undoubtedly Mr. Thorn 199 is telling the truth," said Magnus Ridolph. "The Kolarians will perform violent deeds only when wearing gray pantaloons or the combination of green jacket and red hat. I think you may safely eliminate Mr. Thorn 199."

"Very well," said Pascoglu. "I guess that's all, Mr. Thorn."

Thorn 199 departed, and Pascoglu examined his list with a dispirited attitude. He spoke into the mesh. "Ask Mr. Hercules Starguard to step in."

Hercules Starguard was a young man of great physical charm. His hair was a thick crop of flaxen curls, his eyes were blue as sapphires. He wore mustard-colored breeches, a flaring black jacket, swaggering black short-boots. Pascoglu rose from the chair into which he had sank. "Mr. Starguard, we are trying to learn something about the tragic death of Mr. Bonfils."

"Not guilty," said Hercules Starguard. "I didn't kill the swine."

Pascoglu raised his eyebrows. "You had reason to dislike Mr. Bonfils?"

"Yes, I would say I disliked Mr. Bonfils."

"And what was the cause of this dislike?"

Hercules Starguard looked contemptuously down his nose at Pascoglu. "Really, Mr. Pascoglu, I can't see how my emotions affect your inquiry."

"Only," said Pascoglu, "if you were the person who killed Mr. Bonfils."

Starguard shrugged. "I'm not."

"Can you demonstrate this to my satisfaction?"

"Probably not."

Magnus Ridolph leaned forward. "Perhaps I can help Mr. Starguard."

Pascoglu glared at him. "Please, Mr. Ridolph, I don't think Mr. Starguard needs help."

"I only wish to clarify the situation," said Magnus Ridolph.

"So you clarify me out of all my suspects," snapped Pascoglu. "Very well, what is it this time?"

"Mr. Starguard is an Earthman, and is subject to the influence of our basic Earth culture. Unlike many men and near-men of the outer worlds, he has been inculcated with the idea that human life is valuable, that he who kills will be punished."

"That doesn't stop murderers," grunted Pascoglu.

"But it restrains an Earthman from killing in the presence of witnesses."

"Witnesses? The palaeolithics? What good are they as witnesses?"

"Possibly none whatever, in a legal sense. But they are important indicators, since the presence of human onlookers would deter an Earthman from murder. For this reason, I believe we may eliminate Mr. Starguard from serious consideration as a suspect."

Pascoglu's jaw dropped. "But—who is left?" He looked at the list. "The Hecatean." He spoke into the mesh. "Send in Mr..." He frowned. "Send in the Hecatean to us now."

The Hecatean was the sole non-human of the group, although outwardly he showed great organic similarity to true man. He was tall and stick-legged, with dark brooding eyes in a hard chitin-sheathed white face. His hands were elastic fingerless flaps: here was his most obvious differentiation from humanity. He paused in the doorway, surveying the interior of the room.

"Come in, Mr.—" Pascoglu paused in irritation. "I don't know your name; you have refused to confide it, and I cannot address you properly. Nevertheless, if you will be good enough to enter…"

The Hecatean stepped forward. "You men are amusing beasts. Each of you has his private name. I know who I am, why must I label myself? It is a racial idiosyncrasy, the need to fix a sound to each reality."

"We like to know what we're talking about," said Pascoglu. "That's how we fix objects in our minds, with names."

"And thereby you miss the great intuitions," said the Hecatean. His voice was solemn and hollow. "But you have called me here to question me about the man labeled Bonfils. He is dead."

"Exactly," said Pascoglu. "Do you know who killed him?"

"Certainly," said the Hecatean. "Does not everyone know?"

"No," said Pascoglu. "Who is it?"

The Hecatean looked around the room, and when he returned to Pascoglu, his eyes were blank as holes into a crypt.

"Evidently I was mistaken. If I knew, the person involved wishes his deed to pass unnoticed, and why should I disoblige him? If I did know, I don't know."

Pascoglu began to splutter, but Magnus Ridolph interceded in a grave voice. "A reasonable attitude."

Pascoglu's cup of wrath boiled over. "I think his attitude is disgraceful! A murder has been committed, this creature claims he knows, and will not tell… I have a good mind to confine him to his quarters until the patrol ship passes."

"If you do so," said the Hecatean, "I will discharge the contents of my spore sac into the air. You will presently find your Hub inhabited by a hundred thousand animalcules, and if you injure a single one of them, you will be guilty of the same crime that you are now investigating."

Pascoglu went to the door, flung it aside. "Go! Leave! Take the next ship out of here! I'll never allow you back!"

The Hecatean departed without comment. Magnus Ridolph rose to his feet and prepared to follow. Pascoglu held up his hand. "Just a minute, Mr. Ridolph. I need advice. I was hasty, I lost my head."

Magnus Ridolph considered. "Exactly what do you require of me?"

"Find the murderer! Get me out of this mess!"

"These requirements might be contradictory."

Pascoglu sank into a chair, passed a hand over his eyes. "Don't make me out puzzles, Mr. Ridolph."

"Actually, Mr. Pascoglu, you have no need of my services. You have interviewed the suspects, you have at least a cursory acquaintance with the civilizations which have shaped them."

"Yes, yes," muttered Pascoglu. He brought out the list, stared at it, then looked sidewise at Magnus Ridolph. "Which one? Diasporus? Did he do it?"

Magnus Ridolph pursed his lips doubtfully. "He is a knight of the Dacca, an amateur gladiator evidently of some reputation. A murder of this sort would shatter his self-respect, his confidence. I put the probability at 1 percent."

"Hmph. What about Fiamella of Thousand Candles? She admits she set out to kill him."

Magnus Ridolph frowned. "I wonder. Death by means of amorous attrition is of course not impossible—but are not Fiamella's motives ambiguous? From what I gather, her reputation was injured by Bonfils' disinclination, and she thereupon set out to repair her reputation. If she could harass poor Bonfils to his doom by her charm and seductions, she would gain great face. She had everything to lose if he died in any other fashion. Probability: 1 percent."

"Hymph. What of Thorn 199?"

Magnus Ridolph held out his hands. "He was not dressed in his killing clothes. It is as simple as that. Probability: 1 percent."

"Well," cried Pascoglu, "what of the priests, Banzoso and Impliega? They needed a sacrifice to their god."

Magnus Ridolph shook his head. "The job was a botch. A sacrifice so slipshod would earn them ten thousand years of perdition."

Pascoglu made a half-hearted suggestion. "Suppose they didn't really believe that?"

"Then why trouble at all?" asked Magnus Ridolph. "Probability: 1 percent."

"Well, there's Starguard," mused Pascoglu, "but you insist he wouldn't commit murder in front of witnesses..."

"It seems highly unlikely," said Magnus Ridolph. "Of course we could speculate that Bonfils was a charlatan, that the palaeolithics were impostors, that Starguard was somehow involved in the deception..."

"Yes," said Pascoglu eagerly. "I was thinking something like that myself."

"The only drawback to the theory is that it cannot possibly be correct. Bonfils is an anthropologist of wide reputation. I observed the palaeolithics, and I believe them to be authentic primitives. They are shy and confused. Civilized men attempting to mimic barbarity unconsciously exaggerate the brutishness of their subject. The barbarian, adapting to the ways of civilization, comports himself to the model set by his preceptor—in this case Bonfils. Observing them at dinner, I was amused by their careful aping of Bonfils' manners. Then, when we were inspecting the corpse, they were clearly bewildered, subdued, frightened. I could discern no trace of the crafty calculation by which a civilized man would hope to extricate himself from an uncomfortable situation. I think we may assume that Bonfils and his palaeolithics were exactly as they represented themselves."

Pascoglu jumped to his feet, paced back and forth. "Then the palaeolithics could not have killed Bonfils."

"Probability minuscule. And if we concede their genuineness, we must abandon the idea that Starguard was their accomplice, and we rule him out on the basis of the cultural qualm I mentioned before."

"Well—the Hecatean, then. What of him?"

"He is a more unlikely murderer than all the others," said Magnus Ridolph. "For three reasons: First, he is non-human, and has no experience with rage and revenge. On Hecate violence is unknown. Secondly, as a non-human, he would have no points of engagement with Bonfils. A leopard does not attack a tree; they are different orders of beings. So with the Hecatean. Thirdly, it would be, physically as well as psychologically, impossible for the Hecatean to kill Bonfils. His hands have no fingers; they are flaps of sinew. They could not manipulate a trigger inside a trigger-guard. I think you may dispense with the Hecatean."

"But who is there left?" cried Pascoglu in desperation.

"Well, there is you, there is me and there is—"

The door slid back; the bonze in the red cloak looked into the room.

V

"Come in, come in," said Magnus Ridolph with cordiality. "Our business is just now complete. We have established that of all the persons here at the Hub, only you would have killed Lester Bonfils, and so now we have no further need for the library."

"What!" cried Pascoglu, staring at the bonze, who made a deprecatory gesture.

"I had hoped," said the bonze, "that my part in the affair would escape notice."

"You are too modest," said Magnus Ridolph. "It is only fitting that a man should be known for his good works."

The bonze bowed. "I want no encomiums. I merely do my duty. And if you are truly finished in here, I have a certain amount of study before me."

"By all means. Come, Mr. Pascoglu; we are inconsiderate, keeping the worthy bonze from his meditations." And Magnus Ridolph drew the stupefied Pan Pascoglu into the corridor.

"Is he—is he the murderer?" asked Pascoglu feebly.

"He killed Lester Bonfils," said Magnus Ridolph. "That is clear enough."

"But why?"

"Out of the kindness of his heart. Bonfils spoke to me for a moment. He clearly was suffering considerable psychic damage."

"But—he could be cured!" exclaimed Pascoglu indignantly. "It wasn't necessary to kill him to soothe his feelings."

"Not according to our viewpoint," said Magnus Ridolph. "But you must recall that the bonze is a devout believer in—well, let us call it 'reincarnation'. He conceived himself performing a happy release for poor tormented Bonfils who came to him for help. He killed him for his own good."

They entered Pascoglu's office; Pascoglu went to stare out the window. "But what am I to do?" he muttered.

"That," said Magnus Ridolph, "is where I cannot advise you."

"It doesn't seem right to penalize the poor bonze…It's ridiculous. How could I possibly go about it?"

"The dilemma is real," agreed Magnus Ridolph.

There was a moment of silence, during which Pascoglu morosely tugged at his mustache. Then Magnus Ridolph said, "Essentially, you wish to protect your clientele from further applications of misplaced philanthropy."

"That's the main thing!" cried Pascoglu. "I could pass off Bonfils' death—explain that it was accidental. I could ship the palaeolithics back to their planet…"

"I would likewise separate the bonze from persons showing even the mildest melancholy. For if he is energetic and dedicated, he might well seek to extend the range of his beneficence."

Pascoglu suddenly put his hand to his cheek. He turned wide eyes to Magnus Ridolph. "This morning I felt pretty low. I was talking to the bonze… I told him all my troubles. I complained about expense—"

The door slid quietly aside; the bonze peered in, a half-smile on his benign face. "Do I intrude?" he asked as he spied Magnus Ridolph. "I had hoped to find you alone, Mr. Pascoglu."

"I was just going," said Magnus Ridolph politely. "If you'll excuse me…"

"No, no!" cried Pascoglu. "Don't go, Mr. Ridolph!"

"Another time will do as well," said the bonze politely. The door closed behind him.

"Now I feel worse than ever," Pascoglu moaned.

"Best to conceal it from the bonze," said Magnus Ridolph.

Afterword to "Coup de Grâce"

"No one can teach anybody how to write. People go to writing classes because they want to write and they grab at any straw. The best I think you can do is teach people punctuation, spelling…and conceivably put the idea of rhythm in their heads. Aside from that, what can you teach them? I think the best way you teach someone to be a writer is to force them to read twenty books I would set out for them: *Don Quixote*, *Wind in the Willows*, works of P.G. Wodehouse, the *Oz* books, *The London Times Historical Atlas* (my favorite book—I don't know of anything that's more clutching for the imagination), *Watership Down*—there must be others on that list."

—Jack Vance 1986

Chateau d'If

i

The advertisement appeared on a telescreen commercial, and a few days later at the side of the news-fax. The copy was green on a black background, a modest rectangle among the oranges, reds, yellows. The punch was carried in the message:

Jaded? Bored?

Want ADVENTURE?

Try the Chateau d'If

The Oxonian Terrace was a pleasant area of quiet in the heart of the city—a red-flagged rectangle dotted with beach umbrellas, tables, lazy people. A bank of magnolia trees screened off the street and filtered out most of the street noise; the leakage, a soft sound like surf, underlay the conversation and the irregular thud-thud-thud from the Oxonian handball courts.

Roland Mario sat in complete relaxation, half-slumped, head back, feet propped on the spun-air and glass table—in the same posture as his four companions. Watching them under half-closed lids, Mario pondered the ancient mystery of human personality. How could men be identical and yet each completely unique?

To his left sat Breaugh, a calculator repairman. He had a long bony nose, round eyes, heavy black eyebrows, a man deft with his fingers, methodical and patient. He had a Welsh name, and he looked the pure ancient Welsh type, the small dark men that had preceded Caesar, preceded the Celts.

Next to him sat Janniver. North Europe, Africa, the Orient had combined to shape his brain and body. An accountant by trade, he was a tall spare man with short yellow hair. He had a long face with features that first had been carved, then kneaded back, blunted. He was cautious, thoughtful, a tough opponent on the handball court.

Zaer was the quick one, the youngest of the group. Fair-skinned with red cheeks, dark curly hair, eyes gay as valentines, he talked the most, laughed the most, occasionally lost his temper.

Beside him sat Ditmar, a sardonic man with keen narrow eyes, a high forehead, and a dark bronze skin from Polynesia, the Sudan, or India, or South America. He played no handball, consumed fewer highballs than the others, because of a liver disorder. He occupied a well-paying executive position with one of the television networks.

And Mario himself, how did they see him? He considered. Probably a different picture in each of their minds, although there were few pretensions or striking features to his exterior. He had nondescript pleasant features, hair and eyes without distinction, skin the average golden-brown. Medium height, medium weight, quiet-spoken, quietly dressed. He knew he was well-liked, so far as the word had meaning among the five; they had been thrown together not so much by congeniality as by the handball court and a common bachelorhood.

Mario became aware of the silence. He finished his highball. "Anyone go another round?"

Breaugh made a gesture of assent.

"I've got enough," said Janniver.

Zaer tilted the glass down his throat, set it down with a thud. "At the age of four I promised my father never to turn down a drink."

Ditmar hesitated, then said, "Might as well spend my money on liquor as anything else."

"That's all money is good for," said Breaugh. "To buy a little fun into your life."

"A lot of money buys a lot of fun," said Ditmar morosely. "Try and get the money."

Zaer gestured, a wide fanciful sweep of the arm. "Be an artist, an inventor, create something, build something. There's no future working for wages."

"Look at this new crop of school-boy wonders," said Breaugh sourly. "Where in the name of get-out do they come from? Spontaneous generation by the action of sunlight on slime?…All of a sudden, nothing but unsung geniuses, everywhere you look. De Satz, Coley—atomicians. Honn, Versovitch, Lekky, Brule, Richards—administrators. Gandelip, New, Cardosa—financiers. Dozens of them, none over twenty-three, twenty-four. All of 'em come up like meteors."

"Don't forget Pete Zaer," said Zaer. "He's another one, but he hasn't meteored yet. Give him another year."

"Well," muttered Ditmar, "maybe it's a good thing. Somebody's got to do our thinking for us. We're fed, we're clothed, we're educated, we work at soft jobs, and good liquor's cheap. That's all life means for ninety-nine out of a hundred."

"If they'd only take the hangover out of the liquor," sighed Zaer.

"Liquor's a release from living," said Janniver somberly. "Drunkenness is about the only adventure left. Drunkenness and death."

"Yes," said Breaugh. "You can always show contempt for life by dying."

Zaer laughed. "Whiskey or cyanide. Make mine whiskey."

Fresh highballs appeared. They shook dice for the tab. Mario lost, signed the check.

After a moment Breaugh said, "It's true though. Drunkenness and death. The unpredictables. The only two places left to go—unless you can afford twenty million dollars for a planetary rocket. And even then there's only dead rock after you get there."

Ditmar said, "You overlooked a third possibility."

"What's that?"

"The Chateau d'If."

All sat quiet; then all five shifted in their chairs, settling back or straightening themselves.

"Just what is the Chateau d'If?" asked Mario.

"Where is it?" asked Zaer. "The advertisement said 'Try the Chateau d'If', but it said nothing about how or where."

Janniver grunted. "Probably a new nightclub."

Mario shook his head doubtfully. "The advertisement gave a different impression."

"It's not a nightclub," said Ditmar. All eyes swung to him. "No, I don't know what it is. I know where it is, but only because there's been rumors a couple months now."

"What kind of rumors?"

"Oh—nothing definite. Just hints. To the effect that if you want adventure, if you've got money to pay for it, if you're willing to take a chance, if you have no responsibilities you can't abandon—"

"If—if—if," said Breaugh with a grin. "The Chateau d'If."

Ditmar nodded. "That's it exactly."

"Is it dangerous?" asked Zaer. "If all they do is string a tight-wire across a snake pit, turn a tiger loose at you, and you can either walk tightrope or fight tiger, I'd rather sit here and drink high-balls and figure how to beat Janniver in the tournament."

Ditmar shrugged. "I don't know."

Breaugh frowned. "It could be a dope-den, a new kind of bordello."

"There's no such thing," said Zaer. "It's a haunted house with real ghosts."

"If we're going to include fantasy," said Ditmar, "a time machine."

"If," said Breaugh.

There was a short ruminative silence.

"It's rather peculiar," said Mario. "Ditmar says there've been rumors a couple months now. And last week an advertisement."

"What's peculiar about it?" asked Janniver. "That's the sequence in almost any new enterprise."

Breaugh said quickly, "That's the key word—'enterprise'. The Chateau d'If is not a natural phenomenon; it's a man-created object, idea, process—whatever it is. The motive behind it is a human motive—probably money."

"What else?" asked Zaer whimsically.

Breaugh raised his black eyebrows high. "Oh, you never know. Now, it can't be a criminal enterprise, otherwise the ACP would be swarming all over it."

Ditmar leaned back, swung Breaugh a half-mocking look. "The Agency of Crime Prevention can't move unless there's an offense, unless someone signs a complaint. If there's no overt offense, no complaint, the law can't move."

Breaugh made an impatient gesture. "Very true. But that's a side issue to the idea I was trying to develop."

Ditmar grinned. "Sorry. Go on."

"What are the motives which prompt men to new enterprises? First, money, which in a sense comprises, includes, all of the other motives too. But for the sake of clarity, call this first, the desire for money, an end in itself. Second, there's the will for power. Subdivide that last into, say, the crusading instinct and call it a desire for unlimited sexual opportunity. Power over women. Then third, curiosity, the desire to know. Fourth, the enterprise for its own sake, as a diversion. Like a millionaire's race-horses. Fifth, philanthropy. Any more?"

"Covers it," said Zaer.

"Possibly the urge for security, such as the Egyptian pyramids," suggested Janniver.

"I think that's the fundamental motive behind the first category, the lust for money."

"Artistic spirit, creativeness."

"Oh, far-fetched, I should say."

"Exhibitionism," Ditmar put forward.

"Equally far-fetched."

"I disagree. A theatrical performance is based solely and exclusively, from the standpoint of the actors, upon their mania for exhibitionism."

Breaugh shrugged. "You're probably right."

"Religious movements, missions."

"Lump that under the will to administer power."

"It sticks out at the edges."

"Not far…That all? Good. What does it give us? Anything suggestive?"

"The Chateau d'If!" mused Janniver. "It still sounds like an unnecessarily florid money-making scheme."

"It's not philanthropy—at least superficially," said Mario. "But probably we could fabricate situations that would cover any of your cases."

Ditmar made an impatient gesture. "Talk's useless. What good is it? Not any of us know for sure. Suppose it's a plot to blow up the city?"

Breaugh said coolly, "I appoint you a committee of one, Ditmar, to investigate and report."

Ditmar laughed sourly. "I'd be glad to. But I've got a better idea. Let's roll the dice. Low man applies to the Chateau d'If—financed by the remaining four."

Breaugh nodded. "Suits me. I'll roll with you."

Ditmar looked around the table.

"What's it cost?" asked Zaer.

Ditmar shook his head. "I've no idea. Probably comes high."

Zaer frowned, moved uneasily in his seat. "Set a limit of two thousand dollars per capita."

"Good, so far as I'm concerned. Janniver?"

The tall man with the short yellow hair hesitated. "Yes, I'll roll. I've nothing to lose."

"Mario?"

"Suits me."

Ditmar took up the dice box, cupped it with his hand, rattled the dice. "The rules are for poker dice. One throw, ace high. In other words, a pair of aces beats a pair of sixes. Straight comes between three of a kind and a full house. That suit everybody?…Who wants to roll first?"

"Go ahead, shoot," said Mario mildly.

Ditmar shook, shook, shook, turned the dice out. Five bodies leaned forward, five pair of eyes followed the whirling cubes. They clattered down the table, clanged against a highball glass, came to rest.

"Looks like three fives," said Ditmar. "Well, that's medium good."

Mario, sitting on his left, picked up the box, tossed the dice in, shook, threw. He grunted. A two, a three, a four, a five, a four. "Pair of fours. Ouch."

Breaugh threw silently. "Three aces."

Janniver threw. "Two pair. Deuces and threes."

Zaer, a little pale, picked up the dice. He flashed a glance at Mario. "Pair of fours to beat." He shook the dice, shook—then threw with a sudden flourish. Clang, clatter among the glasses. Five pairs of eyes looked. Ace, deuce, three, six, deuce.

"Pair of deuces."

Zaer threw himself back with a tight grin. "Well, I'm game. I'll go. It's supposed to be an adventure. Of course they don't say whether you come out alive or not."

"You should be delighted," said Breaugh, stuffing tobacco in his pipe. "After all it's our money that's buying you this mysterious thrill."

Zaer made a helpless gesture with both hands. "Where do I go? What do I do?" He looked at Ditmar. "Where do I get this treatment?"

"I don't know," said Ditmar. "I'll ask at the studio. Somebody knows somebody who's been there. Tomorrow about this time I'll have the details, as much as I can pick up, at any rate."

Now came a moment of silence—a silence combined of several peculiar qualities. Each of the five contributed a component, but which the wariness, which the fear, which the quiet satisfaction, it was impossible to say.

Breaugh set down his glass. "Well, Zaer, what do you think? Ready for the tightrope or the tiger?"

"Better take a pair of brass knuckles or a ring-flash," said Ditmar with a grin.

Zaer glanced around the circle of eyes, laughed ruefully. "The interest you take in me is flattering."

"We want a full report. We want you to come out alive."

Zaer said, "I want to come out alive too. Who's going to stake me to the smelling salts and adrenaline, in case the adventure gets really adventurous?"

"Oh, you look fit enough," said Breaugh. He rose to his feet. "I've got to feed my cats. There's the adventure in my life—taking care of seven cats. Quite a futile existence. The cats love it." He gave a sardonic snort. "We're living a life men have dreamed of living ever since they first dreamed. Food, leisure, freedom. We don't know when we're well off."

ii

Zaer was scared. He held his arms tight against his body, and his grin, while wide and ready as ever, was a half-nervous grimace, twisted off to the side. He made no bones about his apprehension, and sat in his chair on the terrace like a prizefighter waiting for the gong.

Janniver watched him solemnly, drinking beer. "Maybe the idea of the Chateau d'If is adventure enough."

"'What is adventure?' asked jesting Zaer, and did not stay for the answer," said Breaugh, eyes twinkling. He loaded his pipe.

"Adventure is just another name for having the daylights scared out of you and living to tell about it," said Zaer wretchedly.

Mario laughed. "If you never show up again, we'll know it wasn't a true adventure."

Breaugh craned his neck around. "Where's Ditmar? He's the man with all the information."

"Here he comes," said Zaer. "I feel like a prisoner."

"Oh, the devil!" said Breaugh. "You don't need to go through with it if you don't want to. After all, it's just a lark. No matter of life or death."

Zaer shook his head. "No, I'll try her on."

Ditmar pulled up a chair, punched the service button, ordered beer. Without preamble he said, "It costs eight thousand. It costs you eight thousand, that is. There's two levels. Type A costs ten million; Type B, ten thousand, but they'll take eight. Needless to say, none of us can go two and a half million, so you're signed up on the Type B schedule."

Zaer grimaced. "Don't like the sound of it. It's like a fun house at the carnival. Some of 'em go through the bumps, others stand around watching, waiting for somebody's dress to blow up. And there's the lad who turns the valves, throws the switches. He has the real fun."

Ditmar said, "I've already paid the eight thousand, so you fellows can write me checks. We might as well get that part over now, while I've got you all within reach."

He tucked the checks from Mario, Janniver and Breaugh into his wallet. "Thanks." He turned to Zaer. "This evening at six o'clock, go to this address." He pushed a card across the table. "Give whoever answers the door this card."

Breaugh and Mario, on either side of Zaer, leaned over, scrutinized the card along with Zaer. It read:

> THE CHATEAU D'IF
> 5600 Exmoor Avenue
> Meadowlands

In the corner were scribbled the words: "Zaer, by Sutlow."

"I had to work like blazes to get it," said Ditmar. "It seems they're keeping it exclusive. I had to swear to all kinds of things about you. Now for heaven's sake, Zaer, don't turn out to be an ACP agent or I'm done with Sutlow, and he's my boss."

"ACP?" Zaer raised his eyebrows. "Is it—illegal?"

"I don't know," said Ditmar. "That's what I'm spending two thousand dollars on you for."

"I hope you have a damn good memory," said Breaugh with a cool grin. "Because—if you live—I want two thousand dollars' worth of vicarious adventure."

"If I die," retorted Zaer, "buy yourself a Ouija board; I'll still give you your money's worth."

"Now," said Ditmar, "we'll meet here Tuesdays and Fridays at three—right, fellows?—" he glanced around the faces "—until you show up."

Zaer rose. "Okay. Tuesdays and Fridays at three. Be seeing you." He waved a hand that took in them all, and stumbling slightly, walked away.

"Poor kid," said Breaugh. "He's scared stiff."

Tuesday passed. Friday passed. Another Tuesday, another Friday, and Tuesday came again. Mario, Ditmar, Breaugh, Janniver reached their table at three o'clock, and with subdued greetings, took their seats.

Five minutes, ten minutes passed. Conversation trickled to a halt. Janniver sat square to the table, big arms resting beside his beer, occasionally scratching at his short yellow hair, or rubbing his blunt nose. Breaugh, slouched back in the seat, looked sightlessly out through the passing crowds. Ditmar smoked passively, and Mario twirled and balanced a bit of paper he had rolled into a cylinder.

At three-fifteen Janniver cleared his throat. "I guess he went crazy."

Breaugh grunted. Ditmar smiled a trifle. Mario lit a cigarette, scowled.

Janniver said, "I saw him today."

Six eyes swung to him. "Where?"

"I wasn't going to mention it," said Janniver, "unless he failed to show up today. He's living at the Atlantic-Empire—a suite on the twentieth floor. I bribed the clerk and found that he's been there over a week."

Breaugh said with a wrinkled forehead, eyes black and suspicious, "How did you happen to see him there?"

"I went to check their books. It's on my route. On my way out, I saw Zaer in the lobby, big as life."

"Did he see you?"

Janniver shrugged woodenly. "Possibly. I'm not sure. He seemed rather wrapped up in a woman, an expensive-looking woman."

"Humph," said Ditmar. "Looks like Zaer's got our money's worth, all right."

Breaugh rose. "Let's go call on him, find out why he hasn't been to see us." He turned to Janniver. "Is he registered under his own name?"

Janniver nodded his long heavy head. "As big as life."

Breaugh started away, halted, looked from face to face. "You fellows coming?"

"Yes," said Mario. He rose. So did Ditmar and Janniver.

The Atlantic-Empire Hotel was massive and elegant, equipped with every known device for the feeding, bathing, comforting, amusing, flattering, relaxing, stimulating, assuaging of the men and women able to afford the price.

At the entry a white-coated flunky took the wraps of the most casual visitor, brushed him, offered the woman corsages from an iced case. The hall into the lobby was as hushed as the nave of a cathedral, lined with thirty-foot mirrors. A moving carpet took the guest into the lobby, a great hall in the Gloriana style of fifty years before. An arcade of small shops lined one wall. Here—if the guest cared little for expense—he could buy wrought copper, gold, tantalum; gowns in glowing fabrics of scarlet, purple, indigo; objets from ancient Tibet and the products of Novacraft; cabochons of green Jovian opals, sold by the milligram, blue balticons from Mars, fire diamonds brought from twenty miles under the surface of the Earth; Marathesti cherries preserved in Organdy Liqueur, perfumes pressed from Arctic moss, white marmoreal blooms like the ghosts of beautiful women.

Another entire wall was a single glass panel, the side of the hotel's main swimming pool. Under-water shone blue-green, and there was the splash, the shining wet gold of swimming bodies. The furniture of the lobby was in shades of the same blue-green and gold, with intimacy provided by screens of vines covered with red, black and white blossoms. A golden light suffused the air, heightened the illusion of an enchanted world where people moved in a high-keyed milieu of expensive clothes, fabulous jewelry, elegant wit, careful lovemaking.

Breaugh looked about with a twisted mouth. "Horrible parasites, posing and twittering and debauching each other while the rest of the world works!"

"Oh, come now," said Ditmar. "Don't be so all-fired intense. They're the only ones left who are having any fun."

"I doubt it," said Breaugh. "They're as defeated and futile as anyone else. There's no more place for them to go than there is for us."

"Have you heard of the Empyrean Tower?"

"Oh—vaguely. Some tremendous building out in Meadowlands."

"That's right. A tower three miles high. Somebody's having fun with that project. Designing it, seeing it go up, up, up."

"There's four billion people in the world," said Breaugh. "Only one Empyrean Tower."

"What kind of a world would it be without extremes?" asked Ditmar. "A place like the inside of a filing cabinet. Breathe the air here. It's rich, smells of civilization, tradition."

Mario glanced in surprise at Ditmar, the saturnine wry Ditmar, whom he would have considered the first to sneer at the foibles of the elite.

Janniver said mildly, "I enjoy coming here, myself. In a way, it's an adventure, a look into a different world."

Breaugh snorted. "Only a millionaire can do anything more than look."

"The mass standard of living rises continuously," reflected Mario. "And almost at the same rate the number of millionaires drops. Whether we like it or not, the extremes are coming closer together. In fact, they've almost met."

"And life daily becomes more like a bowl of rich nourishing mush—without salt," said Ditmar. "By all means abolish poverty, but let's keep our millionaires…Oh, well, we came here to find Zaer, not to argue sociology. I suppose we might as well all go together."

They crossed the lobby. The desk clerk, a handsome silver-haired man with a grave face, bowed.

"Is Mr. Zaer in?" Ditmar asked.

"I'll call his suite, sir." A moment later: "No, sir, he doesn't answer. Shall I page him?"

"No," said Ditmar. "We'll look around a bit."

"About an hour ago I believe he crossed the lobby toward the Mauna Hiva. You might try there."

"Thanks."

The Mauna Hiva was a circular room. At its center rose a great mound of weathered rock, overgrown with palms, ferns, a tangle of exotic plants. Three coconut palms slanted across the island, and the whole was lit with a soft watery white light. Below was a bar built of waxed tropical woods, and beyond, at the periphery of the illumination, a ring of tables.

They found Zaer quickly. He sat with a dark-haired woman in the sheath of emerald silk. On the table in front of them moved a number of small glowing many-colored shapes—sparkling, flashing, intense as patterns cut from butterfly wings. It was a ballet, projected in three-dimensional miniature. Tiny figures leaped, danced, posed to entrancing music in a magnificent setting of broken marble columns and Appian cypress trees.

A moment the four stood back, watching in dour amusement.

Breaugh nudged Mario. "By heaven, he acts like he's been doing it all his life!"

Ditmar advanced to the table; the girl turned her long opaque eyes up at him. Zaer glanced up blankly.

"Hello there, Zaer," said Ditmar, a sarcastic smile wreathing his lips. "Have you forgotten your old pals of the Oxonian Terrace?"

Zaer stared blankly. "I'm sorry."

"I suppose you don't know us?" asked Breaugh, looking down his long crooked nose.

Zaer pushed a hand through his mop of curly black hair. "I'm afraid you have the advantage of me, gentlemen."

"Humph," said Breaugh. "Let's get this straight. You're Pete Zaer, are you not?"

"Yes, I am."

Janniver interposed, "Perhaps you'd prefer to speak with us alone?"

Zaer blinked. "Not at all. Go ahead, say it."

"Ever heard of the Chateau d'If?" inquired Breaugh acidly.

"And eight thousand dollars?" added Ditmar. "A joint investment, shall we say?"

Zaer frowned in what Mario could have sworn to be honest bewilderment. "You believe that I owe you eight thousand dollars?"

"Either that, or eight thousand dollars' worth of information."

Zaer shrugged. "Eight thousand dollars?" He reached into his breast pocket, pulled out a bill-fold, counted. "One, two, three, four, five, six, seven, eight. There you are, gentlemen. Whatever it's for, I'm sure I don't know. Maybe I was drunk." He handed eight thousand-dollar bills to the rigid Ditmar. "Anyway now you're satisfied and I hope you'll be good enough to leave." He gestured to the tiny figures, swaying, posturing, to the rapturous music. "We've already missed the Devotional Dance, the main reason we turned it on."

"Zaer," said Mario haltingly. The gay youthful eyes swung to him.

"Yes?—" politely.

"Is this all the report we get? After all, we acted in good faith."

Zaer stared back coldly. "You have eight thousand dollars. I don't know you from Adam's off ox. You claim it, I pay it. That's pretty good faith on my part."

Breaugh pulled at Mario's arm. "Let's go."

iii

Soberly they sat at a table in an unpretentious tavern, drinking beer. For a while none of the four spoke. Four silent figures—tall strong Janniver, with the rough features, the Baltic hair, the African fiber, the Oriental restraint; Breaugh, the nimble-eyed, black-browed and long-nosed; Ditmar, the sardonic autumn-colored man with the sick liver; Mario, normal, modest, pleasant.

Mario spoke first. "If that's what eight thousand buys at the Chateau d'If, I'll volunteer."

"If," said Breaugh shortly.

"It's not reasonable," rumbled Janniver. Among them, his emotions were probably the least disturbed, his sense of order and fitness the most outraged.

Breaugh struck the table with his fist, a light blow, but nevertheless vehement. "It's not reasonable! It violates logic!"

"Your logic," Ditmar pointed out.

Breaugh cocked his head sidewise. "What's yours?"

"I haven't any."

"I maintain that the Chateau d'If is an enterprise," said Breaugh. "At the fee they charged, I figured it for a money-making scheme. It looks like I'm wrong. Zaer was broke a month ago. Or almost so. We gave him eight thousand dollars. He goes to the Chateau d'If, he comes out, takes a suite at the Atlantic-Empire, buys an expensive woman, shoves money at us by the fistful. The only place he could have got it is at the Chateau d'If. Now there's no profit in that kind of business."

"Some of them pay ten million dollars," said Mario softly. "That could take up some of the slack."

Ditmar drank his beer. "What now? Want to shake again?"

No one spoke. At last Breaugh said, "Frankly, I'm afraid to."

Mario raised his eyebrows. "What? With Zaer's climb to riches right in front of you?"

"Odd," mused Breaugh, "that's just what he was saying. That he was one of the meteoric school-boy wonders who hadn't meteored yet. Now he'll probably turn out to be an unsung genius."

"The Chateau still sounds good, if that's what it does for you."

"If," sneered Breaugh.

"If," assented Mario mildly.

Ditmar said with a harsh chuckle, "I've got eight thousand dollars here. Our mutual property. As far as I'm concerned, it's all yours, if you want to take on Zaer's assignment."

Breaugh and Janniver gave acquiescent shrugs.

Mario toyed with the idea. His life was idle, useless. He dabbled in architecture, played handball, slept, ate. A pleasant but meaningless existence. He rose to his feet. "I'm on my way, right now. Give me the eight thousand before I change my mind."

"Here you are," said Ditmar. "Er—in spite of Zaer's example, we'll expect a report. Tuesdays and Fridays at three, on the Oxonian Terrace."

Mario waved gaily, as he pushed out the door into the late afternoon. "Tuesdays and Fridays at three. Be seeing you."

Ditmar shook his head. "I doubt it."

Breaugh compressed his mouth. "I doubt it too."

Janniver merely shook his head...

Exmoor Avenue began in Lanchester, in front of the Power Bank, on the fourth level, swung north, rose briefly to the fifth level where it crossed the Continental Highway, curved back to the west, slanted under Grimshaw Boulevard, dropped to the surface in Meadowlands.

Mario found 5600 Exmoor to be a gray block of a building, not precisely dilapidated, but evidently unloved and uncared-for. A thin indecisive strip of lawn separated it from the road, and a walkway led to a small excrescence of a portico.

With the level afternoon sun shining full on his back, Mario walked to the portico, pressed the button.

A moment passed, then the door slid aside, revealing a short hall. "Please come in," said the soft voice of a commercial welcome-box.

Mario advanced down the hall, aware that radiation was scanning his body for metal or weapons. The hall opened into a green and brown reception room, furnished with a leather settee, a desk, a painting of three slim wide-eyed nudes against a background of a dark forest. A door flicked back, a young woman entered.

Mario tightened his mouth. It was an adventure to look at the girl. She was amazingly beautiful, with a beauty that grew more poignant the longer he considered it. She was slight, small-boned. Her eyes were cool, direct, her jaw and chin fine and firm. She was beautiful in herself, without ornament, ruse or adornment; beautiful almost in spite of herself, as if she regretted the magic of her face. Mario felt cool detachment in her gaze, an impersonal unfriendliness. Human perversity immediately aroused in his brain a desire to shatter the indifference, to arouse passion of one sort or another...He smothered the impulse. He was here on business.

"Your name, please?" Her voice was soft, with a fine grain to it, like precious wood, and pitched in a strange key.

"Roland Mario."

She wrote on a form. "Age?"

"Twenty-nine."

"Occupation?"

"Architect."

"What do you want here?"

"This is the Chateau d'If?"

"Yes." She waited, expectantly.

"I'm a customer."

"Who sent you?"

"No one. I'm a friend of Pete Zaer's. He was here a couple of weeks ago."

She nodded, wrote.

"He seems to have done pretty well for himself," observed Mario cheerfully.

She said nothing until she had finished writing. Then: "This is a business, operated for profit. We are interested in money. How much do you have to spend?"

"I'd like to know what you have to sell."

"Adventure." She said the word without accent or emphasis.

"Ah," said Mario. "I see…Out of curiosity, how does working here affect you? Do you find it an adventure, or are you bored too?"

She shot him a quick glance. "We offer two classes of service. The first we value at ten million dollars. It is cheap at that price, but it is the dullest and least stirring of the two—the situation over which you have some control. The second we value at ten thousand dollars, and this produces the most extreme emotions with the minimum of immediate control on your part."

Mario considered the word 'immediate'. He asked, "Have you been through the treatment?"

Again the cool flick of a glance. "Would you care to indicate how much you wish to spend?"

"I asked you a question," said Mario.

"You will receive further information inside."

"Are you human?" asked Mario. "Do you breathe?"

"Would you care to indicate how much you have to spend?"

Mario shrugged. "I have eight thousand dollars with me." He pursed his lips. "And I'll give you a thousand to stick your tongue out at me."

She dropped the form into a slot, arose. "Follow me, please."

She led him through the door, along a hall, into a small room, bare and stark, lit by a single cone-shaped floor-lamp turned against the ceiling, a room painted white, gray, green. A man sat at a desk punching a calculator. Behind him stood a filing cabinet. There was a faint odor in the air, like mingled mint, gardenias, with a hint of an antiseptic, medicinal scent.

The man looked up, rose to his feet, bowed his head politely. He was young, blond as beach-sand, as magnificently handsome as the girl was beautiful. Mario felt a slight edge form in his brain. One at a time they were admirable, their beauty seemed natural. Together, the beauty cloyed, as if it were something owned and valued highly. It seemed self-conscious and vulgar. And Mario suddenly felt a quiet pride in his own commonplace person.

The man was taller than Mario by several inches. His chest was smooth and wide, corded with powerful sinew. In spite of almost over-careful courtesy, he gave an impression of over-powering, over-riding confidence.

"Mr. Roland Mario," said the girl. She added dryly, "He's got eight thousand dollars."

The young man nodded gravely, reached out his hand. "My name is Mervyn Allen." He looked at the girl. "Is that all, Thane?"

"That's all for tonight." She left.

"Can't keep going on eight thousand a night," grumbled Mervyn Allen. "Sit down, Mr. Mario."

Mario took a seat. "The adventure business must have tremendous expenses," he observed with a tight grin.

"Oh, no," said Allen with wide candid eyes. "To the contrary. The operators have a tremendous avarice. We try to average twenty million a day profit. Occasionally we can't make it."

"Pardon me for annoying you with carfare," said Mario. "If you don't want it, I'll keep it."

Allen made a magnanimous gesture. "As you please."

Mario said, "The receptionist told me that ten million buys the dullest of your services, and ten thousand something fairly wild. What do I get for nothing? Vivisection?"

Allen smiled. "No. You're entirely safe with us. That is to say, you suffer no physical pain, you emerge alive."

"But you won't give me any particulars? After all, I have a fastidious nature. What you'd consider a good joke might annoy me very much."

Mervyn Allen shrugged blandly. "You haven't spent any money yet. You can still leave."

Mario rubbed the arms of his chair with the palms of his hands. "That's rather unfair. I'm interested, but also I'd like to know something of what I'm getting into."

Allen nodded. "Understandable. You're willing to take a chance, but you're not a complete fool. Is that it?"

"Exactly."

Allen straightened a pencil on his desk. "First, I'd like to give you a short psychiatric and medical examination. You understand," and he flashed Mario a bright candid glance, "we don't want any accidents at the Chateau d'If."

"Go ahead," said Mario.

Allen slid open the top of his desk, handed Mario a cap of crinkling plastic in which tiny wires glittered. "Encephalograph pick-up. Please fit it snugly."

Mario grinned. "Call it a lie-detector."

Allen smiled briefly. "A lie-detector, then."

Mario muttered, "I'd like to put it on you."

Allen ignored him, pulled out a pad of printed forms, adjusted a dial in front of him.

"Name?"

"Roland Mario."

"Age?"

"Twenty-eight."

Allen stared at the dial, frowned, looked up questioningly.

"I wanted to see if it worked," said Mario. "I'm twenty-nine."

"It works," said Allen shortly. "Occupation?"

"Architect. At least I dabble at it, design dog-houses and rabbit hutches for my friends. Although I did the Geraf Fleeter Corporation plant in Hanover a year or so ago, pretty big job."

"Hm. Where were you born?"

"Buenos Aires."

"Ever hold any government jobs? Civil Service? Police? Administrative? ACP?"

"No."

"Why not?"

"Red tape. Disgusting bureaucrats."

"Nearest relative?"

"My brother, Arthur Mario. In Callao. Coffee business."

"No wife?"

"No wife."

"Approximate worth? Wealth, possessions, real estate?"

"Oh—sixty, seventy thousand. Modestly comfortable. Enough so that I can loaf all I care to."

"Why did you come to the Chateau d'If?"

"Same reason that everybody else comes. Boredom. Repressed energy. Lack of something to fight against."

Allen laughed. "So you think you'll work off some of that energy fighting the Chateau d'If?"

Mario smiled faintly. "It's a challenge."

"We've got a good thing here," Allen confided. "A wonder it hasn't been done before."

"Perhaps you're right."

"How did you happen to come to the Chateau d'If?"

"Five of us rolled dice. A man named Pete Zaer lost. He came, but he wouldn't speak to us afterwards."

Allen nodded sagely. "We've got to ask that our customers keep our secrets. If there were no mystery, we would have no customers."

"It had better be good," said Mario, "after all the build-up." And he thought he saw a flicker of humor in Allen's eyes.

"It's cheap at ten million."

"And quite dear at ten thousand?" suggested Mario.

Allen leaned back in his chair, and his beautiful face was cold as a marble mask. Mario suddenly thought of the girl in the front office. The same expression of untouchable distance and height. He said, "I suppose you have the same argument with everyone who comes in."

"Identically."

"Well, where do we go from here?"

"Are you healthy? Any organic defects?"

"None."

"Very well. I'll waive the physical."

Mario reached up, removed the encephalograph pick-up. "Now I can lie again."

Allen drummed a moment on the tabletop, reached forward, tossed the mesh back in the desk, scribbled on a sheet of paper, tossed it to Mario. "A contract relieving us of responsibility."

Mario read. In consideration of services rendered, Roland Mario agreed that the Chateau d'If and its principals would not be held responsible for any injuries, physical or psychological, which he might sustain while on the premises, or as a result of his presence on the premises. Furthermore, he waived all rights to prosecute. Any and all transactions, treatments, experiments, events which occurred on, by or to his person were by his permission and express direction.

Mario chewed doubtfully at his lip. "This sounds pretty tough. About all you can't do is kill me."

"Correct," said Allen.

"A very ominous contract."

"Perhaps just the talk is adventure enough," suggested Allen, faintly contemptuous.

Mario pursed his lips. "I like pleasant adventures. A nightmare is an adventure, and I don't like nightmares."

"Who does?"

"In other words, you won't tell me a thing?"

"Not a thing."

"If I had any sense," said Mario, "I'd get up and walk out."

"Suit yourself."

"What do you do with all the money?"

Mervyn Allen relaxed in his chair, put his hands behind his blond head. "We're building the Empyrean Tower. That's no secret."

It was news to Mario. The Empyrean Tower—the vastest, grandest, heaviest, tallest, most noble structure created or even conceived by man. A sky-piercing star-aspiring shaft three miles tall.

"Why, if I may ask, are you building the Empyrean Tower?"

Allen sighed. "For the same reason you're here, at the Chateau d'If. Boredom. And don't tell me to take my own treatment."

"Have you?"

Allen studied him with narrow eyes. "Yes. I have. You ask lots of questions. Too many. Here's the contract. Sign it or tear it up. I can't give you any more time."

"First," said Mario patiently, "you'll have to give me some idea of what I'm getting into."

"It's not crime," said Allen. "Let's say—we give you a new outlook on life."

"Artificial amnesia?" asked Mario, remembering Zaer.

"No. Your memory is intact. Here it is," and Allen thrust out the contract. "Sign it or tear it up."

Mario signed. "I realize I'm a fool. Want my eight thousand?"

"We're in the business for money," said Allen shortly. "If you can spare it."

Mario counted out the eight thousand-dollar bills. "There you are."

Allen took the money, tapped it on the table, inspected Mario ruminatively. "Our customers fall pretty uniformly into three groups. Reckless young men just out of adolescence, jaded old men in search of new kinds of vice, and police snoopers. You don't seem to fit."

Mario said with a shrug, "Average the first two. I'm reckless, jaded and twenty-nine."

Allen smiled briefly, politely, rose to his feet. "This way, please."

A panel opened behind him, revealing a chamber lit with cool straw-colored light. Green plants, waist-high, grew in profusion—large-leafed exotics, fragile ferns, fantastic spired fungi, nodding spear-blades the color of Aztec jade. Mario noticed Allen drawing a deep breath before entering the room, but thought nothing of it. He followed, gazing right and left in admiration for the small artificial jungles to either side. The air was strong with the mint-gardenia-antiseptic odor—pungent. He blinked. His eyes watered, blurred. He halted, swaying. Allen turned around, watched with a cool half-smile, as if this were a spectacle he knew well but found constantly amusing.

Vision retreated; hearing hummed, flagged, departed; time swam, spun...

iv

Mario awoke.

It was a sharp clean-cut awakening, not the slow wading through a morass of drug.

He sat on a bench in Tanagra Square, under the big mimosa, and the copper peacocks were pecking at bread he held out to them.

He looked at his hand. It was a fat pudgy hand. The arm was encased in hard gray fiber. No suit he owned was gray. The arm was short. His legs were short. His belly was large. He licked his lips. They were pulpy, thick.

He was Roland Mario inside the brain, the body was somebody else. He sat quite still.

The peacocks pecked at the bread. He threw it away. His arm was stiff, strangely heavy. He had flabby muscles. He rose to his feet grunting. His body was soft but not flexible. He rubbed his hand over his face, felt a short lumpy nose, long ears, heavy cheeks like pans full of cold glue. He was bald as the underside of a fish.

Who was the body? He blinked, felt his mind twisting, tugging at its restraint. Mario fought to steady himself, as a man in a teetering canoe tries to hold it steady, to prevent capsizing into dark water. He leaned against the trunk of the mimosa tree. Steady, steady, focus your eyes! What had been done to him no doubt could be undone. Or it would wear off. Was it a dream, an intensely vivid segment of narcotiana? Adventure—ha! That was a mild word.

He fumbled into his pockets, found a folded sheet of paper. He opened it, sat down while he read the typescript. First there was a heavy warning:

MEMORIZE THE FOLLOWING, AS THIS PAPER WILL DISINTEGRATE IN APPROXIMATELY FIVE MINUTES!

You are embarking on the life you paid for.

Your name is Ralston Ebery. Your age is 56. You are married to Florence Ebery, age 50. Your home address is 19 Seafoam Place. You have three children: Luther, age 25, Ralston Jr., age 23, Clydia, age 19.

You are a wealthy manufacturer of aircraft, the Ebery Air-car. Your bank is the African Federal; the pass-book is in your pocket. When you sign your name, do not consciously guide your hand; let the involuntary muscles write the signature Ralston Ebery.

If you dislike your present form, you may return to the Chateau d'If. Ten thousand dollars will buy you a body of our choice, ten million dollars will buy you a young healthy body to your own specifications.

Please do not communicate with the police. In the first place, they will believe you to be insane. In the second place, if they successfully hampered the operation of the Chateau d'If, you would be marooned in the body of Ralston Ebery, a prospect you may or may not enjoy. In the third place, the body of Roland Mario will insist on his legal identity.

With your business opportunities, ten million dollars is a sum well within your reach. When you have it return to the Chateau d'If for a young and healthy body.

We have fulfilled our bargain with you. We have given you adventure. With skill and ingenuity, you will be able to join the group of men without age, eternally young.

Mario read the sheet a second time. As he finished, it crumbled into dust in his hands. He leaned back, aware of nausea rising in him like an elevator in a shaft. The most hateful of intimacies, dwelling in another man's body—especially one so gross and untidy. He felt a sensation of hunger, and with perverse malice decided to let Ralston Ebery's body go hungry.

Ralston Ebery! The name was vaguely familiar. Did Ralston Ebery now possess Mario's own body? Possibly. Not necessarily. Mario had no conception of the principle involved in the transfer. There seemed to be no incision, no brain graft.

Now what?

He could report to the ACP. But, if he could make them believe him, there still would be no legal recourse. To the best of his knowledge, no one at the Chateau d'If had performed a criminal act upon him. There was not even a good case of battery, since he had waived his right to prosecute.

The newspapers, the telescreens? Suppose unpleasant publicity were able to force the Chateau d'If out of business, what then? Mervyn Allen could set up a similar business elsewhere—and Mario would never be allowed to return to his own body.

He could follow the suggestion of the now disintegrated paper. No doubt Ralston Ebery had powerful political and financial connections, as well as great wealth in his own right. Or had he? Would it not be more likely that Ebery had liquidated as much of his wealth as possible, both to pay ten million dollars to the Chateau d'If, and also to provide his new body with financial backing?

Mario contemplated the use of force. There might be some means to compel the return of his body. Help would be useful. Should he report to Ditmar, Janniver, Breaugh? Indeed, he owed them some sort of explanation.

He rose to his feet. Mervyn Allen would not conceivably leave vulnerable areas in his defenses. He must realize that violence, revenge, would be the first idea in a mind shanghaied into an old sick body. There would be precautions against obvious violence, of that he was certain.

The ideas thronged, swirled, frothed, like different-colored paints stirred in a bucket. His head became light, a buzzing sounded in his ears. A dream, when would he awake? He gasped, panted, made feeble struggling motions. A patrolman stopped beside him, tripped his incident-camera automatically.

"What's wrong, sir? Taken sick?"

"No, no," said Mario. "I'm all right. Just dozed off."

He rose to his feet, stepped on the Choreops Strip, passed the central fountain flagged with aventurine quartz, stepped off at the Malabar Pavilion, wandered under the great bay trees out onto Kesselyn Avenue. Slowly, heavily, he plodded through the wholesale florist shops, and at Pacific, let the escalator take him to the third level, where he stepped on the fast pedestrip of the Grand Footway to the Concourse.

His progress had been unconscious, automatic, as if his body made the turns at their own volition. Now at the foot of the Aetherian Block he stepped off the strip, breathing a little heavily. The body of Ralston Ebery was spongy, in poor condition. And Mario felt an unholy gloating as he thought of Ralston Ebery's body sweating, puffing, panting, fasting—working off its lard.

A face suddenly thrust into his, a snarling hate-brimmed face. Teeth showed, the pupils of the eyes were like the black-tipped poison darts of the Mazumbwe Backlands. The face was that of a young-old man—unlined, but gray-haired; innocent but wise, distorted by the inner thrash and coil of his hate. Through tight teeth and corded jaw muscles the young-old man snarled:

"You filthy misbegotten dung-thief, do you hope to live? You venom, you stench. It would soil me to kill you. But I shall!"

Mario stepped back. The man was a stranger. "I'm sorry. You must be mistaken," he said, before it dawned that Ralston Ebery's deeds were now accountable to him.

A hand fell on the young-old man's shoulder. "Beat it, Arnold!" said a hard voice. "Be off with you!" The young-old man fell back.

Mario's rescuer turned around—a dapper young man with an agile fox-face. He nodded respectfully. "Good morning, Mr. Ebery. Sorry that crank bothered you."

"Good morning," said Mario. "Ah—who was he?"

The young man eyed him curiously. "Why, that's Letya Arnold. Used to work for us. You fired him."

Mario was puzzled. "Why?"

The young man blinked. "I'm sure I don't know. Inefficiency, I suppose."

"It's not important," said Mario hurriedly. "Forget it."

"Sure. Of course. On your way up to the office?"

"Yes, I—I suppose so." Who was this young man? It was a problem he would be called on to face many times, he thought.

They approached the elevators. "After you," said Mario. There was such an infinity of detail to be learned, a thousand personal adjustments, the intricate pattern of Ralston Ebery's business. Was there any business left? Ebery certainly would have plundered it of every cent he could endow his new body with. Ebery Air-car was a large concern; still the extracting of even ten million dollars was bound to make a dent. And this young man with the clever face, who was he? Mario decided to try indirectness, a vague question.

"Now let's see—how long since you've been promoted?"

The young man darted a swift side-glance, evidently wondering whether Ebery was off his feed. "Why, I've been assistant office manager for two years."

Mario nodded. They stepped into the elevator, and the young man was quick to press the button. Obsequious cur! thought Mario. The door snapped shut, and there came the swoop which stomachs of the age had become inured to. The elevator halted, the doors flung back, they stepped out into a busy office, filled with clicking machinery, clerks, banks of telescreens. Clatter, hum—and sudden silence with every eye on the body of Ralston Ebery. Furtive glances, studied attentiveness to work, exaggerated efficiency.

Mario halted, looked the room over. It was his. By default. No one in the world could deny him authority over this concern, unless Ralston Ebery had been too fast, too greedy, raising his ten million plus. If Ralston Ebery had embezzled or swindled, he—Roland Mario in Ebery's body—would be punished. Mario was trapped in Ebery's past. Ebery's shortcomings would be held against him, the hate he had aroused would inflict itself on him, he had inherited Ebery's wife, his family, his mistress, if any.

A short middle-aged man with wide disillusioned eyes, the bitter clasp of mouth that told of many hopes lost or abandoned, approached.

"Morning, Mr. Ebery. Glad you're here. Several matters for your personal attention."

Mario looked sharply at the man. Was that overtone in his voice sarcasm? "In my office," said Mario. The short man turned toward a hallway. Mario followed. "Come along," he said to the assistant office manager.

Gothic letters wrought from silver spelled out Ralston Ebery's name on a door. Mario put his thumb into the lock; the prints meshed, the door slid aside; Mario slowly entered, frowning in distaste at the fussy decor. Ralston Ebery had been a lover of the rococo. He sat down behind the desk of polished black metal, said to the assistant office manager, "Bring me the personnel file on the office staff—records, photographs."

"Yes, sir."

The short man hauled a chair forward. "Now, Mr. Ebery, I'm sorry to say that I consider you've put the business in an ambiguous position."

"What do you mean?" asked Mario frostily, as if he were Ebery himself.

The short man snorted. "What do I mean? I mean that the contracts you sold to Atlas Airboat were the biggest money-makers Ebery Air-car had. As you know very well. We took a terrible drubbing in that deal." The short man jumped to his feet, walked up and down. "Frankly, Mr. Ebery, I don't understand it."

"Just a minute," said Mario. "Let me look at the mail." Killing time, he thumbed through the mail until the assistant office manager returned with a file of cards.

"Thank you," said Mario. "That's all for now."

He flicked through them, glancing at the pictures. This short man had authority, he should be somewhere near the top. Here he was—Louis Correaos, Executive Adviser. Information as to salary, family, age, background—more than he could digest at the moment. He put the file to one side. Louis Correaos was still pacing up and down, fuming.

Correaos paused, darted Mario a venomous stare. "Ill-advised? I think you're crazy!" He shrugged. "I tell you this because my job means nothing to me. The company can't stand the beating you've given it. Not the way you want it run, at any rate. You insist on marketing a flying tea-wagon, festooned with ornaments; then you sell the only profitable contracts, the only features to the ship that make it at all airworthy."

Mario reflected a minute. Then he said, "I had my reasons."

Correaos, halting in his pacing, stared again.

Mario said, "Can you conjecture how I plan to profit from these circumstances?"

Correaos's eyes were like poker chips; his mouth contracted, tightened, pursed to an O. He was thinking. After a moment he said, "You sold our steel plant to Jones and Cahill, our patent on the ride stabilizer to Bluecraft." He gazed narrowly askance at Mario. "It sounds like you're doing what you swore you'd never do. Bring out a new model that would fly."

"How do you like the idea?" asked Mario, looking wise.

Louis Correaos stammered, "Why, Mr. Ebery, this is—fantastic! You asking me what I think! I'm your yes-man. That's what you're paying me for. I know it, you know it, everybody knows it."

"You haven't been yessing me today," said Mario. "You told me I was crazy."

"Well," stammered Correaos, "I didn't see your idea. It's what I'd like to have done long ago. Put in a new transformer, pull off all that ormolu, use plancheen instead of steel, simplify, simplify—"

"Louis," said Mario, "make the announcement. Start the works rolling. You're in charge. I'll back up anything you want done."

Louis Correaos's face was a drained mask.

"Make your salary anything you want," said Mario. "I've got some new projects I'm going to be busy on. I want you to run the business. You're the boss. Can you handle it?"

"Yes. I can."

"Do it your own way. Bring out a new model that'll beat everything in the field. I'll check on the final setup, but until then, you're the boss. Right now—clean up all this detail." He pointed to the file of correspondence. "Take it to your office."

Correaos impulsively rushed up, shook Mario's hand. "I'll do the best I can." He left the room.

Mario said into the communicator, "Get me the African Federal Bank…Hello—" to the girl's face on the screen "—this is Ralston Ebery. Please check on my personal balance."

After a moment she said, "It's down to twelve hundred dollars, Mr. Ebery. Your last withdrawal almost wiped out your balance."

"Thank you," said Mario. He settled the thick body of Ralston Ebery into the chair, and became aware of a great cavernous growling in his abdomen. Ralston Ebery was hungry.

Mario grinned a ghastly sour grin. He called food service. "Send up a chopped olive sandwich, celery, a glass of skim milk."

V

During the afternoon he became aware of an ordeal he could no longer ignore: acquainting himself with Ralston Ebery's family, his home life. It could not be a happy one. No happy husband and father would leave his wife and children at the mercy of a stranger. It was the act of hate, rather than love.

A group photograph stood on the desk—a picture inconspicuously placed, as if it were there on sufferance. This was his family. Florence Ebery was a frail woman, filmy, timid, over-dressed, and her face, peering out from under a preposterous hat, wore the patient perplexed expression of a family pet dressed in doll clothes—somehow pathetic.

Luther and Ralston Jr. were stocky young men with set mulish faces, Clydia a full-cheeked creature with a petulant mouth.

At three o'clock Mario finally summoned up his courage, called Ebery's home on the screen, had Florence Ebery put on. She said in a thin distant voice, "Yes, Ralston."

"I'll be home this evening, dear." Mario added the last word with conscious effort.

She wrinkled her nose, pursed her lips and her eyes shone as if she were about to cry. "You don't even tell me where you've been."

Mario said, "Florence—frankly. Would you say I've been a good husband?"

She blinked defiantly at him. "I've no complaints. I've never complained." The pitch of her voice hinted that this perhaps was not literally true. Probably had reason, thought Mario.

"No, I want the truth, Florence."

"You've given me all the money I wanted. You've humiliated me a thousand times—snubbed me, made me a laughing-stock for the children."

Mario said, "Well, I'm sorry, Florence." He could not vow affection. He felt sorry for Florence—Ebery's wife—but she was Ralston Ebery's wife, not his own. One of Ralston Ebery's victims. "See you this evening," he said lamely, and switched off.

He sat back. Think, think, think. There must be a way out. Or was this to be his life, his end, in this corpulent unhealthy body? Mario laughed suddenly. If ten million dollars bought Ralston Ebery a new body—presumably his own—then ten million more of Ralston Ebery's dollars might buy the body back. For money spoke a clear loud language to Mervyn Allen. Humiliating, a nauseous obsequious act, a kissing of the foot which kicked you, a submission, an acquiescence—but it was either this or wear the form of Ralston Ebery.

Mario stood up, walked to the window, stepped out on the landing plat, signaled down an aircab.

Ten minutes later he stood at 5600 Exmoor Avenue in Meadowlands, the Chateau d'If. A gardener clipping the hedges eyed him with distrust. He strode up the driveway, pressed the button.

There was, as before, a short wait, the unseen scrutiny of spy cells. The sun shone warm on his back, to his ears came the shirrrrr of the gardener's clippers.

The door opened.

"Please come in," said the soft commercial voice.

Down the hall, into the green and brown reception room with the painting of the three stark nudes before the olden forest.

The girl of fabulous beauty entered; Mario gazed again into the wide clear eyes which led to some strange brain. Whose brain? Mario wondered. Of man or woman?

No longer did Mario feel the urge to excite her, arouse her. She was unnatural, a thing.

"What do you wish?"

"I'd like to see Mr. Allen."

"On what business?"

"Ah, you know me?"

"On what business?"

"You're a money-making concern, are you not?"

"Yes."

"My business means money."

"Please be seated." She turned; Mario watched the slim body in retreat. She walked lightly, gracefully, in low elastic slippers. He became aware of Ebery's body. The old goat's glands were active enough. Mario fought down the wincing nausea.

The girl returned. "Follow me, please."

Mervyn Allen received him with affability, though not going so far as to shake hands.

"Hello, Mr. Mario. I rather expected you. Sit down. How's everything going? Enjoying yourself?"

"Not particularly. I'll agree that you've provided me with a very stimulating adventure. And indeed—now that I think back—nowhere have you made false representations."

Allen smiled a cool brief smile. And Mario wondered whose brain this beautiful body surrounded.

"Your attitude is unusually philosophical," said Allen. "Most of our customers do not realize that we give them exactly what they pay for. The essence of adventure is surprise, danger, and an outcome dependent upon one's own efforts."

"No question," remarked Mario, "that is precisely what you offer. But don't mistake me. If I pretended friendship, I would not be sincere. In spite of any rational processes, I feel a strong resentment. I would kill you without sorrow—even though, as you will point out, I brought the whole matter on myself."

"Exactly."

"Aside from my own feelings, we have a certain community of interests, which I wish to exploit. You want money, I want my own body. I came to inquire by what circumstances our desires could both be satisfied."

Allen's face was joyous, he laughed delightedly. "Mario, you amuse me. I've heard many propositions, but none quite so formal, so elegant. Yes, I want money. You want the body you have become accustomed to. I'm sorry to say that your old body is now the property of someone else, and I doubt if he'd be persuaded to surrender it. But—I can sell you another body, healthy, handsome, young, for our usual fee. Ten million dollars. For thirty million I'll give you the widest possible choice—a body like mine, for instance. The Empyrean Tower is an exceedingly expensive project."

Mario said, "Out of curiosity, how is this transfer accomplished? I don't notice any scar or any sign of brain graft. Which in any event is probably impossible."

Mervyn Allen nodded. "It would be tedious, splicing several million sets of nerves. Are you acquainted with the physiology of the brain?"

"No," said Mario. "It's complicated, that's about all I know of it—or have cared to know."

Allen leaned back, relaxed, spoke rapidly, as if by rote. "The brain is divided into three parts, the medulla oblongata, the cerebellum—these two control involuntary motions and reflexes—and the cerebrum, the seat of memory, intelligence, personality. Thinking is done in the brain the same way thinking is done in mechanical brains, by the selection of a route through relays or neurons.

"In a blank brain, the relative ease of any circuit is the same, and the electric potential of each and every cell is the same.

"The process is divided into a series of steps—discovered, I may add, accidentally during a program of research in a completely different field. First, the patient's scalp is imbedded in a cellule of what the original research team called golasma—an organic crystal with a large number of peripheral fibers. Between the golasma cellule and the brain are a number of layers—hair, dermal tissue, bone, three separate membranes, as well as a mesh of blood vessels, very complicated. The neural cells however are unique in their high electric potential, and for practical purposes the intervening cells do not intrude.

"Next, by a complicated scanning process, we duplicate the synapses of the brain in the golasma, relating it by a pattern of sensory stimuli to a frame that will be common to all men.

"Third, the golasma cellules are changed, the process is reversed, A's brain is equipped with B's synapses, B with A's. The total process requires only a few minutes. Non-surgical, painless, harmless. A receives B's personality and memories, B takes on A's."

Slowly Mario rubbed his fat chin. "You mean, I—I—am not Roland Mario at all? That thinking Roland Mario's thoughts is an illusion? And not a cell in this body is Roland Mario?"

"Not the faintest breath. You're all—let me see. Your name is Ralston Ebery, I believe. Every last corpuscle of you is Ralston Ebery. You are Ralston Ebery, equipped with Roland Mario's memories."

"But, my glandular makeup? Won't it modify Roland Mario's personality? After all, a man's actions are not due to his brain alone, but to a synthesis of effects."

"Very true," said Allen. "The effect is progressive. You will gradually change, become like the Ralston Ebery before the change. And the same with Roland Mario's body. The total change will be determined by the environment against heredity ratio in your characters."

Mario smiled. "I want to get out of this body soon. What I see of Ebery I don't like."

"Bring in ten million dollars," said Mervyn Allen. "The Chateau d'If exists for one purpose—to make money."

Mario inspected Allen carefully, noted the hard clear flesh, the beautiful shape of the face, skull, expression.

"What do you need all that money for? Why build an Empyrean Tower in the first place?"

"I do it for fun. It amuses me. I am bored. I have explored many bodies, many existences. This body is my fourteenth. I've wielded power. I do not care for the sensation. The pressure annoys me. Nor am I at all psychotic. I am not even ruthless. In my business, what one man loses, another man gains. The balance is even."

"But it's robbery!" protested Mario bitterly. "Stealing the years off one man's life to add to another's."

Allen shrugged. "The bodies are living the same cumulative length of time. The total effect is the same. There's no change but the shifting of memory. In any event, perhaps I am, in the jargon of metaphysics, a solipsist. So far as I can see—through my eyes, through my brain—I am the only true individual, the sole conscious intellect." His eye shadowed. "How else can it be that I—I—have been chosen from among so many to lead this charmed life of mine?"

"Pooh!" sneered Mario.

"Every man amuses himself as best he knows how. My current interest is building the Empyrean Tower." His voice took on a deep exalted ring. "It shall rise three miles into the air! There is a banquet hall with a floor of alternate silver and copper strips, a quarter mile wide, a quarter mile high, ringed with eight glass balconies. There will be garden terraces like nothing else on earth, with fountains, waterfalls, running brooks. One floor will be a fairy-land out of the ancient days, peopled with beautiful nymphs.

"Others will display Earth at stages in its history. There will be museums, conservatories of various musical styles, studios, workshops, laboratories for every known type of research, sections given to retail shops. There will be beautiful chambers and balconies designed for nothing except to be wandered through, sections devoted to the—let us say, worship of Astarte. There will be halls full of toys, a hundred restaurants staffed by gourmets, a thousand taverns serving liquid dreams; halls for seeing, hearing, resting."

Said Mario, "And after you tire of the Empyrean Tower?"

Mervyn Allen flung himself back in the seat. "Ah, Mario, you touch me on a sore point. Doubtless something will suggest itself. If only we could break away from Earth, could fly past the barren rocks of the planets, to other stars, other life. There would be no need for any Chateau d'If."

Mario rubbed his fat jowl, eyed Allen quizzically. "Did you invent this process yourself?"

"I and four others who comprised a research team. They are all dead. I alone know the technique."

"And your secretary? Is she one of your changelings?"

"No," said Mervyn Allen. "Thane is what she is. She lives by hate. You think I am her lover? No," and he smiled faintly. "Not in any way. Her will is for destruction, death. A bright thing only on the surface. Inwardly she is as dark and violent as a drop of hot oil."

Mario had absorbed too many facts, too much information. He was past speculating. "Well, I won't take any more of your time. I wanted to find out where I stand."

"Now you know. I need money. This is the easiest way to get it in large quantities that I know of. But I also have my big premium offer—bank night, bingo, whatever you wish to call it."

"What's that?"

"I need customers. The more customers, the more money. Naturally my publicity cannot be too exact. So I offer a free shift, a free body if you bring in six new customers."

Mario narrowed his eyes. "So—Sutlow gets credit for Zaer and me?"

Allen looked blank. "Who's Sutlow?"

"You don't know Sutlow?"

"Never heard of him."

"How about Ditmar?"

"Ah, he's successful, is Ditmar. Ten thousand bought him a body with advanced cirrhosis. Two more customers and he escapes. But perhaps I talk too much. I can give you no more time, Mario. Good night."

On his way out, Mario stopped in the reception room, looked down into the face of Thane. She stared back, a face like stone, eyes like star sapphires. Mario suddenly felt exalted, mystic, as if he walked on live thought, knew the power of insight.

"You're beautiful but you're cold as the sea-bed."

"This door will take you out, sir."

"Your beauty is so new and so fragile a thing—a surface only a millimeter thick. Two strokes of a knife would make you a horrible sight, one from which people would look aside as you pass."

She opened her mouth, closed it, rose to her feet, said, "This way out, sir."

Mario reached, caught sight of Ralston Ebery's fat flaccid fingers, grimaced, pulled back his hands. "I could not touch you—with these hands."

"Nor with any others," she said from the cool distance of her existence.

He passed her to the door. "If you see the most beautiful creature that could possibly exist, if she has a soul like rock crystal, if she challenges you to take her, break her, and you are lost in a fat hideous porridge of a body—"

Her expression shifted a trifle, in which direction he could not tell. "This is the Chateau d'If," she said. "And you are a fat hideous porridge."

He wordlessly departed. She slid the door shut. Mario shrugged, but Ralston Ebery's face burnt in a hot glow of humiliation. There was no love, no thought of love. Nothing more than the challenge, much like the dare of a mountain to the climbers who scale its height, plunder the secrets of its slopes, master the crest. Thane, cold as the far side of the moon!

Get away, said Mario's brain sharply, break clear of the obsession. Fluff, female bodies, forget them. Is not the tangle of enough complexity?

vi

From the door of the Chateau d'If Mario took an aircab to 19 Seafoam Place—a monster house of pink marble, effulgent, voluted, elaborate as the rest of Ralston Ebery's possessions. He thumbed the lock-hole. The prints meshed with identification patterns, the door snapped back. Mario entered.

The photograph had prepared him for his family. Florence Ebery greeted him with furtive suspicion; the sons were blank, passively hostile. The daughter seemed to have no emotions whatever, other than a constant air of puzzled surprise.

At dinner, Mario outraged Ebery's body by eating nothing but a salad of lettuce, carrots and vinegar. His family was puzzled.

"Are you feeling well, Ralston?" inquired his wife.

"Very well."

"You're not eating."

"I'm dieting. I'm going to take the lard off this hideous body."

Eight eyes bulged, four sets of knives and forks froze.

Mario went on placidly, "We're going to have some changes around here. Too much easy living is bad for a person." He addressed himself to the two young men, both alike with white faces, doughy cheeks, full lips. "You lads now—I don't want to be hard on you. After all, it's not your fault you were born Ralston Ebery's sons. But do you know what it means to earn a living by sweating for it?"

Luther, the eldest, spoke with dignity. "We work with the sweat of our brains."

"Tell me more about it," said Mario.

Luther's eyes showed anger. "I put out more work in one week than you do all year."

"Where?"

"Where? Why, in the glass yard. Where else?" There was fire here, more than Mario had expected.

Ralston Jr. said in a gruff surly voice, "We're paying you our board and room, we don't owe you a red cent. If you don't like the arrangements the way they are, we'll leave."

Mario winced. He had misjudged Ebery's sons. White faces, doughy cheeks, did not necessarily mean white doughy spirits. Better to keep his opinions to himself, base his conversation on known fact. He said mildly, "Sorry, I didn't mean to offend you. Forget the board and room. Spend it on something useful."

He glanced skeptically toward Clydia, Ebery's daughter. She half-simpered. Better keep his mouth shut. She might turn out to be a twelve-hour-a-day social service worker.

Nevertheless, Mario found himself oppressed in Ebery's house. Though living in Ebery's body, the feel of his clothes, his intimate equipment was profoundly disturbing. He could not bring himself to use Ebery's razor or toothbrush. Attending to the needs of Ebery's body was most exquisitely distasteful. He discovered to his relief that his bedroom was separate from that of Florence Ebery.

He arose the next morning very early, scarcely after dawn, hurriedly left the house, breakfasted on orange juice and dry toast at a small restaurant. Ebery's stomach protested the meager rations with angry rumbling. Ebery's legs complained when Mario decided to walk the pedestrip instead of calling down an aircab.

He let himself into the deserted offices of Ebery Air-car, wandered absently back and forth the length of the suite, thinking. Still thinking, he let himself into his private office. The clutter, the rococo junk, annoyed him. He called up a janitor, waved his hand around the room. "Clear out all this fancy stuff. Take it home, keep it. If you don't want it, throw it away. Leave me the desk, a couple of chairs. The rest—out!"

He sat back, thinking. Ways, means.

What weapons could he use?

He drew marks on a sheet of paper.

How could he attack?

Perhaps the law could assist him—somehow. Perhaps the ACP. But what statute did Mervyn Allen violate? There were no precedents. The Chateau d'If sold adventure. If a customer bought a great deal more than he had bargained for, he had only himself to blame.

Money, money, money. It could not buy back his own body. He needed leverage, a weapon, pressure to apply.

He called the public information service, requested the file on 'golasma'. It was unknown.

He drew more marks, scribbled meaningless patterns; where was Mervyn Allen vulnerable? The Chateau d'If, the Empyrean Tower. Once more he dialed into the public information service, requested the sequence on the Empyrean Tower. Typescript flashed across his screen.

> The Empyrean Tower will be a multiple-function building at a site in Meadowlands. The highest level will be three miles above ground. The architects are Kubal Associates, Incorporated, of Lanchester. Foundation contracts have been let to Lourey and Lyble—

Mario touched the shift button; the screen showed an architect's pencil sketch—a slender structure pushing through cloud layers into the clear blue sky. Mario touched the shift button.

Now came detailed information, as to the weight, cubic volume, comparison with the Pyramids, the Chilung Gorge Dam, the Skatterholm complex at Ronn, the Hawke Pylon, the World's Mart at Dar es Salaam.

Mario pushed at his communicator button. No answer. Still too early. Impatient now, he ordered coffee, drank two cups, pacing the office nervously.

At last a voice answered his signal. "When Mr. Correaos comes in, I'd like to speak to him."

Five minutes later Louis Correaos knocked at his door.

"Morning, Louis," said Mario.

"Good morning, Mr. Ebery," said Correaos with a tight guarded expression, as if expecting the worst.

Mario said, "Louis, I want some advice...have you ever heard of Kubal Associates, Incorporated? Architects?"

"No. Can't say as I have."

"I don't want to distract you from your work," said Mario, "but I want to acquire control of that company. Quietly. Secretly, even. I'd like you to make some quiet inquiries. Don't use my name. Buy up as much voting stock as is being offered. Go as high as you like, but get the stock. And don't use my name."

Correaos's face became a humorous mask, with a bitter twist to his mouth. "What am I supposed to use for money?"

Mario rubbed the flabby folds around his jaw. "Hm. There's no reserve fund, no bank balance?"

Correaos looked at him queerly.

"You should know."

Mario squinted off to the side. True, he should know. To Louis Correaos, this was Ralston Ebery sitting before him—the arbitrary, domineering Ralston Ebery. Mario said, "Check on how much we can raise, will you, Louis?"

Correaos said, "Just a minute." He left the room. He returned with a bit of paper.

"I've been figuring up retooling costs. We'll have to borrow. It's none of my business what you did with the fund."

Mario smiled grimly. "You'd never understand, Louis. And if I told you, you wouldn't believe me. Just forget it. It's gone."

"The South African agency sent a draft for a little over a million yesterday. That won't even touch retooling."

Mario made an impatient gesture. "We'll get a loan. Right now you've got a million. See how much of Kubal Associates you can buy."

Correaos left the room without a word. Mario muttered to himself, "Thinks I'm off my nut. Figures he'll humor me..."

All morning Mario turned old files through his desk-screen, trying to catch the thread of Ebery's business. There was much evidence of Ebery's hasty plundering—the cashing of bonds, disposal of salable assets, transference of the depreciation funds into his personal account. But in spite of the pillaging, Ebery Air-car seemed financially sound. It held mortgages, franchises, contracts worth many times what cash Ebery had managed to clear.

Tiring of the files, he ordered more coffee, paced the floor. His mind turned to 19 Seafoam Place. He thought of the accusing eyes of Florence Ebery, the hostility of Luther and Ralston Jr. And Mario wished Ralston Ebery a place in hell. Ebery's family was no responsibility, no concern of his. He called Florence Ebery.

"Florence, I won't be living at home any more." He tried to speak kindly.

She said, "That's what I thought."

Mario said hurriedly, "I think that, by and large, you'd be better off with a divorce. I won't contest it; you can have as much money as you want."

She gave him a fathomless silent stare. "That's what I thought," she said again. The screen went dead.

Correaos returned shortly after lunch. It was warm, Correaos had walked the pedestrip, his face shone with perspiration.

He flung a carved black plastic folder on the desk, baring his teeth in a triumphant smile. "There it is. I don't know what you want with it, but there it is. Fifty-two percent of the stock. I bought it off of old man Kubal's nephew and a couple of the associates. Got 'em at the right time; they were glad to sell. They don't like the way the business is going. Old man Kubal gives all his time to the Empyrean Tower, and he's not taking any fee for the work. Says the honor of the job is enough. The nephew doesn't dare to fight it out with old man Kubal, but he sure was glad to sell out. The same with Kohn and Cheever, the associates. The Empyrean Tower job doesn't even pay the office overhead."

"Hm. How old is Kubal?"

"Must be about eighty. Lively old boy, full of vinegar."

Honor of the job! thought Mario. Rubbish! Old Kubal's fee would be a young body. Aloud he said, "Louis, have you ever seen Kubal?"

"No, he hardly shows his face around the office. He lines up the jobs, the engineering is done in the office."

"Louis," said Mario, "here's what I want you to do. Record the stock in your own name, give me an undated transfer, which we won't record. You'll legally control the firm. Call the office, get hold of the general manager. Tell him that you're sending me over. I'm just a friend of yours you owe a favor to. Tell him that I'm to be given complete and final authority over any job I decide to work on. Get it?"

Correaos eyed Mario as if he expected the fat body to explode into fire. "Anything you like. I suppose you know what you're doing."

Mario grinned ruefully. "I can't think of anything else to do. In the meantime, bring out your new model. You're in charge."

Mario dressed Ralston Ebery's body in modest blue, reported to the office of Kubal Associates, an entire floor in the Rothenburg Building. He asked the receptionist for the manager and was shown in to a tall man in the early forties with a delicate lemonish face. He had a freckled forehead, thin sandy hair, and he answered Mario's questions with sharpness and hostility.

"My name is Taussig…No, I'm just the office manager. Kohn ran the draughting room, Cheever the engineering. They're both out. The office is a mess. I've been here twelve years."

Mario assured him that there was no intention of stepping in over him. "No, Mr. Taussig, you're in charge. I speak for the new control. You handle the office—general routine, all the new jobs—just as usual. Your title is general manager. I want to work on the Empyrean Tower—without any interference. I won't bother you, you won't bother me. Right? After the Empyrean Tower, I leave and the entire office is yours."

Taussig's face unwound from around the lines of suspicion. "There's not much going on except the Empyrean Tower. Naturally that's a tremendous job in itself. Bigger than any one man."

Mario remarked that he did not expect to draw up the entire job on his own bench, and Taussig's face tightened again, at the implied sarcasm. No, said Mario, he merely would be the top ranking authority on the job, subject only to the wishes of the builder.

"One last thing," said Mario. "This talk we've had must be," he tilted Taussig a sidelong wink, "strictly confidential. You'll introduce me as a new employee, that's all. No word of the new control. No word of his being a friend of mine. Forget it. Get me?"

Taussig agreed with sour dignity.

"I want quiet," said Mario thoughtfully. "I want no contact with any of the principals. The interviews with the press—you handle those. Conferences with the builder, changes, modifications—you attend to them. I'm merely in the background."

"Just as you say," said Taussig.

vii

Empyrean Tower became as much a part of Mario's life as his breath, his pulse. Twelve hours a day, thirteen, fourteen, Ebery's fat body sat slumped at the long desk, and Ebery's eyes burned and watered from poring through estimates, details, floor-plans. On the big screen four feet before his eyes flowed the work of twenty-four hundred draughtsmen, eight hundred engineers, artists, decorators, craftsmen without number, everything subject to his approval. But his influence was restrained, nominal, unnoticed. Only in a few details did Mario interfere, and then so carefully, so subtly, that the changes were unknown.

The new building techniques, the control over material, the exact casting of plancheen and allied substances, prefabrication, effortless transport of massive members made the erection of the Empyrean Tower magically easy and swift. Level by level it reached into the air, growing like a macrocosmic bean sprout. Steel, concrete, plancheen floors and walls, magnesium girders, outriggers, buttresses, the new bubble-glass for windows—assembled into precise units, hoisted, dropped into place from freight copters.

All day and all night the blue glare of the automatic welders burnt the sky, and sparks spattered against the stars, and every day the aspiring bulk pushed closer to the low clouds. Then through the low clouds, up toward the upper levels. Sun at one stage, rain far below. Up mile after mile, into the regions of air where the wind always swept like cream, undisturbed, unalloyed with the warm fetor of earth.

Mario was lost in the Empyrean Tower. He knew the range of materials, the glitter of a hundred metals, the silky gloss of plancheen, the color of the semi-precious minerals: jade, cinnabar, malachite, agate, jet, rare porphyries from under the Antarctic ranges. Mario forgot himself, forgot the Chateau d'If, forgot Mervyn Allen, Thane, Louis Correaos and Ebery Air-car, except for spasmodic, disassociated spells when he tore himself away from the Rothenburg Building for a few hours.

And sometimes, when he would be most engrossed, he would find to his horror that his voice, his disposition, his mannerisms were not those of Roland Mario. Ralston Ebery's lifelong reflexes and habits were making themselves felt. And Roland Mario felt a greater urgency. Build, build, build!

And nowhere did Mario work more carefully than on the 900th level—the topmost floor, noted on the index as offices and living quarters for Mervyn Allen. With the most intricate detail did Mario plan the construction, specifying specially-built girders, ventilating equipment, all custom-made to his own dimensions.

And so months in Mario's life changed their nature from future to past, months during which he became almost accustomed to Ralston Ebery's body.

On a Tuesday night Mario's personality had been fitted into Ralston Ebery's body. Wednesday morning he had come to his senses. Friday he was deep in concentration at the office of Ebery Air-car in the Aetherian Block, and three o'clock passed without his awareness. Friday evening he thought of the Oxonian Terrace, his rendezvous with Janniver, Breaugh, the nameless spirit in the sick body named Ditmar. And the next Tuesday at three, Mario was sitting at a table on the Oxonian Terrace.

Twenty feet away sat Janniver, Breaugh, Ditmar. And Mario thought back to the day only a few weeks ago when the five sat lackadaisically in the sun. Four innocents and one man eyeing them hungrily, weighing the price their bodies would bring.

Two of those bodies he had won. And Mario saw them sitting quietly in the warm sunlight, talking slowly—two of them, at least, peaceful and secure. Breaugh spoke with the customary cocksure tilt to his dark head, Janniver was slow and sober, an odd cording of racial vibrants. And there was Ditmar, a foreign soul looking sardonically from the lean dark-bronze body. A sick body, that a man paying ten thousand dollars for adventure would consider a poor bargain. Ditmar had bought adventure—an adventure in pain and fear. For a moment Mario's flinty mood loosened enough to admit that in yearning for his own life in his own body, a man might easily forget decency, fairness. The drowning man strangles a would-be rescuer.

Mario sipped beer indecisively. Should he join the three? It could do no harm. He was detained by a curious reluctance, urgent, almost a sense of shame. To speak to these men, tell them what their money had bought him—Mario felt the warm stickiness, the internal crawling of extreme embarrassment. At sudden thought, Mario scanned the nearby tables. Zaer. He had almost forgotten Pete Zaer. A millionaire's mind lived in Zaer's body. Would Zaer's mind bring the millionaire's body here?

Mario saw an old man with hollow eyes alone at a nearby table. Mario stared, watched his every move. The old man lit a cigarette, puffed, flicked the match—one of Zaer's tricks. The cigarette between his fingers, he lifted his highball, drank, once, twice, put the cigarette in his mouth, set the glass down. Zaer's mannerism.

Mario rose, moved, took a seat. The old man looked up eagerly, then angrily, from dry red-rimmed eyes. The skin was a calcined yellow, the mouth was gray. Zaer had bought even less for his money than Mario.

"Is your name Pete Zaer?" asked Mario. "In disguise?"

The old man's mouth worked. The eyes swam. "How—Why do you say that?"

Mario said, "Look at the table. Who else is missing?"

"Roland Mario," said the old man in a thin rasping voice. The red eyes peered. "You!"

"That's right," said Mario, with a sour grin. "In a week or two maybe there'll be three of us, maybe four." He motioned. "Look at them. What are they shaking dice for?"

"We've got to stop them," rasped Zaer. "They don't know." But he did not move. Nor did Mario. It was like trying to make himself step naked out upon a busy street.

Something rigid surrounded, took hold of Mario's brain. He stood up. "You wait here," he muttered. "I'll try to put a stop to it."

He ambled across the sun-drenched terrace, to the table where Janniver was rolling dice. Mario reached his hands down, caught up the meaningful cubes.

Janniver looked up with puzzled eyes. Breaugh bent his straight Welsh eyebrows in the start of a temper. Ditmar, frowning, leaned back.

"Excuse me," said Mario. "May I ask what you're rolling for?"

Breaugh said, "A private matter. It does not concern you."

"Does it concern the Chateau d'If?"

Six eyes stared.

"Yes," said Breaugh, after a second or two of hesitation.

Mario said, "I'm a friend of Roland Mario's. I have a message from him."

"What is it?"

"He said to stay away from the Chateau d'If; not to waste your money. He said not to trust anyone who suggested for you to go there."

Breaugh snorted. "Nobody's suggesting anything to anybody."

"And he says he'll get in touch with you soon."

Mario left without formality, returned to where he had left Zaer. The old man with the hot red eyes was gone.

Ralston Ebery had many enemies, so Mario found. There were a large number of acquaintances, no friends. And there was one white-faced creature that seemed to live only to waylay him, hiss vileness. This was Letya Arnold, a former employee in the research laboratories.

Mario ignored the first and second meetings, and on the third he told the man to keep out of his way. "Next time I'll call the police."

"Filth-tub," gloated Arnold. "You wouldn't dare! The publicity would ruin you, and you know it, you know it!"

Mario inspected the man curiously. He was clearly ill. His breath reeked of internal decay. Under a loose gray-brown jacket his chest was concave, his shoulders pushed forward like door-knobs. His eyes were a curious shiny black, so black that the pupils were indistinguishable from the iris, and the eyes looked like big black olives pressed into two bowls of sour milk.

"There's a patrolman now," said Arnold. "Call him, mucknose, call him!"

Quickly Mario turned, walked away, and Arnold's laughter rang against his back.

Mario asked Louis Correaos about Letya Arnold. "Why wouldn't I dare have him arrested?"

And Correaos turned on him one of his long quizzical stares. "Don't you know?"

Mario remembered that Correaos thought he was Ebery. He rubbed his forehead. "I'm forgetful, Louis. Tell me about Letya Arnold."

"He worked in the radiation lab, figured out some sort of process that saved fuel. We naturally had a legal right to the patent." Correaos smiled sardonically. "Naturally we didn't use the process, since you owned stock in World Air-Power, and a big block of Lamarr Atomics. Arnold began unauthorized use. We took it to court, won, recovered damages. It put Arnold into debt and he hasn't been worth anything since."

Mario said with sudden energy, "Let me see that patent, Louis."

Correaos spoke into the mesh and a minute later a sealed envelope fell out of the slot into the catch-all.

Correaos said idly, "Myself, I think Arnold was either crazy or a fake. The idea he had couldn't work. Like perpetual motion."

Letya Arnold had written a short preface to the body of the paper, this latter a mass of circuits and symbols unintelligible to Mario.

The preface read:

Efficiency in propulsion is attained by expelling ever smaller masses at ever higher velocities. The limit, in the first case, is the electron. Expelling it at speeds approaching that of light, we find that its mass increases by the well-known effect. This property provides us a perfect propulsive method, capable of freeing flight from its dependence upon heavy loads of material to be ejected at relatively slow velocities. One electron magnetically repelled at near-light speeds, exerts as much forward recoil as many pounds of conventional fuel...

Mario knew where to find Letya Arnold. The man sat brooding day after day in Tanagra Square, on a bench beside the Centennial Pavilion. Mario stopped in front of him, a young-old man with a hysterical face.

Arnold looked up, arose eagerly, almost as if he would assault Mario physically.

Mario in a calm voice said, "Arnold, pay attention a minute. You're right, I'm wrong."

Arnold's face hung slack as a limp bladder. Attack needs resistance on which to harden itself. Feebly his fury asserted itself. He reeled off his now-familiar invective. Mario listened a minute.

"Arnold, the process you invented—have you ever tested it in practice?"

"Of course, you swine. Naturally. Of course. What do you take me for? One of your blow-hard call-boys?"

"It works, you say. Now listen, Arnold: we're working on a new theory at Ebery Air-car. We're planning to put out value at low cost. I'd like to build your process into the new model. If it actually does what you say. And I'd like to have you come back to work for us."

Letya Arnold sneered, his whole face a gigantic sneer. "Put that propulsion into an air-boat? Pah! Use a drop-forge to kill a flea? Where's your head, where's your head? It's space-drive; that's where we're going. Space!"

It was Mario's turn to be taken aback. "Space? Will it work in space?" he asked weakly.

"Work? It's just the thing! You took all my money—you!" The words were like skewers, dripping an acrid poison. "If I had my money now, patent or no patent, I'd be out in space. I'd be ducking around Alpha Centauri, Sirius, Vega, Capella!"

The man was more than half-mad, thought Mario. He said, "You can't go faster than light."

Letya Arnold's voice became calm, crafty. "Who said I can't? You don't know the things I know, swine-slut."

Mario said, "No, I don't. But all that aside, I'm a changed man, Arnold. I want you to forget any injustice I may have done you. I want you back at work for Ebery Air-car. I'd like you to adapt the drive for public use."

Again Arnold sneered. "And kill everything that happened to be behind you? Every electron shot from the reactor would be like a meteor; there'd be blasts of incandescent air; impact like a cannon-ball. No, no—space. That's where the drive must go…"

"You're hired, if you want to be," said Mario patiently. "The laboratory's waiting for you. I want you to work on that adaptation. There must be some kind of shield." Noting the taut clamp to Arnold's mouth, he said hastily, "If you think you can go faster than light, fine! Build a ship for space and I'll test fly it myself. But put in your major effort on the adaptation for public use, that's all I ask."

Arnold, cooler by the minute, now exhibited the same kind of sardonic unbelief Mario had noticed in Correaos. "Blow me, but you've changed your tune, Ebery. Before it was money, money, money. If it didn't make you money, plow it under. What happened to you?"

"The Chateau d'If," said Mario. "If you value your sanity, don't go there. Though God knows," and he looked at Arnold's wasted body, "you couldn't do much worse for yourself than you've already done."

"If it changes me as much as it's changed you, I'm giving it a wide berth. Blow me, but you're almost human."

"I'm a changed man," said Mario. "Now go to Correaos, get an advance, go to a doctor."

On his way to the Rothenburg Building and Kubal Associates it came to him to wonder how Ebery was using his body. In his office he ran down a list of detective agencies, settled on Brannan Investigators, called them, put them to work.

viii

Investigator Murris Slade, the detective, was a short thick-set man with a narrow head. Two days after Mario had called the Brannan agency, he knocked at Mario's workroom at Kubal Associates.

Mario looked through the wicket in the locked door, admitted the detective, who said without preamble, "I've found your man."

"Good," said Mario, returning to his seat. "What's he doing?"

Slade said, in a quiet accentless voice, "There's no mystery or secrecy involved. He seems to have changed his way of living in the last few months. I understand he was quite a chap, pretty well-liked, nothing much to set him apart. One of the idle rich. Now he's a hell-raiser, a woman-chaser, and he's been thrown out of every bar in town."

My poor body, thought Mario. Aloud: "Where's he living?"

"He's got an apartment at the Atlantic-Empire, fairly plush place. It's a mystery where he gets his money."

The Atlantic-Empire seemed to have become a regular rendezvous for Chateau d'If alumni, thought Mario. He said, "I want a weekly report on this man. Nothing complicated—just a summary of where he spends his time. Now, I've got another job for you…"

The detective reported on the second job a week later.

"Mervyn Allen is an alias. The man was born Lloyd Paren, in Vienna. The woman is his sister, Thane Paren. Originally he was a photographer's model, something of a playboy—up until a few years ago. Then he came into a great deal of money. Now, as you probably know, he runs the Chateau d'If. I can't get anything on that. There's rumors, but anybody that knows anything won't talk. The rumors are not in accord with Paren's background, which is out in the open—no medical or psychosomatic training. The woman was originally a music student, a specialist in primitive music. When Paren left Vienna, she came with him. Paren lives at 5600 Exmoor Avenue—that's the Chateau d'If. Thane Paren lives in a little apartment about a block away, with an old man, no relative. Neither one seems to have any intimate friends, and there's no entertaining, no parties. Not much to go on."

Mario reflected a few moments, somberly gazing out the window while Murris Slade sat impassively waiting for Mario's instructions. At last Mario said, "Keep at it. Get some more on the old man Thane Paren lives with."

One day Correaos called Mario on the telescreen. "We've got the new model blocked out." He was half-placating, half-challenging, daring Mario to disapprove of his work.

"I think we've done a good job," said Correaos. "You wanted to give it a final check."

"I'll be right over," said Mario.

The new model had been built by hand at the Donnic River Plant and flown into Lanchester under camouflage. Correaos managed the showing as if Mario were a buyer, in whom he was trying to whip up enthusiasm.

"The idea of this model—I've tentatively called it the Airfarer—was to use materials which were plain and cheap, dispense with all unnecessary ornament—which, in my opinion, has been the bane of the Ebery Air-car. We've put the savings into clean engineering, lots of room, safety. Notice the lift vanes, they're recessed, almost out of reach. No drunk is going to walk into them. Those pulsors, they're high, and the deflection jets are out of reach. The frame and fuselage are solid cast plancheen, first job like this in the business."

Mario listened, nodded appreciatively from time to time. Apparently Correaos had done a good job. He asked, "How about what's-his-name—Arnold? Has he come up with anything useful?"

Correaos bared his teeth, clicked his tongue. "That man's crazy. He's a walking corpse. All he thinks, all he talks, are his pestiferous electrons, what he calls a blast effect. I saw a demonstration, and I think he's right. We can't use it in a family vehicle."

"What's the jet look like?"

Correaos shrugged. "Nothing much. A generator—centaurium powered—a miniature synchrotron. Very simple. He feeds a single electron into the tube, accelerates it to the near-light speed, and it comes roaring out in a gush as thick as your arm."

Mario frowned. "Try to steer him back onto something useful. He's got the brains. Has he been to a doctor?"

"Just Stapp, the insurance doctor. Stapp says it's a wonder he's alive now. Galloping nephritis or necrosis—some such thing." Correaos spoke without interest. His eyes never left his new Airfarer. He said with more life in his voice, "Look into the interior, notice the wide angle of vision; also the modulating glare filter. Look right up into the sun, all you want. Notice the altimeter, it's got a positive channel indicator, that you can set for any given locality. Then the pressurizer, it's built in under the rear seat—see it?—saves about twenty dollars a unit over the old system. Instead of upholstery, I've had the framework machined smooth, and sprayed it with sprinjufloss."

"You've done a good job, Louis," said Mario. "Go ahead with it."

Correaos took a deep breath, released it, shook his head. "I'll be dyed-double-and-throttled!"

"What's the trouble?"

"I don't get you at all," said Correaos, staring at Mario as if he were a stranger. "If I didn't know you stem to stern, I'd say you were a different man. Three months ago, if I'd tried to put something cleanly designed in front of you, you'd have gone off like one of Arnold's electrons. You'd have called this job a flying bread-box. You'd have draped angel's-wings all over the outside, streamlined the dashboard fixtures, built in two or three Louis Fifteenth bookcases. I don't know what-all. If you didn't look so healthy, I'd say you were sick."

Mario said with an air of sage deliberation, "Ebery Air-car has taken a lot of money out of the public. The old Ebery managed to keep itself in the air, but it cost a lot and looked like a pagoda on wings. Now we'll start giving 'em quality. Maybe they'll turn it down."

Correaos laughed exultantly. "If we can't sell ten million of these, I'll run one up as high as she'll go and jump."

"Better start selling, then."

"I hope you don't have a relapse," said Correaos, "and order a lot of fancy fittings."

"No," said Mario mildly. "She'll go out just as she is, so long as I have anything to say about it."

Correaos slapped the hull of the Airfarer approvingly, turned a quizzical face to Mario. "Your wife has been trying to get in touch with you. I told her I didn't know where you were. You'd better call her—if you want to stay married. She was talking about divorce."

Mario looked off into the distance, uncomfortably aware of Correaos's scrutiny. "I told her to go ahead with it. It's the best thing for everybody concerned. Fairest for her, at any rate."

Correaos shook his head. "You're a funny fellow, Ebery. A year ago you'd have fired me a dozen times over."

"Maybe I'm getting you fat for the slaughter," suggested Mario.

"Maybe," said Correaos. "Letya Arnold and I can go into business making electron elephant guns."

Two hundred thousand artisans swarmed over the Tower, painting, plastering, spraying, fitting in pipes, wires, pouring terrazzo, concrete, plancheen, installing cabinets, a thousand kinds of equipment. Walls were finished with panels of waxed and polished woods, the myriad pools were tiled, the gardeners landscaped the hanging parks, the great green bowers in the clouds.

Every week Mervyn Allen conferred with Taussig and old man Kubal, approving, modifying, altering, canceling, expanding. From recorded copies of the interviews Mario worked, making the changes Allen desired, meshing them carefully into his own designs.

Months passed. Now Mervyn Allen might not have recognized this man as Ralston Ebery. At the Ebery Air-car office in the Aetherian Block, his employees were astounded, respectful. It was a new Ralston Ebery—though, to be sure, they noticed the old gestures, the tricks of speech, habits of walking, dressing, involuntary expressions. This new Ralston Ebery had sloughed away fifty pounds of oil and loose flesh. The sun had tinted the white skin to a baby pink. The eyes, once puffy, now shone out of meaty cheeks; the leg muscles were tough with much walking; the chest was deeper, the lungs stronger from the half-hour of swimming every afternoon at four o'clock.

And at last the two hundred thousand artisans packed their tools, collected their checks. Maintenance men came on the job. Laborers swept, scrubbed, polished. The Empyrean Tower was complete—a solidified dream, a wonder of the world. A building rising like a pine tree, supple and massive, overbounding the minuscule streets and squares below. An edifice not intended for grace, yet achieving grace through its secure footing, its incalculable tapers, set-backs, thousand terraces, thousand taxiplats, million windows.

The Empyrean Tower was completed. Mervyn Allen moved in on a quiet midnight, and the next day the Chateau d'If at 5600 Exmoor Avenue, Meadowlands, was vacant, for sale or for lease.

The Chateau d'If was now Level 900, Empyrean Tower. And Roland Mario ached with eagerness, anxiety, a hot gladness intense to the point of lust. He was slowly cleaning off his desk when Taussig poked his head into the office.

"Well, what are you planning to do now?"

Mario inspected Taussig's curious face. "Any more big jobs?"

"Nope. And not likely to be. At least not through old man Kubal."

"How come? Has he retired?"

"Retired? Shucks, no. He's gone crazy. Schizo."

Mario drummed his fingers on his desk. "When did all this happen?"

"Just yesterday. Seems like finishing the Empyrean was too much for him. A cop found him in Tanagra Square talking to himself, took him home. Doesn't know his nephew, doesn't know his housekeeper. Keeps saying his name is Bray, something like that."

"Bray?" Mario rose to his feet, his forehead knotting. Breaugh. "Sounds like senile decay," he said abstractedly.

"That's right," Taussig responded, still fixing Mario with bright curious eyes. "So what are you going to do now?"

"I quit," said Mario, with an exaggerated sweep of the arm. "I'm done, I'm like old man Kubal. The Empyrean Tower's too much for me. I've got senile decay. Take a good look, Taussig, you'll never see me again." He closed the door in Taussig's slack face. He stepped into the elevator, dropped to the second level, hopped the high-speed strip to his small apartment at Melbourne House. He thumbed the lock, the scanner recognized his prints, the door slid back. Mario entered, closed the door. He undressed Ebery's gross body, wrapped it in a robe, sank with a grunt into a chair beside a big low table.

The table held a complex model built of wood, metal, plastic, vari-colored threads. It represented Level 900, Empyrean Tower—the Chateau d'If.

Mario knew it by heart. Every detail of an area a sixth of a mile square was pressed into his brain.

Presently Mario dressed again, in coveralls of hard gray twill. He loaded his pockets with various tools and equipment, picked up his handbag. He looked at himself in the mirror, at the face that was Ebery and yet not quite Ebery. The torpid glaze had left the eyes. The lips were no longer puffy, the jowls had pulled up, his face was a meaty slab. Thoughtfully Mario pulled a cap over his forehead, surveyed the effect. The man was unrecognizable. He attached a natty wisp of mustache. Ralston Ebery no longer existed.

Mario left the apartment. He hailed a cab, flew out to Meadowlands. The Empyrean Tower reared over the city like a fence-post standing over a field of cabbages. An aircraft beacon scattered red rays from a neck-twisting height. A million lights from nine hundred levels glowed, blended into a rich milky shimmer. A city in itself, where two million, three million men and women might live their lives out if they so wished. It was a monument to the boredom of one man, a man sated with life. The most magnificent edifice ever built, and built for the least consequential of motives that ever caused one rock to be set on another. The Empyrean Tower, built from the conglomerate resources of the planet's richest wealth, was a gigantic toy, a titillation, a fancy.

But who would know this? The 221st level housed the finest hospital in the world. The staff read like the Medical Association's list of Yearly Honors. Level 460 held an Early Cretaceous swamp-forest. Full-scale dinosaurs cropped at archaic vegetation, pterodactyls slipped by on invisible guides, the air held the savage stench of swamp, black ooze, rotting mussels, carrion.

Level 461 enclosed the first human city, Eridu of Sumer, complete with its thirty-foot brick walls, the ziggurat temple to Enlil the Earth god, the palace of the king, the mud huts of the peasants. Level 462 was a Mycenaean Island, lapped by blue salt water. A Minoan temple in an olive grove crowned the height, and a high-beaked galley floated on the water, with sunlight sparkling from bronze shields, glowing from the purple sail.

Level 463 was a landscape from an imaginary fantastic world created by mystic-artist Dyer Lothaire. And Level 509 was a private fairyland, closed to the public, a magic garden inhabited by furtive nymphs.

There were levels for business offices, for dwellings, for laboratories. The fourth level enclosed the world's largest stadium. Levels 320 through 323 housed the University of the World, and the initial enrollment was forty-two thousand; 255 was the world's vastest library; 328 a vast art gallery.

There were showrooms, retail stores, restaurants, quiet taverns, theaters, telecast studios—a complex of the world society caught, pillared up into the air at the whim of Mervyn Allen. Humanity's lust for lost youth had paid for it. Mervyn Allen sold a commodity beside which every ounce of gold ever mined, every prized possession, every ambition and goal, were like nothing. Eternal life, replenished youth—love, loyalty, decency, honor found them unfair over-strong antagonists.

ix

Briskly Mario alighted from the aircab at the public stage on the 52nd level, the coordination center of the tower. Among the crowds of visitors, tenants, employees, he was inconspicuous. He stepped on a pedestrip to the central shaft, stepped off at the express elevator to Level 600. He entered one of the little cars. The door snapped shut, he felt the surge of acceleration, and almost at once the near-weightlessness of the slowing. The door flicked open, he stepped out on Level 600, two miles in the air.

He was in the lobby of the Paradise Inn, beside which the Atlantic-Empire lobby was mean and constricted. He moved among exquisitely dressed men and women, persons of wealth, dignity, power. Mario was inconspicuous. He might have been a janitor or a maintenance electrician. He walked quietly down a corridor, stopped at last by a door marked Private. He thumbed the lock; it opened into a janitor's closet. But the janitors for the 600th level all had other storerooms. No other thumb would spring this lock. In case an officious floor-manager forced the door, it was merely another janitor's closet lost in the confusion.

But it was a very special closet. At the back wall, Mario pushed at a widely separated pair of studs, and the wall fell aside. Mario entered a dark crevice, pushed the wall back into place. Now he was alone—more alone than if he were in the middle of the Sahara. Out in the desert a passing aircraft might spy him. Here in the dead spaces alongside the master columns, among elevator shafts, he was lost from every eye. If he died, no one would find him. In the far, far future, when the Empyrean Tower was at last pulled down, his skeleton might be exposed. Until then he had vanished from the knowledge of man.

He shone his flashlight ahead of him, turned to the central spinal cord of elevator shafts, tubes like fibers in a tremendous vegetable. Here he found his private elevator, lost among the others like a man in a crowd. The mechanics who installed it could not recognize its furtive purpose. It was a job from a blueprint, part of the day's work, quickly forgotten. To Mario it was a link to Level 900, the Chateau d'If.

He stepped on the tiny platform. The door snapped. Up he was thrown, up a mile. The car halted, he stepped out. He was in the Chateau d'If—invisible, a ghost. Unseen, unheard, power was his. He could strike from nothingness, unsuspected, unimagined, master of the master of the Chateau d'If.

He breathed the air, exultant, thrilling to his power. This was the ultimate height of his life. He snapped on his torch, though there was no need. He knew these passages as if he had been born among them. The light was a symbol of his absolute authority. He had no need for skulking. He was in his private retreat, secure, isolated, remote.

Mario halted, glanced at the wall. At eight-foot intervals circles of fluorescent paint gleamed brightly. Behind this wall would be the grand foyer to the Chateau d'If. Mario advanced to one of the fluorescent circles. These he himself had painted to mark the location of his spy cells. These were little dull spots hardly bigger than the head of a pin, invisible at three feet. Mario, in the guise of an electrician, had installed them himself, with a pair at every location, for binocular vision.

From his pouch he brought a pair of goggles, clipped a wire to the terminal contacts of the spy cells, fitted the goggles over his eyes. Now he saw the interior of the foyer as clearly as if he were looking through a door.

It was the height of a reception—a housewarming party at the Chateau d'If. Men, old, young, distinguished or handsome or merely veneered with the glow of success; women at once serene and arrogant, the style and show of the planet. Mario saw jewels, gold, the shine and swing of thousand-colored fabrics, and at eye-level, the peculiar white-bronze-brown-black mixture, the color of many heads, many faces—crowd-color.

Mario recognized some of these people, faces and names world-known. Artists, administrators, engineers, bon-vivants, courtesans, philosophers, all thronging the lobby of the Chateau d'If, drawn by the ineffable lure of the unknown, the exciting, the notorious.

There was Mervyn Allen, wearing black. He was as handsome as a primeval sun-hero, tall, confident, easy in his manner, but humble and carefully graceful, combining the offices of proprietor and host.

Thane Paren was nowhere in sight.

Mario moved on. As at 5600 Exmoor, he found a room drenched with amber-white light, golden, crisp as celery, where the broad-leafed plants grew as ardently as in their native humus. The herbarium was empty, the plants suspired numbing perfume for their own delectation.

Mario passed on. He looked into a room bare and undecorated, a work-shop, a processing plant. A number of rubber-wheeled tables were docked against a wall, each with its frock of white cloth. A balcony across the room supported an intricate mesh of machinery, black curving arms, shiny metal, glass. Below hung a pair of translucent balls, the pallid blue color of Roquefort cheese. Mario looked closely. These were the golasma cellules.

No one occupied the chamber except a still form on one of the stretchers. The face was partly visible. Mario, suddenly attentive, shifted his vantage point. He saw a heavy blond head, rugged blunt features. He moved to another cell. He was right. It was Janniver, already drugged, ready for the transposition.

Mario gave a long heavy suspiration that shook Ebery's paunch. Ditmar had made it. Zaer, Mario, Breaugh, and now Janniver, lured into this room like sheep the Judas-goat conducts to the abattoir. Mario bared his teeth in a grimace that was not a smile. A tide of dark rage rose in his mind.

He calmed himself. The grimace softened into the normal loose lines of Ebery's face. Who was blameless, after all? Thane Paren? No. She served Mervyn Allen, the soul in her brother's body. He himself, Roland Mario? He might have killed Mervyn Allen, he might have halted the work of the Chateau d'If by crying loudly enough to the right authorities. He had refrained, from fear of losing his body. Pete Zaer? He might have kept to the spirit of his bargain, warned his friends on the Oxonian Terrace.

All the other victims, who had similarly restrained their rage and sense of obligation to their fellow men? No, Ditmar was simply a human being, as weak and selfish as any other, and his sins were those of commission rather than those of omission, which characterized the others.

Mario wandered on, peering in apartment, chamber and hall. A blonde girl, young and sweet as an Appalachian gilly-flower, swam nude in Allen's long green-glass pool, then sat on the edge amid a cloud of silver bubbles. Mario cursed the lascivious responses of Ebery's body, passed on. Nowhere did he see Thane Paren.

He returned to the reception hall. The party was breaking up, with Mervyn Allen bowing his guests out, men and women flushed with his food and drink, all cordial, all promising themselves to renew the acquaintance on a later, less conspicuous occasion.

Mario watched till the last had left—the last but one, this an incredibly tall, thin old man, dressed like a fop in pearl-gray and white. His wrists were like corn-stalks, his head was all skull. He leaned across Mervyn Allen's shoulder, a roguish perfumed old dandy, waxed, rouged, pomaded.

Now Allen made a polite inquiry, and the old man nodded, beamed. Allen ushered him into a small side-room, an office painted dark gray and green.

The old man sat down, wrote a check. Allen dropped it into the telescreen slot, and the two waited, making small talk. The old man seemed to be pressing for information, while Allen gracefully brushed him aside. The telescreen flickered, flashed an acknowledgment from the bank. Allen rose to his feet. The old man arose. Allen took a deep breath; they stepped into the herbarium. The old man took three steps, tottered. Allen caught him deftly, laid him on a concealed rubber-tired couch, wheeled him forward, out into the laboratory where Janniver lay aready.

Now Mario watched with the most careful of eyes, and into a socket in his goggles he plugged another cord leading to a camera in his pouch. Everything he saw would be recorded permanently.

There was little to see. Allen wheeled Janniver under one of the whey-colored golasma cellules, the old man under another. He turned a dial, kicked at a pedal, flicked a switch, stood back. The entire balcony lowered. The cellules engulfed the two heads, pulsed, changed shape. There was motion on the balcony, wheels turning, the glow of luminescence. The operation appeared self-contained, automatic.

Allen seated himself, lit a cigarette, yawned. Five minutes passed. The balcony rose, the golasma cellules swung on an axis, the balcony lowered. Another five minutes passed. The balcony raised. Allen stepped forward, threw off the switches.

Allen gave each body an injection from the same hypodermic, rolled the couches into an adjoining room, departed without a backward glance.

Toward the swimming pool, thought Mario. Let him go!

At nine o'clock in Tanagra Square, a cab dropped off a feeble lack-luster old man, tall and thin as a slat, who immediately sought a bench.

Mario waited till the old man showed signs of awareness, watched the dawning alarm, the frenzied examination of emaciated hands, the realization of fifty stolen years. Mario approached, led the old man to a cab, took him to his apartment. The morning was a terrible one.

Janniver was asleep, exhausted from terror, grief, hate for his creaking old body. Mario called the Brannan agency, asked for Murris Slade. The short heavy man with the narrow head appeared on the screen, gazed through the layers of ground glass at Mario.

"Hello, Slade," said Mario. "There's a job I want done tonight."

Slade looked at him with a steady wary eye. "Does it get me in trouble?"

"No."

"What's the job?"

"This man you've been watching for me, Roland Mario, do you know where to find him?"

"He's at the Persian Terrace having breakfast with the girl he spent the night with. Her name is Laura Lingtza; she's a dancer at the Vedanta Epic Theater."

"Never mind about that. Get a piece of paper, copy what I'm going to dictate."

"Go ahead, I'm ready."

"'Meet me at eleven p.m. at the Cambodian Pillar, lobby of Paradise Inn, Level Six Hundred, Empyrean Tower. Important. Come by yourself. Please be on time, as I can spare only a few minutes. Mervyn Allen, Chateau d'If.'"

Mario waited a moment till Slade looked up from his writing. "Type that out," he said. "Hand it to Roland Mario at about nine-thirty tonight."

X

Restlessly Mario paced the floor, pudgy hands clasped behind his back. Tonight would see the fruit of a year's racking toil with brain and imagination. Tonight, with luck, he would shed the hateful identity of Ralston Ebery. He thought of Louis Correaos. Poor Louis, and Mario shook his head. What would happen to Louis' Airfarer? And Letya Arnold? Would he go back out into Tanagra Square to lurk and hiss as Ralston Ebery sauntered pompously past?

He called the Aetherian Block, got put through to Louis Correaos. "How's everything, Louis?"

"Going great. We're all tooled up, be producing next week."

"How's Arnold?"

Correaos screwed up his face. "Ebery, you'll think I'm as crazy as Arnold. But he can fly faster than light."

"What?"

"Last Thursday night he wandered into the office. He acted mysterious, told me to follow him. I went. He took me up to his observatory—just a window at the sky where he's got a little proton magniscope. He focused it, told me to look. I looked, saw a disk—a dull dark disk about as large as a full moon. 'Pluto,' said Arnold. 'In about ten minutes, there'll be a little white flash on the left-hand side.' 'How do you know?' 'I set off a flare a little over six hours ago. The light should be reaching here about now.'

"I gave him a queer look, but I kept my eye glued on the image, and sure enough—there it was, a little spatter of white light. 'Now watch,' he says, 'there'll be a red one.' And he's right. There's a red light." Correaos shook his big sandy head. "Ebery, I'm convinced. He's got me believing him."

Mario said in a toneless voice, "Put him on, Louis, if you can find him."

After a minute or so Letya Arnold's peaked face peered out of the screen. Mario said leadenly, "Is this true, Arnold? That you're flying faster than light?"

Arnold said peevishly, "Of course it's true, why shouldn't it be true?"

"How did you do it?"

"Just hooked a couple of electron-pushers on to one of your high-altitude air-cars. Nothing else. I just turned on the juice. The hook-up breaks blazing fury out of the universe. There's no acceleration, no momentum, nothing. Just speed, speed, speed, speed. Puts the stars within a few days' run, I've always told you, and you said I was crazy." His face wrenched, gall burnt at his tongue. "I'll never see them, Ebery, and you're to blame. I'm a dead man. I saw Pluto, I wrote my name on the ice, and that's how I'll be known."

He vanished from the screen. Correaos returned. "He's a goner," said Correaos gruffly. "He had a hemorrhage last night. There'll be just one more—his last."

Mario said in a far voice, "Take care of him, Louis. Because tomorrow I'm afraid maybe things will be different."

"What do you mean—different?"

"Ralston Ebery's disposition might suffer a relapse."

"God forbid."

Mario broke the connection, went back to his pacing, but now he paced slower, and his eyes saw nothing of where he walked...

Mario called a bellboy. "See that young man in the tan jacket by the Cambodian Pillar?"

"Yes, sir."

"Give him this note."

"Yes, sir."

Ralston Ebery had put loose flesh on Mario's body. Pouches hung under the eyes, the mouth was loose, wet. Mario sweated in a sudden heat of pure anger. The swine, debauching a sound body, unused to the filth Ebery's brain would invent!

Ebery read the note, looked up and down the lobby. Mario had already gone. Ebery, following the instructions, turned down the corridor toward the air-baths, moving slowly, indecisively.

He came to a door marked Private, which stood ajar. He knocked.

"Allen, are you there? What's all this about?"

"Come in," said Mario.

Ebery cautiously shoved his head through the door. Mario yanked him forward, slapped a hand-hypo at Ebery's neck. Ebery struggled, kicked, quivered, relaxed. Mario shut the door.

"Get up," said Mario. Ebery rose to his feet, docile, glassy-eyed. Mario took him through the back door, up in the elevator, up to Level 900, the Chateau d'If.

"Sit down, don't move," said Mario. Ebery sat like a barnacle. Mario made a careful reconnaissance. This time of night Mervyn Allen should be through for the day.

Allen was just finishing a transposition. Mario watched as he pushed the two recumbent forms into the outer waiting room, and then he trailed Allen to his living quarters, watched while he shed his clothes, jumped into a silk jerkin, ready for relaxation or sport with his flower-pretty blonde girl.

The coast was clear. Mario returned to where Ebery sat.

"Stand up, and follow me."

Back down the secret corridors inside the ventilation ducts, and now the laboratory was empty. Mario lifted a hasp, pulled back one of the pressed wood wall panels.

"Go in," he said. "Lie down on that couch." Ebery obeyed.

Mario wheeled him across the room to the racked putty-colored brain-molds, wheeled over another couch for himself. He held his mind in a rigid channel, letting himself think of nothing but the transposition.

He set the dials, kicked in the foot-pedal, as Allen had done. Now to climb on the couch, push one more button. He stood looking at the recumbent figure. Now was the time. Act. It was easy; just climb on the couch, reach up, push a button. But Mario stood looking, swaying slightly back and forth.

A slight sound behind him. He whirled. Thane Paren watched him with detached amusement. She made no move to come forward, to flee, to shout for help. She watched with an expression—quizzical, unhuman. Mario wondered, how can beauty be refined to such reckless heights, and still be so cold and friendless? If she were wounded, would she bleed? Now, at this moment, would she run, give the alarm? If she moved, he would kill her.

"Go ahead," said Thane. "What's stopping you? I won't interfere."

Mario had known this somehow. He turned, looked down at his flaccid body. He frowned.

"Don't like its looks?" asked Thane. "It's not how you remember yourself? You're all alike, strutting, boastful animals."

"No," said Mario slowly, "I thought all I lived for was to get back my body. Now I don't know. I don't think I want it. I'm Ebery the industrialist. He's Mario the playboy."

"Ah," said Thane raising her luminous eyebrows, "you like the money, the power."

Mario laughed, a faint hurt laugh. "You've been with those ideas too long. They've gone to your head. There's other things. The stars to explore. The galaxy—a meadow of magnificent jewels...As Ebery, I can leave for the stars next week. As Mario, I go back to the Oxonian Terrace, play handball."

She took a step forward. "Are you—"

He said, "Just this last week a physicist burst through whatever the bindings are that are holding things in. He made it to Pluto in fifteen minutes. Ebery wouldn't listen to him. He's so close to dead right now, you couldn't tell the difference. Ebery would say he's crazy, jerk the whole project. Because there's no evidence other than the word of two men."

"So?" asked Thane. "What will you do?"

"I want my body," said Mario slowly. "I hate this pig's carcass worse than I hate death. But more than that, I want to go to the stars."

She came forward a little. Her eyes shone like Vega and Spica on a warm summer night. How could he have ever thought her cold? She was quick, hot, full-bursting with verve, passion, imagination. "I want to go too."

"Where is this everybody wants to go?" said a light baritone voice, easy on the surface, yet full of a furious undercurrent. Mervyn Allen was swiftly crossing the room. He swung his great athlete's arms loose from the shoulder, clenching and unclenching his hands. "Where do you want to go?" He addressed Mario. "Hell, is it? Hell it shall be." He rammed his fist forward.

Mario lumbered back, then forward again. Ebery's body was not a fighting machine. It was pulpy, pear-shaped, and in spite of Mario's ascetic life, the paunch still gurgled, swung to and fro like a wet sponge. But he fought. He fought with a red ferocity that matched Allen's strength and speed for a half-minute. And then his legs were like columns of pith, his arms could not seem to move. He saw Allen stepping forward, swinging a tremendous massive blow that would crush his jaw like a cardboard box, jar out, shiver his teeth.

Crack! Allen screamed, a wavering falsetto screech, sagged, fell with a gradual slumping motion.

Thane stood looking at the body, holding a pistol.

"That's your brother," gasped Mario, more terrified by Thane's expression than by the fight for life with Allen.

"It's my brother's body. My brother died this morning. Early, at sunrise. Allen had promised he wouldn't let him die, that he would give him a body…And my brother died this morning."

She looked down at the hulk. "When he was young, he was so fine. Now his brain is dead and his body is dead."

She laid the gun on a table. "But I've known it would come. I'm sick of it. No more. Now we shall go to the stars. You and I, if you'll take me. What do I care if your body is gross? Your brain is you."

"Allen is dead," said Mario as if in a dream. "There is no one to interfere. The Chateau d'If is ours."

She looked at him doubtfully, lip half-curled. "So?"

"Where is the telescreen?"

The room suddenly seemed full of people. Mario became aware of the fact with surprise. He had noticed nothing; he had been busy. Now he was finished.

Sitting anesthetized side by side were four old men, staring into space with eyes that later would know the sick anguish of youth and life within reach and lost.

Standing across the room, pale, nervous, quiet, stood Zaer, Breaugh, Janniver. And Ralston Ebery's body. But the body spoke with the fast rush of thought that was Letya Arnold's.

And in Letya Arnold's wasted body, not now conscious, dwelt the mind of Ralston Ebery.

Mario walked in his own body, testing the floor with his own feet, swinging his arms, feeling his face. Thane Paren stood watching him with intent eyes, as if she were seeing light, form, color for the first time, as if Roland Mario were the only thing that life could possibly hold for her.

No one else was in the room. Murris Slade, who had lured, bribed, threatened, frightened those now in the room to the Chateau d'If, had not come farther than the foyer.

Mario addressed Janniver, Zaer, Breaugh. "You three, then, you will take the responsibility?"

They turned on him their wide, amazed eyes, still not fully recovered from the relief, the joy of their own lives. "Yes."…"Yes."…"Yes."

"Some of the transpositions are beyond help. Some are dead or crazy. There is no help for them. But those whom you can return to their own bodies—to them is your responsibility."

"We break the cursed machine into the smallest pieces possible," said Breaugh. "And the Chateau d'If is only something for whispering, something for old men to dream about."

Mario smiled. "Remember the advertisement? 'Jaded? Bored? Try the Chateau d'If.'"

"I am no longer jaded, no longer bored," sighed Zaer.

"We got our money's worth," said Janniver wryly.

Mario frowned. "Where's Ditmar?"

Thane said, "He has an appointment for ten o'clock tomorrow morning. He comes for the new body he has earned."

Breaugh said with quiet satisfaction, "We shall be here to meet him."

"He will be surprised," said Janniver.

"Why not?" asked Zaer. "After all, this is the Chateau d'If."

The Potters of Firsk

The yellow bowl on Thomm's desk stood about a foot high, flaring out
from a width of eight inches at the base to a foot across the rim. The profile showed a simple curve, clean and sharp, with a full sense of completion; the
body was thin without fragility; the whole piece gave an impression of ringing
well-arched strength.

The craftsmanship of the body was matched by the beauty of the glaze—a
glorious transparent yellow, luminescent like a hot summer afterglow. It was the
essence of marigolds, a watery wavering saffron, a yellow as of transparent gold,
a yellow glass that seemed to fabricate curtains of light within itself and fling
them off, a yellow brilliant but mild, tart as lemon, sweet as quince jelly, soothing as sunlight.

Keselsky had been furtively eying the bowl during his interview with Thomm,
personnel chief for the Department of Planetary Affairs. Now, with the interview
over, he could not help but bend forward to examine the bowl more closely. He
said with obvious sincerity: "This is the most beautiful piece I've ever seen."

Thomm, a man of early middle-age with a brisk gray mustache, a sharp but
tolerant eye, leaned back in his chair. "It's a souvenir. Souvenir's as good a name
for it as anything else. I got it many years ago, when I was your age." He glanced
at his desk clock. "Lunch-time."

Keselsky looked up, hastily reached for his brief case. "Excuse me, I had no
idea—"

Thomm raised his hand. "Not so fast. I'd like you to have lunch with me."

Keselsky muttered embarrassed excuses, but Thomm insisted.

"Sit down, by all means." A menu appeared on the screen. "Now—look
that over."

Without further urging Keselsky made a selection, and Thomm spoke into
the mesh. The wall opened, a table slid out with their lunch.

Even while eating Keselsky fondled the bowl with his eyes. Over coffee,
Thomm handed it across the table. Keselsky hefted it, stroked the surface, looked
deep into the glaze.

"Where on earth did you find such a marvelous piece?" He examined the
bottom, frowned at the marks scratched in the clay.

"Not on Earth," said Thomm. "On the planet Firsk." He sat back. "There's a story connected with that bowl." He paused inquiringly.

Keselsky hurriedly swore that nothing could please him more than to listen while Thomm spoke of all things under the sun. Thomm smiled faintly. After all, this was Keselsky's first job.

"As I've mentioned, I was about your age," said Thomm. "Perhaps a year or two older, but then I'd been out on the Channel Planet for nineteen months. When my transfer to Firsk came I was naturally very pleased, because Channel, as perhaps you know, is a bleak planet, full of ice and frost-fleas and the dullest aborigines in space—"

Thomm was entranced with Firsk. It was everything the Channel Planet had not been: warm, fragrant, the home of the Mi-Tuun, a graceful people of a rich, quaint and ancient culture. Firsk was by no means a large planet, though its gravity approached that of Earth. The land surface was small—a single equatorial continent in the shape of a dumbbell.

The Planetary Affairs Bureau was located at Penolpan, a few miles in from the South Sea, a city of fable and charm. The tinkle of music was always to be heard somewhere in the distance; the air was mellow with incense and a thousand flower scents. The low houses of reed, parchment and dark wood were arranged negligently, three-quarters hidden under the foliage of trees and vines. Canals of green water laced the city, arched over by wooden bridges trailing ivy and orange flowers, and here swam boats each decorated in an intricate many-colored pattern.

The inhabitants of Penolpan, the amber-skinned Mi-Tuun, were a mild people devoted to the pleasures of life, sensuous without excess, relaxed and gay, guiding their lives by ritual. They fished in the South Sea, cultivated cereals and fruit, manufactured articles of wood, resin and paper. Metal was scarce on Firsk, and was replaced in many instances by tools and utensils of earthenware, fabricated so cleverly that the lack was never felt.

Thomm found his work at the Penolpan Bureau pleasant in the extreme, marred only by the personality of his superior. This was George Covill, a short ruddy man with prominent blue eyes, heavy wrinkled eyelids, sparse sandy hair. He had a habit, when he was displeased—which was often—of cocking his head sidewise and staring for a brittle five seconds. Then, if the offense was great, he exploded in wrath; if not, he stalked away.

On Penolpan Covill's duties were more of a technical than sociological nature, and even so, in line with the Bureau's policy of leaving well-balanced cultures undisturbed, there was little to occupy him. He imported silica yarn to replace the root fiber from which the Mi-Tuun wove their nets; he built a small cracking plant and converted the fish oil they burned in their lamps into a lighter cleaner fluid. The varnished paper of Penolpan's houses had a tendency to absorb moisture and split after a few months of service. Covill brought in a plastic varnish which protected them indefinitely. Aside from these minor innovations Covill did little. The Bureau's policy was to improve the native standard of living within the framework of its own culture, introducing Earth methods, ideas, philosophy very gradually and only when the natives themselves felt the need.

Before long, however, Thomm came to feel that Covill paid only lip-service to the Bureau philosophy. Some of his actions seemed dense and arbitrary to the well-indoctrinated Thomm. He built an Earth-style office on Penolpan's main canal, and the concrete and glass made an inexcusable jar against Penolpan's mellow ivories and browns. He kept strict office hours and on a dozen occasions a delegation of Mi-Tuun, arriving in ceremonial regalia, had to be turned away with stammered excuses by Thomm, when in truth Covill, disliking the crispness of his linen suit, had stripped to the waist and was slumped in a wicker chair with a cigar, a quart of beer, watching girl-shows on his telescreen.

Thomm was assigned to Pest Control, a duty Covill considered beneath his dignity. On one of his rounds Thomm first heard mentioned the Potters of Firsk.

Laden with insect spray, with rat-poison cartridges dangling from his belt, he had wandered into the poorest outskirts of Penolpan, where the trees ended and the dry plain stretched out to the Kukmank Mountains. In this relatively drab location he came upon a long open shed, a pottery bazaar. Shelves and tables held ware of every description, from stoneware crocks for pickling fish to tiny vases thin as paper, lucent as milk. Here were plates large and small, bowls of every size and shape, no two alike, ewers, tureens, demijohns, tankards. One rack held earthenware knives, the clay vitrified till it rang like iron, the cutting edge chipped cleanly, sharper than any razor, from a thick dripping of glaze.

Thomm was astounded by the colors. Rare rich ruby, the green of flowing river water, turquoise ten times deeper than the sky. He saw metallic purples, browns shot with blond light, pinks, violets, grays, dappled russets, blues of copper and cobalt, the odd streaks and flows of rutilated glass. Certain glazes bloomed with crystals like snowflakes, others held floating within them tiny spangles of metal.

Thomm was delighted with his find. Here was beauty of form, of material, of craftsmanship. The sound body, sturdy with natural earthy strength given to wood and clay, the melts of colored glass, the quick restless curves of the vases, the capacity of the bowls, the expanse of the plates—they produced a tremendous enthusiasm in Thomm. And yet—there were puzzling aspects to the bazaar. First—he looked up and down the shelves—something was lacking. In the many-colored display he missed—yellow. There were no yellow glazes of any sort. A cream, a straw, an amber—but no full-bodied glowing yellow.

Perhaps the potters avoided the color through superstition, Thomm speculated, or perhaps because of identification with royalty, like the ancient Chinese of Earth, or perhaps because of association with death or disease—The train of thought led to the second puzzle: Who were the potters? There were no kilns in Penolpan to fire ware such as this.

He approached the clerk, a girl just short of maturity, who had been given an exquisite loveliness. She wore the *pareu* of the Mi-Tuun, a flowered sash about the waist, and reed sandals. Her skin glowed like one of the amber glazes at her back; she was slender, quiet, friendly.

"This is all very beautiful," said Thomm. "For instance, what is the price of this?" He touched a tall flagon glazed a light green, streaked and shot with silver threads.

The price she mentioned, in spite of the beauty of the piece, was higher than what he had expected. Observing his surprise, the girl said, "They are our ancestors, and to sell them as cheaply as wood or glass would be irreverent."

Thomm raised his eyebrows, and decided to ignore what he considered a ceremonial personification.

"Where's the pottery made?" he asked. "In Penolpan?"

The girl hesitated and Thomm felt a sudden shade of restraint. She turned her head, looked out toward the Kukmank Range. "Back in the hills are the kilns; out there our ancestors go, and the pots are brought back. Aside from this I know nothing."

Thomm said carefully, "Do you prefer not to talk of it?"

She shrugged. "Indeed, there's no reason why I should. Except that we Mi-Tuun fear the Potters, and the thought of them oppresses us."

"But why is that?"

She grimaced. "No one knows what lies beyond the first hill. Sometimes we see the glow of furnaces, and then sometimes when there are no dead for the Potters they take the living."

Thomm thought that if so, here was a case for the interference of the Bureau, even to the extent of armed force.

"Who are these Potters?"

"There," she said, and pointed. "There is a Potter."

Following her finger, he saw a man riding out along the plain. He was taller, heavier than the Mi-Tuun. Thomm could not see him distinctly, wrapped as he was in a long gray burnoose, but he appeared to have a pale skin and reddish-brown hair. He noted the bulging panniers on the pack-beast. "What's he taking with him now?"

"Fish, paper, cloth, oil—goods he traded his pottery for."

Thomm picked up his pest-killing equipment. "I think I'll visit the Potters one of these days."

"No—" said the girl.

"Why not?"

"It's very dangerous. They're fierce, secretive—"

Thomm smiled. "I'll be careful."

Back at the Bureau he found Covill stretched out on a wicker chaise lounge, half-asleep. At the sight of Thomm he roused himself, sat up.

"Where the devil have you been? I told you to get the estimates on that power plant ready today."

"I put them on your desk," replied Thomm politely. "If you've been out front at all, you couldn't have missed them."

Covill eyed him belligerently, but for once found himself at a loss for words. He subsided in his chair with a grunt. As a general rule Thomm paid little heed to Covill's sharpness, recognizing it as resentment against the main office. Covill felt his abilities deserved greater scope, a more important post.

Thomm sat down, helped himself to a glass of Covill's beer. "Do you know anything about the potteries back in the mountains?"

Covill grunted: "A tribe of bandits, something of the sort." He hunched forward, reached for the beer.

"I looked into the pottery bazaar today," said Thomm. "A clerk called the pots 'ancestors'. Seemed rather strange."

"The longer you knock around the planets," Covill stated, "the stranger things you see. Nothing could surprise me any more—except maybe a transfer to the Main Office." He snorted bitterly, gulped at his beer. Refreshed, he went on in a less truculent voice, "I've heard odds and ends about these Potters, nothing definite, and I've never had time to look into 'em . I suppose it's religious ceremonial, rites of death. They take away the dead bodies, bury 'em for a fee or trade goods."

"The clerk said that when they don't get the dead, sometimes they take the living."

"Eh? What's that?" Covill's hard blue eyes stared bright from his red face. Thomm repeated his statement.

Covill scratched his chin, presently hoisted himself to his feet. "Let's fly out, just for the devilment of it, and see what these Potters are up to. Been wanting to go out a long time."

Thomm brought the copter out of the hangar, set down in front of the office, and Covill gingerly climbed in. Covill's sudden energy mystified Thomm, especially since it included a ride in the copter. Covill had an intense dislike of flying, and usually refused to set foot in an aircraft.

The blades sang, grabbed the air, the copter wafted high. Penolpan became a checkerboard of brown roofs and foliage. Thirty miles distant, across a dry sandy plain, rose the Kukmank Range—barren shoulders and thrusts of gray rock. At first sight locating a settlement among the tumble appeared a task of futility.

Covill, peering down into the wastes, grumbled something to this effect; Thomm, however, pointed toward a column of smoke. "Potters need kilns. Kilns need heat—"

As they approached the smoke, they saw that it issued not from brick stacks but from a fissure at the peak of a conical dome.

"Volcano," said Covill, with an air of vindication. "Let's try out there along that ridge—then if there's nothing we'll go back."

Thomm had been peering intently below. "I think we've found them right here. Look close, you can see buildings."

He dropped the copter, and the rows of stone houses became plain.

"Should we land?" Thomm asked dubiously. "They're supposed to be fairly rough."

"Certainly, set down," snapped Covill. "We're official representatives of the System."

The fact might mean little to a tribe of mountaineers, reflected Thomm; nevertheless he let the copter drop onto a stony flat place in the center of the village.

The copter , if it had not alarmed the Potters, at least had made them cautious. For several minutes there was no sign of life. The stone cabins stood bleak and vacant as cairns.

Covill alighted, and Thomm, assuring himself that his gamma-gun was in easy reach, followed. Covill stood by the copter, looking up and down the line of houses. "Cagey set of beggars," he growled. "Well…we better stay here till someone makes a move."

To this plan Thomm agreed heartily, so they waited in the shadow of the copter. It was clearly the village of the Potters. Shards lay everywhere—brilliant bits of glazed ware glinting like lost jewels. Down the slope rose a heap of broken bisque, evidently meant for later use, and beyond was a long tile-roofed shed. Thomm sought in vain for a kiln. A fissure into the side of the mountain caught his eye, a fissure with a well-worn path leading into it. An intriguing hypothesis formed in his mind—but now three men had appeared, tall and erect in gray burnooses. The hoods were flung back, and they looked like monks of medieval Earth, except that instead of monkish tonsure, fuzzy red hair rose in a peaked mound above their heads.

The leader approached with a determined step, and Thomm stiffened, prepared for anything. Not so Covill; he appeared contemptuously at ease, a lord among serfs.

Ten feet away the leader halted—a man taller than Thomm with a hook nose, hard intelligent eyes like gray pebbles. He waited an instant but Covill only watched him. At last the Potter spoke in a courteous tone.

"What brings strangers to the village of the Potters?"

"I'm Covill, of the Planetary Affairs Bureau in Penolpan, official representative of the System. This is merely a routine visit, to see how things are going with you."

"We make no complaints," replied the chief.

"I've heard reports of you Potters kidnapping Mi-Tuun," said Covill. "Is there any truth in that?"

"Kidnapping?" mused the chief. "What is that?"

Covill explained. The chief rubbed his chin, staring at Covill with eyes black as water.

"There is an ancient agreement," said the chief at last. "The Potters are granted the bodies of the dead; and occasionally when the need is great, we do anticipate nature by a year or two. But what matter? The soul lives forever in the pot it beautifies."

Covill brought out his pipe, and Thomm held his breath. Loading the pipe was sometimes a preliminary to the cold sidelong stares which occasionally ended in an explosion of wrath. For the moment however Covill held himself in check.

"Just what do you do with the corpses?"

The leader raised his eyebrows in surprise. "Is it not obvious? No? But then you are no potter—Our glazes require lead, sand, clay, alkali, spar and lime. All but the lime is at our hand, and this we extract from the bones of the dead."

Covill lit his pipe, puffed. Thomm relaxed. For the moment the danger was past.

"I see," said Covill. "Well, we don't want to interfere in any native customs, rites or practices, so long as the peace isn't disturbed. You'll have to understand there can't be any more kidnapping . The corpses—that's between you and whoever's responsible for the body, but lives are more important than pots. If you need lime, I can get you tons of it. There must be limestone beds somewhere on the planet. One of these days I'll send Thomm out prospecting and you'll have more lime than you'll know what to do with."

The chief shook his head, half amused. "Natural lime is a poor substitute for the fresh live lime of bones. There are certain other salts which act as fluxes, and then, of course, the spirit of the person is in the bones and this passes into the glaze and gives it an inner fire otherwise unobtainable."

Covill puffed, puffed, puffed, watching the chief with his hard blue eyes. "I don't care what you use," he said, "as long as there's no kidnapping , no murder. If you need lime, I'll help you find it; that's what I'm here for, to help you, and raise your standard of living; but I'm also here to protect the Mi-Tuun from raiding. I can do both—one about as good as the other."

The corners of the chief's mouth drew back. Thomm interposed a question before he spat out an angry reply. "Tell me, where are your kilns?"

The chief turned him a cool glance. "Our firing is done by the Great Monthly Burn. We stack our ware in the caves, and then, on the twenty-second day, the scorch rises from below. One entire day the heat roars up white and glowing, and two weeks later the caves have cooled for us to go after our ware."

"That sounds interesting," said Covill. "I'd like to look around your works. Where's your pottery, down there in that shed?"

The chief moved not a muscle. "No man may look inside that shed," he said slowly, "unless he is a Potter—and then only after he has proved his mastery of the clay."

"How does he go about that?" Covill asked lightly.

"At the age of fourteen he goes forth from his home with a hammer, a mortar, a pound of bone lime. He must mine clay, lead, sand, spar. He must find iron for brown, malachite for green, cobalt earth for blue, and he must grind a glaze in his mortar, shape and decorate a tile, and set it in the Mouth of the Great Burn. If the tile is successful, the body whole, the glaze good, then he is permitted to enter the long pottery and know the secrets of the craft."

Covill pulled the pipe from his mouth, asked quizzically, "And if the tile's no good?"

"We need no poor Potters," said the chief. "We always need bone-lime."

Thomm had been glancing along the shards of colored pottery. "Why don't you use yellow glaze?"

The chief flung out his arms. "Yellow glaze? It is unknown, a secret no Potter has penetrated. Iron gives a dingy tan, silver a gray-yellow, and antimony burns out in the heat of the Great Burn. The pure rich yellow, the color of the sun…ah, that is a dream."

Covill was uninterested. "Well, we'll be flying back, since you don't care to show us around. Remember, if there's any technical help you want, I can get it for you. I might even find how to make you your precious yellow—"

"Impossible," said the chief. "Have not we, the Potters of the Universe, sought for thousands of years?"

"…But there must be no more taking of lives. If necessary, I'll put a stop to the potting altogether."

The chief's eyes blazed. "Your words are not friendly!"

"If you don't think I can do it, you're mistaken," said Covill. "I'll drop a bomb down the throat of your volcano and cave in the entire mountain. The System protects every man-jack everywhere, and that means the Mi-Tuun from a tribe of Potters who wants their bones."

Thomm plucked him nervously by the sleeve. "Get back in the copter," he whispered. "They're getting ugly. In another minute they'll jump us."

Covill turned his back on the lowering chief, deliberately climbed into the copter. Thomm followed more warily. In his eyes the chief was teetering on the verge of attack, and Thomm had no inclination for fighting.

He flung in the clutch; the blades chewed at the air; the copter rose, leaving a knot of gray-burnoosed Potters silent below.

Covill settled back with an air of satisfaction. "There's only one way to handle people like that, and that is, get the upper hand on 'em; that's the only way they'll respect you. You act just a little uncertain, they sense it, sure as fate, and then you're a goner."

Thomm said nothing. Covill's methods might produce immediate results, but in the long run they seemed short-sighted , intolerant, unsympathetic. In Covill's place he would have stressed the Bureau's ability to provide substitutes for the bone-lime, and possibly assist with any technical difficulties—though indeed, they seemed to be masters of their craft, completely sure of their ability. Yellow glaze, of course, still was lacking them. That evening he inserted a strip from the Bureau library into his portable viewer. The subject was pottery, and Thomm absorbed as much of the lore as he was able.

Covill's pet project—a small atomic power plant to electrify Penolpan— kept him busy the next few days, even though he worked reluctantly. Penolpan, with its canals softly lit by yellow lanterns, the gardens glowing to candles and rich with the fragrance of night-blossoms , was a city from fairyland; electricity, motors, fluorescents, water pumps would surely dim the charm—Covill, however, was insistent that the world would benefit by a gradual integration into the tremendous industrial complex of the System.

Twice Thomm passed by the pottery bazaar and twice he turned in, both to marvel at the glistening ware and to speak with the girl who tended the shelves. She had a fascinating beauty, grace and charm, breathed into her soul by a lifetime in Penolpan; she was interested in everything Thomm had to tell her of the outside universe, and Thomm, young, softhearted and lonely, looked forward to his visits with increasing anticipation.

For a period Covill kept him furiously busy. Reports were due at the home office, and Covill assigned the task to Thomm, while he either dozed in his wicker chair or rode the canals of Penolpan in his special red and black boat.

At last, late one afternoon, Thomm threw aside his journals and set off down the street, under the shade of great kaotang trees. He crossed through the central market, where the shopkeepers were busy with late trade, turned down a path beside a turf-banked canal and presently came to the pottery bazaar.

But he looked in vain for the girl. A thin man in a black jacket stood quietly to the side, waiting his pleasure. At last Thomm turned to him. "Where's Su-then?"

The man hesitated, Thomm grew impatient.

"Well, where is she? Sick? Has she given up working here?"

"She has gone."

"Gone where?"

"Gone to her ancestors."

Thomm's skin froze to stiffness. "*What?*"

The clerk lowered his head.

"Is she dead?"

"Yes, she is dead."

"But—how? She was healthy a day or so ago."

The man of the Mi-Tuun hesitated once more. "There are many ways of dying, Earthman."

Thomm became angry. "Tell me now—what happened to her?"

Rather startled by Thomm's vehemence the man blurted, "The Potters have called her to the hills; she is gone, but soon she will live forever, her spirit wrapped in glorious glass—"

"Let me get this straight," said Thomm. "The Potters took her—alive?"

"Yes—alive."

"And any others?"

"Three others."

"All alive?"

"All alive."

Thomm ran back to the Bureau. Covill, by chance , was in the front office, checking Thomm's work. Thomm blurted, "The Potters have been raiding again—they took four Mi-Tuun in the last day or so."

Covill thrust his chin forward, cursed fluently. Thomm understood that his anger was not so much for the act itself, but for the fact that the Potters had defied him, disobeyed his orders. Covill personally had been insulted; now there would be action.

"Get the copter out," said Covill shortly. "Bring it around in front."

When Thomm set the copter down Covill was waiting with one of the three atom bombs in the Bureau armory—a long cylinder attached to a parachute. Covill snapped it in place on the copter, then stood back. "Take this over that blasted volcano," he said harshly. "Drop it down the crater. I'll teach those murdering devils a lesson they won't forget. Next time it'll be on their village."

Thomm, aware of Covill's dislike of flying, was not surprised by the assignment. Without further words he took off, rose above Penolpan, flew out toward the Kukmank Range.

His anger cooled. The Potters, caught in the rut of their customs, were unaware of evil. Covill's orders seemed ill-advised—headstrong, vindictive, over-hasty. Suppose the Mi-Tuun were yet alive? Would it not be better to negotiate for their release? Instead of hovering over the volcano, he dropped his copter into the gray village, and assuring himself of his gamma-gun, he jumped out onto the dismal stony square.

This time he had only a moment to wait. The chief came striding up from the village, burnoose flapping back from powerful limbs, a grim smile on his face.

"So—it is the insolent lordling again. Good—we are in need of bone-lime, and yours will suit us admirably. Prepare your soul for the Great Burn, and your next life will be the eternal glory of a perfect glaze."

Thomm felt fear, but he also felt a kind of desperate recklessness. He touched his gun. "I'll kill a lot of Potters, and you'll be the first," he said in a voice that sounded strange to him. "I've come for the four Mi-Tuun that you took from Penolpan. These raids have got to stop. You don't seem to understand that we can punish you."

The chief put his hands behind his back, apparently unimpressed. "You may fly like the birds, but birds can do no more than defile those below."

Thomm pulled out his gamma-gun, pointed to a boulder a quarter-mile away. "Watch that rock." And he blasted the granite to gravel with an explosive pellet.

The chief drew back, eyebrows raised. "In truth, you wield more sting than I believed. But—" he gestured to the ring of burnoosed Potters around Thomm "—we can kill you before you can do much damage. We Potters do not fear death, which is merely eternal meditation from the glass."

"Listen to me," said Thomm earnestly. "I came not to threaten, but to bargain. My superior, Covill, gave me orders to destroy the mountain, blast away your caves—and I can do it as easily as I blasted that rock."

A mutter arose from the Potters.

"If I'm harmed, be sure that you'll suffer. But, as I say, I've come down here, against my superior's orders, to make a bargain with you."

"What sort of bargain can interest us?" said the Chief Potter disdainfully. "We care for nothing but our craft." He gave a sign and, before Thomm could twitch, two burly Potters had gripped him, wrested the gun from his hand.

"I can give you the secret of the true yellow glaze," shouted Thomm desperately. "The royal fluorescent yellow that will stand the fire of your kiln!"

"Empty words," said the chief. Mockingly he asked: "And what do you want for your secret?"

"The return of the four Mi-Tuun you've just stolen from Penolpan, and your word never to raid again."

The chief listened intently, pondered a moment. "How then would we formulate our glaze?" He spoke with a patient air, like a man explaining a practical truth to a child. "Bone-lime is one of our most necessary fluxes."

"As Covill told you, we can give you unlimited quantities of lime, with any properties you ask for. On Earth we have made pottery for thousands of years and we know a great deal of such things."

The Chief Potter tossed his head. "That is evidently untrue. Look—" he kicked Thomm's gamma-gun "—the substance of this is dull opaque metal. A people knowing clay and transparent glass would never use material of that sort."

"Perhaps it would be wise to let me demonstrate," suggested Thomm. "If I show you the yellow glaze, then will you bargain with me?"

The Chief Potter scrutinized Thomm almost a full minute. Grudgingly: "What sort of yellow can you make?"

Thomm said wryly: "I'm not a potter, and I can't predict exactly—but the formula I have in mind can produce any shade from light luminous yellow to vivid orange."

The chief made a signal. "Release him. We will make him eat his words."

Thomm stretched his muscles, cramped under the grip of the Potters. He reached to the ground, picked up his gamma-gun, holstered it, under the sardonic eyes of the Chief Potter.

"Our bargain is this," said Thomm, "I show you how to make yellow glaze, and guarantee you a plentiful supply of lime. You will release the Mi-Tuun to me and undertake never to raid Penolpan for live men and women."

"The bargain is conditional on the yellow glaze," said the Chief Potter. "We ourselves can produce dingy yellows as often as we wish. If your yellow comes clear and true from the fire, I agree to your bargain. If not, we potters hold you a charlatan and your spirit will be lodged forever in the basest sort of utensil."

Thomm went to the copter, unsnapped the atom bomb from the frame, discarded the parachute. Shouldering the long cylinder, he said: "Take me to your pottery. I'll see what I can do."

Without a word the Chief Potter took him down the slope to the long shed, and they entered through an arched stone doorway. To the right stood bins of clay, a row of wheels, twenty or thirty lined against one wall, and in the center a rack crowded with drying ware. To the left stood vats, further shelves and tables. From a doorway came a harsh grinding sound, evidently a mill of some sort. The Chief Potter led Thomm to the left, past the glazing tables and to the end of the shed. Here were shelves lined with various crocks, tubs and sacks, these marked in symbols strange to Thomm. And through a doorway nearby, apparently unguarded, Thomm glimpsed the Mi-Tuun, seated despondently, passively, on benches. The girl Su-then looked up, saw him, and her mouth fell open. She jumped to her feet, hesitated in the doorway, deterred by the stern form of the Chief Potter.

Thomm said to her: "You're a free woman—with a little luck." Then turning to the Chief Potter: "What kind of acid do you have?"

The chief pointed to a row of stoneware flagons. "The acid of salt, the acid of vinegar, the acid of fluor spar, the acid of saltpeter, the acid of sulphur."

Thomm nodded, and laying the bomb on a table, opened the hinged door, withdrew one of the uranium slugs. Into five porcelain bowls he carved slivers of uranium with his pocket knife, and into each bowl he poured a quantity of acid, a different acid into each. Bubbles of gas fumed up from the metal.

The Chief Potter watched with folded arms. "What are you trying to do?"

Thomm stood back, studied his fuming beakers. "I want to precipitate a uranium salt. Get me soda and lye."

Finally a yellow powder settled in one of his beakers; this he seized upon and washed triumphantly.

"Now," he told the Chief Potter, "bring me clear glaze."

He poured out six trays of glaze and mixed into each a varying amount of his yellow salt. With tired and slumped shoulders he stood back, gestured. "There's your glaze. Test it."

The chief gave an order; a Potter came up with a trayful of tiles. The chief strode to the table, scrawled a number on the first bowl, dipped a tile into the glaze, numbered the tile correspondingly. This he did for each of the batches.

He stood back, and one of the Potters loaded the tiles in a small brick oven, closed the door, kindled a fire below.

"Now," said the Chief Potter, "you have twenty hours to question whether the burn will bring you life or death. You may as well spend the time in the company of your friends. You cannot leave, you will be well guarded." He turned abruptly, strode off down the central aisle.

Thomm turned to the nearby room, where Su-then stood in the doorway. She fell into his arms naturally, gladly.

The hours passed. Flame roared up past the oven and the bricks glowed red-hot—yellow-hot—yellow-white, and the fire was gradually drawn. Now the tiles lay cooling and behind the bricked-up door the colors were already set, and Thomm fought the impulse to tear open the brick. Darkness came; he fell into a fitful doze with Su-then's head resting on his shoulder.

Heavy footsteps aroused him; he went to the doorway. The Chief Potter was drawing aside the bricked-up door. Thomm approached, stood staring. It was dark inside; only the white gleam of the tiles could be seen, the sheen of colored glass on top. The Chief Potter reached into the kiln, pulled out the first tile. A muddy mustard-colored blotch encrusted the top. Thomm swallowed hard. The chief smiled at him sardonically. He reached for another. This was a mass of brownish blisters. The chief smiled again, reached in once more. A pad of mud.

The chief's smile was broad. "Lordling, your glazes are worse than the feeblest attempts of our children."

He reached in again. A burst of brilliant yellow, and it seemed the whole room shone.

The Chief Potter gasped, the other Potters leaned forward, and Thomm sank back against the wall. "Yellow—"

When Thomm at last returned to the Bureau he found Covill in a fury. "Where in thunder have you been? I sent you out on business which should take you two hours and you stay two days."

Thomm said: "I got the four Mi-Tuun back and made a contract with the Potters. No more raiding."

Covill's mouth slackened. "You *what*?"

Thomm repeated his information.

"You didn't follow my instructions?"

"No," said Thomm. "I thought I had a better idea, and the way it turned out, I had."

Covill's eyes were hard blue fires. "Thomm, you're through here, through with Planetary Affairs. If a man can't be trusted to carry out his superior's orders, he's not worth a cent to the Bureau. Get your gear together, and leave on the next packet out."

"Just as you wish," said Thomm, turning away.

"You're on company time till four o'clock tonight," said Covill coldly. "Until then you'll obey my orders. Take the copter to the hangar, and bring the bomb back to the armory."

"You haven't any more bomb," said Thomm. "I gave the uranium to the Potters. That was one of the prices of the contract."

"*What?*" bellowd Covill, pop-eyed. "*What?*"

"You heard me," said Thomm. "And if you think you could have used it better by blasting away their livelihood, you're crazy."

"Thomm, you get in that copter, you go out and get that uranium. Don't come back without it. Why, you abysmal blasted imbecile, with that uranium, those Potters could tear Penolpan clear off the face of the planet."

"If you want that uranium," said Thomm, "you go out and get it. I'm fired. I'm through."

Covill stared, swelling like a toad in his rage. Words came thickly from his mouth.

Thomm said: "If I were you, I'd let sleeping dogs lie. I think it would be dangerous business trying to get that uranium back."

Covill turned, buckled a pair of gamma-guns about his waist, stalked out the door. Thomm heard the whirr of copter blades.

"There goes a brave man," Thomm said to himself. "And there goes a fool."

Three weeks later Su-then excitedly announced visitors, and Thomm, looking up, was astounded to see the Chief Potter, with two other Potters behind—stern, forbidding in their gray burnooses.

Thomm greeted them with courtesy, offered them seats, but they remained standing.

"I came down to the city," said the Chief Potter, "to inquire if the contract we made was still bound and good."

"So far as I am concerned," said Thomm.

"A madman came to the village of the Potters," said the Chief Potter. "He said that you had no authority, that our agreement was good enough, but he couldn't allow the Potters to keep the heavy metal that makes glass like the sunset."

Thomm said: "Then what happened?"

"There was violence," said the Chief Potter without accent. "He killed six good wheel-men. But that is no matter. I come to find whether our contract is good."

"Yes," said Thomm. "It is bound by my word and by the word of my great chief back on Earth. I have spoken to him and he says the contract is good."

The Chief Potter nodded. "In that case, I bring you a present." He gestured, and one of his men laid a large bowl on Thomm's desk, a bowl of marvelous yellow radiance.

"The madman is a lucky man indeed," said the Chief Potter, "for his spirit dwells in the brightest glass ever to come from the Great Burn."

Thomm's eyebrows shot up. "You mean that Covill's bones—"

"The fiery soul of the madman has given luster to an already glorious glaze," said the Chief Potter. "He lives forever in the entrancing shimmer—"

The Seventeen Virgins

The chase went far and long, and led into that dismal tract of bone-colored hills known as the Pale Rugates. Cugel finally used a clever trick to baffle pursuit, sliding from his steed and hiding among the rocks while his enemies pounded past in chase of the riderless mount.

Cugel lay in hiding until the angry band returned toward Kaspara Vitatus, bickering among themselves. He emerged into the open; then, after shaking his fist and shouting curses after the now distant figures, he turned and continued south through the Pale Rugates.

The region was as stark and grim as the surface of a dead sun, and thus avoided by such creatures as sindics, shambs, erbs and visps, for Cugel a single and melancholy source of satisfaction.

Step after step marched Cugel, one leg in front of the other: up slope to overlook an endless succession of barren swells, down again into the hollow where at rare intervals a seep of water nourished a sickly vegetation. Here Cugel found ramp, burdock, squallix and an occasional newt, which sufficed against starvation.

Day followed day. The sun rising cool and dim swam up into the dark-blue sky, from time to time seeming to flicker with a film of blue-black luster, finally to settle like an enormous purple pearl into the west. When dark made further progress impractical, Cugel wrapped himself in his cloak and slept as best he could.

On the afternoon of the seventh day Cugel limped down a slope into an ancient orchard. Cugel found and devoured a few withered hag-apples, then set off along the trace of an old road.

The track proceeded a mile, to lead out upon a bluff overlooking a broad plain. Directly below, a river skirted a small town, curved away to the southwest and finally disappeared into the haze.

Cugel surveyed the landscape with keen attention. Out upon the plain he saw carefully tended garden plots, each precisely square and of identical size; along the river drifted a fisherman's punt. A placid scene, thought Cugel. On the other hand, the town was built to a strange and archaic architecture, and the scrupulous precision with which the houses surrounded the square suggested a like inflexibility in the inhabitants. The houses themselves were no less uniform, each a construction of two, or three, or even four squat bulbs of diminishing size, one on the other, the lowest always painted blue, the second dark red, the third and fourth respectively a dull mustard ocher and black; and each house terminated in a spire of fancifully twisted iron rods, of greater or lesser height. An inn on the riverbank showed a style somewhat looser and easier, with a pleasant garden surrounding. Along the river road to the east Cugel now noticed the approach of a caravan of six high-wheeled wagons, and his uncertainty dissolved; the town was evidently tolerant of strangers, and Cugel confidently set off down the hill.

At the outskirts to town he halted and drew forth his old purse, which he yet retained though it hung loose and limp. Cugel examined the contents: five terces, a sum hardly adequate to his needs. Cugel reflected a moment, then collected a handful of pebbles which he dropped into the purse, to create a reassuring rotundity. He dusted his breeches, adjusted his green hunter's cap, and proceeded.

He entered the town without challenge or even attention. Crossing the square, he halted to inspect a contrivance even more peculiar than the quaint architecture: a stone fire-pit in which several logs blazed high, rimmed by five lamps on iron stands, each with five wicks, and above an intricate linkage of mirrors and lenses, the purpose of which surpassed Cugel's comprehension. Two young men tended the device with diligence, trimming the twenty-five wicks, prodding the fire, adjusting screws and levers which in turn controlled the mirrors and lenses. They wore what appeared to be the local costume: voluminous blue knee-length breeches, red shirts, brass-buttoned black vests and broad-brimmed hats; after disinterested glances they paid Cugel no heed, and he continued to the inn.

In the adjacent garden two dozen folk of the town sat at tables, eating and drinking with great gusto. Cugel watched them a moment or two; their punctilio and elegant gestures suggested the manners of an age far past. Like their houses, they were a sort unique to Cugel's experience, pale and thin, with egg-shaped heads, long noses, dark expressive eyes and ears cropped in various styles. The men were uniformly bald and their pates glistened in the red sunlight. The women parted their black hair in the middle, then cut it abruptly short a half-inch above the ears: a style which Cugel considered unbecoming. Watching the folk eat and drink, Cugel was unfavorably reminded of the fare which had sustained him across the Pale Rugates, and he gave no further thought to his terces. He strode into the garden and seated himself at a table. A portly man in a blue apron approached, frowning somewhat at Cugel's disheveled appearance. Cugel immediately brought forth two terces which he handed to the man. "This is for yourself, my good fellow, to insure expeditious service. I have just completed an arduous journey; I am famished with hunger. You may bring me a platter identical to that which the gentleman yonder is enjoying, together with a selection of side-dishes and a bottle of wine. Then be so good as to ask the innkeeper to prepare me a comfortable chamber." Cugel carelessly brought forth his purse and dropped it upon the table where its weight produced an impressive implication. "I will also require a bath, fresh linen and a barber."

"I myself am Maier the innkeeper," said the portly man in a gracious voice. "I will see to your wishes immediately."

"Excellent," said Cugel. "I am favorably impressed with your establishment, and perhaps will remain several days."

The innkeeper bowed in gratification and hurried off to supervise the preparation of Cugel's dinner.

Cugel made an excellent meal, though the second course, a dish of crayfish stuffed with mince and slivers of scarlet mangoneel, he found a trifle too rich. The roast fowl however could not be faulted and the wine pleased Cugel to such an extent that he ordered a second flask. Maier the innkeeper served the bottle himself and accepted Cugel's compliments with a trace of complacency. "There is no better wine in Gundar! It is admittedly expensive, but you are a person who appreciates the best."

"Precisely true," said Cugel. "Sit down and take a glass with me. I confess to curiosity in regard to this remarkable town."

The innkeeper willingly followed Cugel's suggestion. "I am puzzled that you find Gundar remarkable. I have lived here all my life and it seems ordinary enough to me."

"I will cite three circumstances which I consider worthy of note," said Cugel, now somewhat expansive by reason of the wine. "First: the bulbous construction of your buildings. Secondly: the contrivance of lenses above the fire, which at the very least must stimulate a stranger's interest. Thirdly: the fact that the men of Gundar are all stark bald."

The innkeeper nodded thoughtfully. "The architecture at least is quickly explained. The ancient Gunds lived in enormous gourds. When a section of the wall became weak it was replaced with a board, until in due course the folk found themselves living in houses fashioned completely of wood, and the style has persisted. As for the fire and the projectors, do you not know the world-wide Order of Solar Emosynaries? We stimulate the vitality of the sun; so long as our beam of sympathetic vibration regulates solar combustion, it will never expire. Similar stations exist at other locations: at Blue Azor; on the Isle of Brazel; at the walled city Munt; and in the observatory of the Grand Starkeeper at Vir Vassilis."

Cugel shook his head sadly. "I hear that conditions have changed. Brazel has long since sunk beneath the waves. Munt was destroyed a thousand years ago by the Dystropes. I have never heard of either Blue Azor or Vir Vassilis, though I am widely traveled. Possibly, here at Gundar, you are the solitary Solar Emosynaries yet in existence."

"This is dismal news," declared Maier. "The noticeable enfeeblement of the sun is hereby explained. Perhaps we had best double the fire under our regulator."

Cugel poured more wine. "A question leaps to mind. If, as I suspect, this is the single Solar Emosynary station yet in operation, who or what regulates the sun when it has passed below the horizon?"

The innkeeper shook his head. "I can offer no explanation. It may be that during the hours of night the sun itself relaxes and, as it were, sleeps, although this is of course sheerest speculation."

"Allow me to offer another hypothesis," said Cugel. "Conceivably the waning of the sun has advanced beyond all possibility of regulation, so that your efforts, though formerly useful, are now ineffective."

Maier threw up his hands in perplexity. "These complications surpass my scope, but yonder stands the Nolde Huruska." He directed Cugel's attention to a large man with a deep chest and bristling black beard, who stood at the entrance. "Excuse me a moment." He rose to his feet and approaching the Nolde spoke for several minutes, indicating Cugel from time to time. The Nolde finally made a brusque gesture and marched across the garden to confront Cugel. He spoke in a heavy voice: "I understand you to assert that no Emosynaries exist other than ourselves?"

"I stated nothing so definitely," said Cugel, somewhat on the defensive. "I remarked that I had traveled widely and that no other such 'Emosynary' agency has come to my attention; and I innocently speculated that possibly none now operate."

"At Gundar we conceive 'innocence' as a positive quality, not merely an insipid absence of guilt," stated the Nolde. "We are not the fools that certain untidy ruffians might suppose."

Cugel suppressed the hot remark which rose to his lips, and contented himself with a shrug. Maier walked away with the Nolde and for several minutes the two men conferred, with frequent glances in Cugel's direction. Then the Nolde departed and the innkeeper returned to Cugel's table. "A somewhat brusque man, the Nolde of Gundar," he told Cugel, "but very competent withal."

"It would be presumptuous of me to comment," said Cugel. "What, precisely, is his function?"

"At Gundar we place great store upon precision and methodicity," explained Maier. "We feel that the absence of order encourages disorder; and the official responsible for the inhibition of caprice and abnormality is the Nolde...What was our previous conversation? Ah yes, you mentioned our notorious baldness. I can offer no definite explanation. According to our savants, the condition signifies the final perfection of the human race. Other folk give credence to an ancient legend. A pair of magicians, Astherlin and Mauldred, vied for the favor of the Gunds. Astherlin promised the boon of extreme hairiness, so that the folk of Gundar need never wear garments. Mauldred, to the contrary, offered the Gunds baldness, with all the consequent advantages, and easily won the contest; in fact Mauldred became the first Nolde of Gundar, the post now filled, as you know, by Huruska." Maier the innkeeper pursed his lips and looked off across the garden. "Huruska, a distrustful sort, has reminded me of my fixed rule to ask all transient guests to settle their accounts on a daily basis. I naturally assured him of your complete reliability, but simply in order to appease Huruska, I will tender the reckoning in the morning."

"This is tantamount to an insult," declared Cugel haughtily. "Must we truckle to the whims of Huruska? Not I, you may be assured! I will settle my account in the usual manner."

The innkeeper blinked. "May I ask how long you intend to stay at Gundar?"

"My journey takes me south, by the most expeditious transport available, which I assume to be riverboat."

"The town Lumarth lies ten days by caravan across the Lirrh Aing. The Isk river also flows past Lumarth, but is judged inconvenient by virtue of three intervening localities. The Lallo Marsh is infested with stinging insects; the tree-dwarfs of the Santalba Forest pelt passing boats with refuse; and the Desperate Rapids shatter both bones and boats."

"In this case I will travel by caravan," said Cugel. "Meanwhile I will remain here, unless the persecutions of Huruska become intolerable."

Maier licked his lips and looked over his shoulder. "I assured Huruska that I would adhere to the strict letter of my rule. He will surely make a great issue of the matter unless—"

Cugel made a gracious gesture. "Bring me seals. I will close up my purse which contains a fortune in opals and alumes. We will deposit the purse in the strong-box and you may hold it for surety. Even Huruska cannot now protest!"

Maier held up his hands in awe. "I could not undertake so large a responsibility!"

"Dismiss all fear," said Cugel. "I have protected the purse with a spell; the instant a criminal breaks the seal the jewels are transformed into pebbles."

Maier dubiously accepted Cugel's purse on these terms. They jointly saw the seals applied and the purse deposited into Maier's strong-box.

Cugel now repaired to his chamber, where he bathed, commanded the services of a barber and dressed in fresh garments. Setting his cap at an appropriate angle, he strolled out upon the square.

His steps led him to the Solar Emosynary station. As before, two young men worked diligently, one stoking the blaze and adjusting the five lamps, while the other held the regulatory beam fixed upon the low sun.

Cugel inspected the contrivance from all angles, and presently the person who fed the blaze called out: "Are you not that notable traveler who today expressed doubts as to the efficacy of the Emosynary System?"

Cugel spoke carefully: "I told Maier and Huruska this: that Brazel is sunk below the Melantine Gulf and almost gone from memory; that the walled city Munt was long ago laid waste; that I am acquainted with neither Blue Azor, nor Vir Vassilis. These were my only positive statements."

The young fire-stoker petulantly threw an arm-load of logs into the fire-pit. "Still we are told that you consider our efforts impractical."

"I would not go so far," said Cugel politely. "Even if the other Emosynary agencies are abandoned, it is possible that the Gundar regulator suffices; who knows?"

"I will tell you this," declared the stoker. "We work without recompense, and in our spare time we must cut and transport fuel. The process is tedious."

The operator of the aiming device amplified his friend's complaint. "Huruska and the elders do none of the work; they merely ordain that we toil, which of course is the easiest part of the project. Janred and I are of a sophisticated new generation; on principle we reject all dogmatic doctrines. I for one consider the Solar Emosynary system a waste of time and effort."

"If the other agencies are abandoned," argued Janred the stoker, "who or what regulates the sun when it has passed beyond the horizon? The system is pure balderdash."

The operator of the lenses declared: "I will now demonstrate as much, and free us all from this thankless toil!" He worked a lever. "Notice I direct the regulatory beam away from the sun. Look! It shines as before, without the slightest attention on our part!"

Cugel inspected the sun, and for a fact it seemed to glow as before, flickering from time to time, and shivering like an old man with the ague. The two young men watched with similar interest, and as minutes passed, they began to murmur in satisfaction. "We are vindicated! The sun has not gone out!"

Even as they watched, the sun, perhaps fortuitously, underwent a cachectic spasm, and lurched alarmingly toward the horizon. Behind them sounded a bellow of outrage and the Nolde Huruska ran forward. "What is the meaning of this irresponsibility? Direct the regulator aright and instantly! Would you have us groping for the rest of our lives in the dark?"

The stoker resentfully jerked his thumb toward Cugel. "He convinced us that the system was unnecessary, and that our work was futile."

"What!" Huruska swung his formidable body about and confronted Cugel. "Only hours ago you set foot in Gundar, and already you are disrupting the fabric of our existence! I warn you, our patience is not illimitable! Be off with you and do not approach the Emosynary agency a second time!"

Choking with fury, Cugel swung on his heel and marched off across the square.

At the caravan terminal he inquired as to transport southward, but the caravan which had arrived at noon would on the morrow depart eastward the way it had come.

Cugel returned to the inn and stepped into the tavern. He noticed three men playing a card game and posted himself as an observer. The game proved to be a simple version of Zampolio, and presently Cugel asked if he might join the play. "But only if the stakes are not too high," he protested. "I am not particularly skillful and I dislike losing more than a terce or two."

"Bah," exclaimed one of the players. "What is money? Who will spend it when we are dead?"

"If we take all your gold, then you need not carry it further," another remarked jocularly.

"All of us must learn," the third player assured Cugel. "You are fortunate to have the three premier experts of Gundar as instructors."

Cugel drew back in alarm. "I refuse to lose more than a single terce!"

"Come now! Don't be a prig!"

"Very well," said Cugel. "I will risk it. But these cards are tattered and dirty. By chance I have a fresh set in my pouch."

"Excellent! The game proceeds!"

➤◄

Two hours later the three Gunds threw down their cards, gave Cugel long hard looks, then as if with a single mind rose to their feet and departed the tavern. Inspecting his gains, Cugel counted thirty-two terces and a few odd coppers. In a cheerful frame of mind he retired to his chamber for the night.

In the morning, as he consumed his breakfast, he noticed the arrival of the Nolde Huruska, who immediately engaged Maier the innkeeper in conversation. A few minutes later Huruska approached Cugel's table and stared down at Cugel with a somewhat menacing grin, while Maier stood anxiously a few paces to the rear.

Cugel spoke in a voice of strained politeness: "Well, what is it this time? The sun has risen; my innocence in the matter of the regulatory beam has been established."

"I am now concerned with another matter. Are you acquainted with the penalties for fraud?"

Cugel shrugged. "The matter is of no interest to me."

"They are severe and I will revert to them in a moment. First, let me inquire: did you entrust to Maier a purse purportedly containing valuable jewels?"

"I did indeed. The property is protected by a spell, I may add; if the seal is broken the gems become ordinary pebbles."

Huruska exhibited the purse. "Notice, the seal is intact. I cut a slit in the leather and looked within. The contents were then and are now—" with a flourish Huruska turned the purse out upon the table "—pebbles identical to those in the road yonder."

Cugel exclaimed in outrage: "The jewels are now worthless rubble! I hold you responsible and you must make recompense!"

Huruska uttered an offensive laugh. "If you can change gems to pebbles, you can change pebbles to gems. Maier will now tender the bill. If you refuse to pay, I intend to have you nailed into the enclosure under the gallows until such time as you change your mind."

"Your insinuations are both disgusting and absurd," declared Cugel. "Innkeeper, present your account! Let us finish with this farrago once and for all."

Maier came forward with a slip of paper. "I make the total to be eleven terces, plus whatever gratuities might seem in order."

"There will be no gratuities," said Cugel. "Do you harass all your guests in this fashion?" He flung eleven terces down upon the table. "Take your money and leave me in peace."

Maier sheepishly gathered up the coins; Huruska made an inarticulate sound and turned away. Cugel, upon finishing his breakfast, went out once more to stroll across the square. Here he met an individual whom he recognized to be the pot-boy in the tavern, and Cugel signaled him to a halt. "You seem an alert and knowledgeable fellow," said Cugel. "May I inquire your name?"

"I am generally known as 'Zeller'."

"I would guess you to be well-acquainted with the folk of Gundar."

"I consider myself well-informed. Why do you ask?"

"First," said Cugel, "let me ask if you care to turn your knowledge to profit?"

"Certainly, so long as I evade the attention of the Nolde."

"Very good. I notice a disused booth yonder which should serve our purpose. In one hour we shall put our enterprise into operation."

Cugel returned to the inn where at his request Maier brought a board, brush and paint. Cugel composed a sign:

THE EMINENT SEER CUGEL
Counsels, Interprets, Prognosticates.
ASK! YOU WILL BE ANSWERED!
consultations: Three Terces.
1S2

Cugel hung the sign above the booth, arranged curtains and waited for customers. The pot-boy, meanwhile, had inconspicuously secreted himself at the back.

Almost immediately folk crossing the square halted to read the sign. A woman of early middle-age presently came forward.

"Three terces is a large sum. What results can you guarantee?"

"None whatever, by the very nature of things. I am a skilled voyant, I have acquaintance with the arts of magic, but knowledge comes to me from unknown and uncontrollable sources."

The woman paid over her money. "Three terces is cheap if you can resolve my worries. My daughter all her life has enjoyed the best of health but now she ails, and suffers a morose condition. All my remedies are to no avail. What must I do?"

"A moment, madam, while I meditate." Cugel drew the curtain and leaned back to where he could hear the pot-boy's whispered remarks, then once again drew aside the curtains.

"I have made myself one with the cosmos! Knowledge has entered my mind! Your daughter Dilian is pregnant. For an additional three terces I will supply the father's name."

"This is a fee I pay with pleasure," declared the woman grimly. She paid, received the information and marched purposefully away.

Another woman approached, paid three terces, and Cugel addressed himself to her problem: "My husband assured me that he had put by a canister of gold coins against the future, but upon his death I could find not so much as a copper. Where has he hidden the gold?"

Cugel closed the curtains, took counsel with the pot-boy, and again appeared to the woman. "I have discouraging news for you. Your husband Finister spent much of his hoarded gold at the tavern. With the rest he purchased an amethyst brooch for a woman named Varletta."

The news of Cugel's remarkable abilities spread rapidly and trade was brisk. Shortly before noon, a large woman, muffled and veiled, approached the booth, paid three terces, and asked in a high-pitched, if husky, voice: "Read me my fortune!"

Cugel drew the curtains and consulted the pot-boy, who was at a loss. "It is no one I know. I can tell you nothing."

"No matter," said Cugel. "My suspicions are verified." He drew aside the curtain. "The portents are unclear and I refuse to take your money." Cugel returned the fee. "I can tell you this much: you are an individual of domineering character and no great intelligence. Ahead lies what? Honors? A long voyage by water? Revenge on your enemies? Wealth? The image is distorted; I may be reading my own future."

The woman tore away her veils and stood revealed as the Nolde Huruska. "Master Cugel, you are lucky indeed that you returned my money, otherwise I would have taken you up for deceptive practices. In any event, I deem your activities mischievous, and contrary to the public interest. Gundar is in an uproar because of your revelations; there will be no more of them. Take down your sign, and be happily thankful that you have escaped so easily."

"I will be glad to terminate my enterprise," said Cugel with dignity. "The work is taxing."

Huruska stalked away in a huff. Cugel divided his earnings with the pot-boy, and in a spirit of mutual satisfaction they departed the booth.

Cugel dined on the best that the inn afforded, but later when he went into the tavern he discovered a noticeable lack of amiability among the patrons and presently went off to his chamber.

The next morning as he took breakfast a caravan of ten wagons arrived in town. The principal cargo appeared to be a bevy of seventeen beautiful maidens, who rode upon two of the wagons. Three other wagons served as dormitories, while the remaining five were loaded with stores, trunks, bales and cases. The caravan master, a portly mild-seeming man with flowing brown hair and a silky beard, assisted his delightful charges to the ground and led them all to the inn, where Maier served up an ample breakfast of spiced porridge, preserved quince, and tea.

Cugel watched the group as they made their meal and reflected that a journey to almost any destination in such company would be a pleasant journey indeed.

The Nolde Huruska appeared, and went to pay his respects to the caravan-leader. The two conversed amiably at some length, while Cugel waited impatiently.

Huruska at last departed. The maidens, having finished their meal, went off to stroll about the square. Cugel crossed to the table where the caravan-leader sat. "Sir, my name is Cugel, and I would appreciate a few words with you."

"By all means! Please be seated. Will you take a glass of this excellent tea?"

"Thank you. First, may I inquire the destination of your caravan?"

The caravan-leader showed surprise at Cugel's ignorance. "We are bound for Lumarth; these are the 'Seventeen Virgins of Symnathis' who traditionally grace the Grand Pageant."

"I am a stranger to this region," Cugel explained. "Hence I know nothing of the local customs. In any event, I myself am bound for Lumarth and would be pleased to travel with your caravan."

The caravan-leader gave an affable assent. "I would be delighted to have you with us."

"Excellent!" said Cugel. "Then all is arranged."

The caravan-leader stroked his silky brown beard. "I must warn you that my fees are somewhat higher than usual, owing to the expensive amenities I am obliged to provide these seventeen fastidious maidens."

"Indeed," said Cugel. "How much do you require?"

"The journey occupies the better part of ten days, and my minimum charge is twenty terces per diem, for a total of two hundred terces, plus a twenty terce supplement for wine."

"This is far more than I can afford," said Cugel in a bleak voice. "At the moment I command only a third of this sum. Is there some means by which I might earn my passage?"

"Unfortunately not," said the caravan-leader. "Only this morning the position of armed guard was open, which even paid a small stipend, but Huruska the Nolde, who wishes to visit Lumarth, has agreed to serve in this capacity and the post is now filled."

Cugel made a sound of disappointment and raised his eyes to the sky. When at last he could bring himself to speak he asked: "When do you plan to depart?"

"Tomorrow at dawn, with absolute punctuality. I am sorry that we will not have the pleasure of your company."

"I share the sorrow," said Cugel. He returned to his own table and sat brooding. Presently he went into the tavern, where various card games were in progress. Cugel attempted to join the play, but in every case his request was denied. In a surly mood he went to the counter where Maier the innkeeper unpacked a crate of earthenware goblets. Cugel tried to initiate a conversation but for once Maier could take no time from his labors. "The Nolde Huruska goes off on a journey and tonight his friends mark the occasion with a farewell party, for which I must make careful preparations."

Cugel took a mug of beer to a side table and gave himself to reflection. After a few moments he went out the back exit and surveyed the prospect, which here overlooked the Isk River. Cugel sauntered down to the water's edge and discovered a dock at which the fishermen moored their punts and dried their nets. Cugel looked up and down the river, then returned up the path to the inn, to spend the rest of the day watching the seventeen maidens as they strolled about the square, or sipped sweet lime tea in the garden of the inn.

The sun set; twilight the color of old wine darkened into night. Cugel set about his preparations, which were quickly achieved, inasmuch as the essence of his plan lay in its simplicity.

The caravan-leader, whose name, so Cugel learned, was Shimilko, assembled his exquisite company for their evening meal, then herded them carefully to the dormitory wagons, despite the pouts and protests of those who wished to remain at the inn and enjoy the festivities of the evening.

In the tavern the farewell party in honor of Huruska had already commenced. Cugel seated himself in a dark corner and presently attracted the attention of the perspiring Maier. Cugel produced ten terces. "I admit that I harbored ungrateful thoughts toward Huruska," he said. "Now I wish to express my good wishes—in absolute anonymity, however! Whenever Huruska starts upon a mug of ale, I want you to place a full mug before him, so that his evening will be incessantly merry. If he asks who has bought the drink you are only to reply: 'One of your friends wishes to pay you a compliment.' Is this clear?"

"Absolutely, and I will do as you command. It is a large-hearted gesture, which Huruska will appreciate."

The evening progressed. Huruska's friends sang jovial songs and proposed a dozen toasts, in all of which Huruska joined. As Cugel had required, whenever Huruska so much as started to drink from a mug, another was placed at his elbow, and Cugel marveled at the scope of Huruska's internal reservoirs.

At last Huruska was prompted to excuse himself from the company. He staggered out the back exit and made his way to that stone wall with a trough below, which had been placed for the convenience of the tavern's patrons.

As Huruska faced the wall Cugel stepped behind him and flung a fisherman's net over Huruska's head, then expertly dropped a noose around

Huruska's burly shoulders, followed by other turns and ties. Huruska's bellows were drowned by the song at this moment being sung in his honor.

Cugel dragged the cursing hulk down the path to the dock, and rolled him over and into a punt. Untying the mooring line, Cugel pushed the punt out into the current of the river. "At the very least," Cugel told himself, "two parts of my prophecy are accurate; Huruska has been honored in the tavern and now is about to enjoy a voyage by water."

He returned to the tavern where Huruska's absence had at last been noticed. Maier expressed the opinion that, with an early departure in the offing, Huruska had prudently retired to bed, and all conceded that this was no doubt the case.

The next morning Cugel arose an hour before dawn. He took a quick breakfast, paid Maier his score, then went to where Shimilko ordered his caravan.

"I bring news from Huruska," said Cugel. "Owing to an unfortunate set of personal circumstances, he finds himself unable to make the journey, and has commended me to that post for which you had engaged him."

Shimilko shook his head in wonder. "A pity! Yesterday he seemed so enthusiastic! Well, we all must be flexible, and since Huruska cannot join us, I am pleased to accept you in his stead. As soon as we start, I will instruct you in your duties, which are straightforward. You must stand guard by night and take your rest by day, although in the case of danger I naturally expect you to join in the defense of the caravan."

"These duties are well within my competence," said Cugel. "I am ready to depart at your convenience."

"Yonder rises the sun," declared Shimilko. "Let us be off and away for Lumarth."

Ten days later Shimilko's caravan passed through the Methune Gap, and the great Vale of Coram opened before them. The brimming Isk wound back and forth, reflecting a sultry sheen; in the distance loomed the long dark mass of the Draven Forest. Closer at hand five domes of shimmering nacreous gloss marked the site of Lumarth.

Shimilko addressed himself to the company. "Below lies what remains of the old city Lumarth. Do not be deceived by the domes; they indicate temples at one time sacred to the five demons Yaunt, Jastenave, Phampoun, Adelmar and Suul, and hence were preserved during the Sampathissic Wars.

"The folk of Lumarth are unlike any of your experience. Many are small sorcerers, though Chaladet the Grand Thearch has proscribed magic within the city precincts. You may conceive these people to be languid and wan, and dazed by excess sensation, and you will be correct. All are obsessively rigid in regard to ritual, and all subscribe to a Doctrine of Absolute Altruism, which compels them to virtue and benevolence. For this reason they are known as the 'Kind Folk'. A final word in regard to our journey, which luckily has gone without untoward incident. The wagoneers have driven with skill; Cugel has vigilantly guarded us by night, and I am well pleased. So then: onward to Lumarth, and let meticulous discretion be the slogan!"

The caravan traversed a narrow track down into the valley, then proceeded along an avenue of rutted stone under an arch of enormous black mimosa trees.

At a mouldering portal opening upon the plaza the caravan was met by five tall men in gowns of embroidered silks, the splendid double-crowned headgear of the Coramese Thurists lending them an impressive dignity. The five men were much alike, with pale transparent skins, thin high-bridged noses, slender limbs and pensive gray eyes. One who wore a gorgeous gown of mustard-yellow, crimson and black raised two fingers in a calm salute. "My friend Shimilko, you have arrived securely with all your blessed cargo. We are well-served and very pleased."

"The Lirrh-Aing was so placid as almost to be dull," said Shimilko. "To be sure, I was fortunate in securing the services of Cugel, who guarded us so well by night that never were our slumbers interrupted."

"Well done, Cugel!" said the head Thurist. "We will at this time take custody of the precious maidens. Tomorrow you may render your account to the bursar. The Wayfarer's Inn lies yonder, and I counsel you to its comforts."

"Just so! We will all be the better for a few days rest!"

However, Cugel chose not to so indulge himself. At the door to the inn he told Shimilko: "Here we part company, for I must continue along the way. Affairs press on me and Almery lies far to the west."

"But your stipend, Cugel! You must wait at least until tomorrow, when I can collect certain monies from the bursar. Until then, I am without funds."

Cugel hesitated, but at last was prevailed upon to stay.

An hour later a messenger strode into the inn. "Master Shimilko, you and your company are required to appear instantly before the Grand Thearch on a matter of utmost importance."

Shimilko looked up in alarm. "Whatever is the matter?"

"I am obliged to tell you nothing more."

With a long face Shimilko led his company across the plaza to the loggia before the old palace, where Chaladet sat on a massive chair. To either side stood the College of Thurists and all regarded Shimilko with somber expressions.

"What is the meaning of this summons?" inquired Shimilko. "Why do you regard me with such gravity?"

The Grand Thearch spoke in a deep voice: "Shimilko, the seventeen maidens conveyed by you from Symnathis to Lumarth have been examined, and I regret to say that of the seventeen, only two can be classified as virgins. The remaining fifteen have been sexually deflorated."

Shimilko could hardly speak for consternation. "Impossible!" he sputtered. "At Symnathis I undertook the most elaborate precautions. I can display three separate documents certifying the purity of each. There can be no doubt! You are in error!"

"We are not in error, Master Shimilko. Conditions are as we describe, and may easily be verified."

"'Impossible' and 'incredible' are the only two words which come to mind," cried Shimilko. "Have you questioned the girls themselves?"

"Of course. They merely raise their eyes to the ceiling and whistle between their teeth. Shimilko, how do you explain this heinous outrage?"

"I am perplexed to the point of confusion! The girls embarked upon the journey as pure as the day they were born. This is fact! During each waking instant they never left my area of perception. This is also fact."

"And when you slept?"

"The implausibility is no less extreme. The teamsters invariably retired together in a group. I shared my wagon with the chief teamster and each of us will vouch for the other. Cugel meanwhile kept watch over the entire camp."

"Alone?"

"A single guard suffices, even though the nocturnal hours are slow and dismal. Cugel, however, never complained."

"Cugel is evidently the culprit!"

Shimilko smilingly shook his head. "Cugel's duties left him no time for illicit activity."

"What if Cugel scamped his duties?"

Shimilko responded patiently: "Remember, each girl rested secure in her private cubicle with a door between herself and Cugel."

"Well then—what if Cugel opened this door and quietly entered the cubicle?"

Shimilko considered a dubious moment, and pulled at his silky beard. "In such a case, I suppose the matter might be possible."

The Grand Thearch turned his gaze upon Cugel. "I insist that you make an exact statement upon this sorry affair."

Cugel cried out indignantly: "The investigation is a travesty! My honor has been assailed!"

Chaladet fixed Cugel with a benign, if somewhat chilly stare. "You will be allowed redemption. Thurists, I place this person in your custody. See to it that he has every opportunity to regain his dignity and self-esteem!"

Cugel roared out a protest which the Grand Thearch ignored. From his great dais he looked thoughtfully off across the square. "Is it the third or fourth month?"

"The chronolog has only just left the month of Yaunt, to enter the time of Phampoun."

"So be it. By diligence, this licentious rogue may yet earn our love and respect."

A pair of Thurists grasped Cugel's arms and led him across the square. Cugel jerked this way and that to no avail. "Where are you taking me? What is this nonsense?"

One of the Thurists replied in a kindly voice: "We are taking you to the temple of Phampoun, and it is far from nonsense."

"I do not care for any of this," said Cugel. "Take your hands off of me; I intend to leave Lumarth at once."

"You shall be so assisted."

The group marched up worn marble steps, through an enormous arched portal, into an echoing hall, distinguished only by the high dome and an adytum or altar at the far end. Cugel was led into a side-chamber, illuminated by high circular windows and paneled with dark blue wood. An old man in a white gown entered the room and asked: "What have we here? A person suffering affliction?"

"Yes; Cugel has committed a series of abominable crimes, of which he wishes to purge himself."

"A total mis-statement!" cried Cugel. "No proof has been adduced and in any event I was inveigled against my better judgment."

The Thurists, paying no heed, departed, and Cugel was left with the old man, who hobbled to a bench and seated himself. Cugel started to speak but the old man held up his hand. "Calm yourself! You must remember that we are a benevolent people, lacking all spite or malice. We exist only to help other sentient beings! If a person commits a crime, we are racked with sorrow for the criminal, whom we believe to be the true victim, and we work without compromise that he may renew himself."

"An enlightened viewpoint!" declared Cugel. "Already I feel regeneration!"

"Excellent! Your remarks validate our philosophy; certainly you have negotiated what I will refer to as Phase One of the program."

Cugel frowned. "There are other phases? Are they really necessary?"

"Absolutely; these are Phases Two and Three. I should explain that Lumarth has not always adhered to such a policy. During the high years of the Great Magics the city fell under the sway of Yasbane the Obviator, who breached openings into five demon-realms and constructed the five temples of Lumarth. You stand now in the Temple of Phampoun."

"Odd," said Cugel, "that a folk so benevolent are such fervent demonists."

"Nothing could be farther from the truth. The Kind Folk of Lumarth expelled Yasbane, to establish the Era of Love, which must now persist until the final waning of the sun. Our love extends to all, even Yasbane's five demons, whom we hope to rescue from their malevolent evil. You will be the latest in a long line of noble individuals who have worked to this end, and such is Phase Two of the program."

Cugel stood limp in consternation. "Such work far exceeds my competence!"

"Everyone feels the same sensation," said the old man. "Nevertheless Phampoun must be instructed in kindness, consideration and decency; by making this effort, you will know a surge of happy redemption."

"And Phase Three?" croaked Cugel. "What of that?"

"When you achieve your mission, then you shall be gloriously accepted into our brotherhood!" The old man ignored Cugel's groan of dismay. "Let me see now: the month of Yaunt is just ending, and we enter the month of Phampoun, who is perhaps the most irascible of the five by reason of his sensitive eyes. He becomes enraged by so much as a single glimmer, and you must attempt your persuasions in absolute darkness. Do you have any further questions?"

"Yes indeed! Suppose Phampoun refuses to mend his ways?"

"This is 'negativistic thinking' which we Kind Folk refuse to recognize. Ignore everything you may have heard in regard to Phampoun's macabre habits! Go forth in confidence!"

Cugel cried out in anguish: "How will I return to enjoy my honors and rewards?"

"No doubt Phampoun, when contrite, will send you aloft by a means at his disposal," said the old man. "Now I bid you farewell."

"One moment! Where is my food and drink? How will I survive?"

"Again we will leave these matters to the discretion of Phampoun." The old man touched a button; the floor opened under Cugel's feet; he slid down a spiral chute at dizzying velocity. The air gradually became syrupy; Cugel struck a film of invisible constriction which burst with a sound like a cork leaving a bottle, and Cugel emerged into a chamber of medium size, illuminated by the glow of a single lamp.

Cugel stood stiff and rigid, hardly daring to breathe. On a dais across the chamber Phampoun sat sleeping in a massive chair, two black hemispheres shuttering his enormous eyes against the light. The grey torso wallowed almost the length of the dais; the massive splayed legs were planted flat to the floor. Arms, as large around as Cugel himself, terminated in fingers three feet long, each bedecked with a hundred jeweled rings. Phampoun's head was as large as a wheelbarrow, with a huge snout and an enormous loose-wattled mouth. The two eyes, each the size of a dishpan, could not be seen for the protective hemispheres.

Cugel, holding his breath in fear and also against the stench which hung in the air, looked cautiously about the room. A cord ran from the lamp, across the ceiling, to dangle beside Phampoun's fingers; almost as a reflex Cugel detached the cord from the lamp. He saw a single egress from the chamber: a low iron door directly behind Phampoun's chair. The chute by which he had entered was now invisible.

The flaps beside Phampoun's mouth twitched and lifted; a homunculus growing from the end of Phampoun's tongue peered forth. It stared at Cugel with beady black eyes. "Ha, has time gone by so swiftly?" The creature, leaning forward, consulted a mark on the wall. "It has indeed; I have overslept and Phampoun will be cross. What is your name and what are your crimes? These details are of interest to Phampoun—which is to say myself, though from whimsy I usually call myself Pulsifer, as if I were a separate entity."

Cugel spoke in a voice of brave conviction: "I am Cugel, inspector for the new regime which now holds sway in Lumarth. I descended to verify Phampoun's comfort, and since all is well, I will now return aloft. Where is the exit?"

Pulsifer asked plaintively: "You have no crimes to relate? This is harsh news. Both Phampoun and I enjoy great evils. Not long ago a certain sea-trader, whose name evades me, held us enthralled for over an hour."

"And then what occurred?"

"Best not to ask." Pulsifer busied himself polishing one of Phampoun's tusks with a small brush. He thrust his head forth and inspected the mottled visage above him. "Phampoun still sleeps soundly; he ingested a prodigious meal before retiring. Excuse me while I check the progress of Phampoun's digestion." Pulsifer ducked back behind Phampoun's wattles and revealed himself only by a vibration in the corded grey neck. Presently he returned to view. "He is quite famished, or so it would appear. I had best wake him; he will wish to converse with you before…"

"Before what?"

"No matter."

"A moment," said Cugel. "I am interested in conversing with you rather than Phampoun."

"Indeed?" asked Pulsifer, and polished Phampoun's fang with great vigor. "This is pleasant to hear; I receive few compliments."

"Strange! I see much in you to commend. Necessarily your career goes hand in hand with that of Phampoun, but perhaps you have goals and ambitions of your own?"

Pulsifer propped up Phampoun's lip with his cleaning brush and relaxed upon the ledge so created. "Sometimes I feel that I would enjoy seeing something of the outer world. We have ascended several times to the surface, but always by night when heavy clouds obscure the stars, and even then Phampoun complains of the excessive glare, and he quickly returns below."

"A pity," said Cugel. "By day there is much to see. The scenery surrounding Lumarth is pleasant. The Kind Folk are about to present their Grand Pageant of Ultimate Contrasts, which is said to be most picturesque."

Pulsifer gave his head a wistful shake. "I doubt if ever I will see such events. Have you witnessed many horrid crimes?"

"Indeed I have. For instance I recall a dwarf of the Batvar Forest who rode a pelgrane—"

Pulsifer interrupted him with a gesture. "A moment. Phampoun will want to hear this." He leaned precariously from the cavernous mouth to peer up toward the shuttered eyeballs. "Is he, or more accurately, am I awake? I thought I noticed a twitch. In any event, though I have enjoyed our conversation, we must get on with our duties. Hm, the light cord is disarranged. Perhaps you will be good enough to extinguish the light."

"There is no hurry," said Cugel. "Phampoun sleeps peacefully; let him enjoy his rest. I have something to show you, a game of chance. Are you acquainted with 'Zampolio'?"

Pulsifer signified in the negative, and Cugel produced his cards. "Notice carefully! I deal you four cards and I take four cards, which we conceal from each other." Cugel explained the rules of the game. "Necessarily we play for coins of gold or some such commodity, to make the game interesting. I therefore wager five terces, which you must match."

"Yonder in two sacks is Phampoun's gold, or with equal propriety, my gold, since I am an integral adjunct to this vast hulk. Take forth gold sufficient to equal your terces."

The game proceeded. Pulsifer won the first sally, to his delight, then lost the next, which prompted him to fill the air with dismal complaints; then he won again and again until Cugel declared himself lacking further funds. "You are a clever and skillful player; it is a joy to match wits with you! Still, I feel I could beat you if I had the terces I left above in the temple."

Pulsifer, somewhat puffed and vainglorious, scoffed at Cugel's boast. "I fear that I am too clever for you! Here, take back your terces and we will play the game once again."

"No; this is not the way sportsmen behave; I am too proud to accept your money. Let me suggest a solution to the problem. In the temple above is my sack of terces and a sack of sweetmeats which you might wish to consume as we continue the game. Let us go fetch these articles, then I defy you to win as before!"

Pulsifer leaned far out to inspect Phampoun's visage. "He appears quite comfortable, though his organs are roiling with hunger."

"He sleeps as soundly as ever," declared Cugel. "Let us hurry. If he wakes our game will be spoiled."

Pulsifer hesitated. "What of Phampoun's gold? We dare not leave it unguarded!"

"We will take it with us, and it will never be outside the range of our vigilance."

"Very well; place it here on the dais."

"So, and now I am ready. How do we go aloft?"

"Merely press the leaden bulb beside the arm of the chair, but please make no untoward disturbance. Phampoun might well be exasperated should he awake in unfamiliar surroundings."

"He has never rested easier! We go aloft!" He pressed the button; the dais shivered and creaked and floated up a dark shaft which opened above them. Presently they burst through the valve of the constrictive essence which Cugel had penetrated on his way down the chute. At once a glimmer of scarlet light seeped into the shaft and a moment later the dais glided to a halt level with the altar in the Temple of Phampoun.

"Now then, my sack of terces," said Cugel. "Exactly where did I leave it? Just over yonder, I believe. Notice! Through the great arches you may overlook the main plaza of Lumarth, and those are the Kind Folk going about their ordinary affairs. What is your opinion of all this?"

"Most interesting, although I am unfamiliar with such extensive vistas. In fact, I feel almost a sense of vertigo. What is the source of the savage red glare?"

"That is the light of our ancient sun, now westering toward sunset."

"It does not appeal to me. Please be quick about your business; I have suddenly become most uneasy."

"I will make haste," said Cugel.

The sun, sinking low, sent a shaft of light through the portal, to play full upon the altar. Cugel, stepping behind the massive chair, twitched away the two shutters which guarded Phampoun's eyes, and the milky orbs glistened in the sunlight.

For an instant Phampoun lay quiet. His muscles knotted, his legs jerked, his mouth gaped wide, and he emitted an explosion of sound: a grinding scream which propelled Pulsifer forth to vibrate like a flag in the wind. Phampoun lunged from the altar to fall sprawling and rolling across the floor of the temple, all the while maintaining his cataclysmic outcries. He pulled himself erect, and pounding the tiled floor with his great feet, he sprang here and there and at last burst through the stone walls as if they were paper, while the Kind Folk in the square stood petrified.

Cugel, taking the two sacks of gold, departed the temple by a side entrance. For a moment he watched Phampoun careering around the square, screaming and flailing at the sun. Pulsifer, desperately gripping a pair of tusks, attempted to steer the maddened demon, who, ignoring all restraint, plunged eastward through the city, trampling down trees, bursting through houses as if they failed to exist.

Cugel walked briskly down to the Isk and made his way out upon a dock. He selected a skiff of good proportions, equipped with mast, sail and oars, and prepared to clamber aboard. A punt approached the dock from upriver, poled vigorously by a large man in tattered garments. Cugel turned away, pretending no more than a casual interest in the view, until he might board the skiff without attracting attention.

The punt touched the dock; the boatman climbed up a ladder.

Cugel continued to gaze across the water, affecting indifference to all except the river vistas.

The man, panting and grunting, came to a sudden halt. Cugel felt his intent inspection, and finally turning, looked into the congested face of Huruska, the Nolde of Gundar, though his face was barely recognizable for the bites Huruska had suffered from the insects of the Lallo Marsh.

Huruska stared long and hard at Cugel. "This is a most gratifying occasion!" he said huskily. "I feared that we would never meet again. And what do you carry in those leather bags?" He wrested a bag from Cugel. "Gold from the weight. Your prophecy has been totally vindicated! First honors and a voyage by water, now wealth and revenge! Prepare to die!"

"One moment!" cried Cugel. "You have neglected properly to moor the punt! This is disorderly conduct!"

Huruska turned to look, and Cugel thrust him off the dock into the water.

Cursing and raving, Huruska struggled for the shore while Cugel fumbled with the knots in the mooring-line of the skiff. The line at last came loose; Cugel pulled the skiff close as Huruska came charging down the dock like a bull. Cugel had no choice but to abandon his gold, jump into the skiff, push off and ply the oars while Huruska stood waving his arms in rage.

Cugel pensively hoisted the sail; the wind carried him down the river and around a bend. Cugel's last view of Lumarth, in the dying light of afternoon, included the low lustrous domes of the demon temples and the dark outline of Huruska standing on the dock. From afar the screams of Phampoun were still to be heard and occasionally the thud of toppling masonry.

Afterword to "The Seventeen Virgins"

"I know I'm writing for people to read, but long ago I decided I wouldn't make concessions to the low end of the readership—that I'd be always writing to the high end of the readership, and the low end would have to look out for themselves. I wouldn't condescend…because that's no fun."

—Jack Vance 1986

Ulward's Retreat

Bruham Ulward had invited three friends to lunch at his ranch: Ted and Ravelin Seehoe, and their adolescent daughter Iugenae. After an eye-bulging feast, Ulward offered around a tray of the digestive pastilles which had won him his wealth.

"A wonderful meal," said Ted Seehoe reverently. "Too much, really. I'll need one of these. The algae was absolutely marvelous."

Ulward made a smiling, easy gesture. "It's the genuine stuff."

Ravelin Seehoe, a fresh-faced, rather positive young woman of eighty or ninety, reached for a pastille. "A shame there's not more of it. The synthetic we get is hardly recognizable as algae."

"It's a problem," Ulward admitted. "I clubbed up with some friends; we bought a little mat in the Ross Sea and grow all our own."

"Think of that,"exclaimed Ravelin. "Isn't it frightfully expensive?"

Ulward pursed his lips whimsically. "The good things in life come high. Luckily, I'm able to afford a bit extra."

"What I keep telling Ted—" began Ravelin, then stopped as Ted turned her a keen warning glance.

Ulward bridged the rift. "Money isn't everything. I have a flat of algae, my ranch; you have your daughter—and I'm sure you wouldn't trade."

Ravelin regarded Iugenae critically. "I'm not so sure."

Ted patted Iugenae's hand. "When do you have your own child, Lamster Ulward?" (*Lamster: contraction of Landmaster—the polite form of address in current use.*)

"Still some time yet. I'm thirty-seven billion down the list."

"A pity," said Ravelin Seehoe brightly, "when you could give a child so many advantages."

"Some day, some day , before I'm too old."

"A shame," said Ravelin, "but it has to be. Another fifty billion people and we'd have no privacy whatever!" She looked admiringly around the room, which was used for the sole purpose of preparing food and dining.

Ulward put his hands on the arms of his chair, hitched forward a little. "Perhaps you'd like to look around the ranch?" He spoke in a casual voice, glancing from one to the other.

Iugenae clapped her hands; Ravelin beamed. "If it wouldn't be too much trouble!"

"Oh, we'd love to, Lamster Ulward!" cried Iugenae.

"I've always wanted to see your ranch," said Ted. "I've heard so much about it."

"It's an opportunity for Iugenae I wouldn't want her to miss," said Ravelin. She shook her finger at Iugenae. "Remember, Miss Puss, notice everything very carefully—and don't touch!"

"May I take pictures, Mother?"

"You'll have to ask Lamster Ulward."

"Of course, of course," said Ulward. "Why in the world not?" He rose to his feet—a man of more than middle stature, more than middle pudginess, with straight sandy hair, round blue eyes, a prominent beak of a nose. Almost three hundred years old, he guarded his health with great zeal, and looked little more than two hundred.

He stepped to the door, checked the time, touched a dial on the wall. "Are you ready?"

"Yes, we're quite ready," said Ravelin.

Ulward snapped back the wall, to reveal a view over a sylvan glade. A fine oak tree shaded a pond growing with rushes. A path led through a field toward a wooded valley a mile in the distance.

"Magnificent," said Ted. "Simply magnificent!"

They stepped outdoors into the sunlight. Iugenae flung her arms out, twirled, danced in a circle. "Look! I'm all alone! I'm out here all by myself!"

"Iugenae!" called Ravelin sharply. "Be careful! Stay on the path! That's real grass and you mustn't damage it."

Iugenae ran ahead to the pond. "Mother!" she called back. "Look at these funny little jumpy things! And look at the flowers!"

"The animals are frogs," said Ulward. "They have a very interesting life-history. You see the little fishlike things in the water?"

"Aren't they funny! Mother, do come here!"

"Those are called tadpoles and they will presently become frogs, indistinguishable from the ones you see."

Ravelin and Ted advanced with more dignity, but were as interested as Iugenae in the frogs.

"Smell the fresh air," Ted told Ravelin. "You'd think you were back in the early times."

"It's absolutely exquisite," said Ravelin. She looked around her. "One has the feeling of being able to wander on and on and on."

"Come around over here," called Ulward from beyond the pool. "This is the rock garden."

In awe, the guests stared at the ledge of rock, stained with red and yellow lichen, tufted with green moss. Ferns grew from a crevice; there were several fragile clusters of white flowers.

"Smell the flowers, if you wish," Ulward told Iugenae. "But please don't touch them; they stain rather easily."

Iugenae sniffed. "Mmmm!"

"Are they real?" asked Ted.

"The moss, yes. That clump of ferns and these little succulents are real. The flowers were designed for me by a horticulturist and are exact replicas of certain ancient species. We've actually improved on the odor."

"Wonderful, wonderful," said Ted.

"Now come this way—no, don't look back; I want you to get the total effect…" An expression of vexation crossed his face.

"What's the trouble?" asked Ted.

"It's a damned nuisance," said Ulward. "Hear that sound?"

Ted became aware of a faint rolling rumble, deep and almost unheard. "Yes. Sounds like some sort of factory."

"It is. On the floor below. A rug-works. One of the looms creates this terrible row. I've complained, but they pay no attention…Oh, well, ignore it. Now stand over here—and look around!"

His friends gasped in rapture. The view from this angle was of a rustic bungalow in an Alpine valley, the door being the opening into Ulward's dining room.

"What an illusion of distance!" exclaimed Ravelin. "A person would almost think he was alone."

"A beautiful piece of work," said Ted. "I'd swear I was looking into ten miles—at least five miles—of distance."

"I've got a lot of space here," said Ulward proudly. "Almost three-quarters of an acre. Would you like to see it by moonlight?"

"Oh, could we?"

Ulward went to a concealed switch-panel; the sun seemed to race across the sky. A fervent glow of sunset lit the valley; the sky burned peacock blue, gold, green, then came twilight—and the rising full moon came up behind the hill.

"This is absolutely marvelous," said Ravelin softly. "How can you bring yourself to leave it?"

"It's hard," admitted Ulward. "But I've got to look after business too. More money, more space."

He turned a knob; the moon floated across the sky, sank. Stars appeared, forming the age-old patterns. Ulward pointed out the constellations and the first-magnitude stars by name, using a pencil-torch for a pointer. Then the sky flushed with lavender and lemon yellow and the sun appeared once more. Unseen ducts sent a current of cool air through the glade.

"Right now I'm negotiating for an area behind this wall here." He tapped at the depicted mountainside, an illusion given reality and three-dimensionality by laminations inside the pane. "It's quite a large area—over a hundred square feet. The owner wants a fortune, naturally."

"I'm surprised he wants to sell," said Ted. "A hundred square feet means real privacy."

"There's been a death in the family," explained Ulward. "The owner's four-great-grandfather passed on and the space is temporarily surplus."

Ted nodded. "I hope you're able to get it."

"I hope so too. I've got rather flamboyant ambitions—eventually I hope to own the entire quarterblock—but it takes time. People don't like to sell their space and everyone is anxious to buy."

"Not we," said Ravelin cheerfully. "We have our little home. We're snug and cozy and we're putting money aside for investment."

"Wise," agreed Ulward. "A great many people are space-poor. Then when a chance to make real money comes up, they're undercapitalized. Until I scored with the digestive pastilles, I lived in a single rented locker. I was cramped—but I don't regret it today."

They returned through the glade toward Ulward's house, stopping at the oak tree. "This is my special pride," said Ulward. "A genuine oak tree!"

"Genuine?" asked Ted in astonishment. "I assumed it was simulation."

"So many people do," said Ulward. "No, it's genuine."

"Take a picture of the tree, Iugenae, please. But don't touch it. You might damage the bark."

"Perfectly all right to touch the bark," assured Ulward. He looked up into the branches, then scanned the ground. He stooped, picked up a fallen leaf. "This grew on the tree," he said. "Now, Iugenae, I want you to come with me." He went to the rock garden, pulled a simulated rock aside, to reveal a cabinet with washbasin. "Watch carefully." He showed her the leaf. "Notice? It's dry and brittle and brown."

"Yes, Lamster Ulward." Iugenae craned her neck.

"First I dip it in this solution." He took a beaker full of dark liquid from a shelf. "So. That restores the green color. We wash off the excess, then dry it. Now we rub this next fluid carefully into the surface. Notice, it's flexible and strong now. One more solution—a plastic coating—and there we are, a true oak leaf, perfectly genuine. It's yours."

"Oh, Lamster Ulward! Thank you ever so much!" She ran off to show her father and mother, who were standing by the pool, luxuriating in the feeling of space, watching the frogs. "See what Lamster Ulward gave me!"

"You be very careful with it," said Ravelin. "When we get home, we'll find a nice little frame and you can hang it in your locker."

The simulated sun hung in the western sky. Ulward led the group to a sundial. "An antique, countless years old. Pure marble, carved by hand. It works too—entirely functional. Notice. Three-fifteen by the shadow on the dial..." He peered at his beltwatch, squinted at the sun. "Excuse me one moment." He ran to the control board, made an adjustment. The sun lurched ten degrees across the sky. Ulward returned, checked the sundial. "That's better. Notice. Three-fifty by the sundial, three-fifty by my watch. Isn't that something now?"

"It's wonderful," said Ravelin earnestly.

"It's the loveliest thing I've ever seen," chirped Iugenae.

Ravelin looked around the ranch, sighed wistfully. "We hate to leave, but I think we must be returning home."

"It's been a wonderful day, Lamster Ulward," said Ted. "A wonderful lunch, and we enjoyed seeing your ranch."

"You'll have to come out again," invited Ulward. "I always enjoy company."

He led them into the dining room, through the living room-bedroom to the door. The Seehoe family took a last look across the spacious interior, pulled on their mantles, stepped into their run-shoes , made their farewells. Ulward slid back the door. The Seehoes looked out, waited till a gap appeared in the traffic. They waved good-bye , pulled the hoods over their heads, stepped out into the corridor.

The run-shoes spun them toward their home, selecting the appropriate turnings, sliding automatically into the correct lift- and drop-pits. Deflection fields twisted them through the throngs. Like the Seehoes, everyone wore mantle and hood of filmy reflective stuff to safeguard privacy. The illusion-pane along the ceiling of the corridor presented a view of towers dwindling up into a cheerful blue sky, as if the pedestrian were moving along one of the windy upper passages.

The Seehoes approached their home. Two hundred yards away, they angled over to the wall. If the flow of traffic carried them past, they would be forced to circle the block and make another attempt to enter. Their door slid open as they spun near; they ducked into the opening, swinging around on a metal grab-bar.

They removed their mantles and run-shoes, sliding skillfully past each other. Iugenae pivoted into the bathroom and there was room for both Ted and Ravelin to sit down. The house was rather small for the three of them; they could well have used another twelve square feet, but rather than pay exorbitant rent, they preferred to save the money with an eye toward Iugenae's future.

Ted sighed in satisfaction, stretching his legs luxuriously under Ravelin's chair. "Ulward's ranch notwithstanding, it's nice to be home."

Iugenae backed out of the bathroom.

Ravelin looked up. "It's time for your pill, dear."

Iugenae screwed up her face. "Oh, Mama! Why do I have to take pills? I feel perfectly well."

"They're good for you, dear."

Iugenae sullenly took a pill from the dispenser. "Runy says you make us take pills to keep us from growing up."

Ted and Ravelin exchanged glances.

"Just take your pill," said Ravelin, "and never mind what Runy says."

"But how is it that I'm 38 and Ermara Burk's only 32 and she's got a figure and I'm like a slat?"

"No arguments, dear. Take your pill."

Ted jumped to his feet. "Here, Babykin, sit down."

Iugenae protested, but Ted held up his hand. "I'll sit in the niche. I've got a few calls that I have to make."

He sidled past Ravelin, seated himself in the niche in front of the communication screen. The illusion-pane behind him was custom-built—Ravelin, in fact, had designed it herself. It simulated a merry little bandit's den, the walls draped in red and yellow silk, a bowl of fruit on the rustic table, a guitar on the bench, a copper teakettle simmering on the countertop stove. The pane had been rather expensive, but when anyone communicated with the Seehoes, it was the first thing they saw, and here the house-proud Ravelin had refused to stint.

Before Ted could make his call, the signal light flashed. He answered; the screen opened to display his friend Loren Aigle, apparently sitting in an airy arched rotunda, against a background of fleecy clouds—an illusion which Ravelin had instantly recognized as an inexpensive stock effect.

Loren and Elme, his wife, were anxious to hear of the Seehoes' visit to the Ulward ranch. Ted described the afternoon in detail. "Space, space and more space! Isolation pure and simple! Absolute privacy! You can hardly imagine it! A fortune in illusion-panes."

"Nice," said Loren Aigle. "I'll tell you one you'll find hard to believe. Today I registered a whole planet to a man." Loren worked in the Certification Bureau of the Extraterrestrial Properties Agency.

Ted was puzzled and uncomprehending. "A whole planet? How so?"

Loren explained. "He's a free-lance spaceman. Still a few left."

"But what's he planning to do with an entire planet?"

"Live there, he claims."

"Alone?"

Loren nodded. "I had quite a chat with him. Earth is all very well, he says, but he prefers the privacy of his own planet. Can you imagine that?"

"Frankly, no! I can't imagine the fourth dimension either. What a marvel, though!"

The conversation ended and the screen faded. Ted swung around to his wife. "Did you hear that?"

Ravelin nodded; she had heard but not heeded. She was reading the menu supplied by the catering firm to which they subscribed. "We won't want anything heavy after that lunch. They've got simulated synthetic algae again."

Ted grunted. "It's never as good as the genuine synthetic."

"But it's cheaper and we've all had an enormous lunch."

"Don't worry about me, Mom!" sang Iugenae. "I'm going out with Runy."

"Oh, you are, are you? And where are you going, may I ask?"

"A ride around the world. We're catching the seven o'clock shuttle, so I've got to hurry."

"Come right home afterward," said Ravelin severely. "Don't go anywhere else."

"For heaven's sake, Mother, you'd think I was going to elope or something."

"Mind what I say, Miss Puss. I was a girl once myself. Have you taken your medicine?"

"Yes, I've taken my medicine."

Iugenae departed; Ted slipped back into the niche. "Who are you calling now?" asked Ravelin.

"Lamster Ulward. I want to thank him for going to so much trouble for us."

Ravelin agreed that an algae-and-margarine call was no more than polite.

Ted called, expressed his thanks, then—almost as an afterthought—chanced to mention the man who owned a planet.

"An entire planet?" inquired Ulward. "It must be inhabited."

"No, I understand not, Lamster Ulward. Think of it! Think of the privacy!"

"Privacy!" exclaimed Ulward bluffly. "My dear fellow, what do you call this?"

"Oh, naturally, Lamster Ulward—you have a real showplace."

"The planet must be very primitive," Ulward reflected. "An engaging idea, of course—if you like that kind of thing. Who is this man?"

"I don't know, Lamster Ulward. I could find out, if you like."

"No, no, don't bother. I'm not particularly interested. Just an idle thought." Ulward laughed his hearty laugh. "Poor man. Probably lives in a dome."

"That's possible, of course, Lamster Ulward. Well, thanks again, and good night."

The spaceman's name was Kennes Mail. He was short and thin, tough as synthetic herring, brown as toasted yeast. He had a close-cropped pad of gray hair, a keen, if ingenuous, blue gaze. He showed a courteous interest in Ulward's ranch, but Ulward thought his recurrent use of the word 'clever' rather tactless.

As they returned to the house, Ulward paused to admire his oak tree.

"It's absolutely genuine, Lamster Mail! A living tree, survivor of past ages! Do you have trees as fine as that on your planet?"

Kennes Mail smiled. "Lamster Ulward, that's just a shrub. Let's sit somewhere and I'll show you photographs."

Ulward had already mentioned his interest in acquiring extraterrestrial property; Mail, admitting that he needed money, had given him to understand that some sort of deal might be arranged. They sat at a table; Mail opened his case. Ulward switched on the wall-screen.

"First I'll show you a map," said Mail. He selected a rod, dropped it into the table socket. On the wall appeared a world projection: oceans; an enormous equatorial landmass named Gaea; the smaller subcontinents Atalanta, Persephone, Alcyone. A box of descriptive information read:

MAIL'S PLANET

Claim registered and endorsed at Extraterrestrial Properties Agency

Surface area:	.87 Earth normal
Gravity:	.93 Earth normal
Diurnal rotation:	22.15 Earth hours
Annual revolution:	2.97 Earth years
Atmosphere:	Invigorating
Climate:	Salubrious
Noxious conditions and influences:	None
Population:	1

Mail pointed to a spot on the eastern shore of Gaea. "I live here. Just got a rough camp at present. I need money to do a bit better for myself. I'm willing to lease off one of the smaller continents, or, if you prefer, a section of Gaea, say from Murky Mountains west to the ocean."

Ulward, with a cheerful smile, shook his head. "No sections for me, Lamster Mail. I want to buy the world outright. You set your price; if it's within reason, I'll write a check."

Mail glanced at him sidewise. "You haven't even seen the photographs."

"True." In a businesslike voice, Ulward said, "By all means, the photographs."

Mail touched the projection button. Landscapes of an unfamiliar wild beauty appeared on the screen. There were mountain crags and roaring rivers, snow-powdered forests, ocean dawns and prairie sunsets, green hillsides, meadows spattered with blossoms, beaches white as milk.

"Very pleasant," said Ulward. "Quite nice." He pulled out his checkbook. "What's your price?"

Mail chuckled and shook his head. "I won't sell. I'm willing to lease off a section—providing my price is met and my rules are agreed to."

Ulward sat with compressed lips. He gave his head a quick little jerk. Mail started to rise to his feet.

"No, no," said Ulward hastily. "I was merely thinking…Let's look at the map again."

Mail returned the map to the screen. Ulward made careful inspection of the various continents, inquired as to physiography, climate, flora and fauna.

Finally he made his decision. "I'll lease Gaea."

"No, Lamster Ulward!" declared Mail. "I'm reserving this entire area—from Murky Mountains and the Calliope River east. This western section is open. It's maybe a little smaller than Atalanta or Persephone, but the climate is warmer."

"There aren't any mountains on the western section," Ulward protested. "Only these insignificant Rock Castle Crags."

"They're not so insignificant," said Mail. "You've also got the Purple Bird Hills, and down here in the south is Mount Cairasco—a live volcano. What more do you need?"

Ulward glanced across his ranch. "I'm in the habit of thinking big."

"West Gaea is a pretty big chunk of property."

"Very well," said Ulward. "What are your terms?"

"So far as money goes, I'm not greedy," Mail said. "For a twenty-year lease: two hundred thousand a year, the first five years in advance."

Ulward made a startled protest. "Great guns, Lamster Mail! That's almost half my income!"

Mail shrugged. "I'm not trying to get rich. I want to build a lodge for my-self. It costs money. If you can't afford it, I'll have to speak to someone who can."

Ulward said in a nettled voice, "I can afford it, certainly—but my entire ranch here cost less than a million."

"Well, either you want it or you don't," said Mail. "I'll tell you my rules, then you can make up your mind."

"What rules?" demanded Ulward, his face growing red.

"They're simple and their only purpose is to maintain privacy for both of us. First, you have to stay on your own property. No excursions hither and yon on my property. Second, no subleasing. Third, no residents except yourself, your family and your servants. I don't want any artists' colony springing up, nor any wild noisy resort atmosphere. Naturally you're entitled to bring out your guests, but they've got to keep to your property just like yourself."

He looked sidewise at Ulward's glum face. "I'm not trying to be tough, Lamster Ulward. Good fences make good neighbors, and it's better that we have the understanding now than hard words and beam-gun evictions later."

"Let me see the photographs again," said Ulward. "Show me West Gaea."

He looked, heaved a deep sigh. "Very well. I agree."

The construction crew had departed. Ulward was alone on West Gaea. He walked around the new lodge, taking deep breaths of pure quiet air, thrilling to the absolute solitude and privacy. The lodge had cost a fortune, but how many other people of Earth owned—leased, rather—anything to compare with this?

He walked out on the front terrace, gazed proudly across miles—genuine unsimulated miles—of landscape. For his home site, he had selected a shelf in the foothills of the Ulward Range (as he had renamed the Purple Bird Hills). In front spread a great golden savannah dotted with blue-green trees; behind rose a tall gray cliff.

A stream rushed down a cleft in the rock, leaping, splashing, cooling the air, finally flowing into a beautiful clear pool, beside which Ulward had erected a cabana of red, green and brown plastic. At the base of the cliff and in crevices grew clumps of spiky blue cactus, lush green bushes covered with red trumpet-flowers, a thick-leafed white plant holding up a stalk clustered with white bubbles.

Solitude! The real thing! No thumping of factories, no roar of traffic two feet from one's bed. One arm outstretched, the other pressed to his chest, Ulward performed a stately little jig of triumph on the terrace. Had he been able, he might have turned a cartwheel. When a person has complete privacy, absolutely nothing is forbidden!

Ulward took a final turn up and down the terrace, made a last appreciative survey of the horizon. The sun was sinking through banks of fire-fringed clouds. Marvelous depth of color, a tonal brilliance to be matched only in the very best illusion-panes!

He entered the lodge, made a selection from the nutrition locker. After a leisurely meal, he returned to the lounge. He stood thinking for a moment, then went out upon the terrace, strolled up and down. Wonderful! The night was full of stars, hanging like blurred white lamps, almost as he had always imagined them.

After ten minutes of admiring the stars, he returned into the lodge. Now what? The wall-screen , with its assortment of recorded programs. Snug and comfortable, Ulward watched the performance of a recent musical comedy.

Real luxury, he told himself. Pity he couldn't invite his friends out to spend the evening. Unfortunately impossible, considering the inconvenient duration of the trip between Mail's Planet and Earth. However—only three days until the arrival of his first guest. She was Elf Intry, a young woman who had been more than friendly with Ulward on Earth. When Elf arrived, Ulward would broach a subject which he had been mulling over for several months—indeed, ever since he had first learned of Mail's Planet.

Elf Intry arrived early in the afternoon, coming down to Mail's Planet in a capsule discharged from the weekly Outer Ring Express packet. A woman of normally good disposition, she greeted Ulward in a seethe of indignation. "Just who is that brute around the other side of the planet? I thought you had absolute privacy here!"

"That's just old Mail," said Ulward evasively. "What's wrong?"

"The fool on the packet set me the wrong coordinates and the capsule came down on a beach. I noticed a house and then I saw a naked man jumping rope behind some bushes. I thought it was you, of course. I went over and said 'Boo!' You should have heard the language he used!" She shook her head. "I don't see why you allow such a boor on your planet."

The buzzer on the communication screen sounded. "That's Mail now," said Ulward. "You wait here. I'll tell him how to speak to my guests!"

He presently returned to the terrace. Elf came over to him, kissed his nose. "Ully, you're pale with rage! I hope you didn't lose your temper."

"No," said Ulward. "We merely—well, we had an understanding. Come along, look over the property."

He took Elf around to the back, pointing out the swimming pool, the waterfall, the mass of rock above. "You won't see that effect on any illusion-pane! That's genuine rock!"

"Lovely, Ully. Very nice. The color might be just a trifle darker, though. Rock doesn't look like that."

"No?" Ulward inspected the cliff more critically. "Well, I can't do anything about it. How about the privacy?"

"Wonderful! It's so quiet, it's almost eerie!"

"Eerie?" Ulward looked around the landscape. "It hadn't occurred to me."

"You're not sensitive to these things, Ully. Still, it's very nice, if you can tolerate that unpleasant creature Mail so close."

"Close?" protested Ulward. "He's on the other side of the continent!"

"True," said Elf. "It's all relative, I suppose. How long do you expect to stay out here?"

"That depends. Come along inside. I want to talk with you."

He seated her in a comfortable chair, brought her a globe of Gluco-Fructoid Nectar. For himself, he mixed ethyl alcohol, water, a few drops of Haig's Oldtime Esters.

"Elf, where do you stand in the reproduction list?"

She raised her fine eyebrows, shook her head. "So far down, I've lost count. Fifty or sixty billion."

"I'm down thirty-seven billion. It's one reason I bought this place. Waiting list, piffle! Nobody stops Bruham Ulward's breeding on his own planet!"

Elf pursed her lips, shook her head sadly. "It won't work, Ully."

"And why not?"

"You can't take the children back to Earth. The list would keep them out."

"True, but think of living here, surrounded by children. All the children you wanted! And utter privacy to boot! What more could you ask for?"

Elf sighed. "You fabricate a beautiful illusion-pane, Ully. But I think not. I love the privacy and solitude—but I thought there'd be more people to be private from."

The Outer Ring Express packet came past four days later. Elf kissed Ulward good-bye. "It's simply exquisite here, Ully. The solitude is so magnificent, it gives me gooseflesh. I've had a wonderful visit." She climbed into the capsule. "See you on Earth."

"Just a minute," said Ulward suddenly. "I want you to post a letter or two for me."

"Hurry. I've only got twenty minutes."

Ulward was back in ten minutes. "Invitations," he told her breathlessly. "Friends."

"Right." She kissed his nose. "Good-bye, Ully." She slammed the port; the capsule rushed away, whirling up to meet the packet.

The new guests arrived three weeks later: Frobisher Worbeck, Liornetta Stobart, Harris and Hyla Cabe, Ted and Ravelin and Iugenae Seehoe, Juvenal Aquister and his son Runy.

Ulward, brown from long days of lazing in the sun, greeted them with great enthusiasm. "Welcome to my little retreat! Wonderful to see you all! Frobisher, you pink-cheeked rascal! And Iugenae! Prettier than ever! Be careful, Ravelin—I've got my eye on your daughter! But Runy's here, guess I'm out of the picture! Liornetta, damned glad you could make it! And Ted! Great to see you, old chap! This is all your doing, you know! Harris, Hyla, Juvenal—come on up! We'll have a drink, a drink, a drink!"

Running from one to the other, patting arms, herding the slow-moving Frobisher Worbeck, he conducted his guests up the slope to the terrace. Here they turned to survey the panorama. Ulward listened to their remarks, mouth pursed against a grin of gratification.

"Magnificent!"

"Grand!"

"Absolutely genuine!"

"The sky is so far away, it frightens me!"

"The sunlight's so pure!"

"The genuine thing's always best, isn't it?"

Runy said a trifle wistfully, "I thought you were on a beach, Lamster Ulward."

"Beach? This is mountain country, Runy. Land of the wide open spaces! Look out over that plain!"

Liornetta Stobart patted Runy's shoulder. "Not every planet has beaches, Runy. The secret of happiness is to be content with what one has."

Ulward laughed gaily. "Oh, I've got beaches, never fear for that! There's a fine beach—ha, ha—five hundred miles due west. Every step Ulward domain!"

"Can we go?" asked Iugenae excitedly. "Can we go, Lamster Ulward?"

"We certainly can! That shed down the slope is headquarters for the Ulward Airlines. We'll fly to the beach, swim in Ulward Ocean! But now refreshment! After that crowded capsule, your throats must be like paper!"

"It wasn't too crowded," said Ravelin Seehoe. "There were only nine of us." She looked critically up at the cliff. "If that were an illusion-pane, I'd consider it grotesque."

"My dear Ravelin!" cried Ulward. "It's impressive! Magnificent!"

"All of that," agreed Frobisher Worbeck, a tall sturdy man, white-haired, red-jowled, with a blue benevolent gaze. "And now, Bruham, what about those drinks?"

"Of course! Ted, I know you of old. Will you tend bar? Here's the alcohol, here's water, here are the esters. Now, you two," Ulward called to Runy and Iugenae. "How about some nice cold soda pop?"

"What kind is there?" asked Runy.

"All kinds, all flavors. This is Ulward's Retreat! We've got methylamyl glutamine, cycloprodacterol phosphate, metathiobromine-4-glycocitrose…"

Runy and Iugenae expressed their preferences; Ulward brought the globes, then hurried to arrange tables and chairs for the adults. Presently everyone was comfortable and relaxed.

Iugenae whispered to Ravelin, who smiled and nodded indulgently. "Lamster Ulward, you remember the beautiful oak leaf you gave Iugenae?"

"Of course I do."

"It's still as fresh and green as ever. I wonder if Iugenae might have a leaf or two from some of these other trees?"

"My dear Ravelin!" Ulward roared with laughter. "She can have an entire tree!"

"Oh Mother! Can—"

"Iugenae, don't be ridiculous!" snapped Ted. "How could we get it home? Where would we plant the thing? In the bathroom?"

Ravelin said, "You and Runy find some nice leaves, but don't wander too far."

"No, Mother." She beckoned to Runy. "Come along, dope. Bring a basket."

The others of the party gazed out over the plain. "A beautiful view, Ulward," said Frobisher Worbeck. "How far does your property extend?"

"Five hundred miles west to the ocean, six hundred miles east to the mountains, eleven hundred miles north and two hundred miles south."

Worbeck shook his head solemnly. "Nice. A pity you couldn't get the whole planet. Then you'd have real privacy!"

"I tried, of course," said Ulward. "The owner refused to consider the idea."

"A pity."

Ulward brought out a map. "However, as you see, I have a fine volcano, a number of excellent rivers, a mountain range, and down here on the delta of Cinnamon River an absolutely miasmic swamp."

Ravelin pointed to the ocean. "Why, it's Lonesome Ocean! I thought the name was Ulward Ocean."

Ulward laughed uncomfortably. "Just a figure of speech—so to speak. My rights extend ten miles. More than enough for swimming purposes."

"No freedom of the seas here, eh, Lamster Ulward?" laughed Harris Cabe.

"Not exactly," confessed Ulward.

"A pity," said Frobisher Worbeck.

Hyla Cabe pointed to the map. "Look at these wonderful mountain ranges! The Magnificent Mountains! And over here—the Elysian Gardens! I'd love to see them, Lamster Ulward."

Ulward shook his head in embarrassment. "Impossible, I'm afraid. They're not on my property. I haven't even seen them myself."

His guests stared at him in astonishment. "But surely—"

"It's an atom-welded contract with Lamster Mail," Ulward explained. "He stays on his property, I stay on mine. In this way, our privacy is secure."

"Look," Hyla Cabe said aside to Ravelin. "The Unimaginable Caverns! Doesn't it make you simply wild not to be able to see them?"

Aquister said hurriedly, "It's a pleasure to sit here and just breathe this wonderful fresh air. No noise, no crowds, no bustle or hurry… "

The party drank and chatted and basked in the sunshine until late afternoon. Enlisting the aid of Ravelin Seehoe and Hyla Cabe, Ulward set out a simple meal of yeast pellets, processed protein, thick slices of algae crunch.

"No animal flesh, cooked vegetation?" questioned Worbeck curiously.

"Tried them the first day," said Ulward. "Revolting. Sick for a week."

After dinner, the guests watched a comic melodrama on the wall-screen. Then Ulward showed them to their various cubicles, and after a few minutes of badinage and calling back and forth, the lodge became quiet.

Next day, Ulward ordered his guests into their bathing suits. "We're off to the beach, we'll gambol on the sand, we'll frolic in the surf of Lonesome Ulward Ocean!"

The guests piled happily into the air-car. Ulward counted heads. "All aboard! We're off!"

They rose and flew west, first low over the plain, then high into the air, to obtain a panoramic view of the Rock Castle Crags.

"The tallest peak—there to the north—is almost ten thousand feet high. Notice how it juts up, just imagine the mass! Solid rock! How'd you like that dropped on your toe, Runy? Not so good, eh? In a moment, we'll see a precipice over a thousand feet straight up and down. There—now! Isn't that remarkable?"

"Certainly impressive," agreed Ted.

"What those Magnificent Mountains must be like!" said Harris Cabe with a wry laugh.

"How tall are they, Lamster Ulward?" inquired Liornetta Stobart.

"What? Which?"

"The Magnificent Mountains."

"I don't know for sure. Thirty or forty thousand feet, I suppose."

"What a marvelous sight they must be!" said Frobisher Worbeck. "Probably make these look like foothills."

"These are beautiful too," Hyla Cabe put in hastily.

"Oh, naturally," said Frobisher Worbeck. "A damned fine sight! You're a lucky man, Bruham!"

Ulward laughed shortly, turned the air-car west. They flew across a rolling forested plain and presently Lonesome Ocean gleamed in the distance. Ulward slanted down, landed the air-car on the beach, and the party alighted.

The day was warm, the sun hot. A fresh wind blew in from the ocean. The surf broke upon the sand in massive roaring billows.

The party stood appraising the scene. Ulward swung his arms. "Well, who's for it? Don't wait to be invited! We've got the whole ocean to ourselves!"

Ravelin said, "It's so rough! Look how that water crashes down!"

Liornetta Stobart turned away with a shake of her head. "Illusion-pane surf is always so gentle. This could lift you right up and give you a good shaking!"

"I expected nothing quite so vehement," Harris Cabe admitted.

Ravelin beckoned to Iugenae. "You keep well away, Miss Puss. I don't want you swept out to sea. You'd find it Lonesome Ocean indeed!"

Runy approached the water, waded gingerly into a sheet of retreating foam. A comber thrashed down at him and he danced quickly back up the shore.

"The water's cold," he reported.

Ulward poised himself. "Well, here goes! I'll show you how it's done!" He trotted forward, stopped short, then flung himself into the face of a great white comber.

The party on the beach watched.

"Where is he?" asked Hyla Cabe.

Iugenae pointed. "I saw part of him out there. A leg, or an arm."

"There he is!" cried Ted. "Woof! Another one's caught him. I suppose some people might consider it sport..."

Ulward staggered to his feet, lurched through the retreating wash to shore. "Hah! Great! Invigorating! Ted! Harris! Juvenal! Take a go at it!"

Harris shook his head. "I don't think I'll try it today, Bruham."

"The next time for me too," said Juvenal Aquister. "Perhaps it won't be so rough."

"But don't let us stop you!" urged Ted. "You swim as long as you like. We'll wait here for you."

"Oh, I've had enough for now," said Ulward. "Excuse me while I change."

When Ulward returned, he found his guests seated in the air-car. "Hello! Everyone ready to go?"

"It's hot in the sun," explained Liornetta, "and we thought we'd enjoy the view better from inside."

"When you look through the glass, it's almost like an illusion-pane," said Iugenae.

"Oh, I see. Well, perhaps you're ready to visit other parts of the Ulward domain?"

The proposal met with approval; Ulward took the air-car into the air. "We can fly north over the pine woods, south over Mount Cairasco, which unfortunately isn't erupting just now."

"Anywhere you like, Lamster Ulward," said Frobisher Worbeck. "No doubt it's all beautiful."

Ulward considered the varied attractions of his leasehold. "Well, first to the Cinnamon Swamp."

For two hours they flew, over the swamp, across the smoking crater of Mount Cairasco, east to the edge of Murky Mountains, along Calliope River to its source in Goldenleaf Lake. Ulward pointed out noteworthy views, interesting aspects. Behind him, the murmurs of admiration dwindled and finally died.

"Had enough?" Ulward called back gaily. "Can't see half a continent in one day! Shall we save some for tomorrow?"

There was a moment's stillness. Then Liornetta Stobart said, "Lamster Ulward, we're simply dying for a peek at the Magnificent Mountains. I wonder—do you think we could slip over for a quick look? I'm sure Lamster Mail wouldn't really mind."

Ulward shook his head with a rather stiff smile. "He's made me agree to a very definite set of rules. I've already had one brush with him."

"How could he possibly find out?" asked Juvenal Aquister.

"He probably wouldn't find out," said Ulward, "but—"

"It's a damned shame for him to lock you off into this drab little peninsula!" Frobisher Worbeck said indignantly.

"Please, Lamster Ulward," Iugenae wheedled.

"Oh, very well," Ulward said recklessly.

He turned the air-car east. The Murky Mountains passed below. The party peered from the windows, exclaiming at the marvels of the forbidden landscape.

"How far are the Magnificent Mountains?" asked Ted.

"Not far. Another thousand miles."

"Why are you hugging the ground?" asked Frobisher Worbeck. "Up in the air, man! Let's see the countryside!"

Ulward hesitated. Mail was probably asleep. And, in the last analysis, he really had no right to forbid an innocent little—

"Lamster Ulward," called Runy, "there's an air-car right behind us."

The air-car drew up level. Kennes Mail's blue eyes met Ulward's across the gap. He motioned Ulward down.

Ulward compressed his mouth, swung the air-car down. From behind him came murmurs of sympathy and outrage.

Below was a dark pine forest; Ulward set down in a pretty little glade. Mail landed nearby, jumped to the ground, signaled to Ulward. The two men walked to the side. The guests murmured together and shook their heads.

Ulward presently returned to the air-car. "Everybody please get in," he said crisply.

They rose into the air and flew west. "What did the chap have to say for himself?" queried Worbeck.

Ulward chewed at his lips. "Not too much. Wanted to know if I'd lost the way. I told him one or two things. Reached an understanding…" His voice dwindled, then rose in a burst of cheerfulness. "We'll have a party back at the lodge. What do we care for Mail and his confounded mountains?"

"That's the spirit, Bruham!" cried Frobisher Worbeck.

Both Ted and Ulward tended bar during the evening. Either one or the other mingled rather more alcohol to rather less esters into the drinks than standard practice recommended. As a result, the party became quite loud and gay. Ulward damned Mail's interfering habits; Worbeck explored six thousand years of common law in an effort to prove Mail a domineering tyrant; the women giggled; Iugenae and Runy watched cynically, then presently went off to attend to their own affairs.

In the morning, the group slept late. Ulward finally tottered out on the terrace, to be joined one at a time by the others. Runy and Iugenae were missing.

"Young rascals," groaned Worbeck. "If they're lost, they'll have to find their own way back. No search parties for me."

At noon, Runy and Iugenae returned in Ulward's air-car.

"Good heavens," shrieked Ravelin. "Iugenae, come here this instant! Where have you been?"

Juvenal Aquister surveyed Runy sternly. "Have you lost your mind, taking Lamster Ulward's air-car without his permission?"

"I asked him last night," Runy declared indignantly. "He said yes, take anything except the volcano because that's where he slept when his feet got cold, and the swamp because that's where he dropped his empty containers."

"Regardless," said Juvenal in disgust, "you should have had better sense. Where have you been?"

Runy fidgeted. Iugenae said, "Well, we went south for a while, then turned and went east—I think it was east. We thought if we flew low, Lamster Mail wouldn't see us. So we flew low, through the mountains, and pretty soon we came to an ocean. We went along the beach and came to a house. We landed to see who lived there, but nobody was home."

Ulward stifled a groan.

"What would anyone want with a pen of birds?" asked Runy.

"Birds? What birds? Where?"

"At the house. There was a pen with a lot of big birds, but they kind of got loose while we were looking at them and all flew away."

"Anyway," Iugenae continued briskly, "we decided it was Lamster Mail's house, so we wrote a note, telling what everybody thinks of him and pinned it to his door."

Ulward rubbed his forehead. "Is that all?"

"Well, practically all." Iugenae became diffident. She looked at Runy and the two of them giggled nervously.

"There's more?" yelled Ulward. "What, in heaven's name?"

"Nothing very much," said Iugenae, following a crack in the terrace with her toe. "We put a booby-trap over the door—just a bucket of water. Then we came home."

The screen buzzer sounded from inside the lodge. Everybody looked at Ulward. Ulward heaved a deep sigh, rose to his feet, went inside.

That very afternoon, the Outer Ring Express packet was due to pass the junction point. Frobisher Worbeck felt sudden and acute qualms of conscience for the neglect his business suffered while he dawdled away hours in idle enjoyment.

"But my dear old chap!" exclaimed Ulward. "Relaxation is good for you!"

True, agreed Frobisher Worbeck, if one could make himself oblivious to the possibility of fiasco through the carelessness of underlings. Much as he deplored the necessity, in spite of his inclination to loiter for weeks, he felt impelled to leave—and not a minute later than that very afternoon.

Others of the group likewise remembered important business which they had to see to, and those remaining felt it would be a shame and an imposition to send up the capsule half-empty and likewise decided to return.

Ulward's arguments met unyielding walls of obstinacy. Rather glumly, he went down to the capsule to bid his guests farewell. As they climbed through the port, they expressed their parting thanks:

"Bruham, it's been absolutely marvelous!"

"You'll never know how we've enjoyed this outing, Lamster Ulward!"

"The air, the space, the privacy—I'll never forget!"

"It was the most, to say the least."

The port thumped into its socket. Ulward stood back, waving rather uncertainly.

Ted Seehoe reached to press the Active button. Ulward sprang forward, pounded on the port.

"Wait!" he bellowed. "A few things I've got to attend to! I'm coming with you!"

"Come in, come in," said Ulward heartily, opening the door to three of his friends: Coble and his wife Heulia Sansom, and Coble's young, pretty cousin Landine. "Glad to see you!"

"And we're glad to come! We've heard so much of your wonderful ranch, we've been on pins and needles all day!"

"Oh, come now! It's not so marvelous as all that!"

"Not to you, perhaps—you live here!"

Ulward smiled. "Well, I must say I live here and still like it. Would you like to have lunch, or perhaps you'd prefer to walk around for a few minutes? I've just finished making a few changes, but I'm happy to say everything is in order."

"Can we just take a look?"

"Of course. Come over here. Stand just so. Now—are you ready?"

"Ready."

Ulward snapped the wall back.

"Ooh!" breathed Landine. "Isn't it beautiful!"

"The space, the open feeling!"

"Look, a tree! What a wonderful simulation!"

"That's no simulation," said Ulward. "That's a genuine tree!"

"Lamster Ulward, are you telling the truth?"

"I certainly am. I never tell lies to a lovely young lady. Come along, over this way."

"Lamster Ulward, that cliff is so convincing, it frightens me."

Ulward grinned. "It's a good job." He signaled a halt. "Now—turn around."

The group turned. They looked out across a great golden savannah, dotted with groves of blue-green trees. A rustic lodge commanded the view, the door being the opening into Ulward's living room.

The group stood in silent admiration. Then Heulia sighed. "Space. Pure space."

"I'd swear I was looking miles," said Coble.

Ulward smiled, a trifle wistfully. "Glad you like my little retreat. Now what about lunch? Genuine algae!"

Seven Exits from Bocz

To the shrouded shape in the back of the car, Nicholas Trasek said, "You understand, then? Three buzzes means come in."

The figure moved.

Trasek turned away slowly, hesitated, looked back. "You're sure you can make it? It's about twenty yards, along a gravel path."

A whirring sound came from the huddled shape.

"Very well," said Trasek. "I'm going in."

But he paused another moment, listening.

Everything was breathlessly quiet. The house stood ghostly white in the moonlight among old trees, three stories of archaic elegance, with lights showing dim yellow along the bottom floor.

Trasek walked up the path, the gravel crunching under his feet. He stopped at the marble porch, and the entry light shone on his face—a harsh tense face with brooding black eyes, a peculiar leaden skin. He mounted the steps gingerly, like a cat on a strange roof, pressed the button.

Presently the door was opened, by a fat middle-aged woman in a pink robe.

"I've come to see Dr. Horzabky," said Trasek.

The woman uncertainly surveyed the pale face. "Couldn't you call some other time? I don't think he'd like to be disturbed this time of night."

"He'll see me," said Trasek.

The woman peered at him. "An old friend?"

"No," said Trasek. "We have—mutual acquaintances."

"Well, I'll see. You'll have to wait a minute." She closed the door, and Trasek was left alone on the moonlit marble.

A few moments later, the door opened, and the woman motioned him in. "This way, if you please."

Trasek followed her down a hall, the woman's slippers scuffing along the dark red carpet. She opened the door and Trasek passed into a long room, lit with golden light from a great crystal chandelier.

The floor was covered by an oriental rug—sumptuous orange, mulberry, indigo—and the furniture was massive antique hardwood. Books in old walnut racks lined one wall—heavy volumes, all sizes, all shapes and colors. Across the room a number of large paintings hung, and a mirror on the far wall reflected the door Trasek had entered.

Dr. Horzabky stood holding a book. He wore a red velveteen smoking jacket over black trousers—a tall narrow-shouldered man with a thin neck, a wide flat head. His chin was small and pointed, his hair sparse. He wore thick-lensed spectacles, under which his eyes showed large and mild blue.

Trasek closed the door behind him, advanced slowly into the room, harsh and fierce as a black wolf.

"Yes?" inquired Dr. Horzabky. "What can I do for you?"

Trasek smiled. "I doubt if you'll do it."

Horzabky raised his eyebrows slightly. "In that case, there was small reason for you to call."

"I might be an art fancier," said Trasek, nodding toward the pictures on the wall. "Although they're something queer for my taste…Mind if I look at them?"

"Not at all." Horzabky lay down his book. "The pictures however are not for sale."

Trasek approached the first, rather more closely than a connoisseur would recommend. It appeared, at first glance, merely a shading of blacks, dull browns and purples. "This one seems dull."

"According to your taste," said Horzabky, looking quizzically back and forth from the picture to Trasek.

"Who is the artist?"

"His name is unknown."

"Ah," and Trasek passed on to the second, an abstraction. "Now this is a nightmare." Indeed, the shapes were unreal, and when the mind reached to grasp them, they slipped away from comprehension; and the colors were equally strange—nameless off-tones, bright tints the eye saw but could not name. Trasek shook his head disapprovingly, to Horzabky's amusement, and passed on to the third, likewise an abstraction, but composed in a quieter spirit—horizontal lines and stripes of gold, silver, copper, and other metallic colors.

Trasek examined this closely. "There's a clever illusion of space and distance here," he said, watching Horzabky from the corner of his eye. "Almost you would think you could reach in, gather up the gold."

"Many have thought so," assented Horzabky, eyes owlish behind the spectacles.

Trasek examined the fourth picture with even greater care. "Another one I can't understand," he said at last. "Are those trees?"

Horzabky nodded. "The artist has painted everything as it would appear inside out."

"Ah, ah…" Trasek nodded wisely and passed on to the fifth picture. Here he found depicted an intricate framework of luminous yellow-white bars on a black background, the framework filling all of space with a cubical lattice, the parallel members meeting at the picture's vanishing point. Without comment Trasek turned to the last picture on the wall, merely a grayish-pink blur, and shook his head silently, then turned away.

"Perhaps now you will reveal your reason for calling," Horzabky put forward, gently.

Trasek looked fiercely toward Horzabky, who blinked in discomfort.

"A friend asked me to find you," said Trasek.

Horzabky shook his flat head. "You still have the advantage of me. Who is the friend?"

"I doubt if you'd recognize his name. He knew yours, though—from the Bocz death-camp, in Kunvasy."

"Ah," said Horzabky softly. "I begin to understand."

Trasek's eyes glowed like eyes seen in the darkness from beside a campfire. "There were sixty-eight thousand devil-ridden slaves. All starved, jellied with beatings, rotten with frost-bite—things that monkeys and jackals would turn away from."

"Come, come," Horzabky protested mildly, lowering his spindly figure into a chair. "Surely—"

"One of the Kunvasian scientists asked for them, was told to do anything he liked; they were too sick and weak to be worked profitably and had been sent to Bocz to be killed." Trasek leaned forward. "Do I interest you?"

"I'm listening," replied Horzabky without emotion.

"The scientist was a man of vision, no question about it. He wished to probe into other dimensions, other universes, but there was no known tool or contrivance to give him a purchase. Any earthly force acted in the bounds of earth dimensions, and he needed a force beyond these bounds. He thought of mental power—of telepathy. All the evidence seemed to indicate that telepathy acted through non-earthly dimensions. Suppose this force were magnified tremendously? Might it not twist open a path into the unknown? Possibly the concentrated effort of a great number of minds might be effective. So he obtained the sixty-eight thousand slaves. He dosed them with drugs that stimulated their concentration but numbed their wills, made them pliable. Into the compound he herded them, massed them cheek on shoulder facing a target painted on a panel of plywood. He told them to will! will! will! To go in but not beyond! Three directions, then a fourth! To imagine the unimaginable!

"The slaves stood there panting, sweating, eyes popping in their efforts. Mist gathered on the target. 'In! In!' yelled the scientist. 'In but not out!' And the target burst open—a three-foot hole into nowhere.

"He let them rest a day, then he brought them out again, and again they broke a way into another space. Seven times he did this, and then catastrophe interrupted him. The Kunvasian General Staff decided that the time had come. On I Day they turned loose their air force, but the United defenses smashed the armada over the Balt Bay; the war was lost the same day it was started.

"The scientist at Bocz was in a quandary. Sixty-eight thousand slaves knew of his seven holes, in addition to a few guards. Silence must be arranged, and death was an excellent arranger. An idea came to him. Why not put all this dying to some use—if only to gratify a whimsical curiosity? So he divided the sixty-eight thousand into seven groups, and on succeeding nights he herded a group through one of the holes.

"By this time the United Army of Occupation was approaching, but when Bocz was liberated, the scientist had disappeared, together with his seven holes. Strangely, all the guards who had aided the scientist were housed in the same barracks, and this barracks was fumigated one night with nocumene. Seems as if the case were closed, doesn't it?"

"I would think so," said Horzabky, casually displaying a small automatic, "but this is your story. Please continue."

"I've about finished my part of it," said Trasek, grinning obliquely at the gun.

"Perhaps you are right." Horzabky rose to his feet. "The accuracy of your knowledge puzzles me, I admit. Possibly you will reveal its source?"

"That's a rather valuable bit of information," said Trasek. "Suppose you talk for a while."

"Hm…" Horzabky hesitated. "Very well. Why not?" He pulled the robe closer around his thin shoulders, as if he were cold. "As you say, it was a grand conception, noble indeed, and no ordinary person can conceive my exultation when success came on the first night of trial…Long after the prisoners had retired to their barracks I stood on the platform, staring into my new universe. I asked myself, what now? I thought, if the hole were fixed in space, the earth's motion would have left it far behind in an instant; evidently it was fixed, part of the plywood panel. And true, when I lifted the panel—cautiously, inch by inch—the hole moved along as well. I carried it to my quarters, and soon I had six others: seven wonderful new universes I could carry around almost in a portfolio." Horzabky gazed at the pictures on the wall. Trasek, if he had leapt at this instant, could have seized the gun; however he chose to keep his distance. "And the prisoners, they had been condemned to die; now wasn't it better that they participated in my grand experiment?"

"Their opinion was not asked," remarked Trasek. "However, I think it likely that they would have preferred to live."

"Pah!" Horzabky pursed his lips, flung his thin arm wide. "Creatures such as they—"

Trasek cut him short, lowered himself into a chair. "Tell me about your universes."

"Ah, yes," said Horzabky. "They're a strange collection, all different, every one, though two of them appear to act by the same set of fundamental laws as our own. This one—" he indicated Picture No. 4 "—is identical to ours, except that it's seen from a versi-dimensional angle. Everything appears inside out. Universe No. 5 now—" this was the space cut into innumerable cubes by the luminous webbing "—is built of the same sort of stuff as our own, but it developed differently. Those bars are actually lines of ions; the whole universe is a tremendous dynamo." He stood back, hands buried in the big pockets of his jacket. "Those two are the only ones susceptible to discussion in our words. Look at No. 1. It appears a mottled crust of black, rusty-purple. The colors are an illusion; there is no light in that universe, and the color is light reflected from our own. What actually is past that blur I don't know. Our words are useless. No word, no thought in our language can possibly be of any use, even ideas like space, time, distance, hard, soft, here, there…A new language, a new set of abstracts is necessary to deal with that universe, and I suspect that, almost by definition, our brains are incapable of dealing with it."

Trasek nodded with genuine admiration. "Well put, doctor. You interest me."

Horzabky smiled slightly. "We have the same difficulty with No. 2, which looks like a particularly frenetic modern painting; also No. 3 and No. 6."

"That's six," Trasek remarked. "Where's the seventh?"

Horzabky smiled again, a small trembling-lipped kewpie-smile. He rubbed his sharp chin, nodded at the mirror. "There."

"Of course," muttered Trasek.

"No. 7—" Horzabky shook his flat bald head "—so alien to our world that light refuses to penetrate it."

"Is it not grotesque," Trasek commented, "that the prisoners of Bocz were denied that option?"

"Only superficially," replied his host. "A moment's reflection solves the paradox. However," he added sadly, "the inflexible nature of light made it impossible for me to observe the experiences of the more obliging prisoners."

"What happens to a stick you push in?"

"It dissolves. Melts to nothing, like tissue paper in a furnace. Conservation of energy falls down in the other universes, where matter and energy are equally unacceptable, and where our laws have no authority."

"And the others?"

"In No. 1 a stick, a bar of iron, crumbles, falls to dust. In No. 2, you can't hold it; it's wrenched from your hands, by whom or what I don't know. In No. 3, the stick may be withdrawn unchanged, and likewise in No. 4. In No. 5 the stick acquires an electric charge, and if released flies off at tremendous speed down one of the corridors. In No. 6—that's the blurred, pinkish-gray place—the stick becomes a new material, though it's structurally the same. The different space alters the electrons and protons, makes the wood as hard as iron, though chemically the substance is still wood. And, in No. 7, as I said, the material merely melts."

Trasek stood up; Horzabky's hand leapt out of the pocket of the robe like a snake, and with it the gun.

"A pity," sighed Horzabky, "that in the discussion these reminders of our tangled lives must intrude. But you appear a passionate man, a bitter man, Mr. Whatever-your-name, and my little weapon, though blunt and unsubtle, is an effectual ally. It is necessary that I be careful. At this moment a number of so-called war-criminals are being rounded up. My innocent activities at Bocz would be misconstrued and I'd suffer a great deal of inconvenience. Perhaps now you had better tell me what you seek here."

Trasek's hand went to his pocket. "Easy!" hissed Horzabky.

Trasek smiled his hard smile. "I have no weapon. I need none. I merely wish to withdraw a small article…This." He displayed a small round box with a button on the lid. "I press this small button three times—so. And presently the reason for my visit will appear."

A long moment the two stared at each other, motionless, as if frozen in crystal; the one suspicious, the other mocking.

"We turn our attention to Universe No. 4," said Trasek, "where recently you commended ten thousand guests. Examine the scene. Does it suggest nothing to you?"

Horzabky forbore to answer, watched Trasek balefully.

"Those are trees, it's evident that they are trees, although the foliage appears to be growing inside the tube of the trunk. We can see we're on dry land, though that's about all we can be sure of, with that lighting…Would you like to know the actual whereabouts of the scene? I'll tell you. It's Arnhem Land, the most isolated part of Australia. It's our own Earth."

The faint buzz of the door-bell sounded.

"You better answer it," said Trasek. "You'll save your housekeeper the worst fright of her life."

Horzabky motioned with his gun. "Go ahead of me, open the door."

As they marched down the hall, the fat woman in the pink robe appeared. "Go back to bed, Martha," said Horzabky. "I'll take care of it." The woman turned, retired.

The bell rang again. Trasek put his hand on the door. "A warning, Doctor. Be careful with that gun. I don't mind a bullet or two at me—but if you injure my brother, the relatively easy death I plan for you will be postponed indefinitely."

"Open the door!" croaked Horzabky.

Trasek threw it wide.

The thing lurched in from the darkness, stood swaying in the hall. Horzabky's breath came as if someone had kicked him in the belly.

"That's a man," said Trasek. "A man inside out."

Horzabky pushed the glasses back up on the ridge of his nose. "Is this—is this one of—"

Trasek had been brightly watching Horzabky's gun. "It's one of your victims, Doctor. You sent him through your No. 4 hole. That's a plastic coverall he's wearing to keep the flies off him, or rather, from inside him, because to himself he's still a normal man, and it's the universe that's backwards."

"How many more are there like him?" inquired Horzabky, casually.

"None. Flies got some, sunburn most of the others, and the natives shot a lot full of reed arrows. A government cattle inspector came along and wanted to know what was going on. How he ever recognized—" Trasek nodded toward his brother "—for a man is a mystery. But he took care of him, as well as he was able, and I finally got a letter…"

Horzabky pursed his small pink mouth. "And what was your plan, relative to him?"

"You and I are going to help him back through Hole No. 4. That should put him right side out again, in relation to the world."

Horzabky smiled thinly. "You're an amazing fellow. You must know that both you and your brother are threats to the quiet life I plan to live here, that I can't possibly permit you to leave alive."

Trasek sprang forward so fast his figure blurred. Before Horzabky could blink, Trasek seized his wrist, jerked the gun free. He turned his head to his brother.

"This way, Emmer." Then to Horzabky: "Back with you, Doctor, back to your art gallery."

They returned down the hall to the library. Trasek motioned to picture No. 4. "Remove the glass, if you please."

Horzabky complied slowly, and with a surly expression. Trasek leaned slightly through the hole, surveyed the country, pulled back. "If this is how things look to you, Emmer, I fail to understand your continued sanity…Well, here's the hole. It's about a six foot drop, but at least you'll be right side to the world. First you'd better take off that plastic playsuit, or you'll have it all wound up in your bowels."

Trasek unzipped the covering, wadded it up, tossed it through the hole. He dragged a chair close under the hole. Emmer climbed awkwardly up, inserted himself, dropped through.

Trasek and Horzabky watched him a moment—still inside out, but one with his environment.

"That's a bad month out of anyone's life," said Trasek. His mouth jerked. "I was forgetting the years he spent as a Kunvasian slave..." A hand was at his pocket; Horzabky seized the gun, stepped away, the weapon leveled.

"You won't snatch it this time, my friend."

Trasek's harsh smile came. "No, you're right there. You may keep the gun."

Horzabky stood staring, half-at, half-past Trasek. "You have given me an upsetting evening," he muttered. "I was sure the entire number had been disposed of." He glanced down the line of pictures.

"Now you're not sure, eh Doctor?" Trasek jeered. "Maybe not all of them died when they passed through...Maybe they're waiting just out of sight, like rats in a hole—"

"Impossible."

"—maybe you've carried them with you everywhere, maybe they steal out during the night to eat and return to hide."

"Nonsense," blurted Horzabky. "I saw them die. In No . 1 they turned stiff and crumbled, vanished off in the murk. In No. 2 they struggled and kicked and finally came all apart and the parts jerked off in all directions. In No. 3 they expanded, exploded. In No. 4—well, as you know. In No. 5 they were picked up and whisked like chaff along the corridors, far down and out of sight. In No. 6—it's impossible to see into the blur, but any object pushed in and withdrawn is changed in every atom, petrified, every bit made part of the new space. In No. 7, matter just melts."

Trasek had been musing. "No . 2 seems disagreeable...No. 4—no, Horzabky, not even for you. I don't believe in torture, for which you can thank your stars...Well, No. 2, shall we say? Will you climb through by yourself, or shall I help you?"

Horzabky's mouth twisted like a mottled rose-bud; his eyes sparked. "You miserable...Insolent..." He spat the words, and they darted through the air like white serpents. He raised his arm; the gun roared—once, twice.

Trasek, still grinning, went to the wall, took down No. 2, propped it against one of the massive tables. The violent shapes of the world within swam, shifted, outraged the mind.

Horzabky was whining in a high-pitched tone. He ran a few steps closer to Trasek, pushed the gun almost into his face, fired again—again—again.

White marks appeared on Trasek's forehead, cheek. Horzabky floundered back.

"You can't kill me," said Trasek. "Not with matter from this world. I'm one of your alumni, too. You sent me through No. 6; I'm like that stick of wood—impervious!"

Horzabky leaned against the table, the gun dangling from his hand. "But—but—"

"The rest of them are dead, Doctor. There is no bottom to this hole; you just fall forever—unless you happen to catch the edge of the opening. I finally climbed back in while you were out gassing the guards. Now, Doctor," he took a soft step closer to the palsied Horzabky, "No. 2 is waiting for you..."

Wild Thyme and Violets

[Outline]

i

The four hundred houses of Gargano, blocks of white- or color-washed stone, occupy numberless tiers and levels up the slopes of a gray limestone mountain. Wisps of smoke float above mouldering tile roofs; a few dispirited trees can be seen: fig, orange, mulberry. At the center of town is the plaza, with the cathedral looming above. Opposite stands the inn, with benches and tables under a trellis. The mayor's mansion looks down a short avenue to the right.

The surrounding country is somewhat bleak. On the hillside grow a few olive trees, wild thyme, asphodel, thistle, groups of slender cypress. Outcroppings of gray limestone scar the slopes; a few poverty-stricken families live in caves, which they have fitted with stout timber doors. Stretching away to the southeast are the marshes, where the folk of Gargano graze their goats and geese. The air is dry and pungent with the odor of herbs. Near the town stands the castle of the Marquis del Torre-Gargano: an extravagant edifice in the rococo style, with mullioned windows, turrets and bartizans, high balconies and skywalks. In the moat grow water-lilies and bulrushes. The gardens are somewhat neglected; the roses bloom profusely but underneath are dry weeds.

In the castle live the saturnine Marquis Paul-Aubry Alcmeone del Torre-Gargano and his seventeen-year-old daughter Alicia, who is dumb. Their life is very quiet; the Marquis chooses to entertain no one. Alicia is something of an enigma: a pensive girl who paints exquisite little pictures of flowers in water-color. No one knows why she cannot speak.

Saturday in Gargano is market day. The plaza is cluttered with color: fabrics and copperware, fruits, melons, spices, glassware, sandals. A blind gypsy plays the guitar. A pair of officers in blue, black and tan uniforms drink wine under the bower outside the inn and ogle the town girls. Mersile, a traveling mountebank, sits on the steps of his horse-drawn caravan, appraising the crowd. Etheny, his idiot helper, erects a booth decorated with thaumaturgical symbols.

A priest, Father Berbolla, darts a frowning side-glance at the booth. He shakes his head at the mountebank and goes his way to the inn.

A blue and gold barouche, the paint faded and the gold-leaf somewhat tarnished, clatters across the square, on its way to the castle. Within, straight and still, sits the Lady Alicia, returning from a visit with her cousin. The folk of Gargano cannot understand her inability to speak. Has she never learned? Or perhaps she is bewitched. Certain devout old ladies cross themselves as the carriage passes.

Behind, running and bounding, comes Lucian, the town ne'er-do-well. He is tall, gaunt, with russet hair, flaming green eyes. Lucian lives in a chronic state of near-starvation. He owns a few frayed brushes, a pot or two of paint; he paints signs, portraits, fences—anything by which to glean a few florins. He runs after the carriage hoping to catch a glimpse of Alicia, whom he adores. He clutches a nosegay of wild thyme and violets which he tosses into the carriage. Alicia pays no heed.

The innkeeper bawls at Lucian, who has been engaged to work a few days at the inn. Lucian regretfully turns aside, and is unlucky enough to jostle Parnasse, the mayor, and is angrily reprimanded for his carelessness.

ii

Parnasse is a large full-blooded man, given to vehement gestures and large curses. Contradictions appear in the character of Parnasse: he is pompous but earthy, generous but mean, shrewd but foolish. His wife Clotilde is barren, and Parnasse has suffered many crude jests on this account. Parnasse longs for a son, but Clotilde obdurately fails to produce even a daughter.

Parnasse goes to his mansion and flings himself on his couch to rest, to concentrate, to muster his energies.

A gong sounds. He marches upstairs to Clotilde in her bed-chamber. "You have taken the extract?"

Clotilde, an amiable woman of good proportions, assents. "To the edge of a surfeit."

"And the exercises?"

"All, everything; the entire regimen."

Parnasse checks a chart on the wall, mumbling and muttering. He pulls out an elaborate watch. "At this instant the moon enters Sagittarius; the hour is at hand!"

iii

At the inn Lucian rushes back and forth in his capacity as roustabout, scullion and waiter. Father Berbolla enters, takes a seat and orders a frugal meal, smiling a small patient smile. Lucian serves this precise meal, at which Father Berbolla stares in astonishment. He calls the innkeeper. "See what this dunderpate has brought me!"

Lucian too late realizes his ungenerous error; the innkeeper's patience is at an end; Lucian is discharged on the instant.

He ambles back to his hut on the marshes. On the road he spies a bit of yellow stone. He takes it home, grinds it to a powder, mixes it with gum, and tests it on a board. Very pale, but nonetheless useful. Lucian's palette by necessity is improvised. For red he uses triturated pomegranate rind; for green, the juice expressed from crushed dock leaves. Saffron stolen from the inn gives him yellow. Soot is black; chalk is white. Muds and slimes provide a range of browns, grays, and even orange. Blue? He uses powdered lichen to doubtful effect.

iv

Marquis Paul-Aubry and Alicia sit at their luncheon. The room is octagonal, very high, and paneled in white wood, with a border of graceful green festoons, from which depend peaches and apricots. A large window overlooks the rose garden and a hazy vista to the south over the marshes. The table is covered with damask; at the center is a low silver vase of yellow roses. Alicia wears a white gown; her skin is pale. She sips verbena tea. Marquis Paul-Aubry is elegantly thin. His skin is as pale as that of Alicia, with a bluish undertone. His hair is black and dressed severely close to his head; his features are stern, austere. His deportment is controlled by a rigid schedule from which he never departs.

He eats half a brandied peach, a biscuit, and takes a glass of white wine.

Footsteps sound in the hall. Into the room rushes the stable-man, in a state of fury. He buffets the Marquis, who topples to the floor. The groom glares and makes a fist, then departs; the Marquis, stern but urbane, picks himself up, dusts his knees with a napkin and resumes his seat. He displays no emotion, because he feels none. How could any person of breeding react to a circumstance so coarse and insipid?

Alicia goes to her bedroom and sits by the window watching the sky. On a nearby branch a bird sings. Alicia listens intently. Suddenly she smiles, and whistles the notes through her teeth.

The bird flies away; Alicia sadly watches it depart over the marshes.

She descends to the rose garden, and sitting on a marble bench pulls petals from blown blossoms. A little heap forms at her feet.

The Marquis saunters to the stables. He instructs the stableman regarding the horses and receives a surly acquiescence.

The Marquis turns and for a moment contemplates the stableman's son. The pink-cheeked boy wears a blue smock; his hair is brown and overlong. With a woebegone face he forks manure into a cart, and will look neither at the Marquis nor his father.

Marquis Paul-Aubry turns away with a sigh. It must be a disease from which he suffers! Other folk feel emotion; why is he so denied?

V

Mersile stands in his booth. He sells balms, elixirs, papers imprinted with magic signs. For those who so require he casts horoscopes, lances boils, pulls teeth. When business is slack he plays a concertina while Etheny, his half-wit helper, performs a jig.

Parnasse approaches the booth. After a glance right and left, he asks in a husky voice: "How may a barren woman be rendered fertile?"

"There is a single certain method," Mersile tells him: "The expert use of hypnosis!"

"Ah!" breathes Parnasse. "This then is the answer! But how do I proceed?"

"Not you! Only an adept can perform the feat!"

Parnasse hires Mersile to do the work, wincing at the price.

"Conditions must be absolutely correct!" Mersile declares.

"So much goes without saying," Parnasse declares. "What do you suggest?"

"A condition where every attribute conduces to the happy consequence we have in mind. Etheny!"

Mersile sends Etheny to the mansion to hang appropriate symbols in Madame Clotilde's bedroom. "Tomorrow the ceremony will take place."

Clotilde has gone to the cathedral. She vows a hundred candles to each of several saints if they will assist her to conceive a child. She implores the advice of Father Berbolla in regard to poor Parnasse, who suffers so many frustrations. "Only today he has gone to take counsel from the thaumaturgist!"

Father Berbolla is shocked. "Here are evil advices. Can you not dissuade him?"

"Only by conceiving, which so far has been beyond my capability."

Father Berbolla will pray for her, and he feels obliged to sprinkle her chamber with holy water, against the possibly baneful influence of Mersile.

vi

Parnasse and Clotilde eat their supper: boiled meat and broth, a brace of roast fowl, pig's feet.

Parnasse tells her of his preparations and admonishes her: "Attend at all times to our goal, which is fecundity! Be fruitful! Bring forth! Conceive! I can only do what is possible; you must do the rest."

"What is left after the possible?" Clotilde inquires somewhat stupidly. "The impossible?"

"You are purposely obtuse," cries Parnasse. "It is not all that difficult!" He sends for Lucian, who presently appears, puzzled and hungry.

"Here is Madame Clotilde," states Parnasse. "Take note: she is without child, flat as a halibut. I wish you to paint her in a state of full gestation, and at once. Is all this clear?"

"What of my fee?"

"A detail! We can arrange the matter at any time. The important thing is that you start work instantly."

"I must buy paint and canvas, but, in all candor, I have no money."

"Obtain what you need; I will pay any reasonable charges. When will you start?"

"I will do my sketches now, if your excellency can provide paper and a bit of charcoal."

"Clotilde will see to your needs."

"A bit of bread and meat, and a bite of cheese—these to steady my hand as I sketch."

vii

One morning before dawn Alicia leaves the castle. The first frost of autumn lies on the land. She walks up the hillside, watches the sky take on color. She seems to be seeking something, but what? Who knows? Least of all Alicia. Overhead a flight of geese fares south croaking and moaning. In the west the full moon grows pale; in the east the sun rises. Alicia suddenly becomes alarmed and hurries back to the castle.

viii

Clotilde is pregnant! Parnasse has confided in no one. Clotilde has provided no information. But the news has suddenly become general property.

Parnasse is irritated to find his intimate business in so many mouths. With rather poor grace he accepts congratulations, then grows proud and, taking a glass of wine here, a taste of plum brandy there, presently he is in good spirits. He knows the remedy for barrenness, he informs his admiring cronies. Indeed! And will he share his secret? Parnasse winks and makes a cryptic sign. Everyone speculates as to which of the expedients proved the most effectual: Prayer? Hypnosis? Cabalistic symbols? The pregnant portrait? Parnasse waggishly shakes his head. "None of these! As your mayor, as your comrade and fellow citizen of Gargano, I will demonstrate the sleight upon any of your wives, nieces or daughters."

ix

The priests engage Lucian to paint an altar-piece. They supply an advance of money sufficient to buy paint and varnish. Lucian instead buys food: bread, cheese, bacon. On his way home a dog steals the bacon. Lucian pursues the dog across the marsh.

x

Lucian paints the altar-piece with paints mixed of pitch, soot, chalk, sulfur, red clay. In the central cartouche sits a madonna and child. Lucian uses Clotilde as a model and absentmindedly includes her pregnancy. The priests are critical; they refuse to pay his fee. Lucian throws up his arms and storms away. The priests inspect the unfinished painting which, for the sake of economy, they decide to use despite the somewhat questionable subject matter.

xi

All-Hallows Eve is at hand: an important festival at Gargano. The priests lock themselves in their cells, and recite troubled Aves and Te Deums.

In Gargano the custom is most rigid: a maid wearing white is deemed innocent and may not be subjected to amorous proposals.

Marquis Paul-Aubry and Alicia appear at the fête. The Marquis wears a black and steel-gray uniform, black shako. His nose is hooked and pinched, his mouth has a sour dyspeptic droop. Alicia is frail as a fairy in a ballerina costume: a tunic of spangled white satin and white tights, a tutu of fluffy white gauze. A cloche of white satin confines her hair; she seems excited and unusually vital. Lucian, costumed as Caliban, sees her and becomes almost faint with longing, but she is swept away by three revelers: a pierrot and two punchinellos. They hoist her upon a table and toast her with goblets of wine, urging her to drink, to dance, to sing; they are young bravos of Montfalcone and unaware of both her identity and her inability to speak. Alicia looks this way and that, wearing a bewildered half-smile. The Marquis, at a little distance, watches with saturnine detachment, envying the revelers their spontaneity. How beautiful is Alicia, this pale dumb creature whom he has sired! How beautiful and how mysterious! But does she feel? Is she sensate? What color are her perceptions? Can she imagine pain? horror? futility?

A cup of wine is upset; a flow of red stains Alicia's stockings; she looks down ruefully.

The two punchinellos lift her down from the table; the pierrot whirls her around in a series of drunken capers. Alicia becomes puzzled and alarmed; her eyebrows raise; her eyes shine in the torchlight.

The Marquis watches from the side. What has she sensed? Does she exult? apprehend?

The three revelers whirl her away, off behind the inn. Alicia makes no sound of protest; the pierrot and the punchinellos believe her acquiescent and take her into a hay-room. Alicia gasps and holds back, to no avail. She no longer wears pure white; the prohibition is dissolved. The Marquis still watches critically from a little distance. Does she realize what is about to happen? He returns to the square and sips a glass of wine.

Lucian in wild anguish comes to tug at his arm; the Marquis thrusts him off with a frown of distaste. Lucian babbles of Alicia's plight; the Marquis turns his back. Lucian rushes to Alicia's aid; he is buffeted back into the darkness.

The Marquis yawns fastidiously. Perhaps after all he will interest himself in the matter. He finishes his wine, and languidly saunters to the hay-room. He stands in the opening waiting for a sensation to come over him. A single cresset illuminates the room. Alicia, her garments in disorder, lays passive in the hay. The two punchinellos have finished with her; the pierrot prepares himself, but now he is annoyed by the Marquis' sneer of disapproval. "Hence troll; we have no need of you here."

The Marquis considers the situation, whips forth a rapier and with the casual ease of a man stepping on an insect, impales the pierrot. The punchinellos croak in dismay and flee. The pierrot lies on his back, kicking and groping like an upturned beetle.

The Marquis watches dispassionately, interested only in the fluctuations of his own awareness. Surely his pulse is beating somewhat faster? Alicia props herself up on her arms, and watches glassy-eyed. Feebly she tries to cover her naked legs. The Marquis orders Lucian to bring up his carriage; Alicia is taken back to the castle.

The Marquis wipes his rapier on the dead pierrot and returns to his table.

xii

Alicia, wearing a night-dress, stands by her window. At Gargano the fête continues, but less exuberantly. The colored lights swing more slowly; the music is fitful. Alicia looks up into the dark sky. The stars are white, remote, pure. Alicia stares up in mournful fascination; how peaceful is the dark sky; how loving are the stars! She steps forward. Dark air rushes past her; she falls into the moat. Lucian, who had followed the carriage and since has been skulking about under the cypress trees, flounders into the water and drags her forth, limp and listless.

Almost beside himself with joy he carries her to his hut on the edge of the marsh, and lays her upon his pallet. He builds up his fire, boils tea, removes her soiled garments and throws them into the fire. He dries her with adoring hands, and talks to her in a soft voice: "You threw your life away; I found it and took it for myself and now you are my very own."

Alicia lies in a half-daze. Lucian speaks on in a husky voice: "Never again will you suffer or know desolation!"

Alicia turns her head and looks at him. Lucian strokes her hand. "Speak to me: tell me that you love me, as I love you."

Alicia's lips twitch: an attempt to speak? A grimace?

xiii

The Marquis sits alone at his breakfast. He drinks coffee from a tall silver cup. Cadwal, his steward, appears with news regarding Alicia. The Marquis considers the situation, but finds no stimulation. He is indifferent.

Cadwal says delicately: "The artist Lucian is notorious both for excessive conduct and indigence."

"The qualities would seem—after a period of disequilibrium—to nullify each other," remarks the Marquis.

The steward bows curtly and withdraws. Marquis Paul-Aubry sips his coffee, eats a slice of fruit-cake. Then he goes to stand by the window. He thinks of the kicking pierrot. Is there such a thing as emotion-by-association? His hands close; his pale knuckles show white.

Father Berbolla presents himself at the castle. Lucian's conduct is an impertinent scandal; what does the Marquis propose to do?

He had not considered the matter from this perspective. The fact that anyone should impute to him a concern, or even an opinion, comes as a notable surprise. He can only affirm and corroborate a condition so self-evident as to seem a banality: the matter is nothing to him. When Alicia sees fit, she will return to the castle. If she chooses to stay, why should she be thwarted? Each person must cut his own trail through the Hyrcanian jungle of the future. Try as he may, he cannot fathom Father Berbolla's evident preoccupation with this matter.

"We are children of the church together," Father Berbolla asserts. "If you refuse to succor a pair of errant souls, then, in all good conscience, I must."

The Marquis offers the priest coffee and fruit-cake, and the conversation shifts to other matters.

Father Berbolla and the Mother Superior go to Lucian's hut. Despite Lucian's pleas they take Alicia away to the convent.

xiv

Father Berbolla talks to Alicia who sits passively. The candles flicker; she is fascinated. Father Berbolla suggests that she take vows, and devote her life to good works. Alicia's eyelids droop.

Lucian meanwhile has contrived a mad plan for the rescue of Alicia. He becomes confused and wanders into the Mother Superior's chamber, where she is washing her feet. Lucian runs wild-eyed from the building. He is seized and taken before the mayor, and consigned to jail. Alicia slips away and returns to the castle.

xv

Marquis Paul-Aubry, in the throes of ennui, wanders about the castle. He shatters a porcelain figurine and studies the shards. Did the act provide a sensation? He secures a volume of illuminated psalms and tears out page after page and feeds each in turn into the fire, watching the colors alter, go dark, shrivel into flakes of soot.

The stable-boy peers through the doorway. The Marquis appraises him from the side of his face, then moves slowly forward. The boy smiles a trembling half-smile. The Marquis kicks him: once, twice, three times. The boy, holding his adorable buttocks, rushes from the castle.

Standing at the window the Marquis sees him wandering off down the hill. He frowns, purses his lips, and selects a dagger from the wall display. Leaving the castle, he strides on long thin legs down the hill.

He waits behind a hedge. The boy comes past. The Marquis chirrups. The boy halts, and peers over the hedge. In a sudden flurry of arms and legs the boy is hacked and slashed.

The Marquis considers the corpse. His nostrils are flared; the pupils of his eyes are dilated. He examines himself. How to distinguish between simple sensation and veritable emotion? If a roaring lion suddenly leapt from behind the hedge, the Marquis no doubt would make a recoil action, to some greater or lesser degree, but could this gross reflex by any device of casuistry be termed an emotion? The Marquis suspects not. Curious, curious. Well, at least the affair had been stimulating. He so seldom went abroad into the fresh air; he must do it more often.

xvi

Gargano is shocked by the murder. Who could commit so monstrous a deed? Parnasse confers with the Marquis, who frowns and taps his chin with his stick. Yes, yes, he will certainly look into the affair.

xvii

The winter passes. Clotilde swells enormously and at the seventh month gives birth to quadruplets. One resembles Mersile the mountebank; the second resembles the priest; the third is gaunt, long-nosed and red-haired like Lucian; the fourth is most like Etheny the idiot.

Parnasse comes to survey the litter. His eyes gleam and he jerks at his beard. Clotilde watches from the corner of her eye.

xviii

The Marquis breakfasts with Alicia, then goes to walk in the countryside, wearing a black and red coat, gray trousers, black boots with moleskin gaiters. The landscape is dark and dreary; the trees have not yet put forth leaves. He passes Lucian's hut and looks within. A stool supports a half-finished portrait of Alicia. The Marquis considers the painting, and prods it with his stick.

He saunters into Gargano and takes a glass of warm tokay with cloves at the inn. Parnasse enters.

The Marquis in his mind's-eye sees himself assaulting Parnasse, cutting the heavy throat, hacking the red cheeks, plunging a great cutlass into the heavy midriff, then standing back as the huge red and pink hoses of Parnasse's guts come tumbling forth. The corpse would smell abominably. The Marquis gives a grimace of fastidious distaste. Parnasse is too strong-blooded, too ruddy and thick; the best murders are delicate and mild. Someday it might be amusing to lower a beautiful young girl by the hair into a vat of perfume.

He returns to the castle. Alicia sits staring into the fire. The Marquis stops to reflect…She would put forth no blood whatever, only a pale ichor, faintly scented of violet. The effort would hardly be worth the nuisance. He goes one step, then pauses again. If they could converse and discuss the matter, what would she say?

Someone has come to the door. Cadwal announces Lucian.

Lucian makes a fervent presentation. "Sir, I have been released from prison only this last hour. My crime, as I construe the argument, is the zeal of my service to the Lady Alicia."

"I wouldn't be too certain of this," replies the Marquis. "As I recall, you were accused of voyeurism at the convent…No matter. What are your present purposes?"

"At one time I begged that she put her life into my keeping. She did not then reject my proposal, and I have come to learn how matters stand now."

The Marquis nods approvingly. "Well spoken. You wish then to resume the custody of the Lady Alicia?"

"If she is of a mind to it."

"Aha, indeed. Well then, I neither render permission nor withhold it. You must persuade the Lady Alicia, as the matter lies between yourselves."

Lucian bows, nearly weeping with gratitude. He turns to where Alicia sits brooding.

The Marquis saunters politely across the room and watches over his shoulder. Lucian smiles down into Alicia's face; she stares into his eyes. He speaks, holds out his hand. Slowly she rises. The Marquis turns and leaves the room. When he comes back they are gone.

The Marquis gazes out the window. Dusk is gathering across the marshes. He goes to a long disused chamber where he dons a harlequin costume and a black domino as well. By a private way he slips out from the castle.

His feet are agile and light; occasionally he cuts a caper. In the lane he hears a sound of singing: three little girls, returning home from taking sheep into paddock.

The harlequin leaps forth; one must escape, which is a pity. With a squirming crying bundle under each arm he jumps the ditch on feet of air, and flits into the dark woods.

xix

Mersile the mountebank declares his competence to find the murderer. He will use hypnosis.

xx

Lucian and Alicia sit in their hut before a small fire. As Alicia looks into the fire tears form in her eyes and stand glistening. Lucian knows why she weeps; he wants to weep himself.

xxi

The Marquis wanders around the castle. He halts before an ancient portrait. With a knife he chips away the paint, flake by flake. After ten minutes he becomes bored with the work and goes to the window. The time is late afternoon. The sun sets in the marshes, a cold vermilion rind.

xxii

Lucian sets forth to earn, beg or steal a few bites of food for himself and Alicia. At the inn he makes caricatures of a group of officers, and receives a silver coin, with which he buys a sausage, a crusty loaf, a cheese and a bottle of wine.

Approaching the hut he stops short, astounded by a flickering of shadows: a frantic motion like the flurry of an enormous moth…Lucian peers through the window. The harlequin stands panting above a crumpled body.

Lucian craftily throws a jug of turpentine upon the harlequin and applies a torch.

The harlequin bounds flaring down the dark road, and off across the marsh.

Lucian is composed and elegant. He arranges Alicia on the couch, and paints a portrait: a face wide-eyed, luminous, glowing with dreams too splendid to be spoken.

xxiii

The funeral takes place in morning mist. Alicia is carried to the crypt of her ancestors, in a little valley above the castle. A few people walk behind the hearse: the Marquis, some aged aunts, the castle servants, Lucian.

When all are departed Lucian comes back to sit by the crypt. His expression is rapt; he seems to be listening.

Rain starts to fall. Lucian shivers and returns to his hut to find a number of angry people waiting for him. The town marshal, acting upon information, has discovered a harlequin suit under his bed.

The townspeople start to cudgel Lucian. He leaps to the roof, roaring in anguish. "I killed no one; I was in jail while the murders occurred!"

Parnasse reluctantly steps forward. "True. He is not the harlequin."

Someone inquires, "Then how to explain these garments under the artist's bed?"

An urchin whispers to Parnasse; he saw Etheny the idiot bringing a parcel to the hut.

xxiv

Etheny is dragged howling to the gibbet. Father Berbolla urges him to confess, that he may be shriven. The Marquis stands to the side, saturnine, dispassionate. Etheny makes a frantic gesticulation: "He gave my orders! There he stands!"

The Marquis laughs. The onlookers are appalled by the scope of Etheny's madness.

Parnasse gives a stern signal; Etheny is hauled aloft, to hang kicking and jerking.

The folk of Gargano take a wan satisfaction in the working of justice. Once more they assure each other that all may sleep soundly in their beds. The

Marquis smiles sadly to himself…Why not? The killings were as tiresome as any other activity. Perhaps for a period he will indulge in charities and good works, and gain the love of the townspeople.

XXV

The evening is calm and still. A new moon hangs over the mountain. Lucian comes across the hillside and approaches the crypt. He stands beside a cypress tree. He hears a soft strange sound, and looks in all directions.

The sound—if it existed—is gone. Lucian slowly returns to his hut. He makes a pack, rolls up the portrait of Alicia. Flinging a cloak around his shoulders, he leaves the hut and walks off down the pale road.

Rumfuddle

I

From *Memoirs and Reflections*, by Alan Robertson:

Often I hear myself declared humanity's preeminent benefactor, though the jocular occasionally raise a claim in favor of the original Serpent. After all circumspection, I really cannot dispute the judgment. My place in history is secure; my name will persist as if it were printed indelibly across the sky. All of which I find absurd but understandable. For I have given wealth beyond calculation. I have expunged deprivation, famine, over-population, territorial constriction: all the first-order causes of contention have vanished. My gifts go freely and carry with them my personal joy, but as a reasonable man (and for lack of other restrictive agency), I feel that I cannot relinquish all control, for when has the human animal ever been celebrated for abnegation and self-discipline?

We now enter an era of plenty and a time of new concerns. The old evils are gone; we must resolutely prohibit a flamboyant and perhaps unnatural set of new vices.

The three girls gulped down breakfast, assembled their homework and departed noisily for school.

Elizabeth poured coffee for herself and Gilbert. He thought she seemed pensive and moody. Presently she said, "It's so beautiful here... We're very lucky, Gilbert."

"I never forget it."

Elizabeth sipped her coffee and mused a moment, following some vagrant train of thought. She said, "I never liked growing up. I always felt strange—different from the other girls. I really don't know why."

"It's no mystery. Everyone for a fact is different."

"Perhaps…But Uncle Peter and Aunt Emma always acted as if I were more different than usual. I remember a hundred little signals. And yet I was such an ordinary little girl…Do you remember when you were little?"

"Not very well." Duray looked out the window he himself had glazed, across green slopes and down to the placid water his daughters had named the Silver River. The Sounding Sea was thirty miles south; directly behind the house stood the first trees of the Robber Woods.

Duray considered his past. "Bob owned a ranch in Arizona during the 1870s: one of his fads. The Apaches killed my father and mother. Bob took me to the ranch, and then when I was three he brought me to Alan's house in San Francisco and that's where I was brought up."

Elizabeth sighed. "Alan must have been wonderful. Uncle Peter was so grim. Aunt Emma never told me anything. Literally, not anything! They never cared the slightest bit for me, one way or the other…I wonder why Bob brought the subject up—about the Indians and your mother and father being scalped and all…He's such a strange man."

"Was Bob here?"

"He looked in a few minutes yesterday to remind us of his 'Rumfuddle'. I told him I didn't want to leave the girls. He said to bring them along."

"Hah!"

"I told him I didn't want to go to his damn Rumfuddle with or without the girls. In the first place, I don't want to see Uncle Peter, who's sure to be there…"

II

From *Memoirs and Reflections*:

I insisted then and I insist now that our dear old Mother Earth, so soiled and toil-worn, never be neglected. Since I pay the piper (in a manner of speaking) I call the tune, and to my secret amusement I am heeded most briskly the world around, in the manner of bellboys jumping to the command of an irascible old gentleman who is known to be a good tipper. No one dares to defy me. My whims become actualities; my plans progress.

Paris, Vienna, San Francisco, St. Petersburg, Venice, London, Dublin surely will persist, gradually to become idealized essences of their former selves, as wine in due course becomes the soul of the grape. What of the old vitality? The shouts and curses, the neighborhood quarrels, the raucous music, the vulgarity? Gone, all gone! (But easy of reference at any of the cognates.) Old Earth is to be a gentle, kindly world, rich in treasures and artifacts, a world of old places: old inns, old roads, old forests, old palaces, where folk come to wander and dream, to experience the best of the past without suffering the worst.

Material abundance can now be taken for granted: our resources are infinite. Metal, timber, soil, rock, water, air: free for anyone's taking. A single commodity remains in finite supply: human toil.

Gilbert Duray, the informally adopted grandson of Alan Robertson, worked on the Urban Removal Program. Six hours a day, four days a week, he guided a trashing-machine across deserted Cupertino, destroying tract houses, service stations and supermarkets. Knobs and toggles controlled a steel hammer at the end of a hundred-foot boom; with a twitch of the finger Duray toppled power-poles, exploded picture-windows, smashed siding and stucco, pulverized concrete. A disposal rig crawled fifty feet behind. The detritus was clawed upon a conveyor-belt, carried to a twenty-foot orifice and dumped with a rush and a rumble into the Apathetic Ocean. Aluminum siding, asphalt shingles, corrugated fiberglass, TVs and barbeques, Swedish Modern furniture, Book-of-the-Month selections, concrete patio-tiles, finally the sidewalk and street itself: all to the bottom of the Apathetic Ocean. Only the trees remained: a strange eclectic forest stretching as far as the eye could reach: liquidambar and Scotch pine; Chinese pistachio, Atlas cedar and gingko; white birch and Norway maples.

At one o'clock Howard Wirtz emerged from the caboose, as they called the small locker room at the rear of the machine. Wirtz had homesteaded a Miocene world; Duray, with a wife and three children, had preferred the milder environment of a contemporary semi-cognate: the popular Type A world on which man had never evolved.

Duray gave Wirtz the work schedule. "More or less like yesterday; straight out Persimmon to Walden, then right a block and back."

Wirtz, a dour and laconic man, acknowledged the information with a jerk of the head. On his Miocene world he lived alone, in a houseboat on a mountain lake. He harvested wild rice, mushrooms and berries; he shot geese, ground-fowl, deer, young bison, and had once informed Duray that after his five year work-time he might just retire to his lake and never appear on Earth again, except maybe to buy clothes and ammunition. "Nothing here I want, nothing at all."

Duray gave a derisive snort. "And what will you do with all your time?"

"Hunt, fish, eat and sleep, maybe sit on the front deck."

"Nothing else?"

"I just might learn to fiddle. Nearest neighbor is fifteen million years away."

"You can't be too careful, I suppose."

Duray descended to the ground and looked over his day's work: a quarter-mile swath of desolation. Duray, who allowed his subconscious few extravagances, nevertheless felt a twinge for the old times, which, for all their disadvantages, at least had been lively. Voices, bicycle bells, the barking of dogs, the slam of doors, still echoed along Persimmon Avenue. The former inhabitants presumably pre-ferred their new homes. The self-sufficient had taken private worlds, the more gre-garious lived in communities on worlds of every description: as early as the Carboniferous, as current as the Type A. A few had even returned to the now uncrowded cities. An exciting era to live in: a time of flux. Duray, thirty-four years old, remembered no other way of life; the old existence, as exemplified by Persimmon Avenue, seemed antique, cramped, constricted.

He had a word with the operator of the trashing-machine; returning to the caboose he paused to look through the orifice across the Apathetic Ocean. A squall hung black above the southern horizon, toward which a trail of broken lumber drifted, to wash ultimately up on some unknown pre-Cambrian shore. There never would be an inspector sailing forth to protest; the world knew no life other than molluscs and algae, and all the trash of Earth would never fill its submarine gorges. Duray tossed a rock through the gap and watched the alien water splash up and subside. Then he turned away and entered the caboose.

Along the back wall were four doors. The second from the left was marked *G. DURAY*. He unlocked the door, pulled it open, and stopped short, staring in astonishment at the blank back wall. He lifted the transparent plastic flap which functioned as an air-seal and brought out the collapsed metal ring which had been the flange surrounding his passway. The inner surface was bare metal; looking through he saw only the interior of the caboose.

A long minute passed. Duray stood staring at the useless ribbon as if hyp-notized, trying to grasp the implications of the situation. To his knowledge no passway had ever failed, unless it had been purposefully closed. Who would play him such a spiteful idiotic trick? Certainly not his wife Elizabeth. She detested practical jokes, and, if anything, like Duray himself, was perhaps a trifle too in-tense and literal-minded. He jumped down from the caboose and strode off across Cupertino forest: a sturdy heavy-shouldered man of about average stature. His features were rough and uncompromising; his brown hair was cut crisply short; his eyes glowed golden-brown and exerted an arresting force. Straight heavy eyebrows crossed his long thin nose like the bar of a T; his mouth, compressed against some strong inner urgency, formed a lower horizontal bar. All in all, not a man to be trifled with, or so it would seem.

He trudged through the haunted grove, preoccupied by the strange and inconvenient event which had befallen him. What had happened to the passway? Unless Elizabeth had invited friends out to Home, as they called their world, she was alone, with the three girls at school…Duray came out upon Stevens Creek Road. A farmer's pick-up truck halted at his signal and took him into San Jose, now little more than a country town.

At the transit center he dropped a coin in the turnstile and entered the lobby. Four portals designated 'Local', 'California', 'North America', 'World', opened in the walls, each portal leading to a hub on Utilis*.

Duray passed into the 'California' hub, found the 'Oakland' portal, returned to the Oakland Transit Center on Earth, passed back through the 'Local' portal to the 'Oakland' hub on Utilis, returned to Earth through the 'Montclair West' portal to a depot only a quarter-mile from Thornhill School**, to which Duray walked.

In the office Duray identified himself to the clerk and requested the presence of his daughter Dolly.

The clerk sent forth a messenger who, after an interval, returned alone. "Dolly Duray isn't at school."

Duray was surprised; Dolly had been in good health and had set off to school as usual. He said, "Either Joan or Ellen will do as well."

The messenger again went forth and again returned. "Neither one is in their classrooms, Mr. Duray. All three of your children are absent."

"I can't understand it," said Duray, now fretful. "All three set off to school this morning."

---

* Utilis: a world cognate to Palaeocene Earth, where, by Alan Robertson's decree, all the industries, institutions, warehouses, tanks, dumps and commercial offices of old Earth were now located. The name 'Utilis', so it had been remarked, accurately captured the flavor of Alan Robertson's pedantic, quaint and idealistic personality.

**Alan Robertson had proposed another specialized world, to be known as 'Tutelar', where the children of all the settled worlds should receive their education in a vast array of pedagogical facilities. To his hurt surprise, he encountered a storm of wrathful opposition from parents. His scheme was termed mechanistic, vast, dehumanizing, repulsive. What better world for schooling than old Earth itself? Here was the source of all tradition; let Earth become 'Tutelar'! So insisted the parents and Alan Robertson had no choice but to agree.

"Let me ask Miss Haig. I've just come on duty." The clerk spoke into a telephone, listened, then turned back to Duray. "The girls went home at ten o'clock. Mrs. Duray called for them and took them back through the passway."

"Did she give any reason whatever?"

"Miss Haig says no; Mrs. Duray just told her she needed the girls at home."

Duray stifled a sigh of baffled irritation. "Could you take me to their locker? I'll use their passway to get home."

"That's contrary to school regulations, Mr. Duray. You'll understand, I'm sure."

"I can identify myself quite definitely," said Duray. "Mr. Carr knows me well. As a matter of fact, my passway collapsed and I came here to get home."

"Why don't you speak to Mr. Carr?"

"I'd like to do so."

Duray was conducted into the principal's office where he explained his predicament. Mr. Carr expressed sympathy and made no difficulty about taking Duray to the children's passway.

They went to a hall at the back of the school and found the locker numbered '382'. "Here we are," said Carr. "I'm afraid that you'll find it a tight fit." He unlocked the metal door with his master key and threw it open. Duray looked inside and saw only the black metal at the back of the locker. The passway, like his own, had been closed.

Duray drew back and for a moment could find no words.

Carr spoke in a voice of polite amazement. "How very perplexing! I don't believe I've ever seen anything like it before! Surely the girls wouldn't play such a silly prank?"

"They know better than to touch the passway," Duray said gruffly. "Are you sure that this is the right locker?"

Carr indicated the card on the outside of the locker, where three names had been typed: *Dorothy Duray, Joan Duray, Ellen Duray.* "No mistake," said Carr, "and I'm afraid that I can't help you any further. Are you in common residency?"

"It's our private homestead."

Carr nodded with lips judiciously pursed, to suggest that such insistence upon privacy seemed eccentric. He gave a deprecatory little chuckle. "I suppose if you isolate yourself to such an extent, you more or less must expect a series of emergencies."

"To the contrary," Duray said crisply. "Our life is uneventful, because there's no one to bother us. We love the wild animals, the quiet, the fresh air. We wouldn't have it any differently."

Carr smiled a dry smile. "Mr. Robertson has certainly altered the lives of us all. I understand that he is your grandfather?"

"I was raised in his household. I'm his nephew's foster son. The blood relationship isn't all that close."

III

From *Memoirs and Reflections*:

I early became interested in magnetic fluxes and their control. After taking my degree I worked exclusively in this field, studying all varieties of magnetic envelopes and developing controls over their formation. For many years my horizons were thus limited, and I lived a placid existence.

Two contemporary developments forced me down from my 'ivory castle'. First: the fearful overcrowding of the planet and the prospect of worse to come. Cancer already was an affliction of the past; heart diseases were under control; I feared that in another ten years immortality might be a practical reality for many of us, with a consequent augmentation of population pressure.

Secondly, the theoretical work done upon 'black holes' and 'white holes' suggested that matter compacted in a 'black hole' broke through a barrier to spew forth from a 'white hole' in another universe. I calculated pressures and considered the self-focusing magnetic sheaths, cones and whorls with which I was experimenting. Through their innate properties, these entities constricted themselves to apices of a cross-section indistinguishable from a geometric point. What if two or more cones (I asked myself) could be arranged in contraposition to produce an equilibrium? In this condition charged particles must be accelerated to near light speed and at the mutual focus constricted and impinged together. The pressures thus created, though of small scale, would be far in excess of those characteristic of the 'black holes': to unknown effect. I can now report that the mathematics of the multiple focus are a most improbable thicket, and the useful service I enforced upon what I must call a set of absurd contradictions is one of my secrets. I know that thousands of scientists, at home and abroad, are attempting to duplicate my work; they are welcome to the effort. None will succeed. Why do I speak so positively? This is my other secret.

Duray marched back to the Montclair West depot in a state of angry puzzlement. There had been four passways to Home, of which two were closed. The third was located in his San Francisco locker: the 'front door', so to speak. The last and the original orifice was cased, filed and indexed in Alan Robertson's vault.

Duray tried to deal with the problem in rational terms. The girls would never tamper with the passways. As for Elizabeth, no more than the girls would she consider such an act. At least Duray could imagine no reason which would so urge or impel her. Elizabeth, like himself a foster-child, was a beautiful passionate woman, tall, dark-haired, with lustrous dark eyes and a wide mouth which tended to curve in an endearingly crooked grin. She was also responsible, loyal, careful, industrious; she loved her family and Riverview Manor. The theory of erotic intrigue seemed to Duray as incredible as the fact of the closed passways. Though, for a fact Elizabeth was prone to wayward and incomprehensible moods. Suppose Elizabeth had received a visitor, who for some sane or insane purpose had forced her to close the passway?…Duray shook his head in frustration, like a harassed bull. The matter no doubt had some simple cause. Or on the other hand, Duray reflected, the cause might be complex and intricate. The thought by some obscure connection brought before him the image of his nominal foster-father, Alan Robertson's nephew, Bob Robertson. Duray gave his head a nod of gloomy asseveration, as if to confirm a fact he long ago should have suspected. He went to the phone booth and called Bob Robertson's apartment in San Francisco. The screen glowed white and an instant later displayed Bob Robertson's alert, clean and handsome face. "Good afternoon, Gil. Glad you called; I've been anxious to get in touch with you."

Duray became warier than ever. "How so?"

"Nothing serious, or so I hope. I dropped by your locker to leave off some books that I promised Elizabeth, and I noticed through the glass that your passway is closed. Collapsed. Useless."

"Strange," said Duray. "Very strange indeed. I can't understand it. Can you?"

"No…Not really."

Duray thought to detect a subtlety of intonation. His eyes narrowed in concentration. "The passway at my rig was closed. The passway at the girls' school was closed. Now you tell me that the downtown passway is closed."

Bob Robertson grinned. "That's a pretty broad hint, I would say. Did you and Elizabeth have a row?"

"No."

Bob Robertson rubbed his long aristocratic chin. "A mystery. There's probably some very ordinary explanation."

"Or some very extraordinary explanation."

"True. Nowadays a person can't rule out anything. By the way, tomorrow night is the Rumfuddle, and I expect both you and Elizabeth to be on hand."

"As I recall," said Duray, "I've already declined the invitation." The 'Rum-fuddlers' were a group of Bob's cronies. Duray suspected that their activities were not altogether wholesome. "Excuse me; I've got to find an open passway or Elizabeth and the kids are marooned."

"Try Alan," said Bob. "He'll have the original in his vault."

Duray gave a curt nod. "I don't like to bother him, but that's my last hope."

"Let me know what happens," said Bob Robertson. "And if you're at loose ends, don't forget the Rumfuddle tomorrow night. I mentioned the matter to Elizabeth and she said she'd be sure to attend."

"Indeed. And when did you consult Elizabeth?"

"A day or so ago. Don't look so damnably gothic, my boy."

"I'm wondering if there's a connection between your invitation and the closed passways. I happen to know that Elizabeth doesn't care for your parties."

Bob Robertson laughed with easy good grace. "Reflect a moment. Two events occur. I invite you and wife Elizabeth to the Rumfuddle. This is event one. Your passways close up, which is event two. By a feat of structured absurdity you equate the two and blame me. Now is that fair?"

"You call it 'structured absurdity'," said Duray. "I call it instinct."

Bob Robertson laughed again. "You'll have to do better than that. Consult Alan and if for some reason he can't help you, come to the Rumfuddle. We'll rack our brains and either solve your problem, or come up with new and better ones." He gave a cheery nod and before Duray could roar an angry expostula-tion the screen faded.

Duray stood glowering at the screen, convinced that Bob Robertson knew much more about the closed passways than he admitted. Duray went to sit on a bench…If Elizabeth had closed him away from Home, her reasons must have been compelling indeed. But, unless she intended to isolate herself permanently from Earth, she would leave at least one passway ajar, and this must be the master orifice in Alan Robertson's vault.

Duray rose to his feet, somewhat heavily, and stood a moment, head bent and shoulders hunched. He gave a surly grunt and returned to the phone booth, where he called a number known to not more than a dozen persons.

The screen glowed white, while the person at the other end of the line scru-tinized his face…The screen cleared, revealing a round pale face from which pale blue eyes stared forth with a passionless intensity. "Hello, Ernest," said Duray. "Is Alan busy at the moment?"

"I don't think he's doing anything particular—except resting."

Ernest gave the last two words a meaningful emphasis.

"I've got some problems," said Duray. "What's the best way to get in touch with him?"

"You'd better come up here. The code is changed. It's MHF now."

"I'll be there in a few minutes."

Back in the 'California' hub on Utilis, Duray went into a side chamber lined with private lockers, numbered and variously marked with symbols, names, colored flags, or not marked at all. Duray went to Locker 122, and ignoring the key-hole, set the code lock to the letters MHF. The door opened; Duray stepped into the locker and through the passway to the High Sierra headquarters of Alan Robertson.

IV

From *Memoirs and Reflections*:

If one Basic Axiom controls the cosmos, it must be this: *In a situation of infinity, every possible condition occurs, not once, but an infinite number of times.*

There is no mathematical nor logical limit to the number of dimensions. Our perceptions assure us of three only, but many indications suggest otherwise: parapsychic occurrences of a hundred varieties, the 'white holes', the seemingly finite state of our own universe, which by corollary, asserts the existence of others.

Hence, when I stepped behind the lead slab and first touched the button I felt confident of success; failure would have surprised me!

But (and here lay my misgivings) what sort of success might I achieve?

Suppose I opened a hole into the interplanetary vacuum?

The chances of this were very good indeed; I surrounded the machine in a strong membrane, to prevent the air of Earth from rushing off into the void.

Suppose I discovered a condition totally beyond imagination?

My imagination yielded no safeguards.

I proceeded to press the button.

Duray stepped out into a grotto under damp granite walls. Sunlight poured into the opening from a dark blue sky. This was Alan Robertson's link to the outside world; like many other persons, he disliked a passway opening directly into his home. A path led fifty yards across bare granite mountainside to the lodge.

To the west spread a great vista of diminishing ridges, valleys and hazy blue air; to the east rose a pair of granite crags with snow caught in the saddle between. Alan Robertson's lodge was built just below the timberline, beside a small lake fringed with tall dark firs. The lodge was built of rounded granite stones, with a wooden porch across the front; at each end rose a massive chimney.

Duray had visited the lodge on many occasions; as a boy he had scaled both of the crags behind the house, to look wondering off across the stillness, which on old Earth had a poignant breathing quality different from the uninhabited solitudes of worlds such as Home.

Ernest came to the door: a middle-aged man with an ingenuous face, small white hands and soft damp mouse-colored hair. Ernest disliked the lodge, the wilderness and solitude in general; he nevertheless would have suffered tortures before relinquishing his post as subaltern to Alan Robertson. Ernest and Duray were almost antipodal in outlook; Ernest thought Duray brusque, indelicate, a trifle coarse and probably not disinclined to violence as an argumentative adjunct. Duray considered Ernest, when he thought of him at all, as the kind of man who takes two bites out of a cherry. Ernest had never married; he showed no interest in women, and Duray, as a boy, had often fretted at Ernest's over-cautious restrictions.

In particular Ernest resented Duray's free and easy access to Alan Robertson. The power to restrict or admit those countless persons who demanded Alan Robertson's attention was Ernest's most cherished perquisite, and Duray denied him the use of it by simply ignoring Ernest and all his regulations. Ernest had never complained to Alan Robertson for fear of discovering that Duray's influence exceeded his own. A wary truce existed between the two, each conceding the other his privileges.

Ernest performed a polite greeting and admitted Duray into the lodge. Duray looked around the interior, which had not changed during his lifetime: varnished plank floors with red, black and white Navaho rugs, massive pine furniture with leather cushions, a few shelves of books, a half-dozen pewter mugs on the mantle over the big fireplace: a room almost ostentatiously bare of souvenirs and mementos. Duray turned back to Ernest: "Whereabouts is Alan?"

"On his boat."

"With guests?"

"No," said Ernest, with a faint sniff of disapproval. "He's alone, quite alone."

"How long has he been gone?"

"He just went through an hour ago. I doubt if he's left the dock yet. What is your problem, if I may ask?"

"The passways to my world are closed. All three. There's only one left, in the vault."

Ernest arched his flexible eyebrows. "Who closed them?"

"I don't know. Elizabeth and the girls are alone, so far as I know."

"Extraordinary," said Ernest, in a flat metallic voice. "Well then, come along." He led the way down a hall to a back room. With his hand on the knob Ernest paused and looked back over his shoulder. "Did you mention the matter to anyone? Robert, for instance?"

"Yes," said Duray curtly, "I did. Why do you ask?"

Ernest hesitated a fraction of a second. "No particular reason. Robert occasionally has a somewhat misplaced sense of humor, he and his 'Rumfuddlers'." He spoke the word with a hiss of distaste.

Duray said nothing of his own suspicions. Ernest opened the door; they entered a large room illuminated by a skylight. The only furnishing was a rug on the varnished floor. Into each wall opened four doors. Ernest went to one of these doors, pulled it open and made a resigned gesture. "You'll probably find Alan at the dock."

Duray looked into the interior of a rude hut with palm-frond walls, resting on a platform of poles. Through the doorway he saw a path leading under sun-lit green foliage toward a strip of white beach. Surf sparkled below a layer of dark blue ocean and a glimpse of the sky. Duray hesitated, rendered wary by the events of the morning. Anyone and everyone was suspect, even Ernest, who now gave a quiet sniff of contemptuous amusement. Through the foliage Duray glimpsed a spread of sail; he stepped through the passway.

V

From *Memoirs and Reflections*:

Man is a creature whose evolutionary environment has been the open air. His nerves, muscles and senses have developed across three million years in intimate contiguity with natural earth, crude stone, live wood, wind and rain. Now this creature is suddenly—on the geologic scale, instantaneously—shifted to an unnatural environment of metal and glass, plastic and plywood, to which his psychic substrata lack all compatibility. The wonder is not that we have so much mental instability but so little. Add to this, the weird noises, electrical pleasures, bizarre colors, synthetic foods, abstract entertainments! We should congratulate ourselves on our durability.

I bring this matter up because, with my little device, so simple, so easy, so flexible, I have vastly augmented the load upon our poor primeval brains, and for a fact many persons find the instant transition from one locale to another unsettling, and even actively unpleasant.

Duray stood on the porch of the cabin, under a vivid green canopy of sunlit foliage. The air was soft and warm and smelled of moist vegetation. Duray stood listening. The mutter of the surf came to his ears and from a far distance a single bird-call.

Duray stepped down to the ground and followed the path under tall palm trees to a river-bank. A few yards downstream, beside a rough pier of poles and planks, floated a white and blue trimaran ketch, sails hoisted and distended to a gentle breeze. On the deck stood Alan Robertson, on the point of casting off the mooring lines. Duray hailed him; Alan Robertson turned in surprise and vexation, which vanished when he recognized Duray. "Hello Gil; glad you're here! For a moment I thought it might be someone to bother me. Jump aboard; you're just in time for a sail."

Duray somberly joined Alan Robertson on the boat. "I'm afraid I am here to bother you."

"Oh?" Alan Robertson raised his eyebrows in instant solicitude. He was a man of no great height, thin, nervously active. Wisps of rumpled white hair fell over his forehead; mild blue eyes inspected Duray with concern, all thought of sailing forgotten. "What in the world has happened?"

"I wish I knew. If it were something I could handle myself I wouldn't bother you."

"Don't worry about me; there's all the time in the world for sailing. Now tell me what's happened."

"I can't get through to Home. All the passways are closed off: why and how I have no idea. Elizabeth and the girls are out there alone; at least I think they're out there."

Alan Robertson rubbed his chin. "What an odd business! I can certainly understand your agitation…You think Elizabeth closed the passways?"

"It's unreasonable—but there's no one else."

Alan Robertson turned Duray a shrewd kindly glance. "No little family upsets? Nothing to cause her despair and anguish?"

"Absolutely nothing. I've tried to reason things out, but I draw a blank. I thought that maybe someone—a man—had gone through to visit her and decided to take over—but if this were the case, why did she come to the school for the girls? That possibility is out. A secret love affair? Possible but so damn unlikely. Since she wants to keep me off the planet, her only motive could be to protect me, or herself, or the girls from danger of some sort. Again this means that another person is concerned in the matter. Who? How? Why? I spoke to Bob. He claims to know nothing about the situation, but he wants me to come to his damned 'Rumfuddle' and he hints very strongly that Elizabeth will be on hand. I can't prove a thing against Bob, but I suspect him. He's always had a taste for odd jokes."

Alan Robertson gave a lugubrious nod. "I won't deny that." He sat down in the cockpit and stared off across the water. "Bob has a complicated sense of humor, but he'd hardly close you away from your world...I hardly think that your family is in actual danger, but of course we can't take chances. The possibility exists that Bob is not responsible, that something uglier is afoot." He jumped to his feet. "Our obvious first step is to use the master-orifice in the vault." He looked a shade regretfully toward the ocean. "My little sail can wait...A lovely world this: not fully cognate with Earth—a cousin, so to speak. The fauna and flora are roughly contemporary except for man. The hominids have never developed."

The two men returned up the path, Alan Robertson chatting light-heartedly: "—thousands and thousands of worlds I've visited, and looked into even more, but do you know I've never hit upon a good system of classification? There are exact cognates—of course we're never sure exactly *how* exact they are. These cases are relatively simple, but then the problems begin... Bah! I don't think about such things any more. I know that when I keep all the nominates at zero the cognates appear. Over-intellectualizing is the bane of this, and every other era. Show me a man who deals only with abstraction and I'll show you the dead futile end of evolution..." Alan Robertson chuckled. "If I could control the machine tightly enough to produce real cognates, our troubles would be over...Much confusion of course. I might step through into the cognate world immediately as a true cognate Alan Robertson steps through into our world, with net effect of zero. An amazing business, really; I never tire of it..."

They returned to the transit room of the mountain lodge. Ernest appeared almost instantly. Duray suspected he had been watching through the passway.

Alan Robertson said briskly, "We'll be busy for an hour or two, Ernest. Gilbert is having difficulties and we've got to set things straight."

Ernest nodded somewhat grudgingly, or so it seemed to Duray. "The progress report on the Ohio Plan has arrived. Nothing particularly urgent."

"Thank you, Ernest, I'll see to it later. Come along, Gilbert; let's get to the bottom of this affair." They went to Door No. 1, and passed through to the Utilis hub. Alan Robertson led the way to a small green door with a three-dial coded lock, which he opened with a flourish. "Very well; in we go." He carefully locked the door behind them and they walked the length of a short hall. "A shame that I must be so cautious," said Alan Robertson. "You'd be astonished at the outrageous requests otherwise sensible people make of me. I sometimes become exasperated...Well, it's understandable, I suppose."

At the end of the hall Alan Robertson worked the locking dials of a red door. "This way, Gilbert; you've been through before." They stepped through a passway into a hall, which opened into a circular concrete chamber fifty feet in diameter, located, so Duray knew, deep under the Mad Dog Mountains of the Mojave Desert. Eight halls extended away into the rock; each hall communicated with twelve aisles. The center of the chamber was occupied by a circular desk twenty feet in diameter: here six clerks in white smocks worked at computers and collating machines. In accordance with their instructions they gave Alan Robertson neither recognition nor greeting.

Alan Robertson went up to the desk, at which signal the chief clerk, a solemn young man bald as an egg came forward. "Good afternoon, sir."

"Good afternoon, Harry. Find me the index for 'Gilbert Duray', on my personal list."

The clerk bowed smartly. He went to an instrument and ran his fingers over a bank of keys; the instrument ejected a card which Harry handed to Alan Robertson. "There you are, sir."

Alan Robertson showed the card to Duray, who saw the code: '4:8:10/6:13:29'.

"That's your world," said Alan Robertson. "We'll soon learn how the land lies. This way, to Radiant 4." He led the way down the hall, turned into the aisle numbered "8", and proceeded to Stack 10. "Shelf 6," said Alan Robertson. He checked the card. "Drawer 13...Here we are." He drew forth the drawer, ran his fingers along the tabs. "Item 29. This should be Home." He brought forth a metal frame four inches square, and held it up to his eyes. He frowned in disbelief. "We don't have anything here either." He turned to Duray a glance of dismay. "This is a serious situation!"

"It's no more than I expected," said Duray tonelessly.

"All this demands some careful thought." Alan Robertson clicked his tongue in vexation. "Tst, tst, tst..." He examined the identification plaque at the top of the frame. "4:8:10 /6:13:29," he read. "There seems to be no question of error." He squinted carefully at the numbers, hesitated, then slowly replaced the frame. On second thought he took the frame forth once more. "Come along, Gilbert," said Alan Robertson. "We'll have a cup of coffee and think this matter out."

The two returned to the central chamber, where Alan Robertson gave the empty frame into the custody of Harry the clerk. "Check the records, if you please," said Alan Robertson. "I want to know how many passways were pinched off the master."

Harry manipulated the buttons of his computer. "Three only, Mr. Robertson."

"Three passways and the master—four in all?"

"That's right, sir."

"Thank you, Harry."

VI

From *Memoirs and Reflections*:

I recognized the possibility of many cruel abuses, but the good so outweighed the bad that I thrust aside all thought of secrecy and exclusivity. I consider myself not Alan Robertson, but, like Prometheus, an archetype of Man, and my discovery must serve all men.

But caution, caution, caution!

I sorted out my ideas. I myself coveted the amplitude of a private, personal, world; such a yearning was not ignoble, I decided. Why should not everyone have the same if he so desired, since the supply was limitless? Think of it! The wealth and beauty of an entire world: mountains and plains, forests and flowers, ocean cliffs and crashing seas, winds and clouds—all beyond value, yet worth no more than a few seconds of effort and a few watts of energy.

I became troubled by a new idea. Would everyone desert old Earth and leave it a vile junk-heap? I found the concept intolerable…I exchange access to a world for three to six years of remedial toil, depending upon occupancy.

A lounge overlooked the central chamber. Alan Robertson gestured Duray to a seat and drew two mugs of coffee from a dispenser. Settling in a chair, he turned his eyes up to the ceiling. "We must collect our thoughts. The circumstances are somewhat unusual; still, I have lived with unusual circumstances for almost fifty years.

"So then: the situation. We have verified that there are only four passways to Home. These four passways are closed, though we must accept Bob's word in regard to your downtown locker. If this is truly the case, if Elizabeth and the girls are still on Home, you will never see them again."

"Bob is mixed up in this business. I could swear to nothing but—"

Alan Robertson held up his hand. "I will talk to Bob; this is the obvious first step." He rose to his feet and went to the telephone in the corner of the lounge. Duray joined him. Alan spoke into the screen. "Get me Robert Robertson's apartment in San Francisco."

The screen glowed white. Bob's voice came from the speaker. "Sorry; I'm not at home. I have gone out to my world Fancy, and I cannot be reached. Call back in a week, unless your business is urgent, in which case call back in a month."

"Mmph," said Alan Robertson returning to his seat. "Bob is sometimes a trifle too flippant. A man with an under-extended intellect…" He drummed his fingers on the arm of his chair. "Tomorrow night is his party? What does he call it…A Rumfuddle?"

"Some such nonsense. Why does he want me? I'm a dull dog; I'd rather be home building a fence."

"Perhaps you had better plan to attend the party."

"That means, submit to his extortion."

"Do you want to see your wife and family again?"

"Naturally. But whatever he has in mind won't be for my benefit, or Elizabeth's."

"You're probably right there. I've heard one or two unsavory tales regarding the Rumfuddlers…The fact remains that the passways are closed. All four of them."

Duray's voice became harsh. "Can't you open a new orifice for us?"

Alan Robertson gave his head a sad shake. "I can tune the machine very finely. I can code accurately for the 'Home' class of worlds, and as closely as necessary approximate a particular world-state. But at each setting, no matter how fine the tuning, we encounter an infinite number of worlds. In practice, inaccuracies in the machine, back-lash, the gross size of electrons, the very difference between one electron and another, make it difficult to tune with absolute precision. So even if we tuned exactly to the 'Home' class, the probability of opening into your particular Home is one in an infinite number: in short, negligible."

Duray stared off across the chamber. "Is it possible that a space once entered might tend to open more easily a second time?"

Alan Robertson smiled. "As to that, I can't say. I suspect not, but I really know so little. I see no reason why it should be so."

"If we can open into a world precisely cognate, I can at least learn why the passways are closed."

Alan Robertson sat up in his chair. "Here is a valid point. Perhaps we can accomplish something in this regard." He glanced humorously sidewise at Duray. "On the other hand—consider this situation. We create access into a 'Home' almost exactly cognate to your own—so nearly identical that the difference is not readily apparent. You find there an Elizabeth, a Dolly, a Joan and an Ellen indistinguishable from your own, and a Gilbert marooned on Earth. You might even convince yourself that this is your very own Home."

"I'd know the difference," said Duray shortly, but Alan Robertson seemed not to hear.

"Think of it! An infinite number of Homes isolated from Earth, an infinite number of Elizabeths, Dollys, Joans and Ellens marooned; an infinite number of Gilbert Durays trying to regain access...The sum effect might be a wholesale reshuffling of families with everyone more or less good-natured about the situation. I wonder if this could be Bob's idea of a joke to share with his Rumfuddlers."

Duray looked sharply at Alan Robertson, wondering whether the man were serious. "It doesn't sound funny, and I wouldn't be very good-natured."

"Of course not," said Alan Robertson hastily. "An idle thought—in rather poor taste, I'm afraid."

"In any event, Bob hinted that Elizabeth would be at his damned Rumfuddle. If that's the case she must have closed the passways from this side."

"A possibility," Alan Robertson conceded, "but unreasonable. Why should she seal you away from Home?"

"I don't know but I'd like to find out."

Alan Robertson slapped his hands down upon his thin shanks and jumped to his feet, only to pause once more. "You're sure you want to look into these cognates? You might see things you wouldn't like."

"So long as I know the truth, I don't care whether I like it or not."

"So be it."

The machine occupied a room behind the balcony. Alan Robertson surveyed the device with pride and affection. "This is the fourth model, and probably optimum; at least I don't see any place for significant improvement. I use a hundred and sixty-seven rods converging upon the center of the reactor sphere. Each rod produces a quantum of energy, and is susceptible to several types of adjustment, to cope with the very large number of possible states. The number of particles to pack the universe full is on the order of ten raised to the power of sixty; the possible permutations of these particles would number two raised to the power of ten raised to the power of sixty. The universe of course is built of many different particles, which makes the final number of possible, or let us say, thinkable states a number like two raised to the power of ten raised to the power of sixty, all times 'x', where 'x' is the number of particles under consideration. A large unmanageable number, which we need not consider because the conditions we deal with—the possible variations of planet Earth—are far fewer."

"Still a very large number," said Duray.

"Indeed yes. But again the sheer unmanageable bulk is cut away by a self-normalizing property of the machine. In what I call 'floating neutral' the machine reaches the closest cycles, which is to say, that infinite class of perfect cognates. In practice, because of infinitesimal inaccuracies, 'floating neutral' reaches cognates more or less imperfect, perhaps by no more than the shape of a single grain of sand. Still 'floating neutral' provides a natural base, and by adjusting the controls we reach cycles at an ever greater departure from Base. In practice I search out a good cycle, and strike a large number of passways, as many as a hundred thousand. So now to our business." He went to a console at the side. "Your code number, what was it now?"

Duray brought forth the card and read the numbers: "4:8:10/6:13:29."

"Very good. I give the code to the computer, which searches the files and automatically adjusts the machine. Now then, step over here; the process releases dangerous radiation."

The two stood behind lead slabs. Alan Robertson touched a button; watching through a periscope Duray saw a spark of purple light, and heard a small groaning rasping sound seeming to come from the air itself.

Alan Robertson stepped forth and walked to the machine. In the delivery tray rested an extensible ring. He picked up the ring, looked through the hole. "This seems to be right." He handed the ring to Duray. "Do you see anything you recognize?"

Duray put the ring to his eye. "That's Home."

"Very good. Do you want me to come with you?"

Duray considered. "The time is Now?"

"Yes. This is a time-neutral setting."

"I think I'll go alone."

Alan Robertson nodded. "Whatever you like. Return as soon as you can, so I'll know you're safe."

Duray frowned at him sidewise. "Why shouldn't I be safe? No one is there but my family."

"Not *your* family. The family of a cognate Gilbert Duray. The family may not be absolutely identical. The cognate Duray may not be identical. You can't be sure exactly what you will find—so be careful."

VII

From *Memoirs and Reflections*:

When I think of my machine and my little forays in and out of infinity, an idea keeps recurring to me which is so rather terrible that I close it out of my mind, and I will not even mention it here.

Duray stepped out upon the soil of Home, and stood appraising the familiar landscape. A vast meadow drenched in sunlight rolled down to wide Silver River. Above the opposite shore rose a line of low bluffs, with copses of trees in the hollows. To the left, landscape seemed to extend indefinitely and at last become indistinct in the blue haze of distance. To the right, the Robber Woods ended a quarter-mile from where Duray stood. On a flat beside the forest, on the bank of a small stream, stood a house of stone and timber: a sight which seemed to Duray the most beautiful he had ever seen. Polished glass windows sparkled in the sunlight; banks of geraniums glowed green and red. From the chimney rose a wisp of smoke. The air smelled cool and sweet, but seemed— so Duray imagined—to carry a strange tang, different—so he imagined—from the meadow-scent of his own Home. Duray started forward, then halted. The world was his own, yet not his own. If he had not been conscious of the fact, would he have recognized the strangeness? Nearby rose an outcrop of weathered gray field-rock: a rounded mossy pad on which he had sat only two days before, contemplating the building of a dock. He walked over and looked down at the stone. Here he had sat, here were the impressions of his heels in the soil; here was the pattern of moss from which he had absently scratched a fragment. Duray bent close. The moss was whole. The man who had sat here, the cognate Duray, had not scratched at the moss. So then: the world was perceptibly different from his own.

Duray was relieved and yet vaguely disturbed. If the world had been the exact simulacrum of his own, he might have been subjected to unmanageable emotions—which still might be the case. He walked toward the house, along the path which led down to the river. He stepped up to the porch. On a deck chair was a book: *Down There, A Study in Satanism*, by J. K. Huysmans. Elizabeth's tastes were eclectic. Duray had not previously seen the book; was it perhaps that Bob Robertson had put through the parcel delivery?

Duray went into the house. Elizabeth stood across the room. She had evidently watched him coming up the path. She said nothing; her face showed no expression.

Duray halted, somewhat at a loss as to how to address this woman.

"Good afternoon," he said at last.

Elizabeth allowed a wisp of a smile to show. "Hello, Gilbert."

At least, thought Duray, on cognate worlds the same language was spoken. He studied Elizabeth. Lacking prior knowledge would he have perceived her to be someone different from his own Elizabeth? Both were beautiful women: tall and slender, with curling black shoulder-length hair, worn without artifice. Their skins were pale with a dusky undertone; their mouths were wide, passionate, stubborn. Duray knew his Elizabeth to be a woman of inexplicable moods, and this Elizabeth was doubtless no different—yet somehow a difference existed, which Duray could not define, deriving perhaps from the strangeness of her atoms, the stuff of a different universe. He wondered if she sensed the same difference in him.

He asked, "Did you close off the passways?"

Elizabeth nodded, without change of expression.

"Why?"

"I thought it the best thing to do," said Elizabeth in a soft voice.

"That's no answer."

"I suppose not. How did you get here?"

"Alan made an opening."

Elizabeth raised her eyebrows. "I thought that was impossible."

"True. This is a different world to my own. Another Gilbert Duray built this house. I'm not your husband."

Elizabeth's mouth drooped in astonishment. She swayed back a step and put her hand up to her neck: a mannerism Duray could not recall in his own Elizabeth. The sense of strangeness came ever more strongly upon him. He felt an intruder. Elizabeth was watching him with a wide-eyed fascination. She said in a hurried mutter: "I wish you'd leave; go back to your own world; do!"

"If you've closed off all the passways, you'll be isolated," growled Duray. "Marooned, probably forever."

"Whatever I do," said Elizabeth, "it's not your affair."

"It is my affair, if only for the sake of the girls. I won't allow them to live and die alone out here."

"The girls aren't here," said Elizabeth in a flat voice. "They are where neither you nor any other Gilbert Duray will find them. So now go back to your own world, and leave me in whatever peace my soul allows me."

Duray stood glowering at the fiercely beautiful woman. He had never heard his own Elizabeth speak so wildly. He wondered if on his own world another Gilbert Duray similarly confronted his own Elizabeth, and as he analyzed his feelings toward this woman before him he felt a throb of annoyance. A curious situation. He said in a quiet voice, "Very well. You, and my own Elizabeth, have decided to isolate yourselves. I can't imagine your reasons."

Elizabeth gave a wild laugh. "They're real enough."

"They may be real now, but ten years from now, or forty years from now, they may seem unreal. I can't give you access to your own Earth, but if you wish, you can use the passway to the Earth from which I've just come, and you need never see me again."

Elizabeth turned away and went to look out over the valley. Duray spoke to her back. "We've never had secrets between us, you and I—or I mean, Elizabeth and I. Why now? Are you in love with some other man?"

Elizabeth gave a snort of sardonic amusement. "Certainly not...I'm disgusted with the entire human race."

"Which presumably includes me."

"It does indeed, and myself as well."

"And you won't tell me why?"

Elizabeth, still looking out the window, wordlessly shook her head.

"Very well," said Duray in a cold voice. "Will you tell me where you've sent the girls? They're mine as much as yours, remember."

"These particular girls aren't yours at all."

"That may be, but the effect is the same."

Elizabeth said tonelessly: "If you want to find your own particular girls, you'd better find your own particular Elizabeth and ask her. I can only speak for myself...To tell you the truth I don't like being part of a composite person, and I don't intend to act like one. I'm just me. You're you, a stranger, whom I've never seen before in my life. So I wish you'd leave."

Duray strode from the house, out into the sunlight. He looked once around the wide landscape, then gave his head a surly shake and marched off along the path.

VIII

From *Memoirs and Reflections*:

The past is exposed for our scrutiny; we can wander the epochs like lords through a garden, serene in our purview. We argue with the noble sages, refuting their laborious concepts, should we be so unkind. Remember (at least) two things. First: the more distant from Now, the less precise our conjunctures, the less our ability to strike to any given instant. We can break in upon yesterday at a stipulated second; during the Eocene plus or minus ten years is the limit of our accuracy; as for the Cretaceous or earlier, an impingement within three hundred years of a given date can be considered satisfactory. Secondly: the past we broach is never our own past, but at best the past of a cognate world, so that any illumination cast upon historical problems is questionable and perhaps deceptive. We cannot plumb the future; the process involves a negative flow of energy, which is inherently impractical. An instrument constructed of anti-matter has been jocularly recommended, but would yield no benefit to us. The future, thankfully, remains forever shrouded.

"Aha, you're back!" exclaimed Alan Robertson. "What did you learn?"

Duray described the encounter with Elizabeth. "She makes no excuse for what she's done; she shows hostility which doesn't seem real, especially since I can't imagine a reason for it."

Alan Robertson had no comment to make.

"The woman isn't my wife, but their motivations must be the same. I can't think of one sensible explanation for conduct so strange, let alone two."

"Elizabeth seemed normal this morning?" asked Alan Robertson.

"I noticed nothing unusual."

Alan Robertson went to the control panel of his machine. He looked over his shoulder at Duray.

"What time do you leave for work?"

"About nine."

Alan Robertson set one dial, turned two others until a ball of green light balanced wavering precisely half-way along a glass tube. He signaled Duray behind the lead slab and touched the button. From the center of the machine came the impact of one hundred and sixty-seven colliding nodules of force, and the groan of rending dimensional fabric.

Alan Robertson brought forth the new passway. "The time is morning. You'll have to decide for yourself how to handle the situation. You can try to watch without being seen; you can say that you have paperwork to catch up on, that Elizabeth should ignore you and go about her normal routine, while you unobtrusively see what happens."

Duray frowned. "Presumably for each of these worlds there is a Gilbert Duray who finds himself in my fix. Suppose each tries to slip inconspicuously into someone else's world to learn what is happening. Suppose each Elizabeth catches him in the act and furiously accuses the man she believes to be her husband of spying on her—this in itself might be the source of Elizabeth's anger."

"Well, be as discreet as you can. Presumably you'll be several hours, so I'll go back to the boat and putter about. Locker Five in my private hub yonder; I'll leave the door open."

Once again Duray stood on the hillside above the river, with the rambling stone house built by still another Gilbert Duray two hundred yards along the slope. From the height of the sun, Duray judged local time to be about nine o'clock: somewhat earlier than necessary. From the chimney of the stone house rose a wisp of smoke; Elizabeth had built a fire in the kitchen fireplace. Duray stood reflecting. This morning in his own house Elizabeth had built no fire. She had been on the point of striking a match and then had decided that the morning was already warm. Duray waited ten minutes, to make sure that the local Gilbert Duray had departed, then set forth toward the house. He paused by the big flat stone to inspect the pattern of moss. The crevice seemed narrower than he remembered, and the moss was dry and discolored. Duray took a deep breath. The air, rich with the odor of grasses and herbs, again seemed to carry an odd unfamiliar scent. Duray proceeded slowly to the house, uncertain whether, after all, he were engaged in a sensible course of action.

He approached the house. The front door was open. Elizabeth came to look out at him in surprise. "That was a quick day's work!"

Duray said lamely, "The rig is down for repairs. I thought I'd catch up on some paperwork. You go ahead with whatever you were doing."

Elizabeth looked at him curiously. "I wasn't doing anything in particular."

He followed Elizabeth into the house. She wore soft black slacks and an old gray jacket; Duray tried to remember what his own Elizabeth had worn, but the garments had been so familiar that he could summon no recollection.

Elizabeth poured coffee into a pair of stoneware mugs and Duray took a seat at the kitchen table, trying to decide how this Elizabeth differed from his own— if she did. This Elizabeth seemed more subdued and meditative; her mouth might have been a trifle softer. "Why are you looking at me so strangely?" she asked suddenly.

Duray laughed. "I was merely thinking what a beautiful girl you are."

Elizabeth came to sit in his lap and kissed him, and Duray's blood began to flow warm. He restrained himself; this was not his wife; he wanted no complications. And if he yielded to temptations of the moment, might not another Gilbert Duray visiting his own Elizabeth do the same? ...He scowled.

Elizabeth, finding no surge of ardor, went to sit in the chair opposite. For a moment she sipped her coffee in silence. Then she said, "Just as soon as you left Bob called through."

"Oh?" Duray was at once attentive. "What did he want?"

"That foolish party of his—the Rumble-menders or some such thing. He wants us to come."

"I've already told him no three times."

"I told him no again. His parties are always so peculiar. He said he wanted us to come for a very special reason, but he wouldn't tell me the reason. I told him thank you but no."

Duray looked around the room. "Did he leave any books?"

"No. Why should he leave me books?"

"I wish I knew."

"Gilbert," said Elizabeth, "you're acting rather oddly."

"Yes, I suppose I am." For a fact Duray's mind was whirling. Suppose now he went to the school passway, brought the girls home from school, then closed off all the passways, so that once again he had an Elizabeth and three daughters, more or less his own; then the conditions he had encountered would be satisfied. And another Gilbert Duray, now happily destroying the tract houses of Cupertino would find himself bereft...Duray recalled the hostile conduct of the previous Elizabeth. The passways in that particular world had certainly not been closed off by an intruding Duray...A startling possibility came to his mind. Suppose a Duray had come to the house and succumbing to temptation had closed off all passways except that one communicating with his own world; suppose then that Elizabeth, discovering the imposture, had killed him...The theory had a grim plausibility, and totally extinguished whatever inclination Duray might have had for making the world his home.

Elizabeth said, "Gilbert, why are you looking at me with that strange expression?"

Duray managed a feeble grin. "I guess I'm just in a bad mood this morning. Don't mind me. I'll go make out my report." He went into the wide cool living room, at once familiar and strange, and brought out the work-records of the other Gilbert Duray...He studied the handwriting: like his own, firm and decisive, but in some indefinable way, different—perhaps a trifle more harsh and angular. The three Elizabeths were not identical, nor were the Gilbert Durays.

An hour passed. Elizabeth occupied herself in the kitchen; Duray pretended to write a report.

A bell sounded. "Somebody at the passway," said Elizabeth.

Duray said, "I'll take care of it."

He went to the passage room, stepped through the passway, looked through the peep-hole—into the large bland sun-tanned face of Bob Robertson.

Duray opened the door. For a moment he and Bob Robertson confronted each other. Bob Robertson's eyes narrowed. "Why hello, Gilbert. What are you doing at home?"

Duray pointed to the parcel Bob Robertson carried. "What do you have there?"

"Oh these?" Bob Robertson looked down at the parcel as if he had forgotten it. "Just some books for Elizabeth."

Duray found it hard to control his voice. "You're up to some mischief, you and your Rumfuddlers. Listen, Bob: keep away from me and Elizabeth. Don't call here, and don't bring around any books. Is this definite enough?"

Bob raised his sun-bleached eyebrows. "Very definite, very explicit. But why the sudden rage? I'm just friendly old Uncle Bob."

"I don't care what you call yourself; stay away from us."

"Just as you like, of course. But do you mind explaining this sudden decree of banishment?"

"The reason is simple enough. We want to be left alone."

Bob made a gesture of mock despair. "All this over a simple invitation to a simple little party, which I'd really like you to come to."

"Don't expect us. We won't be there."

Bob's face suddenly went pink. "You're coming a very high horse over me my lad, and it's a poor policy. You might just get hauled up with a jerk. Matters aren't all the way you think they are."

"I don't care a rap one way or another," said Duray. "Goodbye."

He closed the locker door and backed through the passway. He returned into the living room. Elizabeth called from the kitchen. "Who was it, dear?"

"Bob Robertson, with some books."

"Books? Why books?"

"I didn't trouble to find out. I told him to stay away. After this, if he's at the passway, don't open it."

Elizabeth looked at him intently. "Gil—you're so strange today! There's something about you that almost scares me."

"Your imagination is working too hard."

"Why should Bob trouble to bring me books? What sort of books? Did you see?"

"Demonology. Black magic. That sort of thing."

"Mmf. Interesting—but not all that interesting...I wonder if a world like ours, where no one has ever lived, would have things like goblins and ghosts?"

"I suspect not," said Duray. He looked toward the door. There was nothing more to be accomplished here and it was time to return to his own Earth. He wondered how to make a graceful departure. And what would occur when the Gilbert Duray now working his rig came home?

Duray said, "Elizabeth, sit down in this chair here."

Elizabeth slowly slid into the chair at the kitchen table and watched him with a puzzled gaze.

"This may come as a shock," he said. "I am Gilbert Duray, but not your personal Gilbert Duray. I'm his cognate."

Elizabeth's eyes widened to lustrous dark pools.

Duray said, "On my own world Bob Robertson caused me and my Elizabeth trouble. I came here to find out what he had done and why, and to stop him from doing it again."

Elizabeth asked, "What has he done?"

"I still don't know. He probably won't bother you again. You can tell your personal Gilbert Duray whatever you think best, or even complain to Alan."

"I'm bewildered by all this!"

"No more so than I." He went to the door. "I've got to leave now. Goodby."

Elizabeth jumped to her feet and came impulsively forward. "Don't say goodby. It has such a lonesome sound, coming from you...It's like my own Gilbert saying goodby."

"There's nothing else to do. Certainly I can't follow my inclinations and move in with you. What good are two Gilberts? Who'd get to sit at the head of the table?"

"We could have a round table," said Elizabeth. "Room for six or seven. I like my Gilberts."

"Your Gilberts like their Elizabeths." Duray sighed and said, "I'd better go now."

Elizabeth held out her hand. "Goodby, cognate Gilbert."

IX

From *Memoirs and Reflections*:

The Oriental world-view differs from our own—specifically my own—in many respects, and I was early confronted with a whole set of dilemmas. I reflected upon Asiatic apathy and its obverse, despotism; warlords and brain-laundries; indifference to disease, filth and suffering; sacred apes and irresponsible fecundity.

I also took note of my resolve to use my machine in the service of all men.

In the end I decided to make the 'mistake' of many before me; I proceeded to impose my own ethical point of view upon the Oriental life-style. Since this was precisely what was expected of me; since I would have been regarded as a fool and a mooncalf had I done otherwise; since the rewards of cooperation far exceeded the gratifications of obduracy and scorn: my programs are a wonderful success, at least to the moment of writing.

Duray walked along the riverbank toward Alan Robertson's boat. A breeze sent twinkling cat's-paws across the water and bellied the sails which Alan Robertson had raised to air; the boat tugged at the mooring lines.

Alan Robertson, wearing white shorts and a white hat with a loose flapping brim, looked up from the eye he had been splicing at the end of a halyard. "Aha, Gil! you're back. Come aboard, and have a bottle of beer."

Duray seated himself in the shade of the sail and drank half the beer at a gulp. "I still don't know what's going on—except that one way or another Bob is responsible. He came while I was there. I told him to clear out. He didn't like it."

Alan Robertson heaved a melancholy sigh. "I realize that Bob has the capacity for mischief."

"I still can't understand how he persuaded Elizabeth to close the passways. He brought out some books, but what effect could they have?"

Alan Robertson was instantly interested. "What were the books?"

"Something about satanism, black magic; I couldn't tell you much else."

"Indeed, indeed!" muttered Alan Robertson. "Is Elizabeth interested in the subject?"

"I don't think so. She's afraid of such things."

"Rightly so. Well, well, that's disturbing." Alan Robertson cleared his throat and made a delicate gesture, as if beseeching Duray to geniality and tolerance. "Still, you mustn't be too irritated with Bob. He's prone to his little mischiefs, but—"

"'Little mischiefs'!" roared Duray. "Like locking me out of my home and marooning my wife and children? That's going beyond mischief!"

Alan Robertson smiled. "Here; have another beer; cool off a bit. Let's reflect. First, the probabilities. I doubt if Bob has really marooned Elizabeth and the girls, or caused Elizabeth to do so."

"Then why are all the passways broken?"

"That's susceptible to explanation. He has access to the vaults; he might have substituted a blank for your master orifice. There's one possibility, at least."

Duray could hardly speak for rage. At last he cried out: "He has no right to do this!"

"Quite right, in the largest sense. I suspect that he only wants to induce you to his 'Rumfuddle'."

"And I don't want to go, especially when he's trying to put pressure on me."

"You're a stubborn man, Gil. The easy way, of course, would be to relax and look in on the occasion. You might even enjoy yourself."

Duray glared at Alan Robertson. "Are you suggesting that I attend the affair?"

"Well—no. I merely proposed a possible course of action."

Duray drank more beer and glowered out across the river. Alan Robertson said, "In a day or so, when this business is clarified, I think that we—all of us—should go off on a lazy cruise, out there among the islands. Nothing to worry us, no bothers, no upsets. The girls would love such a cruise."

Duray grunted. "I'd like to see them again before I plan any cruises. What goes on at these Rumfuddler events?"

"I've never attended. The members laugh and joke and eat and drink, and gossip about the worlds they've visited and show each other movies: that sort of thing. Why don't we look in on last year's party? I'd be interested myself."

Duray hesitated. "What do you have in mind?"

"We'll set the dials to a year-old cognate to Bob's world Fancy, and see precisely what goes on. What do you say?"

"I suppose it can't do any harm," said Duray grudgingly.

Alan Robertson rose to his feet. "Help me get these sails in."

X

From *Memoirs and Reflections*:

The problems which long have harassed historians have now been resolved. Who were the Cro-Magnons; where did they evolve? Who were the Etruscans? Where were the legendary cities of the proto-Sumerians before they migrated to Mesopotamia? Why the identity between the ideographs of Easter Island and Mohenjo Daro? All these fascinating questions have now been settled and reveal to us the full scope of our early history. We have preserved the library at old Alexandria from the Mohammedans and the Inca codices from the Christians. The Guanches of the Canaries, the Ainu of Hokkaido, the Mandans of Missouri, the blond Kaffirs of Bhutan: all are now known to us. We can chart the development of every language syllable by syllable, from earliest formulation to the present. We have identified the Hellenic heroes, and I myself have searched the haunted forests of the ancient North and, in their own stone keeps, met face to face those mighty men who generated the Norse myths.

Standing before his machine, Alan Robertson spoke in a voice of humorous self-deprecation. "I'm not as trusting and forthright as I would like to be; in fact I sometimes feel shame for my petty subterfuges; and now I speak in reference to Bob. We all have our small faults, and Bob certainly does not lack his share. His imagination is perhaps his greatest curse: he is easily bored, and sometimes tends to over-reach himself. So while I deny him nothing, I also make sure that I am in a position to counsel or even remonstrate, if need be. Whenever I open a passway to one of his formulae, I unobtrusively strike a duplicate which I keep in my private file. We will find no difficulty in visiting a cognate to Fancy."

Duray and Alan Robertson stood in the dusk, at the end of a pale white beach. Behind them rose a low basalt cliff. To their right the ocean reflected the afterglow and a glitter from the waning moon; to the left palms stood black against the sky. A hundred yards along the beach dozens of fairy lamps had been strung between the trees to illuminate a long table laden with fruit, confections, punch in crystal bowls. Around the table stood several dozen men and women in animated conversation; music and the sounds of gaiety came down the beach to Duray and Alan Robertson.

"We're in good time," said Alan Robertson. He reflected a moment. "No doubt we'd be quite welcome, still it's probably best to remain inconspicuous. We'll just stroll unobtrusively down the beach, in the shadow of the trees. Be careful not to stumble or fall, and no matter what you see or hear, do nothing! Discretion is essential; we want no awkward confrontations."

Keeping to the shade of the foliage, the two approached the merry group. Fifty yards distant, Alan Robertson held up his hand to signal a halt. "This is as close as we need approach; most of the people you know, or more accurately, their cognates. For instance, there is Royal Hart, and there is James Parham and Elizabeth's aunt, Emma Bathurst, and her uncle Peter, and Maude Granger, and no end of other folk."

"They all seem very gay."

"Yes; this is an important occasion for them. You and I are surly outsiders who can't understand the fun."

"Is this all they do, eat and drink and talk?"

"I think not," said Alan Robertson. "Notice yonder; Bob seems to be preparing a projection screen. Too bad that we can't move just a bit closer." Alan Robertson peered through the shadows. "But we'd better take no chances; if we were discovered everyone would be embarrassed."

They watched in silence. Presently Bob Robertson went to the projection equipment and touched a button. The screen became alive with vibrating rings of red and blue. Conversations halted; the group turned toward the screen. Bob Robertson spoke, but his words were inaudible to the two who watched from the darkness. Bob Robertson gestured to the screen, where now appeared the view of a small country town, as if seen from an airplane. Surrounding was flat farm country, a land of wide horizons; Duray assumed the location to be somewhere in the Middle West. The picture changed, to show the local high school, with students sitting on the steps. The scene shifted to the football field, on the day of a game: a very important game to judge from the conduct of the spectators. The local team was introduced; one by one the boys ran out on the field to stand blinking into the autumn sunlight; then they ran off to the pre-game huddle.

The game began; Bob Robertson stood by the screen in the capacity of an expert commentator, pointing to one or another of the players, analyzing the play. The game proceeded, to the manifest pleasure of the Rumfuddlers. At half-time the bands marched and counter-marched, then play resumed. Duray became bored and made fretful comments to Alan Robertson who only said:

"Yes, yes; probably so," and "My word, the agility of that halfback!" and "Have you noticed the precision of the line-play? Very good indeed!" At last the final quarter ended; the victorious team stood under a sign reading:

THE SHOWALTER TORNADOES
CHAMPIONS OF TEXAS
1951

The players came forward to accept trophies; there was a last picture of the team as a whole, standing proud and victorious; then the screen burst out into a red and gold starburst and went blank. The Rumfuddlers rose to their feet and congratulated Bob Robertson who laughed modestly, and went to the table for a goblet of punch.

Duray said disgustedly, "Is this one of Bob's famous parties? Why does he make such a tremendous occasion of the affair? I expected some sort of debauch."

Alan Robertson said, "Yes, from our standpoint at least the proceedings seem somewhat uninteresting. Well, if your curiosity is satisfied, shall we return?"

"Whenever you like."

Once again in the lounge under the Mad Dog Mountains, Alan Robertson said: "So now and at last we've seen one of Bob's famous Rumfuddles. Are you still determined not to attend the occasion of tomorrow night?"

Duray scowled. "If I have to go to reclaim my family, I'll do so. But I just might lose my temper before the evening is over."

"Bob has gone too far," Alan Robertson declared. "I agree with you there. As for what we saw tonight, I admit to a degree of puzzlement."

"Only a degree? Do you understand it at all?"

Alan Robertson shook his head with a somewhat cryptic smile. "Speculation is pointless. I suppose you'll spend the night with me at the lodge?"

"I might as well," grumbled Duray. "I don't have anywhere else to go."

Alan Robertson clapped him on the back. "Good lad! We'll put some steaks on the fire and turn our problems loose for the night."

XI

From *Memoirs and Reflections*:

When I first put the Mark I machine into operation I suffered great fears. What did I know of the forces which I might release?…With all adjustments at dead neutral, I punched a passway into a cognate Earth. This was simple enough; in fact, almost anti-climactic…Little by little I learned to control my wonderful toy; our own world and all its past phases became familiar to me. What of other worlds? I am sure that in due course we will move instantaneously from world to world, from galaxy to galaxy, using a special space-traveling hub on Utilis. At the moment I am candidly afraid to punch through passways at blind random. What if I opened into the interior of a sun? Or into the center of a black hole? Or into an anti-matter universe? I would certainly destroy myself and the machine and conceivably Earth itself.

Still, the potentialities are too entrancing to be ignored. With painstaking precautions and a dozen protective devices, I will attempt to find my way to new worlds, and for the first time interstellar travel will be a reality.

Alan Robertson and Duray sat in the bright morning sunlight beside the flinty blue lake. They had brought their breakfast out to the table and now sat drinking coffee. Alan Robertson made cheerful conversation for the two of them. "These last few years have been easier on me; I've relegated a great deal of responsibility. Ernest and Henry know my policies as well as I do, if not better; and they're never frivolous or inconsistent." Alan Robertson chuckled. "I've worked two miracles: first, my machine, and second, keeping the business as simple as it is. I refuse to keep regular hours; I won't make appointments; I don't keep records; I pay no taxes; I exert great political and social influence, but only informally; I simply refuse to be bothered with administrative detail, and consequently I find myself able to enjoy life."

"It's a wonder some religious fanatic hasn't assassinated you," said Duray sourly.

"No mystery there! I've given them all their private worlds, with my best regards, and they have no energy left for violence! And as you know, I walk with a very low silhouette. My friends hardly recognize me on the street." Alan Robertson waved his hand. "No doubt you're more concerned with your immediate quandary. Have you come to a decision regarding the Rumfuddle?"

"I don't have any choice," Duray muttered. "I'd prefer to wring Bob's neck. If I could account for Elizabeth's conduct, I'd feel more comfortable. She's not even remotely interested in black magic. Why did Bob bring her books on Satanism?"

"Well—the subject is inherently fascinating," Alan Robertson suggested, without conviction. "The name 'Satan' derives from the Hebrew word for 'adversary'; it never applied to a real individual. Zeus of course was an Aryan chieftain of about 3500 B.C., while 'Woden' lived somewhat later. He was actually 'Othinn', a shaman of enormous personal force, who did things with his mind that I can't do with the machine…But again I'm rambling."

Duray gave a silent shrug.

"Well then, you'll be going to the Rumfuddle," said Alan Robertson, "by and large the best course, whatever the consequences."

"I believe that you know more than you're telling me."

Alan Robertson smiled and shook his head. "I've lived with too much uncertainty among my cognate and near-cognate worlds. Nothing is sure; surprises are everywhere. I think the best plan is to fulfill Bob's requirements. Then, if Elizabeth is indeed on hand, you can discuss the event with her."

"What of you? Will you be coming?"

"I am of two minds. Would you prefer that I came?"

"Yes," said Duray. "You have more control over Bob than I do."

"Don't exaggerate my influence! He is a strong man, for all his idleness. Confidentially, I'm delighted that he occupies himself with games rather than…" Alan Robertson hesitated.

"Rather than what?"

"Than that his imagination should prompt him to less innocent games. Perhaps I have been over-ingenuous in this connection. We can only wait and see."

XII

From *Memoirs and Reflections*:

If the Past is a house of many chambers, then the Present is the most recent coat of paint.

>•<

At four o'clock Duray and Alan Robertson left the lodge and passed through Utilis to the San Francisco depot. Duray had changed into a somber dark suit; Alan Robertson wore a more informal costume: blue jacket and pale gray trousers. They went to Bob Robertson's locker, to find a panel with the sign: NOT HOME! FOR THE RUMFUDDLE GO TO ROGER WAILLE'S LOCKER, RC3-96 AND PASS THROUGH TO EKSHAYAN!

The two went on to Locker RC3-96 where a sign read: RUMFUDDLERS, PASS! ALL OTHERS: AWAY!

Duray shrugged contemptuously and parting the curtain looked through the passway, into a rustic lobby of natural wood, painted in black, red, yellow, blue and white floral designs. An open door revealed an expanse of open land and water glistening in the afternoon sunlight. Duray and Alan Robertson passed through, crossed the foyer and looked out upon a vast slow river flowing from north to south. A rolling plain spread eastward away and over the horizon. The western bank of the river was indistinct in the afternoon glitter. A path led north to a tall house of eccentric architecture. A dozen domes and cupolas stood against the sky; gables and ridges created a hundred unexpected angles. The walls showed a fish-scale texture of hand-hewn shingles; spiral columns supported the second- and third-story entablatures, where wolves and bears carved in vigorous curves and masses snarled, fought, howled and danced. On the side overlooking the river a pergola clothed with vines cast a dappled shade; here sat the Rumfuddlers.

Alan Robertson looked at the house, up and down the river, across the plain. "From the architecture, the vegetation, the height of the sun, the characteristic haze, I assume the river to be either the Don or the Volga, and yonder the steppes. From the absence of habitation, boats and artifacts, I would guess the time to be early historic—perhaps 2,000 or 3,000 B.C., a colorful era. The inhabitants of the steppes are nomads; Scyths to the east, Celts to the west, and to the north the homeland of the Germanic and Scandinavian tribes; and yonder the mansion of Roger Waille, and very interesting too, after the extravagant fashion of the Russian Baroque. And, my word! I believe I see an ox on the spit! We may even enjoy our little visit!"

"You do as you like," muttered Duray, "I'd just as soon eat at home."

Alan Robertson pursed his lips. "I understand your point of view, of course, but perhaps we should relax a bit. The scene is majestic, the house is delightfully picturesque; the roast beef is undoubtedly delicious; perhaps we should meet the situation on its own terms."

Duray could find no adequate reply, and kept his opinions to himself.

"Well then," said Alan Robertson, "equability is the word. So now let's see what Bob and Roger have up their sleeves." He set off along the path to the house, with Duray sauntering morosely a step or two behind.

Under the pergola a man jumped to his feet and flourished his hand; Duray recognized the tall spare form of Bob Robertson. "Just in time," Bob called jocosely. "Not too early, not too late. We're glad you could make it!"

"Yes, we found we could accept your invitation after all," said Alan Robertson. "Let me see, do I know anyone here? Roger, hello!…And William…Ah! the lovely Dora Gorski!…Cypriano…" He looked around the circle of faces, waving to his acquaintances.

Bob clapped Duray on the shoulder. "Really pleased you could come! What'll you drink? The locals distill a liquor out of fermented mare's milk, but I don't recommend it."

"I'm not here to drink," said Duray. "Where's Elizabeth?"

The corners of Bob's wide mouth twitched. "Come now, old man; let's not be grim. This is the Rumfuddle! A time for joy and self-renewal! Go dance about a bit! Cavort! Pour a bottle of champagne over your head! Sport with the girls!"

Duray looked into the blue eyes for a long second. He strained to keep his voice even. "Where is Elizabeth?"

"Somewhere about the place. A charming girl, your Elizabeth! We're delighted to have you both!"

Duray swung away. He walked to the dark and handsome Roger Waille. "Would you be good enough to take me to my wife?"

Waille raised his eyebrows as if puzzled by Duray's tone of voice. "She's in primping and gossiping. If necessary I suppose I could pull her away for a moment or two."

Duray began to feel ridiculous, as if he had not been locked away from his world, subjected to harassments and doubts, and made the butt of some obscure joke. "It's necessary," he said. "We're leaving."

"But you've just arrived!"

"I know."

Waille gave a shrug of amused perplexity, and turned away toward the house. Duray followed. They went through a tall narrow doorway into an entry-hall paneled with a beautiful brown-gold wood, which Duray automatically identified as chestnut. Four high panes of tawny glass turned to the west filled the room with a smoky half-melancholy light. Oak settees, upholstered in leather, faced each other across a black, brown and gray rug. Tabourets stood at each side of the settees, and each supported an ornate golden candelabra in the form of conventionalized stag's-heads. Waille indicated these last. "Striking, aren't they? The Scythians made them for me. I paid them in iron knives. They think I'm a great magician; and for a fact, I am." He reached into the air and plucked forth an orange, which he tossed upon a settee. "Here's Elizabeth now, and the other maenads as well."

Into the chamber came Elizabeth, with three other young women whom Duray vaguely recalled having met before. At the sight of Duray, Elizabeth stopped short. She essayed a smile, and said in a light strained voice, "Hello, Gil. You're here after all." She laughed nervously and, Duray felt, unnaturally. "Yes, of course you're here. I didn't think you'd come."

Duray glanced toward the other women, who stood with Waille watching half-expectantly. Duray said, "I'd like to speak to you alone."

"Excuse us," said Waille. "We'll go on outside."

They departed. Elizabeth looked longingly after them, and fidgeted with the buttons of her jacket.

"Where are the children?" Duray demanded curtly.

"Upstairs, getting dressed." She looked down at her own costume, the festival raiment of a Transylvanian peasant girl: a green skirt embroidered with red and blue flowers, a white blouse, a black velvet vest, glossy black boots.

Duray felt his temper slipping; his voice was strained and fretful. "I don't understand anything of this. Why did you close the passways?"

Elizabeth attempted a flippant smile. "I was bored with routine."

"Oh? Why didn't you mention it to me yesterday morning? You didn't need to close the passways."

"Gilbert, please. Let's not discuss it."

Duray stood back, tongue-tied with astonishment. "Very well," he said at last. "We won't discuss it. You go up and get the girls. We're going home."

Elizabeth shook her head. In a neutral voice she said, "It's impossible. There's only one passway open. I don't have it."

"Who does? Bob?"

"I guess so; I'm not really sure."

"How did he get it? There were only four, and all four were closed."

"It's simple enough. He moved the downtown passway from our locker to another, and left a blank in its place."

"And who closed off the other three?"

"I did."

"Why?"

"Because Bob told me to. I don't want to talk about it; I'm sick to death of the whole business." And she half-whispered: "I don't know what I'm going to do with myself."

"I know what I'm going to do," said Duray. He turned toward the door.

Elizabeth held up her hands and clenched her fists against her breast. "Don't make trouble please! He'll close our last passway!"

"Is that why you're afraid of him? If so—don't be. Alan wouldn't allow it."

Elizabeth's face began to crumple. She pushed past Duray and walked quickly out upon the terrace. Duray followed, baffled and furious. He looked back and forth across the terrace. Bob was not to be seen. Elizabeth had gone to Alan Robertson; she spoke in a hushed urgent voice. Duray went to join them. Elizabeth became silent and turned away, avoiding Duray's gaze.

Alan Robertson spoke in a voice of easy geniality. "Isn't this a lovely spot? Look how the setting sun shines on the river!"

Roger Waille came by rolling a cart with ice, goblets and a dozen bottles. Now he said: "Of all the places on all the Earths this is my favorite. I call it 'Ekshayan', which is the Scythian name for this district."

A woman asked, "Isn't it cold and bleak in the winter?"

"Frightful!" said Waille. "The blizzards howl down from the north; then they stop and the land is absolutely still. The days are short and the sun comes up red as a poppy. The wolves slink out of the forests, and at dusk they circle the house. When a full moon shines, they howl like banshees, or maybe the banshees are howling! I sit beside the fireplace, entranced."

"It occurs to me," said Manfred Funk, "that each person, selecting a site for his home, reveals a great deal about himself. Even on old Earth, a man's home was ordinarily a symbolic simulacrum of the man himself; now, with every option available, a person's house is himself."

"This is very true," said Alan Robertson, "and certainly Roger need not fear that he has revealed any discreditable aspects of himself by showing us his rather grotesque home on the lonely steppes of prehistoric Russia."

Roger Waille laughed. "The grotesque house isn't me; I merely felt that it fitted its setting…Here, Duray, you're not drinking. That's chilled vodka; you can mix it or drink it straight in the time-tested manner."

"Nothing for me, thanks."

"Just as you like. Excuse me; I'm wanted elsewhere." Waille moved away, rolling the cart. Elizabeth leaned as if she wanted to follow him, then remained beside Alan Robertson, looking thoughtfully over the river.

Duray spoke to Alan Robertson as if she were not there. "Elizabeth refuses to leave. Bob has hypnotized her."

"That's not true," said Elizabeth softly.

"Somehow, one way or another, he's forced her to stay. She won't tell me why."

"I want the passway back," said Elizabeth. But her voice was muffled and uncertain.

Alan Robertson cleared his throat. "I hardly know what to say. ·It's a very awkward situation. None of us wants to create a disturbance—"

"There you're wrong," said Duray.

Alan Robertson ignored the remark. "I'll have a word with Bob after the party. In the meantime I don't see why we shouldn't enjoy the company of our friends, and that wonderful roast ox! Who is that turning the spit? I know him from somewhere."

Duray could hardly speak for outrage. "After what he's done to us?"

"He's gone too far, much too far," Alan Robertson agreed. "Still, he's a flamboyant feckless sort and I doubt if he understands the full inconvenience he's caused you."

"He understands well enough. He just doesn't care."

"Perhaps so," said Alan Robertson sadly. "I had always hoped—but that's neither here nor there. I still feel that we should act with restraint. It's much easier not to do than to undo."

Elizabeth abruptly crossed the terrace and went to the front door of the tall house, where her three daughters had appeared: Dolly, 12; Joan, 10; Ellen, 8: all wearing green, white and black peasant frocks and glossy black boots. Duray thought they made a delightful picture. He followed Elizabeth across the terrace.

"It's Daddy," screamed Ellen, and threw herself in his arms. The other two, not to be outdone, did likewise.

"We thought you weren't coming to the party," cried Dolly. "I'm glad you did though." "So'm I." "So'm I."

"I'm glad I came too, if only to see you in these pretty costumes. Let's go see Grandpa Alan." He took them across the terrace, and after a moment's hesitation, Elizabeth followed. Duray became aware that everyone had stopped talking to look at him and his family, with, so it seemed, an extraordinary, even avid, curiosity, as if in expectation of some entertaining extravagance of conduct. Duray began to burn with emotion. Once, long ago, while crossing a street in downtown San Francisco, he had been struck by an automobile, suffering a broken leg and a fractured clavicle. Almost as soon as he had been knocked down, pedestrians came pushing to stare down at him, and Duray, looking up in pain and shock had seen only the ring of white faces and intent eyes, greedy as flies around a puddle of blood. In hysterical fury he had staggered to his feet, striking out into every face within reaching distance, man and woman alike. He hated them more than the man who had run him down: the ghouls who had come to enjoy his pain. Had he the miraculous power, he would have crushed them into a screaming bale of detestable flesh, hurled the bundle twenty miles out into the Pacific Ocean...Some faint shadow of this emotion affected him now, but today he would provide them no unnatural pleasure. He turned a single glance of cool contempt around the group, then took his three eager-faced daughters to a bench at the back of the terrace. Elizabeth followed, moving like a mechanical object. She seated herself at the end of the bench and looked off across the river. Duray stared heavily back at the Rumfuddlers, compelling them to shift their gazes, to where the ox roasted over a great bed of coals. A young man in a white jacket turned the spit; another basted the meat with a long-handled brush. A pair of Orientals carried out a carving table; another brought a carving set; a fourth wheeled out a cart laden with salads, round crusty loaves, trays of cheese and herrings. A fifth man, dressed as a Transylvanian gypsy, came from the house with a violin. He went to the corner of the terrace and began to play melancholy music of the steppes.

Bob Robertson and Roger Waille inspected the ox, a magnificent sight indeed. Duray attempted a stony detachment, but his nose was under no such strictures; the odor of the roast meat, garlic and herbs tantalized him unmercifully. Bob Robertson returned to the terrace and held up his hands for attention; the fiddler put down his instrument. "Control your appetites; there'll still be a few minutes, during which we can discuss our next Rumfuddle. Our clever colleague Bernard Ulman recommends a hostelry in the Adirondacks: the Sapphire Lake Lodge. The hotel was built in 1902, to the highest standards of Edwardian comfort. The clientele is derived from the business community of New York. The cuisine is kosher; the management maintains an atmosphere of congenial gentility; the current date is 1930. Bernard has furnished photographs. Roger, if you please…"

Waille drew back a curtain to reveal a screen. He manipulated the projection machine and the hotel was displayed on the screen: a rambling half-timbered structure overlooking several acres of park and a smooth lake.

"Thank you, Roger. I believe that we also have a photograph of the staff…"

On the screen appeared a stiffly posed group of about thirty men and women, all smiling with various degrees of affability. The Rumfuddlers were amused; some among them tittered.

"Bernard gives a very favorable report as to the cuisine, the amenities and the charm of the general area. Am I right, Bernard?"

"In every detail," declared Bernard Ulman. "The management is attentive and efficient; the clientele is well-established."

"Very good," said Bob Robertson. "Unless someone has a more entertaining idea, we will hold our next Rumfuddle at the Sapphire Lake Lodge. And now I believe that the roast beef should be ready: done to a turn as the expression goes."

"Quite right," said Roger Waille. "Tom, as always, has done an excellent job at the spit."

The ox was lifted to the table. The carver set to work with a will. Duray went to speak to Alan Robertson, who blinked uneasily at his approach. Duray asked, "Do you understand the reason for these parties? Are you in on the joke?"

Alan Robertson spoke in a precise manner: "I certainly am not 'in on the joke', as you put it." He hesitated, then said: "The Rumfuddlers will never again intrude upon your life or that of your family. I am sure of this. Bob became over-exuberant; he exercised poor judgment, and I intend to have a quiet word with him. In fact, we have already exchanged certain opinions. At the moment your best interests will be served by detachment and unconcern."

Duray spoke with sinister politeness: "You feel then that I and my family should bear the brunt of Bob's jokes?"

"This is a harsh view of the situation, but my answer must be 'yes'."

"I'm not so sure. My relationship with Elizabeth is no longer the same. Bob has done this to me."

"To quote an old apothegm: 'Least said, soonest mended'."

Duray changed the subject. "When Waille showed the photograph of the hotel staff, I thought some of the faces were familiar. Before I could be quite sure the picture was gone."

Alan Robertson nodded unhappily. "Let's not develop the subject, Gilbert. Instead—"

"I'm into the situation too far," said Duray. "I want to know the truth."

"Very well then," said Alan Robertson hollowly, "your instincts are accurate. The management of the Sapphire Lake Lodge, in cognate circumstances, has achieved an unsavory reputation. As you have guessed, they comprise the leadership of the National Socialist Party during 1938 or thereabouts. The manager of course is Hitler, the desk clerk is Goebbels, the head-waiter is Goering, the bellboys are Himmler and Hess, and so on down the line. They are of course not aware of the activities of their cognates on other worlds. The hotel's clientele is for the most part Jewish, which brings a macabre humor to the situation."

"Undeniably," said Duray. "What of that Rumfuddlers party that we looked in on?"

"You refer to the high-school football team? The 1951 Texas champions as I recall." Alan Robertson grinned. "And well they should be. Bob identified the players for me. Are you interested in the line-up?"

"Very much so."

Alan Robertson drew a sheet of paper from his pocket. "I believe—yes, this is it." He handed the sheet to Duray, who saw a schematic line-up:

LE	LT	LG	C	RG	RT	RE
Achilles	Charlemagne	Hercules	Goliath	Samson	Richard the Lion Hearted	Billy the Kid

Q
Machiavelli

LHB   RHB
Sir Galahad   Geronimo

FB
Cuchullain

Duray returned the paper. "You approve of this?"

"I had best put it like this," said Alan Robertson, a trifle uneasily. "One day, chatting with Bob, I remarked that much travail could be spared the human race if the most notorious evil-doers were early in their lives shifted to environments which afforded them constructive outlets for their energies. I speculated that having the competence to make such changes it was perhaps our duty to do so. Bob became interested in the concept and formed his group, the Rumfuddlers, to serve the function I had suggested. In all candor I believe that Bob and his friends have been attracted more by the possibility of entertainment than by altruism, but the effect has been the same."

"The football players aren't evil-doers," said Duray. "Sir Galahad, Charlemagne, Samson, Richard the Lion Hearted..."

"Exactly true," said Alan Robertson, "and I made this point to Bob. He asserted that all were brawlers and bully-boys, with the possible exception of Sir Galahad; that Charlemagne, for example, had conquered much territory to no particular achievement; that Achilles, a national hero to the Greeks, was a cruel enemy to the Trojans; and so forth. His justifications are somewhat specious perhaps...Still these young men are better employed making touchdowns than breaking heads."

After a pause Duray asked: "How are these matters arranged?"

"I'm not entirely sure. I believe that by one means or another, the desired babies are exchanged with others of similar appearance. The child so obtained is reared in appropriate circumstances."

"The jokes seem elaborate and rather tedious."

"Precisely!" Alan Robertson declared. "Can you think of a better method to keep someone like Bob out of mischief?"

"Certainly," said Duray. "Fear of the consequences." He scowled across the terrace. Bob had stopped to speak to Elizabeth. She and the three girls rose to their feet.

Duray strode across the terrace. "What's going on?"

"Nothing of consequence," said Bob. "Elizabeth and the girls are going to help serve the guests." He glanced toward the serving table, then turned back to Duray. "Would you help with the carving?"

Duray's arm moved of its own volition. His fist caught Bob on the angle of the jaw, and sent him reeling back into one of the white-coated Orientals, who carried a tray of food. The two fell into an untidy heap. The Rumfuddlers were shocked and amused, and watched with attention.

Bob rose to his feet gracefully enough and gave a hand to the Oriental. Looking toward Duray he shook his head ruefully. Meeting his glance, Duray noted a pale blue glint; then Bob once more became bland and debonair.

Elizabeth spoke in a low despairing voice: "Why couldn't you have done as he asked? It would have all been so simple."

"Elizabeth may well be right," said Alan Robertson.

"Why should she be right?" demanded Duray. "We are his victims! You've allowed him a taste of mischief, and now you can't control him!"

"Not true!" declared Alan. "I intend to impose rigorous curbs upon the Rumfuddlers, and I will be obeyed."

"The damage is done, so far as I am concerned," said Duray bitterly. "Come along, Elizabeth, we're going home."

"We can't go home. Bob has the passway."

Alan Robertson drew a deep sigh, and came to a decision. He crossed to where Bob stood with a goblet of wine in one hand, massaging his jaw with the other. Alan Robertson spoke to Bob politely, but with authority. Bob was slow in making reply. Alan Robertson spoke again, sharply. Bob only shrugged. Alan Robertson waited a moment, then returned to Duray, Elizabeth and the three children.

"The passway is at his San Francisco apartment," said Alan Robertson in a measured voice. "He will give it back to you after the party. He doesn't choose to go for it now."

Bob once more commanded the attention of the Rumfuddlers. "By popular request we replay the record of our last but one Rumfuddle, contrived by one of our most distinguished, diligent and ingenious Rumfuddlers, Manfred Funk. The locale is the Red Barn, a roadhouse twelve miles west of Urbana, Illinois; the time is the late summer of 1926; the occasion is a Charleston dancing contest. The music is provided by the legendary Wolverines, and you will hear the fabulous cornet of Leon Bismarck Beiderbecke." Bob gave a wry smile, as if the music were not to his personal taste. "This was one of our most rewarding occasions, and here it is again."

The screen showed the interior of a dance-hall, crowded with excited young men and women. At the back of the stage sat the Wolverines, wearing tuxedos; to the front stood the contestants: eight dapper young men and eight pretty girls in short skirts. An announcer stepped forward and spoke to the crowd through a megaphone: "Contestants are numbered one through eight! Please, no encouragement from the audience. The prize is this magnificent trophy and fifty dollars cash; the presentation will be made by last year's winner Boozy Horman. Remember, on the first number we eliminate four contestants, on the second number two; and after the third number we select our winner. So then: Bix and the Wolverines, and *Sensation Rag*!"

From the band came music, from the contestants agitated motion.

Duray asked, "Who are these people?"

Alan Robertson replied in an even voice: "The young men are locals and not important. But notice the girls: no doubt you find them attractive. You are not alone. They are Helen of Troy, Deirdre, Marie Antoinette, Cleopatra, Salome, Lady Godiva, Nefertiti and Mata Hari."

Duray gave a dour grunt. The music halted; judging applause from the audience, the announcer eliminated Marie Antoinette, Cleopatra, Deirdre, Mata Hari, and their respective partners. The Wolverines played *Fidgety Feet*; the four remaining contestants danced with verve and dedication; but Helen and Nefertiti were eliminated. The Wolverines played *Tiger Rag*. Salome and Lady Godiva and their young men performed with amazing zeal. After carefully appraising the volume of applause, the announcer gave his judgment to Lady Godiva and her partner. Large on the screen appeared a close-up view of the two happy faces; in an excess of triumphant joy they hugged and kissed each other. The screen went dim; after the vivacity of the Red Barn the terrace above the Don seemed drab and insipid.

The Rumfuddlers shifted in their seats. Some uttered exclamations to assert their gaiety; others stared out across the vast empty face of the river.

Duray glanced toward Elizabeth; she was gone. Now he saw her circulating among the guests with three other young women, pouring wine from Scythian decanters.

"It makes a pretty picture, does it not?" said a calm voice. Duray turned to find Bob standing behind him; his mouth twisted in an easy half-smile but his eyes glinting pale blue.

Duray turned away. Alan Robertson said, "This is not at all a pleasant situation, Bob, and in fact completely lacks charm."

"Perhaps at future Rumfuddles, when my face feels better, the charm will emerge…Excuse me; I see that I must enliven the meeting." He stepped forward. "We have a final pastiche: oddments and improvisations, vignettes and glimpses, each in its own way entertaining and instructive. Roger; start the mechanism, if you please."

Roger Waille hesitated and glanced sidelong toward Alan Robertson.

"The item number is sixty-two, Roger," said Bob in a calm voice. Roger Waille delayed another instant then shrugged and went to the projection machine.

"The material is new," said Bob, "hence I will supply a commentary. First we have an episode in the life of Richard Wagner, the dogmatic and occasionally irascible composer. The year is 1843; the place is Dresden. Wagner sets forth on a summer night to attend a new opera *Der Sängerkrieg* by an unknown composer. He alights from his carriage before the hall; he enters; he seats himself in his loge. Notice the dignity of his posture; the authority of his gestures! The music begins: listen!" From the projector came the sound of music. "It is the overture," stated Bob. "But notice Wagner: why is he stupefied? Why is he overcome with wonder? He listens to the music as if he has never heard it before. And in fact he hasn't; he has only just yesterday set down a few preliminary notes for this particular opus, which he planned to call *Tannhäuser*; today, magically, he hears it in its final form. Wagner will walk home slowly tonight, and perhaps in his abstraction he will kick the dog Schmutzi…Now, to a different scene: St. Petersburg in the year 1880 and the stables in back of the Winter Palace. The ivory and gilt carriage rolls forth to convey the Czar and the Czarina to a reception at the British Embassy. Notice the drivers: stern, well-groomed, intent at their business. Marx's beard is well-trimmed; Lenin's goatee is not so pronounced. A groom comes to watch the carriage roll away. He has a kindly twinkle in his eye, does Stalin." The screen went dim once more, then brightened to show a city street lined with automobile showrooms and used car lots. "This is one of Shawn Henderson's projects. The four used-car lots are operated by men who in other circumstances were religious notables: prophets and so forth. That alert keen-featured man in front of 'Quality Motors', for instance, is Mohammed. Shawn is conducting a careful survey, and at our next Rumfuddle he will report upon his dealings with these four famous figures."

Alan Robertson stepped forward, somewhat diffidently. He cleared his throat. "I don't like to play the part of spoil-sport, but I'm afraid I have no choice. There will be no further Rumfuddles. Our original goals have been neglected and I note far too many episodes of purposeless frivolity and even cruelty. You may wonder at what seems a sudden decision, but I have been considering the matter for several days. The Rumfuddles have taken a turn in an unwholesome direction, and conceivably might become a grotesque new vice, which of course is far from our original ideal. I'm sure that every sensible person, after a few moments' reflection, will agree that now is the time to stop. Next week you may return to me all passways except those to worlds where you maintain residence."

The Rumfuddlers sat murmuring together. Some turned resentful glances toward Alan Robertson; others served themselves more bread and meat. Bob came over to join Alan and Duray. He spoke in an easy manner. "I must say that your admonitions arrive with all the delicacy of a lightning bolt. I can picture Jehovah smiting the fallen angels in a similar style."

Alan Robertson smiled. "Now then, Bob, you're talking nonsense. The situations aren't at all similar. Jehovah struck out in fury; I impose my restrictions in all good will, in order that we can once again turn our energies to constructive ends."

Bob threw back his head and laughed. "But the Rumfuddlers have lost the habit of work. We only want to amuse ourselves, and after all, what is so noxious in our activities?"

"The trend is menacing, Bob." Alan Robertson's voice was reasonable. "Unpleasant elements are creeping into your fun, so stealthily that you yourself are unaware of them. For instance, why torment poor Wagner? Surely there was gratuitous cruelty, and only to provide you a few instants of amusement. And, since the subject is in the air, I heartily deplore your treatment of Gilbert and Elizabeth. You have brought them both an extraordinary inconvenience, and in Elizabeth's case, actual suffering. Gilbert got something of his own back, and the balance is about even."

"Gilbert is far too impulsive," said Bob. "Self-willed and egocentric, as he always has been."

Alan held up his hand. "There is no need to go further into the subject, Bob. I suggest that you say no more."

"Just as you like, though the matter, considered as practical rehabilitation, isn't irrelevant. We can amply justify the work of the Rumfuddlers."

Duray asked quietly, "Just how do you mean, Bob?"

Alan Robertson made a peremptory sound, but Duray said, "Let him say what he likes, and make an end to it. He plans to do so anyway."

There was a moment of silence. Bob looked across the terrace to where the three Orientals were transferring the remains of the beef to a service cart.

"Well?" Alan Robertson asked softly. "Have you made your choice?"

Bob held out his hands in ostensible bewilderment. "I don't understand you! I want only to vindicate myself and the Rumfuddlers. I think we have done splendidly. Today we have allowed Torquemada to roast a dead ox instead of a living heretic; the Marquis de Sade has fulfilled his obscure urges by caressing seared flesh with a basting brush, and did you notice the zest with which Ivan the Terrible hacked up the carcass? Nero, who has real talent, played his violin; Attila, Genghis Khan, and Mao Tse Tung efficiently served the guests. Wine was poured by Messalina, Lucrezia Borgia, Delilah, and Gilbert's charming wife Elizabeth. Only Gilbert failed to demonstrate his rehabilitation, but at least he provided us a touching and memorable picture: Gilles de Rais, Elizabeth Báthory and their three virgin daughters. It was sufficient. In every case we have shown that rehabilitation is not an empty word."

"Not in every case," said Alan Robertson, "specifically that of your own."

Bob looked at him askance. "I don't follow you."

"No less than Gilbert, are you ignorant of your background. I will now reveal the circumstances so that you may understand something of yourself and try to curb the tendencies which have made your cognate an exemplar of cruelty, stealth and treachery."

Bob laughed: a brittle sound like cracking ice. "I admit to a horrified interest."

"I took you from a forest a thousand miles north of this very spot, while I traced the phylogeny of the Norse gods. Your name was Loki. For reasons which are not now important I brought you back to San Francisco and there you grew to maturity."

"So I am Loki."

"No. You are Bob Robertson, just as this is Gilbert Duray, and here is his wife Elizabeth. Loki, Gilles de Rais, Elizabeth Báthory: these are names applied to human material which has not functioned quite as well. Gilles de Rais, judging from all evidence, suffered from a brain tumor; he fell into his peculiar vices after a long and honorable career. The case of Princess Elizabeth Báthory is less clear, but one might suspect syphilis and consequent cerebral lesions."

"And what of poor Loki?" inquired Bob with exaggerated pathos.

"Loki seemed to suffer from nothing except a case of old-fashioned meanness."

Bob seemed concerned. "So that these qualities apply to me?"

"You are not necessarily identical to your cognate. Still, I advise you to take careful stock of yourself, and, so far as I am concerned, you had best regard yourself as on probation."

"Just as you say." Bob looked over Alan Robertson's shoulder. "Excuse me; you've spoiled the party and everybody is leaving. I want a word with Roger."

Duray moved to stand in his way, but Bob shouldered him aside and strode across the terrace, with Duray glowering at his back.

Elizabeth said in a mournful voice, "I hope we're at the end of all this."

Duray growled, "You should never have listened to him."

"I didn't listen; I read about it in one of Bob's books; I saw your picture; I couldn't—"

Alan Robertson intervened. "Don't harass poor Elizabeth; I consider her both sensible and brave; she did the best she could."

Bob returned. "Everything taken care of," he said cheerfully. "All except one or two details."

"The first of these is the return of the passway. Gilbert and Elizabeth, not to mention Dolly, Joan and Ellen, are anxious to return home."

"They can stay here with you," said Bob. "That's probably the best solution."

"I don't plan to stay here," said Alan Robertson in mild wonder. "We are leaving at once."

"You must change your plans," said Bob. "I have finally become bored with your reproaches. Roger doesn't particularly care to leave his home, but he agrees that now is the time to make a final disposal of the matter."

Alan Robertson frowned in displeasure. "The joke is in very poor taste, Bob."

Roger Waille came from the house, his face somewhat glum. "They're all closed. Only the main gate is open."

Alan Robertson said to Gilbert: "I think that we will leave Bob and Roger to their Rumfuddle fantasies. When he returns to his senses we'll get your passway. Come along then, Elizabeth! Girls!"

"Alan," said Bob gently. "You're staying here. Forever. I'm taking over the machine."

Alan Robertson asked mildly: "How do you propose to restrain me? By force?"

"You can stay here alive or dead; take your choice."

"You have weapons then?"

"I certainly do." Bob displayed a pistol. "There are also the servants. None have brain tumors or syphilis, they're all just plain bad."

Roger said in an awkward voice, "Let's go and get it over."

Alan Robertson's voice took on a harsh edge. "You seriously plan to maroon us here, without food?"

"Consider yourself marooned."

"I'm afraid that I must punish you, Bob, and Roger as well."

Bob laughed gaily. "You yourself are suffering from brain disease— megalomania. You haven't the power to punish anyone."

"I still control the machine, Bob."

"The machine isn't here. So now—"

Alan Robertson turned and looked around the landscape, with a frowning air of expectation. "Let me see: I'd probably come down from the main gate; Gilbert and a group from behind the house. Yes; here we are."

Down the path from the main portal, walking jauntily, came two Alan Robertsons with six men armed with rifles and gas grenades. Simultaneously from behind the house appeared two Gilbert Durays and six more men, similarly armed.

Bob stared in wonder. "Who are these people?"

"Cognates," said Alan smiling. "I told you I controlled the machine, and so do all my cognates. As soon as Gilbert and I return to our Earth, we must similarly set forth and in our turn do our part on other worlds cognate to this…Roger, be good enough to summon your servants. We will take them back to Earth. You and Bob must remain here."

Waille gasped in distress. "Forever?"

"You deserve nothing better," said Alan Robertson. "Bob perhaps deserves worse." He turned to the cognate Alan Robertsons. "What of Gilbert's passway?"

Both replied, "It's in Bob's San Francisco apartment, in a box on the mantelpiece."

"Very good," said Alan Robertson. "We will now depart. Goodby, Bob. Goodby, Roger. I am sorry that our association ended on this rather unpleasant basis."

"Wait!" cried Roger. "Take me back with you!"

"Goodby," said Alan Robertson. "Come along then, Elizabeth. Girls! Run on ahead!"

XIII

Elizabeth and the children had returned to Home; Alan Robertson and Duray sat in the lounge above the machine. "Our first step," said Alan Robertson, "is to dissolve our obligation. There are of course an infinite number of Rumfuddles at Ekshayans and an infinite number of Alans and Gilberts. If we visited a single Rumfuddle, we would, by the laws of probability, miss a certain number of the emergency situations. The total number of permutations, assuming that an infinite number of Alans and Gilberts makes a random choice among an infinite number of Ekshayans, is infinity raised to the infinite power. What percentage of this number yields blanks for any given Ekshayan, I haven't calculated. If we visited Ekshayans until we had by our own efforts rescued at least one Gilbert and Alan set, we might be forced to scour fifty or a hundred worlds, or more. Or we might achieve our rescue on the first visit. The wisest course, I believe, is for you and I to visit, say, twenty Ekshayans. If each of the Alan and Gilbert sets does the same, then the chances for any particular Alan and Gilbert to be abandoned are one in twenty times nineteen times eighteen times seventeen, etcetera. Even then I think I will arrange that an operator check another five or ten thousand worlds to gather up that one lone chance…"

A Different View of Jack Vance

By Norma Vance

Most of you reading this have probably read at least one biography of Jack or, if not, you have some acquaintance with his writing. As his wife, I have the inside track and instead of enumerating all his literary achievements, I have decided to write about the person you may not know very well, but who I hope you will enjoy getting to know.

My first impression of Jack was that he was—different. Certainly he was daring: to appear on a girl's doorstep with a bag of donuts and ask if I could make some coffee? The 56 years since have not altered my opinion. He is still daring, but his most notable quality is persistence; somehow the two seem to belong together. Persistence is what accomplishes things like excavating tons and tons of dirt to make room to build a house, or writing books, lots of books.

The rustic little house and property we bought in Oakland was not ideal, but it was cheap. The terrain was a challenge, hardly any space on which to build. Using a pick-axe, shovel, wheelbarrow and hard work, Jack created a building site. Wall by wall the rustic cabin disappeared and in affordable stages became a really comfortable place to live. All the while Jack made time to write. This could not have happened without his drive (or persistence).

During the time the contours of our property were being changed, there was general concern that a nuclear war might develop. What did Jack do? He was already moving tons of dirt, so he dug a tunnel into the hillside: a few feet forward, then a turn to the left for about five feet, then a turn to the right and another turn left, terminating in a chamber of about eight square feet. He shored up walls and ceiling with heavy timbers, installed a small fireplace for comfort and light, a chimney to vent smoke. Before heaping extra dirt over the top of the excavation, he laid heavy black plastic over all. With lanterns and candles the space began to look inviting.

One day, when noise and activity in the house made concentration difficult, Jack retreated to the cave. He brought with him a thermos bottle of hot coffee, a canvas slingback chair, a pillow to rest his clipboard on. He made a fire in the fireplace, lit a lantern and set to work. Peace at last!

But as luck, or Mother Nature, would have it, rain began to fall. Not long after a trickle of water found its way down to the plastic, then underneath it and finally into the cave. Drip-drip-drip! Onto Jack's head and shoulders, clipboard and paper. That was enough! The fall-out shelter was a failure.

A more successful venture was the treehouse. We had lots of big eucalyptus trees and our son John, as many boys do, wanted a treehouse. Jack chose a huge old tree which, about fifteen feet up, had branches suited to supporting a platform. He installed a ladder, then a platform made from two sheets of ¾"x 4' x 8' plywood. The walls also were plywood, with two windows and a door. There was a front porch with access through a hole in the platform.

John and his friends enjoyed this playhouse for enough years so that, when a terrific windstorm blew it to the ground along with its supporting branches, there was no great sorrow—just a little sadness.

One of Jack's most enduring interests is in the culinary arts. He likes to read recipes, read about memorable banquets such as in the *Epicurean*, concoct his own recipes and feasts, cook; take note of the latest best dining spots and of the talented chefs who make simple ingredients divine. Naturally this interest has its downside and dieting is the result. Luckily for him our son is not so affected. Jack has been known to make a detour, even, to a place like La Pyramide in Vienne whose repast was so memorable that I'm sure it will never be equaled.

When John was about six months old, I went back to work. Jack did much of the cooking for several years; one of his favorite activities was to create beautiful, delicious breakfasts for John. Some were so appetizing he took pictures of them, I guess to remind himself of what a pleasurable thing it was to nurture his son.

Boats. They represented Jack's dreams of travel and adventure. Boats have always been at the forefront of everything for Jack; always studying plans to build his favorite, always looking for the safest, most seaworthy craft. At one time he bought plans to build a Piver 36' trimaran, even got so far as to finishing and fiberglassing the three hulls. Then Mr. Piver disappeared during a coastwise jaunt to the south in his trimaran. He was never found. This rather dampened Jack's anxiety to own a trimaran. He sold the three hulls and began his search anew.

We bought a 17' cutter-rigged Venture for our son to learn about sailing and be part of Jack's crew; at the age of 16 John sailed this boat on San Francisco Bay with friends. Somewhat later Jack bought a 35' Columbia; then a 45' Explorer designed by Stanley Huntingford because the Columbia didn't seem as seaworthy. The Explorer was documented and named *Hinano*. One of the happiest periods of Jack's life was spent in the company of John, rigging *Hinano*, installing all sorts of hull-strengthening devices, a global position locator, running lights, safety net and railings, choosing sails and planning itineraries. Sadly, at the same time glaucoma was stealing his eyesight and financial realities were asserting themselves. The dream was eventually set aside, and John started his studies at U.C. Berkeley.

Jack reluctantly decided to sell *Hinano*. Berth rental and upkeep—along with continued construction expenses at home—were just too expensive for us. As luck would have it a man named Jack Storer fell in love with *Hinano* and was thrilled to buy her. For a shakedown Jack Storer invited a couple of friends to go with him to Half Moon Bay. On their arrival drinks of congratulation were consumed and when the supply ran out, his friends retired. But Mr. Storer decided to take the dinghy ashore for another bottle. Upon his return it appeared that his foot became entangled in a mooring-line; poor Jack Storer never made it back on-board. He was found in the morning, floating dead beside the boat. If this isn't a cautionary tale, I don't know what is!

Years before, when John was still a baby, Jack drew plans for a houseboat. He was pals with Frank Herbert and Poul Anderson; both being of an adventurous nature, it wasn't difficult to entice them into a partnership to build the houseboat. This was a very happy time. Jack built the pontoons in our driveway and fiber-glassed them there as well. Finally they were ready to be moved to a beach on the bay. Several friends had now joined in the work, enjoying the sunshine, salt air and companionship. Every stage completed was cause for celebration; a party atmosphere prevailed.

Poor Frank Herbert could not stay the course due to medical problems. Also he and his family were planning a move further north, which meant he must give up being a partner. Eventually his place was taken by our guitar-playing friend Albert Hall, who had been joining us regularly to work. After the work-day was finished, Albert's songs and guitar struck just the right mood.

After the platform and under-pinnings were joined to the hulls, the next step was to move it to the water, where the cabin was built. One evening the owners of the little restaurant on the pier brought a bottle of champagne to christen the houseboat, which was done immediately, though it never was given a name—just houseboat.

An outboard motor was installed at the stern and connected to the steering wheel in the forward cabin, by a Jack Vance innovation of two long reinforcing rods enclosed in an aluminum pipe. The mechanism performed remarkably well. (Incidentally, the nautical wheel was a gift from Frank Herbert.)

The houseboat was painted white with blue trim inside and out. Six foam mattresses were installed on the bunks, curtains were hung, toilet and wash-basin installed in the head and a potbellied stove for the kitchen-living-room.

Now it was time for relocation to the sloughs of the Sacramento-San Joaquin-Mokelumne Rivers delta. Jack and six other men and boys made the maiden voyage up the Sacramento River. An overnight at Dalrelio's Yacht Harbor and an early start the next morning, brought them in good time to Moore's Riverboat Yacht Haven on the Mokelumne River. This same moorage is where 'Houseboat' met its demise a few years later, but not before many happy memories were earned.

Our houseboat was ideal for life on the sloughs: vacations, parties and overnights, which usually were spent away from the harbor. The houseboat glided along the sloughs to find an ideal anchorage. Then, lounging on the porch with feet on the railing, a favorite night-cap in hand, we listened to the sounds of insects, animals and bird calls; it was sheer delight. Mornings were usually cold, but after stoking and lighting the little wood-burning stove, we soon had the cabin warm and cozy.

Jack and I were planning a trip to Ireland with John and likely would be away for a year or more. We would have to transfer ownership of the houseboat to our friend Ali Szantho, whose pleasure was fishing, and he chose another partner who also enjoyed fishing. They felt the houseboat sat too low in the water for fishing, so they removed the heavy ceiling panels. The boat popped up in the water at least a foot, maybe more. This little alteration may have caused the houseboat's demise or perhaps it was a misadventure of some kind. We will never know.

I have mentioned Jack's daring and persistence and now I'd like to refer back to a younger Jack Vance—before Norma—for further evidence.

At the age of 18 Jack was living with his Aunt Nellie (his father's sister) in San Francisco, right next door to the twin house his mother had owned at one time. This privilege was afforded him in exchange for doing minor chores around the house. Along with almost everyone else Jack was fascinated with the construction of the San Francisco-Oakland Bay Bridge. Before, there had been only a ferry-boat fleet to convey cars and passengers from the San Francisco side of the bay to the Oakland side and vice versa. The only alternative was to drive to San Jose; then cross the city from west to east to join highway 680 north and on to Oakland.

Steel towers were already anchored at intervals into the floor of the bay and soared upward very high; I'm guessing at least 200 or even 300 feet. Cables also were being put in place between the towers.

One evening Jack rode his motorcycle to the building site. He secured it to a pole, then looked around, neither seeing nor hearing anyone. There may have been a sign warning the would-be trespasser to Keep Out, but he did not see one. Work on the bridge continued day and night; it would be a challenge to not be seen, since his plan was to climb the cable to the top of the first tower.

At the beginning the cable presented a gentle slope, and as he neared the tower the slope became steeper and steeper. The cable was approximately two feet wide with a wire rope on each side to grasp for security. The mere thought of being in such a situation would scare me so much I wouldn't even be able to grasp the rope, whereas, according to Jack, he felt no fear at all. He reached the tower in about twenty minutes and almost immediately heard voices coming toward him from the direction of the second tower. The only thing that gave Jack pause was the thought of being caught where he knew he should not be, so he turned around without hesitation and carefully made his way back to the ground. Why did he do it? Because of the thrill.

Sam Wainwright was a student at UC Berkeley when Jack first met him as a reporter for the *Daily Californian*. Sam's brain worked overtime. He was brilliant and at the same time a bit mad. He was always doing something new, planning and organizing. Everyone knew of him because he made news, but not many friends. He was ridiculed more than appreciated. Jack saw past Sam's quirkyness, appreciated his wit and became his friend.

Sam organized the Thumbwagger's Club. So far only two persons had joined. Jack did not become a member but went along with the first competition to get the story for the *Daily Cal*. The game was to see who could thumb a ride from the foot of University Avenue, all the way to Salt Lake City, and back to Berkeley first. There were four people so Sam ordained two teams: Sam's and Jack's. All four wore T-shirts with a thumb on the front.

Jack's team got the first ride. The driver actually recognized them: "Oh! You guys are the Thumbwaggers! Late afternoon the first day they made it to Reno. Sam's team made it to Sparks, Nevada. In the morning Sam's team got a ride with an Indian (American) driver who claimed to be going in the direction of Salt Lake City, but after driving 50 miles into the desert, he said goodbye and took off on a side road. What a predicament! Jack's team got a ride to Winnemucca. The fun had waned for both teams.

Jack had heard that the Santa Fe Railroad was nice to hoboes and let them ride without bother, so he and his partner headed for the railroad tracks. No one seemed to be about, so they entered the caboose and made themselves comfortable, even built a fire in the stove. They were beginning to feel drowsy when the railroad 'bull' entered the caboose, brandishing his club and shouting.

"Who do you think you are? Get out of here! Now!" (This was not a Santa Fe train.)

"But the train is moving too fast."

"It will go faster!"

"You heard me. Jump!"

"Gulp. Let's get off now; it might not be too bad."

"Jump! I mean now!"

The train was rumbling along at 15 or 20 miles per hour. They jumped and received a few bumps and scrapes but were not incapacitated. Jack's team made it back to Berkeley the next day and Sam's team finally arrived a day and a half later in some disgruntlement.

Jack remained friends with Sam for many years, but he eventually became annoyed with him because no matter how many times Sam consulted him about various problems, especially with the ladies, he never was able to act on the advice. Later, when Jack heard him on the phone to me, asking for the same advice as previously, he lost all respect for him and forbade him to call again. Poor Sam! Great potential, but unable to use it where it counted.

Jack had many friends while attending UC, some of them full of the Old Nick. Thinking up tricks and mischief seemed to ameliorate some of the pressures of getting an education. Jack and three of his friends theorized that they could hoist a communist flag to the top of the Campanile by doing the following: first they should place some stout twine around the four corners of the tower, tie the ends together, leaving a bit of slack. Next a cluster of five helium balloons should be tied to the string at each corner. Then the flag should be attached to the twine on the side visible to the most people. Each of the four mischief-makers held a stick with a string attached to a hook, the idea being to place the hook over the twine and jiggle it to keep the balloons moving upward and thus raise the flag. What was not counted on was a very strong wind which came up and almost at the same time the campus cops came by on their normal rounds. The wind alone could have spoiled the fun but when the boys saw the cops they scattered in every direction. There was so much noise and confusion with the wind that no one ever guessed who the culprits were.

Well, I could write more but I don't have the time right now—and maybe that's a good thing.

A Jack Vance Biography

By Norma Vance

1.

I wrote a JV biography last year for Norwescon which was based on events experienced personally and others gleaned from conversations with Jack, concerning his life before our marriage, parts of which could have been termed amusing escapades. This was fun, but I would rather not repeat myself. So I have decided to place him in the background (foreground?) of his parents and grandparents. I hope it won't prove to be a bore.

Jack's maternal grandfather, L.M. Hoefler, was a prominent lawyer who represented the San Francisco breweries, among other clients. He was a member of the Olympic Club and the Bohemian Club. On a visit to Italy, he shipped two marble statues of athletes, as a gift, to the Olympic Club. They are, to this day, still placed on either side of the Club's entrance, on Post Street. He counted among his friends other lawyers, judges, mayors, politicians, Hollywood types, successful businessmen and everyday, ordinary workmen, as well as more affluent members of society. Everyone seems to have known him, by sight if not personally.

L.M. Hoefler lived on Haight Street, rather a steep hill, which had trolley service. Normally the trolley stopped at intersections. Jack remembers that, wherever his grandfather stood along the block to hail the trolley, the driver would stop for him to climb aboard; the same policy applied wherever he wished to disembark. Jack's brother, David, recalls that when he was only 10 L.M. would require him to drive. On one occasion, probably to get around slow traffic, he asked David to drive on the left side of the street. David complained that they might be hit by an oncoming car, but his grandfather refused to listen, and David was compelled to do as he was told. Even though L.M. Hoefler had many friends, was kind and generous, he had no idea how to relate to children; he expected only obedience. Jack remembers being teased by his grandfather about 'four eyes', with no concern for Jack's discomfort. In those days this was a rather common tease, practiced by children against children who needed to wear glasses. I'm not sure that L.M. was being deliberately unkind but Jack has never forgotten it.

2.

I seem to have moved too far ahead in the story so will return in time a bit. Ludwig Mathias Hoefler married Emma Madeline Altemus. Jack's mother, Edith, was their only child. 'Edy', as we all knew her, had many advantages and to her credit she was never selfish. She was good-natured, intelligent and popular. Her schooling came at Miss Sarah Hamlin's, where she excelled in all her studies, especially History. Her memory for important dates was phenomenal. Another talent was for playing the piano by ear. This was very much appreciated years later, after the move to Oakley, when she played for country dances and not much sheet-music was available.

Edy was 16 when the San Francisco earthquake and fire* occurred. The earthquake was devastating, but the fire was even worse. Her father's house was so badly damaged that a small cook-shack had to be built to the side of the street, in front of the house, to cook meals. Someone took a snapshot of Edy, her mother and her mother's mother sitting on the pavement, leaning against the shack—a treasured memento today.

Now, to the paternal side of Jack's parentage. The Vance family owned several furniture stores in San Francisco, Benecia, Stockton, Sacramento, perhaps at other sites as well. Charles Albert Vance, Jack's father, was born in Benecia. Edy and Charles Albert probably met at a party, or some such social function. Both the Hoeflers and the Vances were well-established members of San Francisco Society and the two young people were considered newsworthy. It was no surprise to anyone when the engagement was announced and a wedding date set. The wedding was a grand event. Extravagant and beautiful gifts arrived, as well as others more practical. John Vance, Jack's grandfather and Charles Albert's father, gave the newlyweds a large lot on Filbert street, which still is one of the best neighborhoods of San Francisco. He also saw to the building of a large two-story house. It seemed that the couple could only anticipate a long and happy life. At least it was fruitful: there were five children in about ten years, or a bit longer.

Footnote:
*Another memorable event occurring in Edy's lifetime was the attack on Pearl Harbor, December 7, 1941. December 7 was Edy's birthday.

3.

After Prohibition was voted into law, the breweries of San Francisco shut down their operations and never re-opened, or if they did so, it wasn't until more recent times and the beverage was most likely a soft drink. L.M. Hoefler had lost his greatest source of income; nonetheless, he had other clients and investments. He was not in danger of becoming destitute at this point. Over the horizon, however, loomed the Depression.

'Society' has never impressed Jack very much. Intelligence, drive, courage and mastery of special skills are what appeal to him. New Orleans Jazz is an example of a special skill: the playing of ensemble music, often without written scores, or without sheet-music, by talented masters of their particular instrument. Each musician must be alert to the performance of every other musician playing in the ensemble. Jack also enjoys lively conversations with friends, about anything and everything, a type of 'brainy' competition derived from scientific knowledge of all kinds. He is thankful for the recorded books and magazines which keep him abreast of a great variety of subjects. Humor and friends are essential elements to Jack's idea of a good life.

Jack does not remember his father with any kindness, only as a self-indulgent, negligent, authoritarian person, to be avoided for the most part. Charles Albert owned a ranch of 23,000 acres in a beautiful part of Mexico, near the city of Tepic. On his periodic visits to the ranch, he sometimes took his second son, Louie, along for company. Eventually the property was nationalized, which must have been a terrible blow to Charles Albert.

4.

The Depression held the U.S. in a tight grip. Jack's grandfather, L.M. Hoefler, began to realize that something had to be done to economize. He knew of a man with substantial means who was relocating, or starting, a business in San Francisco and needed a suitable residence. L.M. had been thinking of ways to cut expenses and also had thought the Sacramento Delta region might be a healthy environment for Edy and her children. He himself relished the idea of a weekend retreat in the country. He scouted around and found a small ranch in the area of Oakley. There was a house that was large enough and, with very little effort, would be perfect for the whole family. He approached Edy and his son-in-law with the idea, explaining that the rental of their Filbert Street home would pay the rent in Oakley and much of their other living expenses. Edy expressed no disagreement and so the move was made. All five children, the nurse, Allie, even Charles Albert lived there when he wasn't in Mexico.

To Jack's mind, the move to the country at that time was the single most important event in his life. Life was just about perfect. All five children attended the one-room Iron House School. The school and the ranch house were both about a half-mile off the edge of a slough, the ranch house a half-mile further east and not far from a dairy. Jack absorbed everything within sight, sound and smell. He has remembered it all when writing his books. The experience has been a perfect resource for descriptive prose: of place, of mood, and sensation. His bedroom had a large screened window just beside his bed. The view was of rolling hills, fruit orchards, eucalyptus, firs of various kinds, shrubs, flowers and weeds in dun-colored soil. The backdrop was kingly Mount Diablo, a former volcano, now extinct (or so we should hope). Jack found this scene so enchanting that he painted it on a plaster batt to make it visible to him even when the sky was overcast. It was lost when everyone moved away to gain a higher education or find employment.

Editor Bios

Terry Dowling

Terry Dowling is one of Australia's most acclaimed and best-known writers of science fiction, fantasy and horror, the award-winning author of *Rynosseros, Blue Tyson, Twilight Beach, Rynemonn, Wormwood, The Man Who Lost Red, An Intimate Knowledge of the Night, Blackwater Days, Basic Black: Tales of Appropriate Fear* and co-editor of *Mortal Fire: Best Australian SF, The Essential Ellison, The Jack Vance Treasury* and *The Jack Vance Reader*. He has also written a number of articles on Jack's writing, among them "Kirth Gersen: The Other Demon Prince" (which won the 1983 William Atheling Award for Criticism) and his 28,000 word "The Art of Xenography: Jack Vance's 'General Culture' Novels" (*Science Fiction # 3*, December 1978). Terry is a close friend of the Vances and a frequent visitor to their home in the Oakland hills. Jack wrote an Introduction to *Blue Tyson*, Terry's 1992 collection of Tom Rynosseros stories, and refers to a "Terence Dowling's World" in *Throy*. In *Ports of Call*, he mentions a drink called a "Wild Dingo Howler, which was invented by a reckless smuggler named Terence Dowling." Terry counts these things among his most treasured possessions.

Jonathan Strahan

Jonathan Strahan is an editor, anthologist and reviewer from Perth, Western Australia. He established one of Australia's leading semiprozines before moving to work for *Locus* as an editor and book reviewer. He has been Reviews Editor for *Locus* since 2002, and he has had reviews published in *Locus, Eidolon*, Ticonderoga and *Foundation*. He has won the William J Atheling Jr Award for Criticism and Review, the Ditmar Award a number of times, and is a recipient of The Peter McNamara Award. As a freelance editor, he has edited or co-edited 22 anthologies, with a number still set for publication. He is editor of the *The Best Science Fiction and Fantasy of the Year* and *Eclipse* anthology series. He also edited the Locus Award-winning anthology *The New Space Opera* with Gardner Dozois and stand-alone YA SF anthology *The Starry Rift*, amongst others. He was a 2008 Hugo Award nominee for Best Editor, Short Fiction.